MW01248535

About the Author

Esmirna R. Pratt, author of *Who is That Woman in the Mirror?*
She was born in the Dominican Republic and migrated to the
USA in 1989 when she was still an adolescent. She learned
English fluently and assimilated the American culture rather well
meanwhile keeping the essence of her own culture and traditions.
Life was not as she thought or dreamt it would be living in the
USA; economic challenges of the time and adopting to a new
way of life, was really difficult for her. She currently has a BSN
degree and works as an RN caring for terminally ill patients.

Who is that Woman in the Mirror?

Esmirna R. Pratt

Who is that Woman in the Mirror?

Olympia Publishers
London

www.olympiapublishers.com
OLYMPIA PAPERBACK EDITION

A CIP catalogue record for this title is
available from the British Library.

ISBN: 978-1-80074-933-7

First Published in 2023

Olympia Publishers
Tallis House
2 Tallis Street
London
EC4Y 0AB

Printed in Great Britain

Dedication

I dedicate this book to my special son who has taught me a great lesson in life by forcing me to be a little bit humbler each day; and discovering that the most significant things in life are not necessarily the most important ones.

Acknowledgements

I thank my husband and children [you know who you are] for allowing me to isolate myself from time to time, to focus and indulge in my writings.

Chapter 1

Cinderella for a Day

The arduous plan

She finally found the one; she was perplexed for a moment due to the decision which ought to be made, in disbelief that she could have just met her match. Her baby sister, Anne Marie, the one who was almost the voice in her conscience because Esmeralda would seek for her approval under circumstances such as this one, also did not hesitate to utter, "That's it... that's the one!" Esmeralda took a glance at this 'thing', and imagined herself a fulfilled woman, happy, admired by everyone who was going to stand up when the bridal music interrupted with an uplifting beat to let her enter angelically, wearing this gown on her path to the altar.

Just about three months before her own wedding, Esmeralda had witnessed that of her cousin and she was a bridesmaid in three previous friends' weddings, in less than two years. She and her boyfriend of a couple of years had talked about getting married one day, but no engagement, no kneeling, and no ring until one day they just decided to put a date for the wedding without the normal romantic rituals that should come first. Esmeralda tried to break up with Valentino a few too many times. However, she got to the inevitable conclusion that he should be the one she should marry, for many reasons; he was quiet −not a womanizer– a hardworking guy, the type her father would approve of. Most importantly, they shared the same faith. To Esmeralda her father was this untouchable figure, wise, and a man of God. Therefore, she had to marry a man who was going to, like her, admire and respect him. Valentino had characteristics that made him suitable for marriage. He also had a college education, and was moldable to some extent to Esmeralda's desires. She nevertheless, deep inside of her most torturous thoughts, found NOT a good reason – romantic reason – why she should marry this guy. But her feelings abated and she went on with her plan; a plan to have a normal family with kids, going to church on the Sabbath and so on and so forth.

Esmeralda was a huge soñadora – her enormous ability to create scenarios of vivencias – things she had not experienced yet, definitively set her apart. Since she was an adolescent, she would spend many waking hours just fantasizing how she was going to meet her 'príncipe azul'. So, she used to imagine every possible situation, moment and place where the magical experience might one day take place. She did have real moments such as the one when she felt in love with her high school sweetheart. She was just fifteen years old when he appeared into her simple, solitary life. Nothing happened the way she imagined it before. She was new in town, this little, unsophisticated and technology-lacking town served as the vehicle to transport her to feelings and emotions she only dreamed of thus far. So let me introduce you to Esmeralda's first real love experience when she was an adolescent and living with her mother in the countryside, back in her native island. A big rain storm had taken down some trees and the electricity went out in the whole town. The next morning a neighbor who possessed the only pick-up truck in miles, invited some kids in the neighborhood to go to the river shore as it was customary to go there to collect water in plastic containers to bring home for use, and at the same time everybody had fun in the process. They all jumped into the back of the truck, and as Esmeralda was lifting one leg while the other one was resting on the bumper and she was awkwardly looking down, a hand extended and an offer was made to hold it. She did and simultaneously looked at these bright, smiley eyes. She was quickly pulled in and forced to sit down on the bare warm metal surface. The naturally appearing confident boy had his eyes fixed on her, always with a smile, almost as if that was an act of defiance toward the constant up and down motion of the old machine on the bumpy gravel roads. She was just feeling gratitude for his kind gesture, but he seemed to want something more. A country boy was not what she had in mind to be her first love experience; she liked that type of guy who was given to reading – that is, one who had intellectual curiosity; this local boy sounded like he had not ever put foot at the door of a library, and his poor diction revealed a below average general knowledge of literacy. Eventually her desires would take a detour from that ideal guy she used to dream of, after realizing that she had fallen in love for the very first time in her little life; he conquered her with a romanticism that was unsophisticated but yet effective enough to make her melt down. He would send pieces of paper with little love thoughts written in them, or citations to find each other in an infrequent part of town at a certain time. He would pass by the front of her house and walk very slowly just to see her sitting on the front porch. If she was not there, he would throw little rocks at her bedroom window. So, if you ask her to describe her attraction for him, she would not be able to say; it just happened, mysteriously happened. Sadly, Esmeralda had to leave her first love behind to migrate to a totally different country with her family; abandoning a life that she had not appreciated until she was very far and away in a different world. She would one day miss the quiet lazy afternoons when she indulged on that guano rocking chair while lost in her thoughts and looking at the beautiful sun sluggishly disappearing behind the mountains located just a few miles away from home. Unbeknownst to her these moments were going to be one of −if not the most− harmonious and special moments in her life.

Back to her pre-wedding planning and hectic moments in her life, in her work place, a co-worker one day asked, "Esmeralda, you are looking too thin and pale, aren't you exaggerating a little with that diet?"

She replied, "No, I am just fine; I have gone from size eight to six in about two months and I just need to get to size four. You see? I need to fit in this beautiful wedding dress. It is unique and I like it a lot, but they only had a size four and the wedding is coming soon." Esmeralda was absorbed in the planning of her wedding so much that all she did day in and day out was related somehow to preparing for the perfect wedding. She would get up from bed at least two hours earlier than her usual routine and jog for a couple of miles; she would talk about her wedding details such as church decoration stuff with friends and co-workers whenever she had a chance, at the cafeteria and even while working. She would come home from work and hurry to the garage to hand-paint with little brushes the aisle runner; she drew with a template Fleur de Lys symbol inside diamond shapes and painted them with a variety of dusty pink hues. She never said it aloud, but she wanted to feel at least for one day, like a princess. She sometimes reflected on her life changing events and thought that she actually never had any opportunity to feel exceptionally beautiful and special. She remembered with melancholy the fact that she never had a 'fiesta de quinceañera' back in her native island, due in part to financially difficult times. Even more disappointing for her was the fact that attending a prom party was never an option for her, owing to her family's precarious situation as new comers to the United States of America. She did not go to a regular high school once living in the USA; she worked full time during the day in a factory filled with black dusty floors and doing mechanical types of jobs – getting her hands all greased up, at least for the first two years in this land of dreamers, or until she got to be proficient in the English language good enough to find a more delicate job. She went to an adult school at night to complete her GED, and in this way, obtained a high school diploma. She used to watch with tearful eyes kids of her age on their way to high school, some walking cheerfully and others with not an apparent interest to ever get there. She many times thought, "If only I could go back to my old life… just worry about my school assignments, have a boyfriend and eventually attend my prom?" But that never was possible for her. Now, she saw an opportunity with her wedding of becoming that flawless beautiful woman — at least for a day.

The groom was in Esmeralda's subconscious thoughts another important ornament in the wedding. So, she imposed her influence that is, she practically made the decision of the clothing he ought to wear. She intended to give as much importance and pay attention to any minute detail to improve the groom's appearance just as she invested on her own ajuar. "This gray vest and dark black suit and pants go well with your dark hair, honey," Esmeralda said softly and looking at the suit that was hanging in the shop, she did not even bother to look at her fiancé's face for any reaction to what she was proposing; it was just as if she had the absolute privilege and rights to do whatever the heck she wanted to do in her wedding, and Valentino was just there to please her, after all, after everything was said and done, after the wedding euphoria was evaporated from her senses, who knows what she would become? There was the possibility that she would have to resign herself to a simple, bitter life as a dedicated wife. Esmeralda did not know for sure nor did she perpend the fatal consequences of jumping into a marriage that was destined to fail before it even started. She did not want to hesitate, fearing that if she stopped to think, really think what she was doing, things were going to come suddenly to a halt and she would feel lost not knowing how to start all over again; how was it going to be possible for her to find a new 'viable husband'? That sounded way too complicated to her; a task that would require enormous effort and energy to say the least.

You could say that Esmeralda did not have much luck in love matters before she met Valentino and her luck did not seem to change with his appearance. Not that the following experience has anything to do with anything, however, it is a curiosity, one of those things in life that you just don't know what to make of it. One day Esmeralda found a letter addressed to her with an anonymous sender; she quickly opened it and the message was basically a request to resend this letter to seven more people otherwise facing the possibility of seven years of bad luck in love relationships. Of course, she just laughed and also felt annoyed by such a porquería that just took five precious minutes away from her life; she tore it apart and feeling disappointed and upset pitched it into the kitchen's trash can. Time passed as it usually does, without waiting for anyone to catch up with their lives, without rendering a chance to compensate for lost times and without regards to one's disadvantages that life just decides to assign to you. One night after her last class in college, a younger

Esmeralda [about nineteen years of age] is quickly going down the stairs of the large main hall like trying to reach somebody; she yelled, "Hey, hey... Ah, ah, I just wanted to ask you..." She tried to catch her breath and continued, "Do you need a ride home?" She had noticed that this guy stood up on the bus stop in front of the college building after class every Thursday night. Her mind used to wander and her body floated in the classroom when she contemplated the 'beauty' sitting a couple of seats from her. His dark wavy hair, big brown eyes, milky soft skin, well defined arms, tall and svelte young man. She wished he approached her and asked her out, but she grew impatient and that night she just went for it, without much thought.

The guy looked at her kind of surprised and with a big melting smile said, "Yes!... That would be great!" Once inside the 1978 Plymouth Horizon tiny light blue car, the handsome creature on the passenger side keenly stated, "There is a park on the way to my apartment that we can stop by and chat a little if you want."

Esmeralda's pupils dilated and her heart pumped ten times stronger; she took a deep breath and tilting her head while fixing her hair with her fingers firmly said, "Of course, that's an excellent idea!" At that time, the park was officially closed but they did not care and parked the car close to the little lake, got out and sat on the huge roots of an old tree while looking up at the huge moon that was watching these two careless-nocturne young college students. Esmeralda waited nervously for a romantic expression of his feelings or just a kiss that night, but it was as if he was merely testing the waters and he did not make a move. She was so confused; why he made her come to this isolated romantic place just to stare at the ever-present firmament? Obviously, this guy was more than what met the eyes; he was a very clever guy with intentions that only he knew and the oblivious romantic girl was going to be inevitably swayed away by a deceptive charming force, in no time.

Another night after class when Esmeralda was going to take Mike home as it became the custom, he proposed to her the following, "Esmeralda would you do me a huge favor? That would be so cool…"

Esmeralda, very interested on what he was about to say, replied, "Yes, what is it? What can I do for you?"

He added, "You, see? I just got my permit to drive, but I don't have a car and nobody to let me practice; would you let me drive you home tonight?" She was a little bit uneasy, but could not say 'no' to this attractive young man. She nodded yes and he quickly got out of the car and they switched positions. He was driving nice and easy and then a couple of blocks from his destination, about one hundred feet from a big traffic light intersection which was green precisely at the time when he rashly and eagerly asked, "Do you think I could make a left turn… What do you think, what do you think?"

Esmeralda nervously answered, "Sure, if you hurry, and no car is coming." She was not sure why he was reacting that way. All of a sudden, she saw a car fast approaching the light on the opposite side of the road. Mike quickly made a left turn and in a blink of an eye, boom! She felt the big impact that made her hit the front glass; luckily nothing major happened other than a little bump on her forehead. Before she had a chance to recuperate from her frightened state, the guy asked her very nervously to switch seats again. She did not understand and asked, "Why?" He then confessed that he did not have a permit as he said before and the police were going to come soon and they would get in trouble if the cops found out that he was driving without a license or permit to drive. Still baffled she had no choice but to quickly do what he said.

As expected just a few minutes later the police arrived; the accident report was written, "Female driver by the name of Esmeralda Gomez, nineteen years old…" That was how her first car and witness of so many crazy moments and the one thing, which granted her independence, came abruptly to its sad end.

Esmeralda was able to find another used car, one that her stepfather, Santiago, was going to abandon in the local junkyard. So, as usual, the cynical guy who amazingly was still having Esmeralda under a spell got a ride home with her and this time, he invited her to come in to his place. She did, she was excited and happy. Once there, she saw a typical guy's room, unorganized, a huge bed in the middle of the apartment, clothes everywhere. He did not hesitate to kiss her all over and rushed to remove her clothes; she asked to go to the bathroom not sure for what maybe just to pee, but she got distracted and started looking into the medicine cabinet; he showed up and she felt surprised and then while grabbing her shoulders and kissing them persuaded her to go out of the bathroom to the center of the room. Esmeralda started to feel anxious, not necessarily a good anxiety; she was actually petrified, perhaps she intuited what was about to happen right there and then – it was not rocket science – sex was on the horizon; however, her intuition encompassed much more than that; Esmeralda was sexually molested when she was a little girl and even later during her adolescence, she endured a couple of attempts of rape. So, it is not a surprise that she would react in a negative way just when she realized this guy, she hardly knew, wanted to have sex with her. All of a sudden, she felt this agonizing frightening feeling as opposed to any desire to get laid. She got into her survival mode and one more time had a peculiar idea: she stopped him and put on a serious face and stated, "There is something I got to confess to you before we do anything, it is very important…"

He smiled and asked, "What is it? You're making me nervous."

She went ahead and told him the following story, "I was once raped by this older guy on the streets, I suspect that he might have HIV or something, it was just a few months ago. I'm sorry but I felt you needed to know this…" The guy's sudden paleness and the way he quickly got off her and put on his clothes denounced how terrified he was to listen to such a confession. Esmeralda had accomplished what she intended to do – discourage him from having sexual intercourse at that moment. She was not prepared for this yet, but she did not want to sound as the typical young girl who innocently says 'let us wait for the right moment'. Perhaps if he had taken the time to conquer her with some romantic talks or actions there would have been a different outcome; either this guy did not have the gift of the gab or he was such a jerk, one of those who think they are entitled to anything they desire just for their mere looks. The semester quickly ended and they never saw each other again. About three months later, Esmeralda received a letter from an attorney stating that she was being sued for putting in danger the life of Michael Lopez, that she was driving irresponsibly that night of the accident when 'the passenger of same name above on 03/15/1990 at 10:45 pm was in the car with her…' She could not believe what her eyes were looking at, but she was forced to come to the obvious conclusion that this guy used her; he carefully planned the whole thing; it was a setup and he was going to gain a lot of money as a result of her stupidity, her naivety and rushed desire for passion and romance. This guy was already in his twenties and no driving license yet? Esmeralda did not think of that; she was used to seeing a lot of people in her community who learned to drive much later in life than the average American. Esmeralda was eighteen years of age when she got her driving license herself. She was not mature enough for her age; the way she was brought up in her strict religion could explain her oafishness dealing with guys. She would eventually learn slowly and painfully the rules of the love game; however, that process needed to run its due course.

If you think just for a minute that the story previously narrated was a bitter experience for Esmeralda, wait until you read the following. There was this time when a theologian student who came from abroad to work in the USA for a short period of time — a practice of many young men every summer who belonged to Esmeralda and her father's religious denomination, this guy rented precisely Esmeralda's uncle's basement apartment. This time around Esmeralda was no longer living in the same place as her mother's; she went to live with her father and uncle for some time. She would stay with them until her mom could get back on her feet because she just had separated from her second husband and got no financial help from him. One evening, a younger and full of life, Esmeralda, is rushing trying to finish getting ready to go when she hears the doorbell. "I'm opening the door… or!" she shouted as she was running down the steep stairs from the attic – her temporary bedroom – and almost breathlessly signaled the young guy with her unoccupied hand to come inside while with the other hand tried to open a bobby pin with her teeth to fix her hair. For a moment she stood there, kind of frozen – like not sure what to do next; the guy quickly grabbed her by her waist and pulled her close to him, but had to quickly let her go when they heard somebody approaching.

"Hello! Mr. Guzman... like I promised I'm here at seven p.m.; whenever you're ready, we can go." Esmeralda's father could not be ready on time for hardly anything, but church was a different story, so after ten minutes they headed out. Once all inside the tiny brown old car, Enrique switched around the worn-out leather stick to manually start the car which produced way more noise and dark smoke than actually velocity. About five minutes away the car stopped and never again was able to be restarted, it was dead, never to be resuscitated. They all had to walk back home in the cold, kind of disappointed; Esmeralda's father tried to conceal his annoyance and Esmeralda felt a relief because she did not have to listen to another interminable boring sermon that night. Esmeralda's father goes, "Enrique, why don't you come inside and sit down with us? It behooves us to converse a bit, don't you think?"

Enrique, "Sure! Mr. Gomez... that would be my pleasure." They went up the stairs to the second apartment and sat on the old and ugly, oversized for the room, sofas; they were sitting across from each other. Esmeralda went to hang the coats on the crowded and disorganized stand in a corner of the room. She then went and sat on the arm of the sofa her father was sitting on and kind of wondering if her father was planning to keep on talking for much longer or if they were going to have a moment alone.

After a good while it seemed to Esmeralda, her father finally excused himself. "Oh! Boy I am really tired, I will have to retire to bed... please don't stay long, muchachos, Esmeralda?"

"Yes, Daddy," said Esmeralda.

"Remember you work tomorrow," her loving father said.

She nodded a yes with a smile, and Jeremias kissed her forehead. "Bendición Papi," she asked for his blessing as she did since she could ever remember and jumped to sit next to Enrique the minute the old man turned his back. She was growing fond of Enrique; he was a very smart and funny guy; He did not have 'donde caerse muerto' but she was not minding his economic hardship status, at all. Enrique purported this sort of personification of cleverness; the way he told her short stories and narrated anecdotes enticed her very much. He had managed to steal from her a few passionate kisses even around her strict father, a very astute guy for sure; that made her feel as if they were having this little adventure, and getting a big dose of adrenaline every time, they were together.

One afternoon, Esmeralda came home earlier than usual from work and found her father was not home; he was out doing some errands, her uncle was still at work, so she decided to lay down comfortably on the sofa while eating a cup of ice cream, just trying to chill out after such a long day at work and coming from the heat outside that summer. A few minutes into her so-desired solitude, the bell rang. She opened the door and there was Enrique. She was surprised to see him there and invited him to come in; she quickly let him know that nobody was home and waited for his reaction while still holding the door open half way; he rushed to enter the small living room and sat on the sofa without waiting to be asked. He then extended his arm, asking her to sit next to him. She timidly went and sat down quietly, she was a little bit nervous because she knew better than that; she was not supposed to stay alone with a guy and she knew her father or uncle would come soon. Enrique, however, he did not look preoccupied at all; on the contrary, he started hugging Esmeralda and at one point grabbed her by her shoulders, positioned her laying down and proceeded to unbutton her blouse; he pulled down his pants and her underwear. Esmeralda started to breathe heavily and asked him, "Please get off me… I don't want to do this! … Get off me!" She was frantically screaming and kicking her legs, the only part of her body she could still move since Enrique's body was pressing down the rest of her skinny and fragile body. All of a sudden… somebody was knocking at the door very hard as if in a state of emergency. Enrique quickly got up and they both fixed themselves up. Esmeralda asked, "Who is it?" She knew it could not be her father or uncle since they both always had the key with them and the manner this person was hitting the door was suspicious.

"It's your neighbor on the first floor… ah, I heard a lot of noise… is everything all right in there?"

Esmeralda, "Everything is okay here; I was jumping, doing aerobics… gracias por preocuparse, Señora Perez." Esmeralda took advantage of this and firmly told him, "Look! If you don't get out of here right now… I will change my mind and call the neighbors and tell them what really is going on."

Enrique, "Why are you behaving like a puritan all of a sudden?" Those words penetrated her like a knife; she was heartbroken when she realized this guy just wanted to play with her —no real intentions to love her, ever. Esmeralda looked pale as if she had just seen a ghost; she then opened the door for him while indicating with a swift movement of her head the way out and looking very angry.

Who would have thought that the guy who was able to deceive Mr. Gomez to the point that he thought Enrique could very well be a good match for her daughter —just imagine his daughter married to a church minister, how splendid! This guy was a real imbecile? It is worth mentioning that Mr. Gomez had told Esmeralda about a dream he had a couple of nights before and which made him feel uneasy in general; he said, "I was watching how this huge and strong tree was slowly coming down and splashing on a river's waters..." And that was it! Esmeralda just stood there like waiting for her dad to finish how the dream ended, but he just jumped to say, "Daughter, in the bible *trees* have a special meaning, *'life'* and *waters* is associated with *'people'* or *'crowds'*; and I interpret this dream as that tree being you and the fact that is falling down on water —and in a mysterious way— because I did not see how it was cut, as a premonition that you could go through something shameful in front of many people." Esmeralda looked pensive for a moment; still at that time, a young Esmeralda would take heed of her loving father's counsel. However, this weird dream her father had did not affect her sleep and she continued with her normal life. After all, this dream was so ambiguous that she did not see how knowing about it could help her, but she did not want to be disrespectful toward her father and just left it at that. It could be debatable whether this dream materialized in Esmeralda's future experiences, but she did ponder the dream after this last sad experience and even later in her life when once again she would feel ashamed and disvalued.

After this last episode of an attempt to be forced to have intercourse with a man, Esmeralda was very afraid to trust guys again, and even more fixed with the idea of avoiding sex all together, even when later on she might like a guy very much. It felt to her as if she was cursed because she just could not find a guy who wanted her for what she was instead of what they could take from her. You have to scratch your head thinking why Esmeralda did so badly in love relationships? Was she sending the wrong signals? Well, it is true that she was all smiles when she liked a guy and to make matters worse, she tended to be way too credulous and it showed. So, this combination of apparent foolishness and coquettish personality on her part did not help at all. The thing is that Esmeralda just wished she could be loved and appreciated by a guy; but she ended up trusting too much and too quickly and was beguiled into doing the unconceivable, in her mind, way too often. Now she had to resign herself to whatever was left out there and always be on the lookout to avoid or confront unforeseeable trouble in future love matters.

Unfortunately, this was not the first time Esmeralda was fooled in love and certainly was not going to be the last. There were a few more sad and humiliating love episodes coming her way while she was still a young and immature person. Like when she was dating this gorgeous blue-eyed, tan-skinned, curly-blond-hair young guy who made her laugh her heart out with his silly jokes. The situation was that he was dating another girl, a new church member who started frequenting the same church that he and Esmeralda visited; at the same time, he was secretly seeing Esmeralda at his basement apartment in that old industrial city, in the USA. One day, he had the audacity to sit down on a bench at church with the girl and hold her hands —a distinctive sign announcing that she was his girlfriend; who knows what he was thinking…? Maybe that Esmeralda was not supposed to be there that day? Or simply… since they did not have any official commitment, he cowardly assumed that she would not mind. Whatever twisted reason he thought he had, for Esmeralda what she saw, where she saw it and when she saw it, made her wish the earth could open up right there and swallow her; all their mutual friends knew there was something going on between them, this was not a secret. She was 'so in love with him' and he had even taken her one Saturday after the church service to have lunch on his mother's; Esmeralda thought she was a lovely woman. How could he have the nerve to do this monstrous horrendous act to her? Needless to say, Esmeralda cried inconsolably for days every time anything reminded her of him and the humiliation she suffered. She finally had the courage to confront him; she wrote a well thought out letter stating something like this, 'You are a big coward. You could have let me know that you liked another girl and even heartbroken I would have accepted it. You told me that you needed a Christian girl because you wanted to be closer to God and one day form a Christian family. You are so full of shit! Go and be happy with her; I give you, my blessing. No, don't you look down when you see me at church again. I will look right into your eyes because I don't fear you and I will go ahead with my life. I forgive you, have a happy life!' This last love disappointment was a turning point in Esmeralda's life; she promised to herself that the next guy who dared to cross her path was going to have to love her more than what she loved him. "Nobody is going to break my heart ever, ever, again!" she groaned. The following summer she met Valentino and in this emotional environment is when their relationship took roots. So, going back to the present situation of her wedding preparations, and analyzing the groom's personality a little closer: Valentino was a taciturn kind of guy, he could be easily shaped to her own ways once living together, she thought. Perhaps, she flirted with the idea that after the wedding her life was going to miraculously change for the better, away from her dysfunctional family; Esmeralda never went to live on her own as many American young adults do; she would stay with her mom and her non-married siblings until the day of her wedding. Esmeralda presumed that once married she was going to have a new and fresh start, so she continued day-dreaming of a better life after marriage. It could not be any other way —as a single young woman and proceeding from such a strict religious background, it was considered an indecent act to live alone. So, her only way of acquiring independence, ironically, was going to be via her marriage. Indeed, a very wrong and stupid idea. Now, this independence was going to consist mostly and among other things, of having sex with Valentino without the pressure to be discovered, that is right! They could not even do that without a feeling that they had an invisible observer looking over them all the time. It is not like Esmeralda was looking forward to having sex per se those days, but she got to know and trust Valentino so much that given the opportunity, she was not likely to object to this, maybe because she had assumed he would be the one with whom she inevitably would end up with for the rest of her life. Just to have an idea of their situation, analyze the following story: there was this time when her cousin, Martha, and her boyfriend visited a motel and were seen by a member of their church, as they were innocently going inside; this incident was disclosed and their names were taken to the elders in church for them to be reprimanded. Esmeralda remembered her anguish when seeing this nineteen-year-old girl being embarrassed in front of everyone there who had the guts to witness such a humiliating act. So, yes, she was probably preoccupied with all those piercing eyes from church constantly fixed on her; or even more important, a perception of a father's romantic dream of seeing his daughter marry a Christian man and/or perhaps her own tortuous thoughts of approaching the end of her youth, all of these factors always pressuring her to do the right and proper thing at the propitious time. Then when she had reached that milestone of becoming a successful married woman, perhaps all the lights which once were directed at her were going to be shut down at last and she could be free to be herself. After all, she did not think Valentino had what it takes to subdue her will. Therefore,

Esmeralda continued with her plan, with the illusion that she was going to be able to detach from her former life and be a mature, adult and independent woman; this was what she was longing for quite some time.

Weeks before her wedding, she had this conversation with her current supervisor: "Esmeralda, you have been assigned to work the last weekend of the month, as part of the Y2K team," her boss told her quietly in this dark, cold room, filled with computer monitors everywhere, seven guys and two more ladies, wearing headphones either working with clients or waiting for them to call. She tried to talk him out of this assignment by stating that by that time she would be a newlywed woman and she wanted to invite her relatives over that last weekend, New Year's Eve, in that way have her first holiday event in her new home. Esmeralda worked at a computer help desk, troubleshooting for network users over the phone. The plan was to be prepared and have computer technicians available for the unforeseen events or problems that might take place on the eve of the new millennium [year 2000]. Ironically, in the months prior to the wedding the sentiment of some people was wanting to fulfill their last wishes – sort of speaking, just in the event the end of all things known to men were about to finally arrive. Did she feel this way as well? She did not give any indication that this was indeed the case; she did not make any mention alluding to such an idea. The only thing getting close to an end for her was her own chronological clock, at least that was her perception of her situation because in her culture a woman quickly approaching her thirties and not married or planning to be soon married, is considered a 'Solterona' meaning a lady who is way past her young-good years to marry and is no longer looking attractive to most men in search of a señorita; who wants a withered flower even though it once was so beautiful? Her boss responded to Esmeralda's excuses with what seemed an irrelevant remark, "Is he loaded?"

She replied, "What do you mean by that?"

He paraphrased his comment by saying; "You know... Does he have a lot of money?" Esmeralda smiled, nervously, and just nodded. She thought of that remark that day on her way home, wondering why her boss made such a silly question. She even commented with Valentino, kind of joking about it, but as usual, he reacted indifferent and was not amused by it. That was the end of the money talk and she never thought of her fiancé's financial status again, not before the wedding, anyway.

Esmeralda continued with the arduous plan –her wedding preparation– steadily and without second guessing or asking for any advice. She concentrated with taking care of every detail of the wedding itself, and anything else was not worth her attention. Those months, weeks and days before the wedding, Anne Marie had been going through a tough emotional state where she was in love with a complicated man and she kept it secret from her parents; Esmeralda knew little about the guy and did not have time to be that confident friend her baby sister needed at that time. Esmeralda did not know the intricate details of what was going on in her sister's life or she just pretended to listen while having her mind filled with 'alas de cucarachas' –Spanish saying– having cockroach wings in one's head, that is what her mother used to tell her often when she noted Esmeralda was distracted. Once again, she was behaving as if she was hypnotized by her own obsession of getting married or simply having this huge fantasy of being Cinderella for one day. Therefore, the person who once exercised the most influence over her, the one who had a strong personality and unlike

Esmeralda was not submissive in character or action, her sister Anne Marie, at this point, was merely a blurry background image or for that matter, so was everybody else; Esmeralda's mother was absent, at least emotionally. They were never that close and she never trusted her mother that much to confide in her with any worries or doubts she might have. Her father, that being that she had put on a pedestal, even he tried to make her come to her senses; he told her just a few weeks before the big day, "Daughter, I want you to remember what the prophetess stated about marriage: 'Anyone can back off honestly from marrying a person —even at the altar if it came to that, if one becomes unsure or finds a powerful reason to do so because it is far better to break a commitment even when it is of this magnitude than to go into a marriage and be unhappy for the rest of your life'. Those words that her father enunciated were profound and right to the point, relevant to her situation. Esmeralda frowned her forehead, looked at her father silently and pensively for a few seconds, then quickly shook her head and assured him that she was doing the right thing, no need to worry. That was it! If Esmeralda ignored her father's advice, there was nothing else or anyone else who was going to prevent her from doing what she was determined in her mind to do. This titanic was going down soon, very soon, but no alerts were strong enough for her. Esmeralda's three brothers, Emmanuel, the older responsible one, the middle and troubled one, Pedro, and the youngest of all and clueless one, Tobias, did not tell her what they were thinking regarding her decision to marry that guy; however, if she had paid attention to their body language, and facial expressions, she would have realized that they did not approve of what she was about to do, either. They liked her fiancé; they considered him a good person, but just not the right man for their sister. It was like anyone who really knew

Esmeralda and saw them together got a sense that something was not quite right with this picture. She could deceive co-workers, acquaintances and even the people from church, and that she did. Esmeralda did not look happy with him; on the contrary, she was always finding fault with him and they were arguing about trifles all the time, it seemed. So, again nobody who really knew her understood her hurry to marry under these circumstances.

By the time of the wedding rehearsal, a spirit of resignation prevailed, that is, no one attempted to persuade Esmeralda to resist jumping into the abyss. It was as if they were all participating in a theatrical play; everybody had a role to play and had to perform to the best of their abilities. Or perhaps, Esmeralda finally convinced them she could be happy with Valentino; she never showed any ambivalence and her enthusiasm in the latter months had been so obvious. So, they had no choice but to hope for the best. The mystery remains, why would she succumb to an insipid life, deprived of passion and anything that she always desired her life to be? And why would she relinquish the idea of marrying the man of her dreams?

The great entrance

It was a chilly, breezy and sunny, autumn afternoon, one p.m. to be precise. The trees had started their transition, after leaving their healthy green foliage and becoming half way alive and half way dead. Almost like a vivid representation of what Esmeralda was experiencing herself, but she preferred to detach from her reality. Nevertheless, in the midst of all, there was solace; a mix of golden, orange, red, yellow, plum, mulberry, and wine hues adorned her path to the church. Esmeralda contemplated all this beauty; she was enjoying herself. She absorbed every minute and did not take a glimpse of what the near future would bring. Sitting in the back of the white limousine, she surprised the chauffeur quietly looking at her through the rearview mirror and they both smiled; he then asked her politely, "Are you ready?"

She took a deep breath in and out through pursed lips, and then firmly said, "Yes, I'm ready." He opened the door for her and she looked at him again while he was holding her hand to help her get out of the vehicle. For a few seconds, they were both on their feet, parallel to each other, very close to each other and making eye contact. It was then when it crossed her mind that this attractive man was the last man, she would have a chance to interact with before signing her life away in marriage. She felt something… that something that makes one flirt with someone if only for a little while. Was it attraction? Too late and too nervous to even contemplate such an idea. A few minutes later she will have to make her great entrance at the church and let the show begin.

At the high-celling altar with light pink and white lily flowers refreshing the atmosphere and an obviously nervous −as a typical man would be under these circumstances− awaited the groom. Esmeralda's father looked at her with admiration and took her hand. She immediately said, "Daddy, almost time to go in; we have to pay attention to the music when it changes." They could not see inside the church from the room they were waiting in; Esmeralda was hoping that everything went the way it was planned and carefully rehearsed. The pastor, the best man and the groom would be there already and then would walk in a little boy holding a huge bible, at least it must had seemed to him; he was only five years of age. He was Esmeralda's nephew, her older brother's son. The boy was brave and smart; he walked slowly and steadily and kept looking forward just as Aunty Esmeralda had instructed him. Normally this boy would carry the rings in a regular Spanish wedding, but in this case, Esmeralda opted for the boy to carry the holy book that the pastor was going to read at the ceremony because in this couple's religion people did not wear jewelry except for a watch or a modest decorative pin and although a wedding band was optional, it normally took no part in the church ceremony.

Then the maid of honor, who was of course Anne Marie, made her entrance. She wore a long gown — reaching her ankles and semi-straight, it accentuated her small waist and showed a discreet nice cleavage; it was not a Cinderella type of dress, that wouldn't go with her personality. The light was dancing over her subtle curves, reflecting varied hues of a dusty pink and a sort of translucent bronze brownish or greenish color, giving the fabric of this gown a metallic feeling although this material was fine and not metallic at all; a sense of classic and simplicity beauty was shown in the haute couture of her gown; it was a very expensive and elegant dress, the one that she picked and paid for; she would not settle for anything cheap-looking and of poor taste. Her petite figure looked svelte and she appeared taller in this gown. Her make-up and hair-do could have looked much better, but things were not going that smoothly for her lately. Her stylist, who happened to be her friend as well, had treated her hair with a chemical to make it both lighter and straight, this would break most of it. So, she thought that cutting it really short, was going to disguise the obviously bad-hair-do. On top of this unfortunate episode, the make-up artist that Anne Marie also contracted to fix the bride, mother and herself, failed to accomplish her mission of doing the best make-up they could ever get. This woman had gone to a party the night before, got drunk and woke up the next day with a resaca so bad that she was not being herself that morning. Esmeralda did not know for sure what was happening because this was the first time with her, but quickly realized that she was not doing that great and she had to ask her, "Please, I would like my make-up to be more subdued, do you understand?

More natural, but I also would like to look different today, kind of special." Esmeralda remained surprisingly calm, perhaps because she did not want her sister to feel bad. She managed to pass that moment in the beauty salon and after a few trials of different types of color blushes, lipstick, eyebrow pencils and mascara, etc., etc. at the end she felt satisfied with her own face. The truth was that no amount of make-up or lack of thereof was going to change the unchangeable, the fake happy faces and the disappointment of seeing the first woman to be married in the family probably have her own misfortune from that day on.

Then appeared las damitas who were four girls ranging from six to eight years of age. They were wearing long cream dresses with a dusty pink double skirt separated and picked up in intervals with a little bunch of artificial flowers; these elaborate flower girls' dresses also had a tulle underneath the taffeta skirt and a wide dusty pink bow. These made the little girls look like they were taken from a royal magazine. These dresses were costume made; all the girls had their measurements taken more than once. Esmeralda emphasized to la modista, "Is it possible for the girls to have a high waist... you know... So, their waist would appear smaller...? I think this way they will have sort of a royalty look; don't you think?" The modista nodded with a smile. "And the bow... I wish it does not move; I want it to stay neatly put on their backs." Esmeralda also asked her to make a flower-crown for each of the girls and clarified, "I want them to have the same pink and cream of the fabric used for the dresses... could you please do that for me?" The modista replied she was going to do her very best. "Oh! I bought these round baskets that I would really like you to decorate with small flowers and ribbons to be folded around the handles and wrap the round bottom of these baskets with the same fabric used for the little dresses; that could go well with the theme colors... Is that at all possible?" added Esmeralda, anxiously waiting for a positive response.

"That is also possible," said the patient dressmaker, with a smile. The girls gracefully walked down the beautiful, carefully hand-painted aisle runner that Esmeralda had invested so much time on; they sprinkled pale pink rose petals, slowly taking them from their baskets all the way to the altar, preparing the path for the bride to walk on. In case you wonder, no, there were no bridesmaids because most of Esmeralda's female friends were married or working on their soon to be wedding and besides it occurred to her that her wedding would be even more interesting and unique if she opted for the flower girls instead of the typical young ladies.

At one point, the pianist abruptly stopped the music, turned her head to look at the rear of the church, quickly turned her head again and immediately and enthusiastically stroked the piano keys with a new and uplifting music that signaled the appearance of the bride. Everybody stood up and turned to see her; they were impressed to see her so beautiful and elegant, at least that was what she perceived and that was how she felt. Los noviecitos were walking right behind her; they are an important part of a Spanish wedding tradition where the couple's youngest relatives accompany the bride during that epoch when the wedding dresses had a long train, los noviecitos would hold the bride's train, and Esmeralda had witnessed this so many times while growing up in her native country. A seven-year-old boy and a six-year-old girl, the boy wearing similar clothing to that of the groom and the girl wearing a white dress that loosely reached to her knees and wore a veil and even carried a bouquet of flowers because 'lo noviecitos' literally means the little bride and groom or couple. Esmeralda walked proudly and with a big smile, thinking that everything so far had gone as planned. When father and daughter reached the edge of the stairs that would take her to the final destination, the place where her future was going to be sealed for better or for worst, her father lifted up a side of her veil and softly kissed her cheek — the undeniable signal that he was giving his beloved daughter away in marriage; she smiled at her dad and walked up to meet her man.

The moment of truth

There in that spot which is the most holy place in a church, the priest started his discourse. He did not say anything unusual, otherwise Esmeralda would have remembered weeks, months or even years later, at least the essence of what she heard at one of the most important moments in her life. Again, she was lost in her thoughts and not really paying attention; it was just one more sermon of many she heard over the years. She just picked up clues as this moment was rehearsed the night before and she knew the key things that demanded her participation, so she acted accordingly. This same pastor who was now directing the ceremony was the same one who once counseled the couple in preparation for marriage. This holy man might have been knowledgeable in theology matters, but he was oblivious to Esmeralda's indifference and her real motives to get married. So, he continued with his inspirational biblical phrases and moving anecdotes; eventually the bride and groom repeated the vows after him; she did not know how she got to that point, but she did. How could she assent to this so far? The explanation might rely on her tendency or practice of putting herself in unsafe situations; like one time when she was a brand-new immigrant to one of the most dangerous cities in New Jersey, USA, and a clueless and naive seventeen-year-old girl. One winter afternoon when the sun was still shining, Esmeralda decided to go for a walk in the neighborhood and eventually found herself in the downtown mall. She got in and out of different departmental clothing stores and then getting out of a store she met darkness, in all the sense of the word. She was literally lost; night fell and she had not noticed it while inside the stores filled with so many material things that attracted her. She did not remember which way she came from. How was she going to return home? She did not carry a cellular phone with her – no such thing existed for regular people at the time – and she did not have a penny on her to even place a phone call on those public phones and on top of that, she did not remember the home's phone number or even her now temporary home address. While she was wandering on a busy corner in downtown, and probably giving the impression of being one of those women who provided sex pleasures to men in exchange for money in that area – the naïve young lady unaware of this – and looking in all directions, she spotted a skyline of a cathedral and remembered that it was located a couple of blocks from her aunt's house where she was staying; at that precise moment in time, a man, an older man stopped his car and rolled down his car's window. He called her while waving his hands as if he was desperate to catch her attention. She looked around not sure he was talking to her. She timidly approached him and she tried hard to understand what he was saying, but her English was very limited at the time and this man had a heavy accent. She did guess that this stranger was offering her a ride; she hesitated for a few minutes, but then thought, "If he could take me to that church, I will easily get home from there." So, she quickly got into the car and while he was still talking and Esmeralda still trying to understand him, she kept smiling nervously. She always smiled no matter what, she was wired that way; she was una muchacha risueña. She tried to explain to the man where she was heading and pointed to the cathedral. The guy quickly took off and about two blocks down the hill he suddenly put one hand on Esmeralda's lap and left it resting there; she froze for a few seconds, her semblance of innocence changed drastically, and with no words coming out of her mouth, she just realized that she was in big trouble. She thought of something quickly, so she turned her head to look at him and with a smile, slowly said, "Me forget, a bag in store, over there." That was all she could articulate at the time due to both the language barrier and her frightened state. Almost like a miracle, he stopped the car and she said, "Me come back," got out of the car and flew away 'Como alma que se lleva el diablo'. She started running and lost the guy; she managed to get home that night guided by the cathedral that was still there in the same place she left it before unconsciously getting into that car. She cried all the way home and told nobody about this horrible experience. Oh yes! Esmeralda was notorious for getting into perilous situations. It seems that she learned her way in life like scientists conduct trials, trying one thing and then the other; in her case she got no regards for safety, most of the time anyway. Only that this time, this was not an experiment, it was the real thing. How couldn't she see that? They were married just like that, and Esmeralda continued in that state of stupor through the whole ceremony and beyond.

The reception from hell

"Ladies and Gentlemen, please welcome with a big applause, the newlyweds: Mr. and Mrs. Valentino Ignacio Vignota and Esmeralda Daniela Vignota!" exclaimed the disk jockey. Esmeralda could not help but notice that the hall was overcrowded; she sent out invitations with the number of chairs in the room in mind. The problem was that she invited practically the whole church besides her relatives, who were numerous to begin with. Some couples from church brought their youngsters even though the invitations stated: 'For couples only', obviously a culture misunderstanding. She was not happy with this situation, but she did not panic — coming from a large family, people were creative. So, everybody found a seat; there were kids sitting on their parents' laps or on the floor, they did not care, they all mingled together, spoke loudly and cheerfully, typical of their blithesome culture. Oh! The cake; Esmeralda took a good look at the cake, took a deep breath, she tried to conceal her reaction, however, for a few minutes she could not smile. She noted the cake which consisted of a castle like theme; one of the towers was tilted, and made it look asymmetrical, and she did not like that. This was just the beginning of an evening filled with not so pleasant surprises for Esmeralda. The bride and groom finally sat down and after doing a brindis with what resembled champagne, but indeed was just a non-alcoholic drink which bottle looked as sparkling and sophisticated as a champagne bottle since in their religion the consumption of alcohol was also prohibited. Traditionally, in the weddings from her church that Esmeralda attended before, nobody drank a toast, but she intended in her wedding to go a step ahead of tradition in order to stand out, I suppose. Was she attempting to compensate for something that was not there… her lack of enamoramiento, perhaps? No matter how hard she tried to convince everyone that this was the perfect union, the fact of the matter is that she was not emotionally committed to him; he was not the love of her life. Esmeralda needed to not dwell on this little problem of hers; she just wanted a normal life with a faithful husband and kids to love. Esmeralda had a huge problem; she had not recognized and or accepted that she was addicted to that feeling of infatuation… you know? When one feels butterflies in one's stomach and wish to look at his eyes forever. In reality that was going to be the one thing that would one day make her regret what she was doing now. Esmeralda's feelings could remain dormant for a while until awakened abruptly one day when the anesthesia of her enchanted wedding wears off. Meanwhile she had no qualms about correcting her actions and like a horse with blinkers, just kept looking ahead to the path to her perdition.

Already in the wedding reception, Esmeralda started to feel what could be an indication of what her life with Valentino might turn out to be; in one word: CHAOS. Going back to this wedding reception from hell... somehow this couple did not make sufficiently clear who the padrino [best man in Spanish] was going to be. Yes, I mentioned before that the best man was waiting at the altar –Valentino's brother. However, Esmeralda's older brother also participated in the wedding and he was the one who went to the podium and threw a speech and made a formal 'brindis'. Esmeralda witnessed with astonishment this moment with total perplexity. Thinking, "is not the best man who owed this pivotal moment?" While Emmanuel was giving his inspirational little discourse, Esmeralda took a look at her brother-in-law... the official best man. She spotted him quickly and awkwardly trying to put away a piece of paper; it seemed, and it was just logical, that he was ready to fulfill his role of expressing in public some anecdotes and good wishes typically enunciated by a man in his position at a time like this. Esmeralda tried to make sense of this predicament, reflecting on a recent conversation with her beloved brother when she told him that it would be a great honor to have him at her wedding; maybe this created the illusion that he was asked to be that special person in her sister's wedding. Emmanuel never attended Esmeralda's church ceremonies and was not aware of the usual ceremony of a Protestant Christian church. Now, he did go to and even participated in non-church weddings and weddings from the most popular denomination in their culture [Catholic Church] a few times before since he was so loved and popular among his many friends. Emmanuel was to his sister that person who was more than an older brother; even though he was just a year older than Esmeralda, sometimes he assumed those responsibilities proper of a father in Esmeralda's life. Their parents got divorced at their tender ages of seven and six. Their mother went through harsh times as a single mother, and was even afflicted by an illness that at one point she looked skinny as young bulimic women look nowadays. Emmanuel was the only one from his siblings to stay with her mother in that little town while his two sisters and younger brother lived with their father who had custody of them, at the time, in the city. Once they all migrated to this great and dreamed country, the United States of America, Emmanuel continued to help provide the financial and emotional support his family demanded. Esmeralda's mother had re-married a guy about ten years younger than her back in her native country. He seemed to love her and respect her at the beginning and accepted her kids and they adopted a boy who Esmeralda loved just like her other blood siblings; Esmeralda's stepfather, Santiago, would treat them warmly when they came over on vacation in summer time to see her mom, back there in their country of origin. However, he was still somehow immature and when faced with harsh times typical of new comers to this new country, he simply did not hesitate to abandon her with kids and all and replace her with a younger chick. Once again, the older brother assumed the position of a father figure to his siblings and provided all the help he could possibly give his mother. Esmeralda's father, Jeremias, was physically disabled, incapable of giving any financial support and as usual submerged in his religion. So, Emmanuel was a very good candidate to be the padrino. Valentino's younger brother, Florencio, as per Valentino's own account when he and

Esmeralda talked about their family's experiences and personality that each possessed, described his brother as distant from his own world; they were not close brothers. It seemed that Valentino could not think of a better person to be the best man, given that he did not have any close friends in this new land and he was a very socially anxious type of guy to make new friends. Also, Valentino may have just thought of this opportunity to show his brother the love that he was incapable of expressing to him ever. This is a very case in point type of situation that clearly demonstrated how disconnected this couple was. This was just the beginning and was not going to get any better. Esmeralda never knew whether her husband ever apologized to his brother for the miscommunication and emotionally precarious and uncomfortable position his brother was put through. Esmeralda didn't think she was in a position to go and clear things up with her brother-in-law or simply she was way too embarrassed to approach him with this nonsense. Esmeralda and his new partner for life never re-visited together this episode not even to figure out what caused it to happen. Unfortunately, this couple would continue to be in the future as out of sync as they were this day.

One last thing that cannot be ignored in this reception was the very ridiculous moment that one of the guests kindly and uninvited just went ahead and created. This young woman was Esmeralda's second cousin's daughter, yes, the whole extended family — they all were there. This crazy one – all of a sudden, it seemed to Esmeralda – appeared on stage and announced she was interpreting a song dedicated to the bride and groom. The mariachi musicians who were contracted without Esmeralda's knowledge by a couple of girlfriends, accompanied the 'singer' in a song that Esmeralda deemed totally inappropriate and of bad taste; those canciones de amargue that people listen to while getting drunk when they have suffered a love disappointment. Who in the world invited her to sing at her carefully arranged wedding? "What the hell just happened here?" Esmeralda quietly thought while trying with a fake smile to keep her composure. And how can this single episode translate into her future married life? I would say that could very well represent the little nasty surprises that life would throw at a married couple and if their love is not strong enough, these bitter moments can shake them up and they can no longer find a real meaningful purpose to continue sharing a life with the person each one swore to spend the rest of their life with.

La luna de ~~hiel~~ miel

All of a sudden Esmeralda found herself crouched on the white sand of the beautiful Fort Lauderdale beach. A chilly breeze played with her hair while she was picking up little shells and time seemed to have come to a halt. She had left her husband sleeping and went for a walk on the hotel's ocean front. This was the first morning she faced after the wedding; this was day #1 of her honeymoon. This sunny, but yet cold, morning Esmeralda couldn't help it and felt a sudden rush of melancholy and despair. She felt so lonely; she finally started to realize that she was not in a desirable position, that she did not belong in that space and time, that this was not what she dreamed of or even imagined and not because her situation was so magical, on the contrary because it was so sad.

Perhaps in an attempt to jettison some frustrations caused by the reality that she insisted on putting herself through, Esmeralda so desperately needed to be by herself if just for a couple of hours. Scenes from a sweet and tender love experience she was so lucky to be part of were released from her most precious trunk of memories that morning; she reminisced of the young man who came one summer to stay at her aunt's house where she was living for a while. He was a Theologian major student in a university in Puerto Rico – one of many who have come throughout the years to Esmeralda's church – the young man came to New Jersey to work for a couple of months. His work consisted of selling religious, spiritual and health related books in this way contributing to the payment of his college tuition. One nice evening they were sitting on the backyard terrace, T.V. area; Esmeralda was watching her little cousin absorbed in his Nintendo Super Mario game and across her were these eyes contemplating her silhouette; she was wearing a white cotton simple dress and one could appreciate her small chest and flesh lacking clavicles, meanwhile a front lace was accentuating her small waist; she wore these brown leather roman sandals that reached her calves, giving her a sort of renaissance appearance; her cinnamon curly hair that rested on her shoulders was unrestrained that day and she was distilling this healthy glow typical of a young girl accompanied by that almost permanent smile of hers. At one point their gazes coincided and he signaled her to go to sit down next to him on the weaker love-seat. She timidly but happily consented and he continued to look at her semblance of innocence and natural beauty; he got even closer to her and almost without thinking stole a kiss from her. She did not react; she was paralyzed and felt this warm feeling on her face. The young fellow must have taken Esmeralda's demeanor as a sign of disapproval and with embarrassment apologized for his imprudence. She nodded in a noticeable way, but with a frozen flat face, almost as if by wanting him to desist of his misunderstanding; she could not feel happier and more pleased but her sympathetic nervous system rendered her incapable of showing her real feelings. How could she not be attracted to this young fellow? His beauty consisted not only of his generous and sincere spontaneous laugh so very often, but the devotion reflected in his big brown eyes when he looked at her. His skin was soft and immaculately fair, like a heavenly being. The way he would run his fingers softly through his night-black hair when a gentle breeze tousled it meanwhile inclining his head forward — a natural tendency of his; this mere action would provoke something inside her so mysteriously disturbing and gratifying at the same time. So, again... why in the world he would think that she did not welcome that incredible kiss?

Fabio had this peaceful look at his face all the time; always solicitous about people's spiritual wellbeing and Esmeralda must have felt attracted to such a noble character. One afternoon, after Esmeralda came from work and she was sitting in the front porch leisurely, he was ready to go with his briefcase full of books and asked her if she would like to accompany him to knock on a couple of doors in their neighborhood. She with a big smile nodded a 'yes' and looking vibrant and enthusiastic both of them stood at the door of one neighbor; an elderly woman opened it and let them in after the handsome young salesman enunciated an introductory, convincing, powerful phrase. The way he conversed with this woman was as if they had known each other for a long time; she even offered them a cup of tea. He did not get to sell her anything that day, the elderly, poor lady could not afford it, but he was welcomed to come again anytime for another nice talk. Esmeralda sensed from the soon-to-be spiritual missionary pastor that feeling of abnegation and willingness to make a difference in people's lives. He did not cease to amaze her; one day when he was looking for her upstairs in the house and did not find her, he went down and knocked at the basement

46

door where she lived with her mother, stepfather and older brother –her younger siblings came to the USA later on when the family settled in a more suitable place for a large family. There was nobody else in the whole house, but he was not aware of this and besides he wanted to see her if only for a few minutes. Esmeralda took a while to finally come to the door; she was pleasantly surprised to see him standing there. She quickly grabbed his hand and asked him to come inside; he got very nervous when he saw her with her hair wet and only wearing a bathrobe and when realizing she was home alone, out of the blue he pronounced these words, "Chamita [little girl in Venezuelan colloquial language], you have to keep your innocence; I want you to remain pure…" Esmeralda did not quite comprehend why he was saying that precisely at that moment; for her that was a moment that was not probably going to repeat itself; that was their chance to be alone and show their affection in a more intimate fashion. She was not at all afraid and just desiring to be with him — not sexually speaking, though, just being able to finally be alone and cuddle together romantically. The young and yet mature man had elevated inclinations; he tended to act with the 'consequences' principle always fixed in the frontal lobe of his brain. He did not wish to harm her in any way, not physically nor emotionally. They kissed briefly only because Esmeralda initiated it. He nonetheless, was very strong spiritually speaking and while taking his enamorada's arms from around his neck, with sad eyes told her he had to go back upstairs and they could see each other again when other members of the family arrived home. He was just trying to avoid something that they could regret later. Esmeralda put this face of disappointment on, but did get it. She was an easy target for guys who would try to take advantage of her vulnerability in an attempt to satisfy their low sexual urges; just like that other minister college student attempted to violate her some time before and fortunately for this fragile girl, this time was different.

That summer quickly got to an end and the young college student needed to return to finish one more semester. A couple of days before his departure while sitting at the dining room table – on her aunt's floor – and just the two of them, Fabio looking very serious stated, "Esmeralda, I have to leave in two days as you know and then..."

Esmeralda interrupted him and said, "We will keep in touch, we will write to each other all the time, right?"

He continued where he left off, "I will finish my studies and I will become a pastor, but one that travels around the world to remote places where people need a lot of help... I won't be that typical minister who is assigned a church and lives comfortably with his family in a nice house. My question is and I need you to be frank with me, would you be willing to leave this country, your family and come with me in my missionary work?" Esmeralda was shocked; she was not prepared for this; and Fabio took her utter silence as a sign that she was not going to be able to be his partner in life – at least she was not mature enough to make such a major decision at that point in time – and he seemed to not have much time left to embark on his important mission. That morning that Esmeralda helped her loving angel put his precarious belongings in her uncle's old wagon to be taken to the airport, Esmeralda again asked Fabio if he was going to send letters to her and one day they would meet again; this time his silence said it all and with half a smile and tender hug and kiss on her cheek he said good bye. Esmeralda kept looking at the distance with a premature melancholic and saddened expression on her face as the car disappeared and her most precious love thus far.

Esmeralda never forgot about that summer and the man who treated her with respect and unmarred love. Months later she did receive something from him; it was a postcard addressed to the whole family. She felt sad because he did not send anything just for her and this way, she accepted the fact that Fabio was a closed chapter in her life. This marked the beginning of a journey for Esmeralda when she was going to resign to true love altogether and be receptive to anything else which was able to mitigate just a little her love devastation, but was anybody going to ever supplant her angel's pure love?

The main reason she was reminded of this particular period in her life explains a lot; she was probably comparing her present life with the one offered to her and that she had forgone years back. Her reflection was, "Maybe I would have been very happy with him even living in a shack, eating whatever we could find or afford but here I am enduring this senseless life I chose for myself." She finally sauntered back to the quiet lonely villa where Valentino waited, wondering where his wife had disappeared to. She could not and did not dare to make her feelings known to her husband; she put on a positive face and told Valentino, "Well? This cold front that is hitting South Florida is not going to ruin our plans, honey!" She continued, "What are we going to do now? You know that I was looking forward to a nice, warm vacation and instead we got this?" Valentino quickly suggested that they could rent a car and go to Walt Disney World Resort, Orlando, FL. They both had not been there before and this could be a great opportunity. They did not hesitate and went on with the plan. Even in this great resort, they felt the chilly meddling wind that only served to annoy their already disturbed senses. If you see their honeymoon photo album, you would appreciate that what looks romantic at first glimpse, however, it was something they did out of necessity; Esmeralda and Valentino would alternate wearing the only two sweaters that Esmeralda's mother insisted she put in her suit case, 'just in case'. What an irony, that a place that was supposed to be a tropical resort turned out to be as cold as a chilly autumn on the East coast where they ran away from that late November. Was this unforeseen climate change yet another sign? For Esmeralda, this was just a mere inconvenience and of course provoked more tension between them than the usual. They would quarrel often during their stay there over silly things such as the restaurant to visit for dinner or what attractions to choose for the day. The only thing that remotely resembled a romantic couple's actions was when they timidly asked someone passing by to take a picture of them. In one instance, an older couple stopped by and Valentino told them they were on their honeymoon, that they came from New Jersey, blab, blab, blab… This was big for Valentino being that he was such a shy person or should I say… introverted? Or maybe he was just thinking aloud and, in this way, intended to remind her new wife of their current status and that they needed to act accordingly or at least try.

This honeymoon trip far from being a pleasant and remarkable time for this newlywed couple was going to be a subject of unending dispute in the near future. Not only had they ended up suffering a cold front in the midst of their 'tropical' retreat, but apparently, Valentino reserved [online] a villa which consisted of a master room, a large twin-bedded bedroom, a small living room with TV area, and small kitchen instead of the hotel suite he was supposed to get and ended up paying for one night at the villa what they would have paid for five days in one of the hotel's rooms. This mistake, Esmeralda was not going to forgive and / or forget. She would mention it to try to prove a point often later on. This is how their honeymoon became their 'Bitter Moon'. What should have they expected, anyway? With every hour that passed by Esmeralda felt soberer; the detoxification period after the drunkenness with her desire to celebrate a wonderful wedding or in reality to have a magical day – pure fantasy no reality involved – started to have a reverse effect on her. She now started feeling sort of ashamed — that typical feeling that one has when one realizes how badly one behaved in front of many people while under the influence a night before. Moreover, it was so painful to finally and secretly admit to a grave mistake. From now on she would live her days trying to make the best of her decision and hoping that time was going to bring something she wished above anything else, a solid and loving family. She now had the chance to create a new beginning, a new destiny. She sincerely thought that the unconditional and eternal love that a mother should feel for a child was going to serve as the catalyst to a satisfying life. She was willing to try to go on −llevar la fiesta en paz− with Valentino. But you should know that time is more powerful than even an ardent desire or will, so time in its due time was going to accomplish something it does very well, create a monotony that would destroy everything still standing in its path. Esmeralda was not able to conceive the idea that perhaps she needed to relinquish to that need of 'planning her life' to really enjoy the beauty that only spontaneous moments and sincere actions can bring.

Why if Esmeralda felt in her heart so early on in her fateful marriage that she had committed a terrible mistake, she did not seem to reconsider and annul the whole thing? Strangely enough, Esmeralda had faith that she could learn to love Valentino and since they were supposed to have a couple of key components which guaranteed the solidification of their union such as their religious ideas and practices – these were important to form a family with strong values – so she thought everything was going to be just fine. Esmeralda totally negated how crucial it was for her to acknowledge her true feelings and be guided by them before time goes and make a bad situation worse, much worse. Esmeralda had many reflections during her honeymoon; she remembered when Jenny, this young girl, probably in her early twenties, told her one day, "Esmeralda, are you sure you want to marry him? You don't look happy." Jenny was a Psychology major student so that might have contributed to her conclusion though frankly it did not take a college degree to notice that. Perhaps all her other friends were just afraid to tell her what they really thought and now she regretted totally ignoring this clever and sincere friend's advice. Jenny tried to alert her of an imminent misstep, but Esmeralda was way too stubborn to consider what she was doing and exasperated by unending love dissolutions. She got no motivation to wait for love and at the same time afraid to see it knock at her heart –only to see 'it' ridicule her once again; hence, she would go and attempt to trick life by fatuously wanting to take command of her feelings as if her reason or logic were going to do the job this time instead of her silly and vulnerable heart. However, the trickery was all on her, poor thing; indeed, she did not have the most remote idea of the damage she was self-inflicting; how pain was going to rip her from inside out; how life was going to turn so unbearable to the point of not fearing hell itself since she would visit it while still living her cruel existence. Here, on her honeymoon, she still did not imagine how she was going to be transformed soon enough into this woman who would eventually lose her dignity, in all the depth and amplitude that this word implies because she was going to disregard the intrinsic value of her own life, one of the most precious gifts from the Creator to mankind. She nullified dignity in her life and one needs this virtue in order to have respect for others and self-respect as well. When one has no longer that capability to place one's life in high regards, anything else has no purpose or reason to be. Yes, one can say that Esmeralda's honeymoon was the prelude to an inferno fast-approaching.

Chapter 2

It's *Not* a Tele-Novela

For whom was the pleasant surprise?

About fourteen months into Esmeralda and Valentino's marriage, something huge is about to hit them. Esmeralda seems to be more neurotic than usual and easily and too often bursts into tears. Her husband as usual is aloof of her real feelings and only judges by what he superficially is able to perceive. It is common for them to have a fracas every time she wants her husband to understand her position. Esmeralda continues wishing that Valentino could understand her better without the need of telling him explicitly how she feels about something, all the time! Esmeralda always thought that when a man loves a woman, he ought to –almost as if by a telepathic means– deduce how or why she is feeling the way she is feeling. Valentino's lack of sensitivity toward his wife because he would not bother to ask her how she really felt or what was causing her anxiety, was a real problem. If he had shown at least interest in her feelings that would have been helpful and would had made her feel more at ease.

One morning, Esmeralda finally brings home a pregnancy test since she had missed her menstrual period for a couple of weeks now. The test was positive and she is not shocked; nevertheless, she went into a pensive mode, looked around while standing in front of the bathroom sink with the evidence still fresh on top of the toilet tank cover. She begins to appreciate this tiny space and how unsophisticated and unattractive it looks; the black smoke's marks on the walls serve as a constant reminder of the time when her brother, Pedro, used to occupy that place and caused a fire. He got himself barricaded –not wanting to talk or allowing anybody to enter there for days– while he was submerged in a deep depression until the local police and fire department interfered. Then she goes into her bedroom where she has to lower herself to the mattress on the floor and it becomes a real ordeal just to open one of the dresser's drawers which was adjacent to the bed; she got exhausted and suddenly throws herself back, her arms folded on the back of her head and looking at the low celling, an inevitable claustrophobic sentiment involved her. After a while, could have been minutes or hours it did not matter –of what seemed to be reflections– Esmeralda snapped out of it and started preparing a special dinner during which she was going to give her husband the good news.

Esmeralda inherited from her mother the habit of watching tele-novelas, these Spanish soap operas which consist of no more than three to four months of ongoing suffering on the part of the protagonist and at the end the typical beautiful and of lower class but of good character young lady finally marries her beloved rich powerful man. Watching tele-novelas, she also has moments and / or episodes from them that interweave with her own memories or even her own dreams. At times it is hard for her to separate reality from fantasy; one of the scenes she enjoyed the most was when la dulce muchacha conceived a baby and the man who impregnated her, the impossible to reach guy, but who also loved her to death reacted so romantically and wanted to treat her as special as she could possibly be treated... only that other obstacle forbade him from doing so until 'El Fin'. At one point, it crossed her mind that when Valentino knew she was pregnant he would as if by a miracle change his behavior completely and start treating her in a special way, you know, he would pamper her...

concede to all her demands... or just a few.

Slowly but surely, it was the evening; Esmeralda anxiously had waited for Valentino – that long day she had a day off from work – to show up at the door and *she could now surprise him with a sweet and tender naturally wrapped gift*, she thought. The obviously tired husband muttered a hello with his eyes fixed in the opposite direction to hers and as if wanting to put her out of his way, quickly and steadily proceeded to succumb onto the old couch, automatically reached for the TV remote control and without noticing the look on his wife's face – a mixture of deep sadness and disappointment, he started watching his favorite food channel show. After a few seconds of staring at that passive aggressive type of husband of hers, Esmeralda feeling kind of abdicated slowly turned around and started finishing up dinner. No news was delivered that evening; she decided it was better to wait until 'the right time'. The problem had nothing to do with the timing of the telling rather it was related to the event itself. When Esmeralda finally updated him with their new status, the news provoked something in Valentino only that he went ahead and disguised that something the only way he knew how to do it — he tried to ignore her. Why was he reacting this way? It was good news... they were expecting their first child! So, for whom was the pleasant surprise? Certainly not for Valentino.

Esmeralda found no justification for his harsh behavior toward her or worst the innocent creature growing in her. "Why did you go and do something like this? Are you out of your mind?" Esmeralda heard Valentino say these words while she did not say a word; she felt something cold that traveled up and down her spine. She was used to always having a prompt response for him and this time around she simply opted for a profound silence, at least for a few minutes. Oh, no, no! That is not exactly how it happened. Valentino was not happy about the news; however, he did not say much at all; his feelings were pretty much stoic as usual. But, to Esmeralda his behavior – the silence, the lack of emotions and no physical demonstration of affection – were one of the most insulting and cruel actions her husband could display in moments such as these. She was expecting a warm hug accompanied by a wide smile at the minimum once he was given this wonderful news, instead she received a cold look and a posterior panorama of her husband's silhouette. Perhaps she had imagined a scene generated by her subconscious tormented mind when Valentino supposedly uttered his discontent with the news; she had reasons to suspect her husband would not agree to have a responsibility this enormous amidst their current situation. So, in a way she did expect him to be very upset with the news, but she preferred to go and take the denial road. As customary for Esmeralda she did not want to wait for things to duly accommodate into place and/or time rather she would take action by impulse without caressing reason. For fairness' sake, it has to be mentioned that Valentino's sense of urgency was almost non-existent; as per Esmeralda's perception, he is that type of guy that procrastinates to even reach to the bathroom on time; he takes long naps on Sunday afternoons and to get him to take the garbage out, Esmeralda has to mention the word 'divorce' in a sentence filled with other angry sounding words. Perhaps, Esmeralda lost hope that things were going to ever change and / or improve and her time to be fruitful on this earth was going to pass waiting for the 'good' times to finally come. After all, she saw other people around her, some of them friends and relatives of hers, who had already one or more kids and they had a lower income than theirs. She would use this argument to try to convince or change Valentino's negative view of their 'situation' to no avail.

The situation was that this couple planned before they married to rent a house from Esmeralda's mother. She had two standalone houses in two different towns; they rented one of them, it was nice and big — perfect to start a family. They had been living in it ever since they returned from their honeymoon. To everybody's surprise, just a few months after Valentino and Esmeralda were situated in this house, her mother decided to retire back to her native country and sell these dwellings. The house that Valentino and Esmeralda lived in sold quicker than expected and this disconcerted young couple were suddenly left on the streets, so they had the 'clever' idea of renting the other house – a mother and daughter type of house Esmeralda's mother had – which still was not sold and stay there until they found a new suitable place. They stayed in the lower part of the house [the upper floor was occupied] which was a small area with only a small bedroom, very tiny bathroom, the kitchen and small living/dining area with an old, filthy carpet to name just a few of the many negatives and the only entrance or exit was over the backyard. Yes, Valentino had a point after all. Now... it is not clear when Esmeralda decided to get pregnant; it might have been when they were still in the other house which was huge, beautiful, with a decent nice backyard and her mother had not announced her sudden decision to abandon everything and fly away. Anyway, Esmeralda neglected to inform her husband her intentions of getting pregnant. Perhaps she tacitly let him know, but she should have known better that her husband was not a good listener and definitively not a man who easily comprehended the sensible thoughts of a woman like her.

When her mom came to the rescue

Esmeralda's baby shower was in full swing when the doorbell rang and there was her mother who came from her country where she had been for a good while. Esmeralda was pleasantly surprised to see her mother, precisely now when she needed her the most. Esmeralda was going to have her first baby already due in a couple of weeks; she burst into tears and ran to receive her with a big hug. During her pregnancy, she had moments when she felt this sense of impending doom. If there was going to be a time when Esmeralda was going to empathize with her mother, the time had arrived; Esmeralda did not understand why she was feeling that way when she was supposed to feel happier than ever. The reason of her persistent depressed mood could naturally be the result of many factors including her drastically changed body image, but certainly all the hormonal changes typical of the state she was in. However, the situation of her marriage since the very beginning, I would say that was the most influential cause. It was during this important time in her life when one of Esmeralda's most splendid of all times dreams crumbled; she had this idea that her husband was going to treat her as delicately and gentle as one would handle a rose's petals, in response to this 'magical' period in the soon to be new parents' lives. Instead, she met face to face with indifference in its most archaic form; she felt a coldness that would numb her vitality and sadness in its cruel and unmerciful pure state. It was now when she was convinced that Valentino did not love her; he might have believed he did, but in reality, Valentino did not have the slightest idea of how to love a woman. How could him? He never saw his own father showing any love and affection to her mom. On the contrary, he witnessed at the tender age of seven the emotional abuse his poor mother suffered because Valentino's father did not seem to love her, evidenced by his coldness toward her and later on the abandonment his father provoked in his family when he replaced her mom with another woman. Also, her mother's second husband would inflict this submissive woman with physical abuse whenever he felt like it. This guy would be Valentino's stepfather for a few years — during a time when Valentino was a tender boy in need of a good father figure.

It was now while 'walking through The Valley of Shadows' herself that Esmeralda had pity on her mom, thinking that perhaps she had a similar experience with her father. Her mother had told her a little bit about her first marriage with Esmeralda's father and it sounded like she had her tough times with him as well. There was this time when Esmeralda casually commented to her mom, "Do you know that I learned to put on make-up watching you?" Her mother smiled and Esmeralda continued, "Yes, I would watch you when you were getting ready to go out on special occasions... you managed to make your eyes look amazing." [During her mother's second marriage]

Esmeralda's mother had a flashback — way back and told Esmeralda, "You are so lucky! I didn't have so much freedom when I was so young and still married to your father." She told her that one of those days when she looked pale after so much vomiting when she was pregnant, she dared to put on her cheeks this light rosy blush only to hear her husband ask her, 'Go wash that off your face, you look like an impious woman!' She just wanted to look healthy, but her ignorant, preoccupied with religion, pathological fanatic husband could not see her need. He was incapable of lowering himself to his wife's vulnerable emotional level. Instead, this woman felt psychologically abandoned by the one who was supposed to love her, respect her and above of all, have charity. Was not he as a man of God supposed to show charity, mercy to anyone, most of all, his wife? Because without this biblical attribute there cannot be love, these two concepts have a propensity to get interwoven and you cannot have one without the other. Now, he as a God's follower and obedient to his holly commandments should have known better. But you might wonder: was Valentino like Esmeralda's father?

No, they were very different; however, they both had a distinct particular behavior that would trigger the same damaging effects on mother and daughter. First of all, Esmeralda –the woman, a victim or simply a product of her era– had special needs which she was not willing to forgo. This woman did not agree, contrary to what it might seem, unite in marriage solely to reproduce and preserve the species. She did not get out of her father's watch to get incarcerated in another cage. To Esmeralda's surprise as well as dislike, her husband provoked this weird feeling of entrapment because once again and perhaps in a much higher degree this time, she was not free. How could she be free? This is the thing… when one person decides to join another one with the intention to love and cherish each other forever this does not mean they are going to relinquish their individual freedom; what it means is that their love, which is supposed to be not forced or imposed, will surpass any other feeling even that tendency that one has to want to be free. In Esmeralda's case, it was impossible for her not to want to be completely free when there was no love involved from either part. Her desire to acquire free rein to love and be loved by another man is what came to govern her life, late into her farce marriage. Valentino became this torturer that was not going to allow her to open her wings and fly away in search of her happiness. Their lives together made no sense to her; she was annoyed by the simplest gesture, choice of words and behavior her husband demonstrated these latter days. Just to have an idea of the things that Esmeralda abhorred was the arrogance her husband displayed when he was accusing her of mismanaging the money, or pointing out that the reason she did not know how to handle technology, like troubleshooting a problem with the computer, this was due to her lack of interest in learning. Nothing could have been further from the truth since Esmeralda was for about four years a computer networking person who provided assistance to hundreds of remote users, a task that demanded indeed a constant acquisition of new technology knowledge; she just did not enjoy that type of job, her calling was something else. Indeed, it was like the writing was on the wall; the culmination of an era where Esmeralda would resign herself to be just a lousy wife and frustrated mother was finally around the corner. Ines was finally attempting to make up for the lost times when she should have been closer to her daughter and sensitive to her emotional needs; the reappearance of Esmeralda's mother into her life and her supporting presence when she had her child, gave her the strength to even consider the possibility of one day, not too far away, to abandon the sinking boat and find a secure port where she could anchor her love until the end of her days.

Like daughter like father

"Look at those tiny hands, oh my Gosh! her fingers are just like her father's," said Esmeralda with a smile and a singing tone on her voice while putting Valentino's hand together with her newborn baby girl's hand. Another perfect tender picture is what one could appreciate when these inexperienced parents saw their little angel falling asleep way too early in the evening and they tried to desperately keep her awake by making noise and all kind of silly stuff; a futile attempt to prevent another sleepless night. Yet another magical moment was when one night Valentino fell asleep laying on the couch with the baby and Esmeralda quietly took a picture of them. The years passed so quickly that in no time, it seemed to Esmeralda, her baby transformed into this thirteen-year-old with 'a stubborn personality, procrastination incarnate, and indolent in action… a replica of her father', Esmeralda would repeat to herself way too often. She was

Esmeralda's first born, an extremely timid girl named Emma Natasha. Emma was a natural artist of the small brush; she would draw all kinds of cartoon like characters as a professional, both hand-written and with her inseparable Wacom tablet and styluses. She undoubtedly got this gift from her father; he could paint very well and that is one of the things that Esmeralda felt attracted to when they were getting to know each other. Esmeralda was impressed by a painting which awarded Valentino a recognition in the strict Jesuit Catholic School that he attended when he was about fifteen years old. This black and white picture of what looked like a ten-year-old boy with profound deep dark sunken sad eyes and holding another kid maybe two to three years of age; these kids were dressed in rags with dirt visible in their faces and hands; and looking emaciated, clearly conveyed the suffering that hunger and abandonment can cause.

Valentino talked to Esmeralda about the making of this picture. "I knew about this contest at school and immediately felt like really doing this, but I had no decent painting and tools material; I used a thick carbon pencil that I managed to get and a piece of drawing paper that was given to me by another kid who did not want it... I saw a picture of what seemed to be two poor brothers who only had each other on the newspaper and I tried to capture this image... can you believe that my parents were not present at school that day or ever to any other significant event?" Needless to say, Esmeralda was deeply touched by this. Yes, amazingly Esmeralda did find something in this guy at one point; he was also a good cook –he would actually cook for her when they were dating– and yes... he went to college back in his native country, remember how Esmeralda preferred an intellectual type of guy? He was an Economist major student and also learned to speak English on his own when he was a teenager by listening to singers like Elton John, Billy Joel and Percy Sledge many years before arriving at the land where he found his love. Esmeralda only wished that her husband could show more passion, a least a drop of ambition and could put his talent to good use; in vain she begged him to draw pictures for them to hang in the house or dedicate a few hours a week to teach her daughter his painting techniques. Well… Valentino did attempt to teach her daughter, but they would end up fighting.

Esmeralda would roll her eyes in disbelief and frustration and think, "How two beings that have so much in common can't stand each other?" Fortunately, Emma self-developed her artistic side, so there was light at the end of the tunnel. After all, Emma went from being this toddler who refused to utter a single word way past her fourth birthday – a psychiatrist suggested a tentative 'Selective Mutism' diagnosis – and being a very socially anxious girl – slow to warm up to obtain new friends, a psychologist once explained – to being a followed-teenager artist on Instagram. Far from understanding her husband through her daughter's character, Esmeralda had grown more intolerant to her husband's personality and daily burst of apathy and with each day she felt more and more distant from him — not that she was ever that close, but she did at one point at least have some tenderness and respect for him. Now she felt trapped like a bird in a cage and saw Valentino as the sole reason she was so disgusted with life to the point that there were days when she wished not ever to have met him. Not only did she feel submerged in the monotonous routine that each day would bring, but meagerness in the love and passion arena was driving her to madness. There were moments she felt she could literally die of boredom and desperately looked for a way to abandon her solitude state; she would fall into her old-dreamer-soul and start fantasizing that man who could still save her from herself and transport her to the stars.

Before and after Mateo

Fifteen months after receiving their first child, Esmeralda and Valentino found themselves again with the same dilemma... Valentino's face turned pale and he had to sit down at the obvious approaching fainting spell; all this provoked by Esmeralda's confession of expecting the unexpected — once again. This time Esmeralda did not intend to get pregnant but she did. How could she want to repeat nine or so more months of pure anguish and desolate moments that she had undergone only a few months before? Well, this is Esmeralda's theory of what happened, "Remember the night before my trip...? Yes, that night when I was exhausted after preparing for my sudden vacation all on my own?" Esmeralda's voice filled with sarcasm and a marked accentuation on each syllable she pronounced while informing her husband of the real account of things, according to her calculations, anyway. She added, "That night, you threw yourself at me disregarding my plea to leave me the hell alone! Because I was tired and not in the mood... but because you were already drunk did not pay attention to a word I said and you also obviously forgot that I was not on any kind of birth control method... but, no, no, no, you did not care at all... you animal!" This time around she was not going to be blamed for being an irresponsible immature person; she was not going to stand the disdain and the insult. In spite of such undesirable circumstances, she bravely went on with the whole painful process all over again.

At one point Esmeralda was more than likely suffering from post-partum depression. When she went back to work and left her baby girl behind, she felt so miserable a woman. It was bad enough that she was not capable of breastfeeding: 'a lack of milk' according to her mom, Inez; her mother knew a lot about 'producing milk' – she breastfed Esmeralda until she was a year of age and she herself was still breastfed, as per her own report, when she was able to speak and walk – about four to five years. "Oh! Please stop milking yourself as if you were a cow! That pump is going to ruin your breasts… I want you to understand that you are one of those women who simply don't produce enough milk," insisted Inez. Also, Emma's lack of engagement did not help; Emma showed her inclination to a slothfulness type of personality since she was a newborn baby; she would prefer to sleep over sucking her mom's breasts; it seems that the effort she needed to make to open up the nipple for the first time was too much for her. The first two nights after Esmeralda gave birth to Emma, her nurse kept waking her up every two to three hours to breastfeed her baby.

At one point Esmeralda was so exhausted that she told the nurse, putting on a sad face and in a pleading voice, "Please, don't bring her to me to be fed any more tonight, she does not know how to suck on my breasts and she is sleeping all the time… can you give her some kind of formula in a bottle? I will continue to try to breastfeed her once we get home." The nurse firmly explained the need to keep trying in order for the baby to get used to her nipples instead of the bottle's rubber artificial nipples, so she sent a 'lactation counselor nurse' to her room; she went over the steps to follow to get Emma to latch on her breast. Well, it did not help. A few days later, Emma finally was able to latch on and suck, but at about four or so weeks into this agonizing activity, Esmeralda's breasts were engorged, she had high fevers and pain; her OBGYN prescribed antibiotics and in this way, she had to put an end to the breastfeeding once and for all. So, this situation put Esmeralda in an even more vulnerable condition because this experience exasperated her already depressive mood. One day at work her workmate, and who also happened to become Esmeralda's friend and confidante, advised her to go on vacation because she could use some time to distract herself, sort of 'a reboot'. They worked as computer technicians, but there was nothing technical in their behavior; they were purely sensitive women trying to survive a harsh male-dominated professional world. When Esmeralda got home that evening from work and mentioned her intentions, Valentino reacted to this mostly by attacking with sarcastic criticism; he viewed her rushed decision as a 'witticism' that only Esmeralda was capable of coming up with. Once again, the turbid waters that were their relationship were disturbed. Valentino did not approve of going on vacation when Esmeralda had 'just returned from maternity leave' being afraid that she might end up losing her job and he did not want to take time off either, given he had a new job — more than a year. Valentino was not persuaded to go with her even when Esmeralda begged him to do so; he let her go alone with their baby, an 'act of cruelty' that he was going to lament later on.

A few days after Esmeralda and baby returned from their sort-of-vacation type of trip, is when she suspected of her pregnancy and went through the ritual of finding out once again. This time, she felt kind of disappointed since the trip served if nothing else to 'clear her mind' and she was determined to ask him for 'the divorce'. However, she had to shift gears and face a new and challenging phase.

"This is the most handsome baby boy I've ever seen!" said the labor and delivery nurse; everybody who went to visit Esmeralda and her baby had to say something about his pleasant physic; even as a newborn baby his attractiveness was that apparent and most people who witnessed it were not quiet about it. If Esmeralda were a superstitious person, she would have had ample reason to believe that her child could easily be given a 'mal de ojo'. But she was not, as a matter of fact, she hated anything that remotely resembled or was associated with superstition; she had fresh in her mind very strange scenes of her mother doing certain rituals that she found absurd and that she thought only a perfectly ignorant person would do.

Mateo was such a good baby; he did not cry that much except when he was hungry or wet as any other baby would do. This was a great advantage for Esmeralda because she decided to go back to college and become a registered nurse. She was laid off her job just a month before her actual due date to deliver her son – Valentino's fears materialized after all, but she did get a large check for leaving her employer quietly. These studies she decided to pursue were going to demand a lot of time; she could study and do assignments while her precious little boy entertained himself with music from Beethoven and Mozart and observed colorful mobile toys hanging either from his stationary chair or crib.

It was Mateo's second year check-up; the pediatrician asked some questions regarding his developmental stage, among them, "Does he have any eye contact?"

To which Esmeralda replied, "What do you mean by that? I was not aware kids this age had eye contact."

The doctor affirmed that yes... they do and asked, "Do you notice that when people come to visit if he lifts up his head to see them or follow them with his eyes?"

"Oh! now that you put it that way, no, he never does that," answered Esmeralda with her face showing some reserved curiosity.

"Does he play with other kids or does he stay isolated?" the pediatrician asked again, and again Esmeralda had a negative answer. Esmeralda was not cognizant of the ominous signs his little adoration was showing. Mateo was given a referral to see a specialist in developmental pediatric, therefore Esmeralda diligently sought for the best professional she could find and afford. Mateo was given a diagnosis of a severe type of autism spectrum disorder. As devastating as it might have sounded, Esmeralda did not take this news as something that she could not overcome; she was of course upset by the news and immediately started looking for answers to things like what could possibly have caused this condition. The oblivious parents like any lay person would do this time and age consulted the endless and 'trusted' sources of information that is available to everyone, the internet, what else? And as expected this untamable monster created more doubts and frustration than ever.

"Aha... I knew it!" exclaimed Valentino while his eyes still were glued to the crystal ball; with a couple of fingers striking the magical tablet more and more data would reveal undiscernible information. Valentino found articles alluding to the relationship between vaccines given at an early age and autism; allegedly the mercury used to preserve them was the culprit. Esmeralda had already found and read about this 'misleading information' as she called it; and of course, there they went again — a dispute originated between the two of them as it was their habitual thing to do. Esmeralda was already on her third semester of nursing and had studied about the importance of adhering to the recommended vaccination at the proper age to prevent dangerous childhood diseases most of which have been eradicated thanks to this method of infection prevention. Valentino was blinded by his anger and accused Esmeralda that as usual she would prefer to take sides with anybody else but him.

"Yes, Valentino… I am getting good money for defending the scientific community!" Esmeralda shot her ironic remark and continued saying, "So, now I am a terrible mother because I took my kids to have administered their scheduled vaccines? You are such an imbecile!"

And Valentino belittling his wife's argument went on to insinuate, "This government is covering the pharmaceutical companies… those thieves!" To which Esmeralda still had the energy to object by saying that so far, no scientific study has found a relation between the vaccines and autism and finally walked away leaving Valentino talking to himself.

You can say that Esmeralda had a late reaction to her son's diagnosis. This couple went through the normal stages of grieving. At first, they were in denial; Esmeralda had hopes that the results the Child Developmental Specialist came up with were inaccurate.

Her mother once told her, "He will start talking eventually; your uncle was a seven-year-old and still was not able to talk and now you cannot shut him off…" Esmeralda's obstinacy with the idea that Mateo only had a speech delay helped her cope with this unfortunate situation that life had put her through, if just for a while. Later they would experience the angry and bargaining stages which at times overlapped with each other and subsequent ones as well. When Mateo was bigger, Esmeralda secretly and probably unconsciously envied mothers whose boys were around Mateo's age —these youngsters could 'talk back to them' and go on the neighborhood with their skateboards or bicycles; she would have tearful eyes when she saw these fortunate mothers interacting normally with their kids. When her sister spoke about her own son alluding to his intelligence or reaching a normal developmental stage, Esmeralda simply listened though she was trying hard to contain her desire to ask her to 'please stop, stop torturing me!' Esmeralda was indeed happy for her sister – that her little nephew was a perfect normal boy – but she was equally and in the opposed direction unhappy that hers was not. When Esmeralda was pregnant, she would daydream of taking her son to a soccer game and instructing him to be a good boy so later he could be the perfect husband to someone. Eventually she would have to resign these dreams, but that was not going to happen overnight. The process of having to relinquish to the concept of having a 'normal' boy was painful; she would have to learn to deal with the pain that a mother suffers when she has lost a child because even though he did not die, that ideal boy she had in mind even way before he was conceived — ceased to exist.

On many occasions Esmeralda's guilt would come to the surface and torment her; she would call into question such things as her nutritional diet while she was pregnant – whether she ate too much fish that probably contained mercury; or maybe she should not have dyed her hair or even not gone on a trip abroad; or perhaps if she had been present at that crucial moment when a consent was requested to have her infant boy have performed a lumbar puncture (spinal tap) to rule out meningitis due to the high fevers, without an apparent cause, he was having. Esmeralda was taking a course in college every Saturday, so missing just one school day was a big deal; that is why she decided to finish that day and let Valentino and her sister, Anne Marie, take Mateo to the emergency room with the intention to meet them later since the wait in that place was usually so long. Esmeralda not only was angry at herself but also at that superior being that is supposed to answer every believer's prayers in this fallen world. She forgot, though those prayers are supposed to be answered according to God's will even when it is unknown or not understood the reason why sometimes one's requests seem to be ignored by God. There was a time when Esmeralda was much younger that for some unexplained reason, she had this little secret prayer which stated, 'God, if I am going to bring to this world children who will suffer greatly, or would cause me unbearable suffering, please do not allow it... I would prefer to be a sterile woman.' After Mateo, she was questioning God for not answering her prayers. She would in the most intimate space of her heart and soul resent her heavenly father; the one that she learned ever since she had her first memories to love and praise because he is such a merciful and synonymous of love, Lord and Savior. Esmeralda became even more indignant when her father once mentioned in a casual conversation, "Daughter, according to the Holy Scripture, children pay for the sins of their parents... the consequences generated by bad choices and/or sins from our ancestors can reach up to the fourth generation far into the future..." These words of course subject to different interpretations were powerful enough to open a door for Esmeralda where she found even more dark thoughts and discontent with both her heavenly and worldly fathers. With every day of watching her son behave like that new puppy you bring home and need to potty train [and Mateo was already six to eight years of age]; witness him painting the living room's walls with his feces; hear him screaming so loud that she had to cover her ears — a noise that provoked uncontrollable rage to all her senses; physically hurting himself by biting his arms and throwing himself at the walls; and not hear him pronounce the simple and desired word: Mom; she then would look up and exclaim, "What did I ever do that was so bad to deserve this? God! that is if you even exist!" Now and then, Esmeralda would reconcile with her God; there were times that she would come to the conclusion, "Who am I to complain about my situation while there are mothers out there who are going through the same or even far worse circumstances?" She would recognize that there were people going through some rough times and facing real challenges with children such as a seven-year-old with cancer undergoing endless chemotherapy; kids confined to a wheelchair and wishing to run like anybody else; babies being fed through horrible tubes in their tiny nostrils or a stoma in their tummies just to name a few. What about the case of those parents that have a perfectly normal child and it is not until past his / her seventh birthday that a terrible disease develops or its destructive symptoms are known? This could be even more painful given that these parents got to enjoy being the proud parents of talented and gracious children to then watching in astonishment these kids becoming blind, losing drastically their verbal and cognitive skills, declining physical dexterity, and other devastating changes. However, one cannot go and compare people's different problems or sufferings like when you compare apples and pineapples; an individual's specific suffering is just that… 'suffering' and to be perfectly frank about this ambiguous concept, the person experiencing it will not normally find consolation in the comparison of the 'suffering-quantity-ratio' of a certain group of people, not without consciously preparing themselves to do that, anyway. Nonetheless, Esmeralda would normally put on that face of resignation and behave as if she had accepted her destiny. What else could she do…? Other than survive every single day and try to make her innocent boy as happy as he could possibly be; if he preferred French fries with maple-blueberry syrup on top instead of ketchup, so be it. Mateo's happiness she could only estimate by his smile since he would never express his feelings verbally or even with sign language, you, see? His problem was not just a matter of speech but also of comprehension. You could never know how much Mateo understood the world around him and his own mysterious world which seemed to collide with the real one, Esmeralda thought, might just be a better place than the reality of her world. She reasoned that perhaps Mateo was one of the lucky ones to live in this harsh place and yet be so disconnected from it. She even settled in her mind that if he were an average boy he would have had more chances of ending up either killed, depressed and unhappy a teenager or adult and/or with even a worse diagnosis — he could be like his Uncle Pedro who suffered from a schizophrenia disorder and bipolar depressive tendencies; he was declared incapacitated to sustain a job in his late twenties due to his persistent formulations in his head of false conspiracy theories and his supposed persecution of people who only intended to hurt him. She witnessed her brother's disconcerting behavior when they were little though nobody knew exactly what the problem was at the time, he was just viewed as a very conflicted kid. She could see how his mental illness caused so much pain and discomfort to his parents and siblings and how he could never have a family of his own in spite of being a handsome and an intelligent guy. When she went to visit him to that remote place after he had a major crisis and the police took him against his will to the nearest emergency room and consequently transferred to a mental illness institution, she was about seven months pregnant with Mateo. She would feel so sad to see her younger brother, the one with whom she would spend so many hours under the hot sun in their tropical native land, trying to build a little house or put together pieces of wood to make a 'skating board' when they were kids, now life escaping from his eyes. There in that solitude that a place of this sort would typically and inevitably transmit and his constant state of 'conscious sedation', Esmeralda felt so sad and frustrated because there seemed nothing, she could do to help him. At some point she felt she was grieving a loss, a loss she could not describe because her brother, the one who looked so much like her – she had an affinity to him due mostly for being so closed in age, both being middle children and their fondness to enjoy outdoors-activities when they were kids, even though his body was responding to the everyday routines, walking like a zombie, but walking, barely talking, no more ardent arguments about the political issues of the day, though, and mostly staring at a wall, he was pretty much gone!

In the news, she would watch in disbelief and at the same time with a certain grade of illogical gratitude those cases of kids killing or being killed by their cohorts. She would think that Mateo could not be one of them since he was so in his own world and not able to interact with anyone to the extent that he could be brainwashed or influenced to do 'those things those poor tormented kids were doing.' Events such as the one when a youngster massacred students and staff in a USA high school would remind her of an analogy type of story that she came across while reading a matutinal spiritual book many years back; it read like this: 'A mother found her little boy dead in his bed one morning… in her grief she desperately asked God why such a suffering came upon her… why did he not have any mercy on her innocent son?' This mother was then presented with a scenario, kind of a vision type of experience; she witnessed this young adult man stealing and killing innocent people; being an unhappy and lonely person. God then asked her, "Do you know who that man is?" And without giving her a chance to answer, he stated, "That would have been your son if he had lived to be a grown man." The poor woman burst into tears and thanked God for being so merciful. So, yes you might agree or disagree with the old adage that the end justifies the means. In the case of Esmeralda's situation with her autistic son she might have fixed the moral of this story to apply to her life and that of her son by reasoning that maybe Mateo could have had the potential to be a person so undesirable or be so unhappy that his life as is now would be probably far better. This forced spiritual resolution was not going to resolve her emotional conflict in a perfect way, but it helped increase her resignation and way of coping without desperation. Apart from all the tantrums and periods of over activity Mateo experienced, his mother got to enjoy the affectionate side of him; he was such a loving kid, he would frequently give her mommy and daddy kisses and hugs [or perhaps he was just 'stimulating his senses' by smelling them, not actually kissing them] and he seemed to love to be reciprocated. Mateo was not the typical aloof autistic kid because without words he would attempt to impart his love and his parents found joy in the unconditional loving attitude of this angel that came into their lives perhaps with a mysterious mission. These clueless and often frustrated parents would need to discover on their own what their son was here to teach them.

Once you put in your mind that your life is the way it is and that you only can change those things under your control then you will be a little bit happier and even more each day the more you put this concept into practice. Sure, there are days that you go back to square one on the field of uncertainties and anguish. And then you pick up where you left off even when you have to drag the time –a minute after minute– to transport yourself to a better state of mind and/or existence. And it will sound as a cliché, but yes you can do it! That was one of Esmeralda's favorite inspirational phrases, so was 'No por mucho madrugar amanece más temprano' literal meaning: getting up earlier won't make the sun rise sooner, again another philosophy that Esmeralda adopted during the difficult times in her life. Esmeralda would eventually learn that one should not force things to happen because in its due time all things happen anyway [Lo que sera, sera] and it is a real waste to spend time mortifying oneself with the what ifs. Lastly, in her philosophy repertoire was the thought that the present time is the only thing certain because the past won't come back and the future, there is no way of knowing if one will get to live it. So, learn to be happy with what you have now and that was the end of one of her many sort-of-self-talk discourses.

Is it the darkest moment, yet?

"Please fill out these forms and then you can come in," the young receptionist informed Esmeralda and her husband. Valentino grabbed her gently by her arm and assisted her to sit down in that frigid waiting area; space which did not absorb the heat that a room filled to its capacity would normally generate; one can say that the coldness of the souls of so many couples with their different reasons to end up precisely there and at that time was the impediment. Esmeralda's eyes seemed to be fixed – looking toward a single direction, almost without blinking; she was not talking not even to respond to the office manager. Valentino had to answer the tedious questionnaire while she continued looking into the emptiness that the room provoked in her and her body being slowly elevated to another dimension of an existence so cruel to even begin to understand. Esmeralda felt like a goat on its path to the slaughterhouse; however, this goat had the option to escape — at least physically run way from that place, that moment, that decision. Esmeralda was more submissive than ever, as a matter of fact, she was never that submissive; it was as if her soul was stripped away from her and a different entity possessed her. After signing any necessary papers, Esmeralda consented once again to something that she did not really want to do; she just failed to see a way out of it and she had lost an argument with her inner logical self and ignored the sensitive side of her. At one point, she was taken to a room and asked to lie down on an examination table and once on a supine position with her head slightly elevated, she saw the monitor; the doctor quickly put on some blue gloves, proceeded to gently rub this cold gel on Esmeralda's lower abdomen and pressed firm the probe against her skin with a circular motion. A fetal Doppler was also applied and she immediately heard sounds than in no time were clear heart beats. As if it was not a torture act that of going through this, she had to also hear her unborn child's unique sound of evidence of life. Esmeralda never understood that step and she thought it was totally unnecessary; but that was the method the clinic used to deduce the exact size and age of the embryo and / or fetus, she reasoned; however, years later she found out in a reading by mere chance, that it was a government mandatory procedure for abortion clinics to routinely adhere to such a step. If she had been warned about this, she would have refused but she did not listen to any of the instructions about the whole process before she found herself witnessing one more time a miracle of life. Esmeralda was given a bottle with two pills to take at a certain time and was told the things expected to happen shortly after she had taken them. They went home and Valentino in association with his mother-in-law did not waste time and went to Esmeralda who was lying in bed; Valentino encouraged her to sit on the edge of the bed to take the pills, but she with her head down, in tears, and sobbing suddenly looked at him with very sad eyes like hoping to change his mind at the last minute. Valentino noticed his wife's intentions that probably she was not going to be compliant with what was already agreed upon. So, he looked at Esmeralda's mother as if asking for help; she said something like, 'what has to be done has to be done' with this look as if saying, 'I can't help you with this one'. Esmeralda still with tears in her eyes looked at her, but her mother was not persuaded, on the contrary she encouraged her to take the pills. She finally did and a couple of hours later she went to the toilet where she bled for a long while; she did not complain of major physical discomfort. Esmeralda's real pain was the pain that eventually goes and transforms a woman into a cynic, bitter, lonely, and miserable one. That was what she saw in the mirror when she dared to stand in front of one — those days.

Be kind to one another

In spite of all the sadness and remorse caused by a decision and action she later on would regret, Esmeralda still was convinced that a woman should have her own voice because for one thing, everyone goes through unique circumstances; no outside earthly authority ought to impose on them rules and apply punishment based on religious convictions of a group of people. Esmeralda remembered that instance when her current OBGYN at the time told her, "No, I cannot perform a procedure to prevent you from having kids at this time."

Esmeralda, "Why not? I will already have two kids by the time of the operation... All I'm asking you is to cut, burn my tubes, whatever you need to do that same day I give birth and in that way, it would be less expensive and more convenient because I won't have to take even more time off from work to do this thing later on."

Doctor, "I understand, Mrs. Vignota. The thing is that I am associated with a Catholic hospital and their policy does not allow me to sterilize a woman who has no more than three kids."

Esmeralda thought this was a preposterous action and an arbitrary position on the part of the institution that came up with this absurd rule; Esmeralda would think aloud, "Shouldn't a couple decide how many children they desire to have?" and as usual applied a biblical reference to this issue, "It is true that God once said: 'And you, be ye fruitful, and multiply; bring forth abundantly in the earth, and multiply therein'. (Genesis 9:7). And she would conclude that these words were stated at a time when the earth was practically empty – as opposed to the situation we are experiencing where there are so many millions living inhumanely and where those who benefit from the comfort of a capital society do not seem to care that much for the rest of humanity; indeed, very different circumstances to that of the times when a family consisting of about eight members had the whole, still healthy, earth for themselves. "Why then 'God's people' apparently do not use their God given intellect or at least use common sense to deduce that such a mandate does not apply any longer?" she thought. On the other hand, Esmeralda found that there was an enormous irony involved in the way partisan politicians would act upon. "How can they be so adamant at abortion all together and at the same time not give a damn about the general wellbeing of a child?"

Esmeralda was talking to other women and one of them said, "Todo niño viene con un pan bajo el brazo." She was sounding optimistic; however, for Esmeralda this Spanish adage is just a hopeful and yet primitive or even naïve sentimental expression that conveys that the birth of a child brings along with him / her blessings regardless of the way and in the condition, they are brought to this world. Esmeralda did not treasure this sentiment in her heart; on the contrary, she thought that it was an irresponsible and senseless act that of abandoning a tender and innocent kiddo to the harshness of an environment that would eventually and prematurely kill them if not physically at least emotionally and even worse create a vicious cycle where these kids given their unprivileged upbringing would in turn have kids of their own with the same fateful end.

Something that was even more tormenting to her was the idea that other women tended to be so forgiving when it came down to other moral issues in their society; issues that were or should have been in utter contradiction to their 'Christian values'. Examples of this would be sexual assault not necessarily physical aggression, but also denigrating or verbal abusive behavior on the part of a man that would demoralize a woman and this goes for both single women and married women alike even when the aggressor is the husband. Once again, Esmeralda was in that beauty parlor among women proudly standing by their pro-life posture. She goes, "So, don't you know that the same holy book which teachings you profess to follow clearly states? 'Likewise, husbands, live with your wives in an understanding way, showing honor to the woman as the weaker vessel, since they are heirs with you [not after you] of the grace of life, so that your prayers may not be hindered'". (1Peter 3:7). To Esmeralda's point, if God is persuading men to recognize that women are as valuable in his eyes as men are and to the extent where he would not bother to listen to their prayers if they do not treat women with the respect and sensibility they deserve, why then you go and totally ignore this? Oh! That is because these women might interpret this piece of Holy Scripture and many others at the same time they are being influenced by men, yes, many times the same male figure who mistreats and disvalues a woman. These women might be thinking that the verse previously mentioned literally means that 'women are weaker than men', and that is all that is to it! No, not the case here. What about the 'honor' word ingrained in these divine verses? That should be the main focus of the whole conversation that God is intending to establish with men [people in general] on earth. "Don't you care about the impact of belittling men's disrespectful talks and acts toward women? Isn't this a dangerous threat to the dignity and basic human rights of your own daughters and granddaughters?" Esmeralda continued with her plea, but it is what it is, many women are so absorbed in men's made assumptions and convenient truths, that they will undermine their own value as a woman in order to elevate an inculcated male-fabricated religion dogma.

So, going back to the hot topic, one can debate forever the reasons one might have to take a position regarding abortion. However, one thing is for sure, just as the oldest illicit profession according to the known history of humans, prostitution, is not going away, so will abortion remain with us irrespective of your contentious stand – either personal or public, against this 'immoral act'. Esmeralda went and made another remark, or should I say, one of her extended monologues? and not so much to try to convince them to change their views, but because she was indeed intrigued by their immutable thought process and perhaps just needed to vent out some repressed feelings. "What would you rather have... a society where many, many women would go secretly to have abortions in an unsafe way, risking their own lives – for the most part out of desperation? – Or to have a formal support system financed by government which would allow these unfortunate women or parents of underage girls, facing such a difficult decision be given other viable alternatives by obtaining important and needed guidance and help on how to give their babies for adoption, health education and paid health preventive measures? And why not also provide women with affordable or free means of contraception? Here in the USA and in many parts of the planet there are millions of women living in abject poverty and many millions more who cannot afford to have a large family or even afford one child when they cannot provide themselves with basic needs care and nutrition. These women are your sisters according to the same Holy Book from where you deduce your ideas. Oh! I forgot this is also a sin [contraception]. How the hell a woman goes and has ten kids when she is not able to even afford health insurance or have three meals or even one a day, and who might also have the stars solely as their roof? Isn't' that a very cruel thing to allow to happen? Perhaps you, yes! You holding that horrible sign in front of an abortion clinic, will go and adopt one of those poor kids who are all over the planet and even here close to you –they could be in your neighborhood, without hope and nobody to have compassion for them. Nonetheless, in a second thought, even if you all adopt one of them, there will still be left more millions in abandonment. Heeding the inhumane condition of innumerable groups of people in this world and trying to put aside your own proud resolutions, that would be more in agreement with God's announcement through his word: 'Put on therefore, as the elect of God, holy and beloved, bowels of mercies, kindness, humbleness of mind, meekness, longsuffering'. (Colossians 3:12). Then we should ask ourselves: do I suffer together with those who are mourning? Can I count myself as being 'poor in spirit' (Matthew 5:3) — something the divine inspired words purport to be a good attribute of a Christ's follower? Or... your self-righteousness overflows? What do you care? You have your perfect nice family sitting all around the table with a delicious meal on Sundays after church, very nice indeed! And the leaders you pick to represent your political party have this way of supporting policies/legislations that would enrich even more the big covetous corporations at the expense of the poor and middle classes... oh! Please, don't let me touch on your double standards when it comes to your position on the death sentence where we are running the risk of assassinating an innocent and wrongfully convicted person and lastly, what about that innocent twelve-year-old girl who has been raped and gets pregnant...? doesn't she deserve to live? Yes, because chances are she could very well lose her life during the course of the pregnancy or in childbirth; being that she is unlikely to be ready either physically or mentally to undergo such a thing. Why are you so obsessed with only the unborn? what about the ones already here? Oh! I might know why... because many of your political leaders are simply regurgitating on a controversial topic such as abortion with the sole intention to wrongly attract masses to their political views or party." Yes, Esmeralda felt strongly about this left wing/liberal ideology at the same time that she was sensitive to the spiritual concepts she was exposed to most part of her life.

If there was a thing Esmeralda accidentally inferred from a life-time of religious impregnated teachings was that one should not dwell in an absolutism sort of state; that one should be compassionate toward one another regardless of our choices in practices and beliefs. To illustrate, this other biblical reference would come to her mind: 'For the whole law can be summed up in this one command: Love your neighbor as yourself'. (Galatians 5:14). Esmeralda was trying to appeal to these women's hearts utilizing the same weapon that Christians or even other religious entities have at their disposal, that is 'the spiritually discerning capability'. She learned since she was able to reason 'good and evil' what the word of God says: 'But the natural man receiveth not the things of the Spirit of God: for they are foolishness unto him: neither can he know them, because they are spiritually discerned'. (1 Corinthians 2:14). And so, many religious authorities, denominations or what have you, proclaim they are able to discern God's word and that they have 'the truth'. Seriously? The same people who are unmerciful, intolerable to other fellow human beings just because of their preferences in the way they conduct themselves; these apparently pious people simply go and take shelter on the promise that they are 'God's chosen people' totally negating a principle that Jesus Christ made clear while walking on this planet among imperfect human beings: 'So when they continued asking him, he lifted up himself, and said unto them, He that is without sin among you, let him first cast a stone at her'. (John 8:7). So, how can they be spiritually discerning people when they cannot show any evidence that they indeed understand God's love and mercy for all his creatures – both the believers and non-believers? At the end of all arguments Esmeralda would sadly conclude, "If some Christians would reflect God's loving character instead of the hatred that escapes from their pores when fanatically voicing utterances and acting upon uncharitably based assumptions that only push people away, a totally outcome would result." There were those in her female audience who would just roll their eyes and others would show a serious pensive face while listening to Esmeralda's passionate remarks.

From her own past experience Esmeralda could say that it is not easy to be in a situation where you feel trapped against a wall, a wall that only she saw and felt, but that it was a cruel and real thing to her at that particular moment in her life, a mystery since she did not know exactly why she felt the way she did or arrived to such a decision; it is indeed a very personal decision that of deciding to have an abortion. In that particular moment when she made that drastic decision, she might have been a different person to the one she was three days before and three days after. and to expand a little bit more on this, I should say that the person you were ten years ago might not be the same person you are today or who you think you are today will be different to the one you will become tomorrow. Because the experiences you have shape you; they modify your way of seeing things. However, if you did not suffer deep, drastic changes in your life, you might never experience such a metamorphosis in character or thoughts and that might be good for you, but not necessarily to the people around you. In order to be able to empathize with the sufferings of others you should either have gone through the same experience or a similar one or have an extremely natural tendency to put yourself in somebody else's shoes.

Speaking again about Esmeralda's spiritual views, if you will, she did believe that everyone under the sun will have to one day respond to a supreme being regarding their actions taken during their path on this earth, so then again it is not the duty of a few to pass judgment and / or obligate anybody to be subjugated to their personal religious beliefs. Besides, a woman's decision to go through an abortion should not affect anyone else – other than herself, in the society she is part of as opposed to other decisions and actions that people take that do affect in a negative way other members of their community and or society at large; things such as depriving the vulnerable ones from their health insurance, not even considering to do something to stop the increasing amounts of victims of gun violence and other factors that hinder the wellbeing of young people; for instance, their ability to obtain a less expensive education and quality of such, just to name a few. So, to Esmeralda's point about giving others a chance despite their 'wrongful' actions, she often thought that God is undeniably more compassionate with 'sinners' than many of these people with their different views on spiritual or moral laws. Think hard about this... many Christian faiths have at their core the notion of a place where 'condemned by God' souls would end up when they die and will burn forever, in this way paying for their sins; Esmeralda would express this very intimate thought often, "I cannot conceive the idea that my God would be so cruel as to allow a creature of his burn forever and ever... besides, according to the Holy Book, 'the wages of sin is death'; that is why Jesus Christ was sacrificed, so he could solve the debt of sin and for those who will never accept his gift of forgiveness of their sins, they shall pay by suffering an eternal death – not staying in limbo or in hell forever." Esmeralda did not believe in an inferno type of place commonly called 'hell'. In her interpretation of the Holy Scriptures with respect to this subject she found no theological grounds to deduce that indeed a place of souls perpetually burning exists. Partly because she concluded that the original Greek word for hell 'hades' and even the Hebrew word 'Sheol' with the same literal translation had a different meaning to what the modern word 'hell' denotes today. Originally, Hades and Sheol, meant a tranquil place where dead people remained until their bodies totally decomposed and nothing else. There are a few parables related to 'hell' in the Bible meant to convey a moral or spiritual concept / teachings, but they are fictitious in character, therefore not to be taken literally; I suppose intellectual writers such as Saul of Tarsus – better known in the Christian world as the apostle Paul [Jewish in origin], still employed in his writing a literacy style in the manner he learned while in his previous world as a Roman Citizen [the Roman Empire being a Pagan Society]; similarly, one could appreciate within the Greek culture, stories referring to hell and a study of the early Christian Church should not fail to mention the influences brought into their origins by pagan cultures that would amalgamate with their new adopted religion. And sure, the Bible does allude to 'hellfire' that will burn those who will be found guilty at judgment day; that would be real fire, and therefore 'hell' due to the seriousness that such a day should mean to everyone. But even this fire would not stay burning forever – just until everything in this contaminated earth and everyone who will be condemned to suffer an eternal death [final death; will not resuscitate again] be consumed entirely, se terminado, acabado. Also, something else about the word 'forever' which is used together with hell in several biblical readings meant to Esmeralda something different to what it means to most Christian denominations; it meant that the final result of the action of burning [death] will be eternal or for eternity – finished, consumed, burned forever [not actually burning forever]. To Esmeralda's point, there are many verses in the bible where 'forever' is used and is not meant to be taken literally, an example is when Jonah said that he was in the belly of the fish 'forever' (Jonah 2:6), but we know that he suffered this frightening experience beneath the sea for 'three days and three nights' only (Jonah 1:17). Yet other relevant words in the discussion of 'hell' are 'spirit' and 'soul' – they are used interchangeably many times and these words are one of the reasons people believe in 'hell'. Esmeralda interpreted the meaning of these words mainly by analyzing the story that narrates how God created Adam [the first man on earth]; 'God molded a man out of clay [earth] and then gave him a breath into his nostrils and in this way the body became a living being'. (Genesis 2:7). Therefore, a person ceases to exist all together when that combination of the body and breath no longer exist – this being is no longer living and all that is left is a body. The air [Spirit or pneúma in Greek] goes to the atmosphere [to God] who gave it and the body [corpse] returns to the earth [becomes dust] where it came from. (Ecclesiastes 12:7). So, for Esmeralda when a person dies, she / he simply does not exist – not even his / her soul. This sounds horrible because we all have the hope that when one of our loved ones dies something about them will stay forever and that is true! Their love, and the memories we have of them that will not go away and by the way the Bible explains the following about the dead: 'For the living know that they shall die: but the dead know not anything, neither have they any more a reward; for the memory of them is forgotten'. (Ecclesiastes 9:5). So, this clearly negates the truthfulness of those accounts of people who have talked or / and seen a dead person; in reality, they might have seen something, anything, but a dead person. Esmeralda would try to shed some light when having a doctrine type of argument by saying things like this, "There are many holy scripture's references that if studied carefully and in context and as a whole – not a piece of isolated information – will depict that when a person dies, she / he will not go to heaven nor to hell; a person while dead or 'sleeping' will await the second coming of the Lord and with a loud noise [the trumpet of God] those who died believing their sins were forgiven will resuscitate, will be transformed into immortal beings and live with God and their saved loved ones for eternity. Moreover, the main reason many Christians believe in hell is because they have misinterpreted Paul's writings. The way this loving apostle spoke about his desire to be with Christ was almost as if trying hard to skip death altogether, therefore, giving the impression that once dead a person would go directly to heaven. Many Christians deduce that Paul is talking about a place one goes after you die, if this was at all truth, then he would be in contradiction with the remaining inspired words. So, again a closer look will show that Paul's wonderful news did not include 'a hell'." There was a time when Esmeralda was very young and vibrant and she would be tireless speaking of how she understood certain biblical readings to those who had a different spiritual view to hers; the topic of death and hell was one of her most visited. "What a waste of saliva!" she would say to herself later on when she was exhausted and lacking spiritual vitality due to so many years heading on into an unhappy married life.

But the most beautiful thing about that former, young and spirited Esmeralda was her hope that 'when that mortal being that at one point became dust gets totally restored by God into a whole incorruptible body and the same being [personality wise], but with renewed inclinations to do good and naturally detest evil – the way God intended originally – that he / she was before dying, one day this person will be transformed into a perfect immortal being... as God has promised' (1 Corinthians 15:52-53). So, she firmly believed that she would enjoy of that person's company once again and then for eternity; she longed for one day seeing her loving grandpa and caressing his soft white hair as she did so many times when she was a little girl.

"The heart of the matter is that one should not obey God's commands out of fear for burning eternally in hell; it should be out of love for God... And this belief in eternal condemnation goes to explain how some Christians seem to have so little compassion for their fellow human beings because they cannot see how merciful God really is. God's love is so easy to understand, just think for instance about this: if your child disobeyed you, would you punish him / her for as long as you or they shall live? No, you would perhaps put them in time-out if they are small kids or ban them from going out a weekend if they are teenagers… and that is it. So, being that we are imperfect, sinners, and just humans and yet we do not let our kids suffer a punishment for long, much less our loving heavenly father will! You as a Christian do not need to even begin to understand what ultimately leads a woman and sometimes her partner to take such a path because no! you do not need to help God; he opts for using you so you can be molded and refined as gold is — through fire, the fire of love, the process of bringing someone to God by love and mercy alone. Just be kind to one another and everything else will fall into their own and proper places. You will be more convincing and influential merely by demonstrating love and compassion toward your brothers and sisters than by imposing laws that they simply cannot follow given their mental state, circumstances and yes, personal choice — even God gave his children the power of libre albedrío. God has the power to touch a person's heart and convince him / her to change the direction of their lives; only a loving heavenly father would be able to do that." This was the final conclusion of Esmeralda's whole argument about, yes! Abortion.

It's always darkest before the dawn
Esmeralda was sitting down, concentrating on listening to the teacher who was reading a paragraph of an essay in her literature elective course when her cell phone buzzed; she noticed it was from her OBGYN's office, so she excused herself and quickly headed out to the ladies' room. The voice on the other side

sounded courteous, but yet the content of what she attempted to explain to Esmeralda was not well received by her. "… You mean to say that Dr. Patel is cancelling my surgery one more time? What's the reason this time? Don't tell me her assistant is not available again… this is unbelievable!"

The bearer of bad news had to stop her abruptly and pronounced the words, "Mrs. Vignota, you are pregnant therefore the procedure cannot be performed." [A tubal legation to prevent pregnancy].

Esmeralda had a brief sarcastic laugh and replied, "I am not pregnant… that is impossible!" The receptionist assured her that the last time she came to see the doctor to plan the operation, she had her blood drawn and one of the exams that tested for pregnancy revealed unequivocal results. While sluggishly sliding her back against the pale wall of the depressive unattractive bathroom, she lowered herself to the cold bare floor, assuming a fetal position and unable to continue a futile argument, Esmeralda ended the call. For a few minutes, her world was once again disintegrating like when a put together puzzle is shaken and all the pieces get spread out. In this fatidic moment, Esmeralda sobbed until people started coming into this basic and unavoidable room. She went out to the front door and out to the sidewalk of this old building which faced a community park, she paced back and forward on the lonely sidewalk, being bathed by the morning sun's rays. Esmeralda did not fail to quietly observe the luxuriant park vegetation and to listen to the sweet melodic chirping of birds. From about a half-way block distance, she looked at people waiting on the corner for the next bus and elderly and / or disabled people being dropped off their mobile-assist transportation to the community clinic. Esmeralda got closer to the busy corner as if searching for something, something to clarify her cloudy thoughts or at least bring her out of that damp and dark cisterna which was filled with this enormous agonizing sentiment; that is when she saw a mother pushing a baby in a stroller with two more youngsters grabbing her skirt and crossing the street; the little girl smiled at Esmeralda while still sucking her thumb and she could not help it to smile back. After a mixture of conflicting thoughts and deep reflections, Esmeralda took a deep needed breath, reached out for her cell phone and re-dialed the last call.

"This is the office of Dr. Patel; how may I assist you?" said the receptionist to which Esmeralda replied, "I am Mrs. Vignota and I would like to set up an appointment to see the doctor as soon as possible." The astonished receptionist — who had provided the pregnancy news to Esmeralda a few minutes before and heard her fiery reaction... asked her if she was all right and what the reason was for the visit. Esmeralda enthusiastically stated, "Well, I am pregnant, so I need a prescription for prenatal vitamins right away. I need everything to go smoothly with this pregnancy," and without hesitation the lady gave her the soonest appointment she could arrange for her. What in the world made Esmeralda experience such a drastic change in direction? She went from pure anguish and desperation to hope... just that: HOPE. That simple four-letter-word changed everything in her debilitated mind, obviously she did not lose her mind to an irreversible point. All of this metamorphosis of thoughts and actions transpired before anybody — not even her husband, knew of 'the news'. It was as if she needed to analyze the situation to come to her own conclusion and decide without any external interference what she should do next. She did not dwell on the fact that she was a full-time nurse student; she had decided to go back to school to obtain a higher degree in nursing. The thing is that she did not get to finish her last semester of the Registered Nurse [RN] program some years back, mostly due to the difficulties of dealing with her son newly Severe Autistic

Disorder diagnosis, so she took the nursing exam to become an LPN in the City of New York which accepted people who had completed three semesters of Nursing to sit for the NY License exam. This was the only state close to her offering this program. She also had a full-time stressful job in the City of New York as a Licensed Practical Nurse and therefore needed to commute daily from New Jersey, where she lived. She spent over twelve daily hours away from her family at least five days a week – that included every other weekend. This time around, she got this surge of energy apparently from nowhere. I don't need to go into details of how her husband reacted to the news; however, it is worth mentioning that he as expected had already the logical plan in his head, that is another act of 'undoing' what was not intended in the first place. Before he had a chance to say anything, Esmeralda made it completely clear that she was going ahead with all her plans and the unplanned ones as well. She continued living her life as if she was not a vulnerable woman, but very aware that she was carrying a life inside her, so she tried to eat as healthy as she possibly could, but as far as getting up before sunrise on the bitter winter to wait for the bus to take her to the city and once there boarding two crowded local trains and then suffering the side effects of the rush hours going back home, that she had to endure. The most important factor that helped Esmeralda during this phase in her life was the simple fact that she did not feel sorry for herself. She became sort of this magnanimous woman — at least for the time being; she was constantly motivated by everyone around her because people could appreciate her dedication and passion in what she did at work – to care for vulnerable people, especially the elderly – and she went the extra mile very often in order to make them feel appreciated and valued. She did not get that same motivation from her husband, though. As usual Valentino was that distant and cold guy and Esmeralda kind of got used to his personality

— in other words, she did not let it bother her or interfere with working toward meeting her goals. There was something else beyond Esmeralda's behavior; something that could possibly pertain to that place where that feeling of unconscious revenge dwells. She was in a way punishing him for what he did to her a couple of years back where she was put in this situation of feeling totally out of control, lost and disvalued as a person. She felt she lost something of great value and she would never know how that could have changed her life and although it was her prerogative to go ahead with the terrible act, she would forever, secretly adjudicate the blame mostly to her husband even when realizing that this was not fair. Perhaps because she felt he should have been brave and found out how she really felt and then support her in whatever decision she made. Instead, he went ahead and took advantage of her temporary insanity and emotional vulnerability, completely disregarding any clues she might be showing — that is, her ambivalence and deep sadness state while tacitly agreeing to such a major and brutal decision. Now she was going to partake without any outside intervention of her destiny; she was going to confront whatever was coming her way — once she decided to again experiment what it was like to be a mother of a newborn baby… you know, that feeling that makes an expectant mother imagine the ideal little person that in a few months will fill her days with gurgles, oohs, and coos; the sounds of joy! This time she did not stop for a minute to worry about the possibility of having another child like Mateo. On the contrary, she secretly wished this baby were a boy too; a boy that she was going to have the privilege to teach him to make a neck tie for his prom night; advise him how to treat a lady and hear him say 'I love you mom'. "Is that too much to ask?" She debated with that inner voice — that had the tendency to wake her up to reality. She probably felt at times that she had been given a second chance to exercise her faith and go ahead with a decision without pondering on the possible negative consequences. Her husband had all the reason to be terrified about having another kid. After all, you could say that Mateo was like a combination of Dennis the Menace and Roadrunner [the cartoon]; he would do really crazy things in the house such as emptying a toothpaste in thirty seconds, spilling the dish detergent on the kitchen floor – grandma slipped over once and almost broke her back, taking the electrical outlets from the walls with his bare hands, ripping up his sister's homework; there were no decorative or photo pictures hanging on the walls any more — the little mischievous one would not allow it; there was furniture missing either an arm or leg in their house, all the time, and he would make a hole in the wall by throwing himself with such an impact that nobody knows to what this phenomenon can be attributed to and much more. Euphoria often followed by weeping with tears was something he would experiment as well; he could be spontaneously laughing aloud without provocation and the next minute he would show a face of sadness. To his parents this was pure torture not knowing what was going through his mind and not knowing how to help him. As a matter of fact, they never knew when he had a headache or belly ache because he was not able to verbalize anything; he would run a high fever that would dissipate in one or two days, again no idea what caused it. It was nearly impossible to make him swallow a teaspoon of Tylenol other than when they restrained his extremities to apply a suppository. No, one should not judge Valentino for not wanting a duplicate of this type of life. I guess it takes a unique kind of person such as Esmeralda to be willing to accept whatever life had in reserve for her, or you might think that she even sometimes incited life's anger with her own incautiousness; one thing is for sure, she was brave to defy life and its occurrences all together. She had this desire to experience life in different dimensions even when taking the risk to be burnt in the tormenting flames of disillusions, frustrations, and spiritual misery. Valentino was a methodical type of guy and he was not going to flirt with uncertainty and the unexpected on purpose. Nevertheless, he would eventually have to adjust to his wife's decisions and accept deep, deep inside that it was now her turn to decide the directions their lives would take for better or for worse.

Un Lucerito

Esmeralda is staring at the bold red LED numbers on the alarm clock on her night table: it is 4:13 a.m.; she gets up and goes to the closet, and reaches for a small suitcase. Then takes out some clothes from the dresser, goes to the bathroom and brushes her teeth, shaves her legs and armpits. She gets all her essential items from the bathroom and sits on the toilet with her legs extended and resting on the bathroom tub; looking at the celling, other times at the floor, and other times standing up at the medicine cabinet mirror like anxiously waiting for something to happen any minute. She was silently counting her contractions and once they were about five minutes apart, she goes and wakes him up. "Valentino, wake up, wake up!... It's time, the baby is on its way, please wake up and get ready to go!" The disturbed poor man finally woke up and was forced to quickly head out to the hospital which was about ten to fifteen minutes away without traffic. They got to the emergency room through the Women's Pavilion entrance and in an unhurried way – she had already pre-registered a few weeks before – went to the receptionist who assigned a wheelchair right away and put on her an identification wrist band. They were taken to a preparation room with a registered nurse to take her vital signs and put her in her hospital gown. Everything is going smoothly; they look like normal happy expectant parents; no signs of mental disturbance and just a calm smile on their faces, kind of… "Well, we have been here before – twice –

let's do it one more time!"

Esmeralda's cervix was dilated almost ten centimeters and the waters had not broken yet, but this was normal for her; the doctor had to break her waters in the last two pregnancies. A couple of hours later the experienced obstetrician — this Indian lady who Esmeralda trusted so much and who made her feel at ease even during these stressful circumstances, acting so calm and smiling told Esmeralda to start to push. Esmeralda never got good at breathing or pushing, and this time was not an exception. Something peculiar happened this time; as expected the doctor asked her to push whenever the machine signaled a contraction was coming, but no significant progress was achieved when Esmeralda tried to push and the simple fact that she was coughing so often did not allow her to concentrate and give a good push. Esmeralda had been suffering with a dry non-productive cough for a few weeks now — the primary doctor thought it was her habitual seasonal allergy whose symptoms were mostly relieved with antihistamine medicine and when it got too bad, she would take a narcotic syrup and this obviously she could not take while pregnant. The wise doctor soon noticed that every time Esmeralda coughed, she pushed the baby as if she were pushing exceptionally well, so she asked Esmeralda to cough instead of pushing and with every cough the baby was pushed even further out and that is how Bianca was born. She cried very strongly and Esmeralda felt as if she was looking at her with this look as if saying, "What are you waiting for to feed me? I am starving!" Her skin was as fair as milk, her head full of dark soft hair and big brown eyes. She looked so healthy and Esmeralda could not believe it was so easy to deliver her and wondered if she was going to be a 'good' baby because as excited as she could be about her little sunshine she was also exhausted as every woman normally is after labor.

Remember that Esmeralda was attending nursing school with this pregnancy. Well, I will try to tell you all about it — how she managed a newborn baby, her other kids and husband and final exams, etc. Esmeralda is situated comfortably in her room, a private beautiful room, at the right side of her bed is the baby in her bassinet and at the left side table is a big textbook with the title 'Psychiatric Nursing'. The evening nurse comes in to do her usual assessment and did not miss the book staring at her. She could not control her curiosity and asked Esmeralda what she was doing with that book. Esmeralda very enthusiastically explained that she had a Psych final exam the very next day. The nurse's jaw dropped and her eyes widened and she proceeded to exclaim, "What did you say? An exam tomorrow? You just gave birth last night!"

To which Esmeralda replied, "Yes, and you are going to help me." The woman still in disbelief and waiting for what Esmeralda had to say next, heard the following, "I need you to please make sure the pediatrician comes first thing in the morning to check my baby; I will need to be discharged as early as possible in the day because I need to be in Harlem, NY by one thirty p.m.... you know? For the test."

At this point the poor nurse plummeted into the love seat and with a hand on her forehead and leaning forward like trying to make sense of what her ears heard, asked one more time, "How exactly are you planning to do this?"

"Simple," she answered, and added, "My husband will pick us up at around ten forty-five a.m. and drop the baby at home where her grandmother will be taking good care of her and then he will drive me to New York City, comprendes?" The news of Esmeralda's ambitious plans quickly divulged through the whole nursing unit and as planned the next day she was out of that place at the predicted time and got to college right on time to sit for the exam. Oh!… Just one small detail was still hanging in the air — Esmeralda had not informed anybody at school that she had given birth; she thought and had good reason to believe that if anybody from the faculty found out, she was not going to be allowed to take the final exam that day and she did not wish to extend her time of graduation, not a bit longer. So, she omitted telling the news for the time being and as typical of a woman who just gave birth her belly was still prominent and since she was wearing the same maternity clothes she wore before to school, nobody suspected anything unusual — besides her classmates were all way too nervous and anxious with their own situations to notice her. Oh, no! Esmeralda forgot about something else… and she realized it once sitting in the toilet when she went, "Oops… oh darn it! I forgot to bring sanitary pads, shit!" and immediately called her ~~servant~~ husband to come to the rescue; he had to turn around and go to the nearest pharmacy to get the precious merchandise and promptly deliver it to his beloved wife. The fact of the matter is that whenever Esmeralda got something stuck between her two eyebrows, she would not rest, not even blink until it was finished, terminado, finito, wan!

Bebé Bianca, the bully

"Stop it… get out of here! Mateo." One could hear the four-year-old little girl yell angrily this phrase to her older brother [eight years older], very often. Bianca was the cleverest member of the family at least it seemed that way. At her tender age, she seemed to have already deduced that there was something insidious related to Mateo's bizarre behavior. Mateo would scream in such a loud and annoying voice and at the same time project himself toward the walls and jump high and then come down to the floor with such an impact that the whole house would shake — and the poor little girl would get terrified; however, she would react in a defensive way and actually try to reprimand him — as if she were his mother, in lieu of going to Mommy's lap. Bianca would chase Mateo out of her sight whenever she felt like – sometimes even when he was quiet and not bothering her at all – so Esmeralda had to frequently intercede in Mateo's favor. She tried to convince this little sponge that Mateo even though he was her big brother, he was a unique kind of boy who needed a lot of love and patience. The thing is that at such an age, a kid does not understand abstractness, that is, the meaning of terms like 'understanding' or 'compassion'; she only could perceive and comprehend what was tangible such as Mateo's intolerable episodes of meltdowns. Therefore, even when Mateo was in a tranquil temporary mode, she would still be on the lookout as if her intentions were of 'no darle gabela' [Spanish for: Don't give the advantage to someone] to his untamed erratic conduct. On the other hand, she would approach Mateo and try to entice him to do what she needed him to do for her. Mateo had the proper height and physical dexterity and Bianca realized she could use these features to her advantage; it was like Mateo was the muscles and Bianca the brain and combined they both were a dangerous force. So, she would with a sweet voice call his name and with her tiny cute fingers point to what she needed to reach, open, turn on or off, whatever her desire was at the time and Mateo would satisfy her unconditionally — sometimes he looked at her with the most tender smile and one could sense a bit of curiosity in his facial expression; it was as if he were thinking, "What is this little thing… how can she be so powerful and adorable at the same time?" But, make no mistake, Mateo was to be feared nonetheless; there were a couple of instances that he would thrust the lightweight Bianca by grabbing her little fragile arms and making a circular type of movement with her little body while he was laughing uncontrollably; he must have thought this was a fun activity. It was a miracle that she did not get hurt — not physically, but obviously emotionally she was either getting her nervous system exercised and developing stronger or just getting traumatized.

Bebé Bianca — the little sister

"Bebé you're so cute... I love you!" Emma, Esmeralda's eldest child would spontaneously utter to the sweet little pie when the rebelde sin causa teenager was in a favorable mood; other times when the moon was full, she would say the reverse, "You're ugly and nasty." She was supposedly just kidding when she pronounced these phrases to her little sister; but that was not at all appropriate and Esmeralda would reproach such a behavior of hers by making her aware that she was in no condition to interact with her baby sister as if they were the same age; she had to behave like the mature older sister that ought to teach her by setting a good example. Emma would just roll her eyes and walk away — an act that Esmeralda so much detested and did not tolerate. Esmeralda remembered that when Emma was Bianca's age, she was very protective of her and showed her a lot of affection, so now she does not understand why she was being such a brat and not sensitive enough with her sister. Personality is the key here; people are born with intrinsic characteristics that are somehow moldable to a point – but in no way eradicated completely from our beings – of course this is only a theory and I am inclined to believe in it. Now, for fairness's sake, Emma did have good attributes of her own only that she was constantly so entrapped in her solitude and virtual world that when she finally decided to come out, she could no longer interact appropriately with the rest of the humans out there. Esmeralda had flashbacks of her own rebellious adolescent years and now she was indeed very afraid to become her mother. She would panic when she recalled how hateful she seemed to feel about practically everything her mom did or said. Still, Esmeralda would analyze the situation at the present time and conclude that she needed to show Emma 'tough love'; after all, she was not doing good in middle school mostly because of her tendency to procrastinate — she was late with assignments and even had some missing altogether to the point where a notice was sent from school to the effect that the possibility of Emma having to attend summer school. This was like a nightmare for Esmeralda, she was so applied a student and never failed a grade even when she did not have her mother with her all the way from first grade to seventh; she lived with her father and paternal grandparents — her father did pay attention to her study habits but he did not have to make a great effort to keep her in good standing at school. Esmeralda had yet another secret that if revealed would hurt her daughter, Emma Natasha, very much; Bianca was at such a young age already indicating she would have a personality with more affinity to her mother's own personality. So, Esmeralda had to try to hide her enthusiasm and refrain from demonstrating way too much attention and praise to this little one, especially in Emma's presence. Esmeralda did not want to repeat her childhood story where her mother would make comments and behave in a certain way which created tension and jealousy between her and her little sister. However, it was undeniable that Bianca had won her heart and she could see her one day become a young lady with a character and even a disposition to be involved in practicing and experiencing things very similar to her own character and passion in everything she put her mind to do.

An empty nest with kids still home
Oh… Yes! As noted, before when she decided to marry without love, Esmeralda had this concept of happiness — which is a

result of acquiring the greatest gift of all by creating a big family whom to love and care for and obtain the reciprocal affection or love from them as 'everything' in life albeit the unforeseen troubles and frustrations it might bring with it. However, in a much more advanced level of comprehension, she at some instance in her married life with kids started entertaining the possibility that she needed something more in order to feel totally accomplished and a happy woman at least in that field that we call LOVE or the emotional state where a person has a deep feeling for someone in a way that is not related to the familial type of love or the love you feel for a fellow brother — human being. The Ancient Greeks introduced four terms to describe different types of love; as exposed in the Journal of Moral Theology, Volume1, number 2: Love [Page 48-55] I will focus on three types of love as it is explained in this book: 'Descending, oblative [sacrifice] love – agape – would be typically Christian, while... ascending, possessive or covetous love – eros – would be typical of non-Christian, and Greek culture... and – Philia – (commonly translated as friendship)'. The book expands on the definition of these terms: '... eros is acquisitive desire an 'upward longing' that is 'man's way to God'; an 'egocentric love' even if 'of the highest, noblest, sublimest kind'; a 'man's love', which, even if ascribed to God, is 'patterned on human love'. Eros finally 'recognizes value in its object' and then loves it; hence it may be called 'evoked' or 'motivated'... agape is 'sacrificial giving'. It is 'unselfish love' that 'gives itself away... ' So, it can be said that Esmeralda needed to experience love in its different dimensions or characteristics as these original concepts of love described. She was not going to be content with practicing only the philia and agape type of love even though they are both crucial in the path a human being needs to walk on during their life span.

The kind of love Esmeralda was longing for was the 'eros' love; and to go even more in depth, the Journal of Moral Theology also pointed out: '… Constantly distinguishing philia from eros, Lewis claims that whereas in eros lovers stand face to face, gazing at each other, in philia, friends stand side by side, absorbed in a common interest… Lewis understands eros from what has already been said about its contrast to philia… eros is romantic love, or the 'State of being in love'. Esmeralda strived with this love because it gave her energy to go on in life and do things, from an aerobic exercise routine to being inspired to write a romantic poem; this type of feeling or sensation was like an addictive drug or stimulant to her. She became a new woman whenever she felt 'enamorada' and this woman was able to conquer all. This new woman could reach occult and forbidden places where she felt free to be herself or better yet what she herself did not even imagine she could be.

Another factor that would contribute to Esmeralda's unhappiness or simply put, her dissatisfaction with her insipid life has to do with a term called vanity. She could not describe how disvalued and undesired a woman she felt whenever her husband went and totally neglected her, in other words, he did not see the need nor cared to elevate her spirit; even when he thought he was doing so, he was a hundred thousand miles away from accomplishing it. This clueless man was not even able to employ the proper adjective when attempting to pay a complement to her; like one time when she wore this nice and simple long dress and she asked him how she looked and he replied, "I like it… you look very wifey." A woman, in order to be completely happy or close to that, she needs to simultaneously play a role in different categories; one of them being that attractive, seductive and beautiful woman we all aspire to be. If you as a woman or a person with a sex / gender preference other than that of the typical male heterosexual and you have doubts about the relevance of this concept in a woman's life then you or someone you know may do the following experiment: line up all your shoes in the closet and soon you will see at least a pair of them looking very provocative almost as if you have not chosen them yourself for you. At that particular time when you decided to grab them, try them on and felt so distinct and fabulous, you were ambitioning to be that 'seductive woman' even if unaware of it. So, I will throw this question out there, shouldn't a man at least pretend to like his old-time partner? Is that too much to ask when one has dedicated the tender years of one's life, one's youth to a man who needed a mom, a friend, a shrink? Well, Esmeralda is not that different from the rest of us — womanhood, after all. I believe there is an intrinsic value in the act of dedicating one's most tender years to someone; Esmeralda accepted Valentino into her life in her early twenties when she didn't know herself that much yet because there was a woman in the process of developing inside her. You could say that she was kind of molded to some extent by the experiences she lived with him at the same time when she was learning to be an adult woman. So, you can be safe to deduce that the way she came to experience life at his side played a major role in the definition and direction her own character adopted. Valentino was responsible in a way of who she ultimately would become as a human being. Therefore, if she turned out to be a bitter woman, most part of the time, anyway, it could be assumed that she paid her dues staying with him for as long as she did. For clarification's sake it must be stated that there was a time when Esmeralda even when she was not cognizant of her real feelings for Valentino, she would behave in such a way that showed a sweet and caring personality the way she interacted with Valentino before the catastrophe of their union and even for a while after that; she would call him 'honey' instead of a cold and dry 'Valentino', but one day she stopped sugaring her words employed to address him and Valentino did not seem to notice or appreciate the difference between his woman tenderly looking at him while pronouncing an affectionate noun to name him and the dull or sometimes harsh way she would enunciate his name when calling him. Valentino did not realize that at some point Esmeralda was rendered incapable of feeling anything remotely close to that peaceful sentiment that is evoked by daily interactions that people who love each other should have. To Esmeralda her husband's obliviousness was in and of itself a key component in getting to the realization that he never cared about her feelings and he never paid attention to details in their relationship, demonstrating in this way his lack of interest in making her happy or understanding her. So, yes there was this hole in her heart that was as vacant as an old and unattractive little apartment in a major criminalized city is; nobody would go there — not even around it, and if and when that person dares to get in, it is only to quickly get out. It is no surprise that her husband could not fill that void either — if ever he possessed a key to open that apartment, he had already lost it, way back. Esmeralda felt utterly and completely alone in an existence that was perhaps in a parallel universe with that of her husband's and millions of light-years apart. The days and hours were long and tedious when she was with him; besides the commonalities that they had in great part due to having their kids and the necessity to talk to each other in order to co-exist, there was nothing else left to enjoy, really enjoy. Esmeralda was living for the sake of living or to be more practical, just for the sake of her kids; she was never that selfish a person so she was going to endure this life and stay being that mother their kids needed. But, for how long was she going to remain just that? A woman who felt she had failed to be that ideal mother for the most part — at least that is how she perceived herself; she had this black veil on her face sparkled with guilt due to her lack of motivation to give herself one hundred per cent to her kids. For instance, going to the town park with them was such a major undertaking, kind of a duty and just that, as opposed to feeling the normal and expected enjoyment a loving mother would feel just watching their children laugh and play. She would now and then be bathed with this secret desire to undo everything — that is, going back in time to that chapter in her life when she was simply Esmeralda, no marriage name, no mammy title, just a free woman. Esmeralda had a fantasy that one day she could take off to a faraway place alone leaving everything and everybody in her life — even her kids, behind. She then would start a new life, a totally different life as if the universe decided to give her another chance to recreate a new path where she felt happy, loved and accomplished as a woman. This act of suddenly disappearing, she did not consider it abandonment rather something that would actually benefit everyone because she was not fit to be the mother and wife their family needed, anyway. She of course would eventually wake up to her reality and realize that her kids did need her even as imperfect as she was. This feeling their kids provoked in her was probably the only thing keeping her from making her fantasy a dream come true.

Esmeralda's heart was an empty nest, she did try to occupy it with the love for her loving squabs, but one day they would acquire their wings and all their feathers and leave her lonely and wondering: what's next? This process seemed so premature; how could she be feeling this way when their kids were still so young and she was still providing them with basic needs care? Esmeralda employed way too much time feeling life was passing by in front of her eyes without her having any control of it and watching how it took away all her energy and desire to go on. She was secretly convinced she had obtained the title of 'unhappy wife' mostly via her own efforts although it seemed she found satisfaction in blaming her husband for this — in a regular basis. Time was going to definitely tell the unfolding of her life with her frustrations and failed dreams; her desires to have 'more' both quantitatively and qualitatively speaking in the love arena. So, her life could not be expected to get any easier or less complicated, on the contrary, her unrestrained emotions and deep lonely sentiments elicited by the unknown or a life she was not experiencing at all — not just yet, were going to monopolize her life and nothing would prevent the snowball from getting bigger and bigger...

Chapter 3

Is Love a State of Mind?

And one day out of the blue...

It is about five forty-five p.m., almost time for Esmeralda's medical surgical clinical rotation at one of the main hospitals in that city where she spent most of her youth after she came to the United States of America. She is walking with advance and firm steps entering the Emergency Department entrance road to this hospital as this would serve as a shortcut. Suddenly through the corner of her eye she saw the glimmer of a body which looked very familiar to her the more she kept staring at it. After proceeding about two to three steps she abruptly stopped and suspiciously turned her head, now she saw that man quickly coming in the same direction she was standing like the Statue of Salt. In what seemed to be a flash to her, he was standing right in front of her; she was in utter disbelief and got way too nervous to initiate the proper salutation typical of when one runs into someone you know. He was the one to gracefully say, "Hi, Esmeralda, it is so nice to see you! What are you doing here dressed like ah...?"

To which she finally warmed up enough to respond, "... like a nurse? I am going now to a clinical rotation at this hospital; I am studying to be a registered nurse, you know? A change in career... what about you... Do you work here?" He explained that he had worked in the Radiology Department for a few years already. "That's right... you told me you wanted to go into that field when we took that prerequisite course together in college, remember?" said Esmeralda.

He replied, "How could I forget?" Esmeralda exhaled and frowned her forehead when she apologized by saying that she had to get going and she could not be late — 'the instructor was an intolerable bitter woman'. They did have a chance to and they did exchange their phone numbers and say good bye with a kiss on the cheeks.

From that unexpected but pleasant encounter with that young man from the past, Esmeralda could not stop thinking about that summer they met and spent time together. As you might have already noticed, she was a sucker for romance, anything romantic. So, one of the first memories that came to the surface now was once when they were both in an unoccupied classroom in that Community College and Jason went and wrote on the whiteboard with a marker a huge heart with their names inside, Esmeralda was sitting by the large window sill facing a view of the marginal and declining industrial city. He approached her with this look as if saying, 'I want you... and desire you!' and without asking grabbed her face and kissed her lips with passion until they were interrupted by the students entering the room for a class that was about to start. They both laughed kind of embarrassed and ran out of the room. Yes, she loved moments like these ones; those were the moments in her life that kept her alive and made her want to spend one more minute breathing and hoping for another moment like these ones.

Jason was a young guy with a spirit and desires to become more than what his parents could ever be; he aspired and worked hard to graduate from college and have a better life than he had so far. He came from a humble family with low financial resources, first generation of immigrants to the USA — just regular people who lived pay-check by pay-check.

Finally, Esmeralda could not resist and fell into the temptation; she grabbed the phone and called him. He sounded surprised but with a cheerful tone of voice and they agreed to see each other to 'talk about old times'. The day came and they got to their destination, parked their vehicles and Esmeralda was impressed by what she saw; he was driving a Lexus, it looked like one of the last models if not the newest one. He was looking tall and svelte and his bronze skin tone with his big brown eyes, fleshy well shaped lips and elegant pose elevated Esmeralda to the clouds. They met half way on the streets full with cars on both sides and old tired buildings inhabited mostly by people from many countries of Latin America and other parts of the world; there were competing businesses such as bodegas in the under privileged community of a city that once distilled great splendor — a place where history tells us the industrial revolution was born, and people as its main resource. He invited her to enter his car while distilling gallantry and gracefully opened the car's door to let her in. They sat there with the engine off while another engine was just igniting — Esmeralda was gradually getting this tension building up on her insides and any minute the steam of passion was going to evaporate from her pores; so, before he could finish another sentence, she asked him, "What are you waiting for... to kiss me?" He smiled the way only he knew how, so enchanting and sensual and he kissed her... it was a long and passionate kiss.

Of course, the topic of their current life status was going to be touched and when they both with innate curiosity inquired about each other, he said he got married three years back and had a three-year-old little girl — his eyes sparkling while saying this.

She told him she married Valentino and had a four-year-old girl and a three-year-old boy. For Jason hearing that she married precisely this guy must have bothered him no end. He probably had fresh in his mind the way they broke up toward the end of that magical summer. One evening when sitting on the front porch's stairs – in the house she lived with her family when she was single – and the night quickly approaching, Esmeralda very solemnly expressed what was eating her for the last couple of days. She had decided to go back with Valentino and break up 'this ardent love experience but that she was convinced was as ephemeral as the tulips that bloom in spring' she did not say it like this, but those were her thoughts. While she was 'tactfully' breaking up with him — he could not help it and immediately his beautiful eyes filled with tears; he could not pronounce a single word, he jumped to get up, trying to not lose his balance while standing on one leg with arms in the air and half twirl later sadly looked at her and moved his lips — no sound, to say 'Good bye' at the same time waving his hand and walking away. Back to their present time, they talked and kissed for a while and then said good bye to each other, but not before making plans to meet again — perhaps in a suitable place where they could freely demonstrate what their bodies were anxiously waiting to release, unrestrained selfish passion. They did try to accomplish this, however, this time for Esmeralda's dismay, Jason was not the same guy she met years back when they were both so young and dreamers. He was acting as if his only intension was to have a cursory affair where only the physical aspect of it was going to be utilized. Esmeralda in vain tried to search into his real feelings, looking for a vestige of the love that once was by observing his every move and everything he uttered when they were together or conversing on the phone. But her 'he is just not the same' hypothesis concluded with irrefutable evidence when she only felt his cold careless and rushed caresses — not a pure sentiment of love or resemblance of romance perceived by the eternally in love with LOVE Esmeralda.

"Do you love her?" Esmeralda asked Jason one day to which he replied, "My wife? Yes, I do," sounding very relaxed and oblivious to the reason she had to ask him such a question. She asked the question hoping that he was going to say no, 'I am just with her because of my daughter', but instead got the cruel truth; she realized that she was alone in another love fantasy, wrongly assuming that he was as unhappy in his marriage as she was. There is an old Spanish adage, 'El ladrón juzga por su condición' meaning: A thief believes everyone else steals; this phrase very well could serve as an analogy to describe Esmeralda's most inner thoughts and intentions. She organized this whole story in her mind that went like this... 'He must be with her out of habit, living his life for the sake of living, without feeling real love, attached to a duty to a custom' and she was determined to help him get out of that situation and at the same time she could do that as well. The rude awakening that his cold and direct response caused her, sent her one more time to the abyss, darkness and loneliness, yes, she was indeed loving alone and not being loved back. You can say that this was the 'perfect revenge' for the rejection he felt years back when Jason was so in love with Esmeralda. That day she felt so devastated that after she left him and drove home almost hit another car in the highway. Days, months and maybe a year or so went by and she as usual got over him and even got to the conclusion that she was not really in love with him anyway; it must have been just a mirage and felt ashamed that she could mistake true love with a lousy temporary filthy love affair. She might not have found any relationship between her behavior and actions while indulging her emotions deep into this ave de paso love affair with the words of St. John the Evangelist when he mentions the famous: 'Concupiscence of the flesh'; but Esmeralda's behavior was reflecting just that, the desire that the flesh unavoidably and naturally seeks. She should had deduced this right away being that she had a Christian background, but she was in denial and only trying to avoid one more time her own reality; a reality deprived of true love.

They say that habit is stronger than love…
In case you are wondering why Esmeralda went back with Valentino when she had decided to break up with him after a long-term relationship of more than three years, your guess is as good as mine. But, understanding what disillusioned her about the attractive and smart young guy with whom she had an adventure, would certainly explain it. Jason and Esmeralda had a lot in common; their immigration status, a big family and an extraordinary desire to be successful in this new land. However, there was one single thing which the young Esmeralda would demand from the guy she was going to choose as her eternal companion, he had to be at least willing to join her in her religious beliefs and practices. Therefore, that summer when they were going out together and he even visited with Esmeralda and all her immediate family, she would try to introduce Jason to her way of thinking — spiritually speaking. An evening when they were sitting at the kitchen table studying for an exam, she brought to him a big book. On the cover was a portrait of Jesus Christ; her intentions? You guessed it. She was testing the waters; she wanted to have an idea how sensitive he was when it came down to spirituality or religion. She wanted to know if he could one day convert to her religion. When she noticed his total indifference,

she then decided to cut him off as if trying quickly to get rid of a gangrenous toe before it was too late. And that is exactly what she did, in this way she decided to prematurely stop a relationship in which she could very well had gotten to know him and even loved this young man. Instead, she went back to a more comfortable place, a place where she was able to contemplate herself in a not so far future with a husband with whom she would share one faith, one religion.

One morning while a younger Esmeralda is at her job, placing phone calls to customers in a billing department she got this call from downstairs; the operator informed her that a visitor was waiting for her in the lobby area. As soon as she got out of the elevator, she saw Valentino pacing back and forth and as she got closer, she realized he was holding a bible which made absolutely no sense to her; he quickly got on his knees and asked her to swear while extending the black book out, 'that she was not in love with another guy'. He looked like he had been crying, his eyes were red and he looked horrible, disheveled, with a stained shirt, and long and messy hair and beard. She could not believe her eyes. She begged him to get up and assured him they were going to meet later in another place to talk. Those days after their breakup, Valentino was frequenting some of Esmeralda's relatives; he would just show up in their homes without an invitation. One day Esmeralda's uncle asked her what was going on with them? Because Valentino came and started talking nonsense about Esmeralda, things like: 'she has no shame… now she is going out with a different guy every night', he was obviously drunk. Most people in their circle of friends and even many relatives of Esmeralda were not yet aware of the fact that for Esmeralda Valentino was out of the picture and she just wanted to move on. But he was not out of the picture; quite contrary, he was very much everywhere Esmeralda went. One evening when she was coming down the large stairs from one of the Community College's buildings, she was surprised by Valentino. "So, this is the new guy you're seeing now?" said Valentino to Esmeralda while trying to ignore the young man next to her. He followed them to the parking lot and at this point Jason — yes, the same one she broke up with to only go and accept Valentino back in her life. Jason decided to walk away and let them resolve the obvious unfinished situation they had.

Esmeralda spoke sincerely and frankly with Valentino; she tried hard to make him understand why she was breaking up with him. "If this is the way we are going to treat each other ten, fifteen, twenty or fifty years from now, I prefer to end it now." Esmeralda told Valentino this self-fulfilling prophecy and she continued, "I feel very unhappy with you, all we do is fight and I don't even feel any joy hanging around with you any more... Don't you ever wonder how it would be like if you could meet someone and she could make you feel totally different to how you're feeling now?... I can see you are not happy, either." If Valentino had a clue of what Esmeralda was talking about, he simply acted as if he did not care. It was not until he saw her evaporate from his side and interact with another man that he started to freak out and tried to convince her to get back together. Esmeralda had that brief but yet intense romance with Jason and then one day without a good or logical explanation finished it and days later called Valentino's house to invite him out and talk.

Valentino's mother answered the phone and as soon as she realized it was Esmeralda, in a defensive kind of way told her, "Please, Esmeralda... don't hurt my son again... you have no idea what I have been through in the last couple of months with him; he does not stop crying and he is just out of it." Esmeralda was very touched by his mother's confession and thought that if he indeed loved her that much maybe they had a chance to be happy... that his love would suffice for both of them and maybe he could change. Valentino and Esmeralda resumed their relationship and as you know, got married and got children and only God knows how their story will end up? One thing is for sure, Valentino signified security because she was not dealing with a stranger, emotional stabilization — meaning her feelings were going to remain stagnant and not experiencing that euphoria sort of feeling proper of when she falls crazy in love with someone to later suffer a disappointment, and she did care about him a great deal. After all they had been together for such a long time that she learned to love him just as she loves a very good friend and she did not want to hurt him. However, she did not admit to this, instead she must have gotten confused thinking that if she started missing him, it was because she had strong feelings for him. And that is why they say that 'Habit is stronger than love'.

And that: Donde hubo fuego cenizas quedan...

"Señor, where are we? Why are you stopping here?" said Esmeralda to the chauffeur; he told her that they had arrived at her destination. Esmeralda was in front of the house that she lived in when she was a kid back in her native country. Her mother had completely remodeled it — now it had a tall elegant metal fence that enclosed all the front yard with just the sidewalk separating it from the busy street. She remembered playing with the neighborhood's kids in the large terrain in front of her house. She got out of the car with her baby in arms and was received by her mother standing on the big front door. The whole atmosphere of the house itself and even the town felt strange to her; she was searching for something that could make her feel at home once again. However, nothing was the way she imagined it was going to be in this old town that so desperately at one time she wanted to leave because it lacked attractiveness and nothing ever changed. But now she wished she could see that old town again to attempt to revive an era that now she could appreciate she was very happy, in harmony with her senses and free compared to her current life. Then one evening as she used to do before, she went and sat at her favorite place –the front porch of the house – and after a while as if she had seen a ghost, saw this guy passing in front of the house with his eyes fixed on it and when he got under the tall wood-post street light she recognized him. It was him, her high school sweetheart. Just as old times, he attempted to get in and talk to her. Now a fence was between them, but Esmeralda did not hesitate to open the gate for him to come inside. She was holding her baby girl and he got closer to see her and touched her cheeks; Esmeralda quickly asked him, "Do you have kids of your own, yet?" He immediately got out his wallet and showed her a picture of a little boy; he said 'that's my son'. They both smiled and looked at each other's eyes with tenderness. She asked, "What about your son's mother?" to which he replied, "She's back there [USA] we are not together; I don't have any feelings for her." Esmeralda feared that her mom was going to find out of his presence there and all of a sudden said adios to him and they timidly gave each other a quick kiss on their lips. Just like old times, again he availed himself of Esmeralda's high school best friend's assistance to send her a note: 'Esmeralda, I will be waiting for you by the river shore at six p.m., please don't fail to come, with love, Antonio." Even though she was extremely uneasy about this encounter with her primer amor, she did dare to go and meet him as he had proposed. They did not talk that much that evening — they just kissed, intensely kissed. Esmeralda was on vacation just for two weeks and she had already employed one week visiting her cousins in two major cities, a few hours away from this town and now was on her day before departing back home [USA]. Part of her wished she could have found him sooner; that way she could have spent more time with him. Esmeralda asked for his phone number and told him that she wanted to keep in touch with him. One more time, Esmeralda seemed to have this illusion that now she could leave her husband and live happily with her old love, again she thought Antonio was going to fight and wait for her. And again, she perceived herself being in love and being loved back.

Esmeralda took the plane back to the USA and once there attempted to call the number Antonio had given her. She would call every day and every day she got either a voice mail or another person answering and taking her message. "Please tell Antonio that I need to speak with him, it is very important." Perhaps she had not realized yet that for Antonio to come back to the USA was practically impossible; he must have had some problems with justice back in the old city, New Jersey. Yes, he had lived there for a while, but he was an undocumented immigrant and after committing a criminal act involving drugs, he was deported to his country of origin. Esmeralda was oblivious to both the incredible geographic proximity that at one point they had while Antonio used to stay next to the town where Esmeralda lived and the troubles he faced. Now, she was just concentrated on this idea of making up for the old times; maybe she could help him gain legal status in the land of opportunities once she got her divorce. Esmeralda could not be further from reality, but as usual she was going to be startled out of her comfortable dreams. A couple of weeks after her return from her conflicting vacation, Esmeralda had again the need to use a pregnancy test. While she is at the bathroom door and Valentino is at the living room, but visible, she shouts, "Valentino… come quickly, I need to show you something!" Yes, indeed, she was pregnant and Valentino got so shaken by the news that he just kept saying, "What are we supposed to do now, Esmeralda, what?" Esmeralda had tried to be 'sincerer' with him those last weeks and somehow made him aware that something changed her during that trip and now she had new plans with her life that did not include him. But, as usual due to his subdued temperament, he did not react that much to her comments. She did insist that they needed to at least get separated; she needed some space to realize what to do with her life. She even dared to confess that she had seen 'him' and mentioned his name. Valentino knew about Esmeralda's first love; she had mentioned the story to him a couple of times before — thinking it was part of her past and just a beautiful love experience. Letting Valentino know about what took place this time around was her worse mistake. Now, he got rankled by her confession and even made him suppose that this baby might not even be his. He would not say it aloud, though; perhaps he feared that Esmeralda could use this as a powerful reason to leave him once and for all. The way Valentino 'loved' Esmeralda was very strange, it looked like he wanted her with him in spite of the fact she didn't seem to love him or it could be that he thought he knew her more than what she knew herself. He might have thought that she was once again 'confused' and she was going to eventually desist of the crazy idea of leaving and starting fresh without him. Therefore, after his anger dissipated and the waters settled down and Esmeralda finally realized that she did not stand a chance with her old-time love, Valentino and Esmeralda stayed together and had their baby. Only ashes remained of that old flame… only ashes. So, yet again, Esmeralda's persistent infatuation and illogical emotional turmoil positioned her at a place where she had to question her ability to love someone for real and wondered if she has ever experienced true love.

Crazy, Irrational, Immature lovers!

It is five forty-five a.m., this rainy winter morning, it is still dark outside; Esmeralda is standing in line — waiting for the bus with destination to New York City. The cold drizzling rain suddenly became a torrential one. "Hey, I can share my umbrella with you if you want, it's big enough for the two of us," boldly asked Esmeralda to a travelling peer standing next to her who was getting soaked by the unforgiving steady rain.

He smiled and asked, "Are you sure?" as if with fear that she was offering just trying to be courteous and he did not wish to bother her. But Esmeralda insisted and, in this way, he got under her wings. Esmeralda had seen this young guy on the bus stop and inside the bus a few times before, so she did get a chance to notice him and he did the same. They got on the bus that morning and sat in different seats. Public transportation seats are unpredictable and funny looking; in a large bus, you will typically see about ninety-five per cent of the two-passenger seats occupied by a single person and the other seat empty –even though eventually all the seats are taken; so, unless there are people who know each other who get in the bus together, that is pretty much how the picture looks like at least for a while. It's interesting to try to figure out to what cause this phenomenon can be related to; perhaps people are afraid to get stuck with a very talkative person when all they want to do is sleep all the way to their final stop or people fear getting to know a stranger in a more in-depth way… because you know what that means? Eventually you get involved in their private lives without you even realizing it. Most people have plenty of issues going on with their own lives and don't need more.

Every morning they saw each other either standing in line and other times just coming back from work. They would smile and wave at each other even when they were each in an extreme point of the line; other times they would have small talks while patiently waiting for the bus and yet another time they were lucky to sit one seat away from each other. There was this time when Elijah was sitting just behind Esmeralda even though she was alone in her double seat; maybe they were shy to purposely show closeness. However, he tried to interact with her and asked her, "Could you do me a favor?"

"Sure!" said Esmeralda.

"Please wake me up when we're close… you know, as soon as we're out of the Lincoln Tunnel." Esmeralda nodded with a smile and turned her head facing to the front.

This guy would ask Esmeralda for the same favor a few many times until one morning, she told him, "Why don't you sit right here next to me? I can do a better job at waking you up in this way." He released a quick and nervous laugh and jumped into her seat. They looked at each other directly into their eyes and something happened that was going to change the way they saw each other from this instance forward. Esmeralda, feeling chilly due to the bus's strong air conditioning, asked him if they could sit even closer so she could benefit from his body's heat and he happily did just that. In a few seconds, their heads turned to see each other and this time without any warning they kissed on their lips — that morning there were not many passengers, so they felt very comfortable. This same experience would repeat itself very often whenever the atmosphere was clear of any witness, that is, people they would normally see every day in their daily trips.

One day, Elijah was holding Esmeralda's hands and caressing them with devotion when out of the blue he said, "Esmeralda, I would like us to have something more formal, you know, I want you to be my girlfriend." Esmeralda could not believe what she just heard and even though she felt extremely flattered, she came to the realization that it was about time her identity became undisguised. She hated to have to make him aware this way; all this time she had been pretending to be this super young chic playing around with this fascinating young guy.

So, she went like this, "I am married with two kids and I am not as young as you supposed I am."

Bum! the news hit him hard judging by the face he put, but quickly showed resilience by admitting, "I have a little girl, too… she is two-years-old." Esmeralda was surprised to hear this because this guy was so young — probably in his early 20's, it seemed to her.

So, she in an inquiring sort of way asked him, "So… you have a wife… a woman in your life?"

He replied, "No, we are separated, she lives in NY and you know… I live here [in New Jersey]." Esmeralda had a sigh of relief, but did not hesitate to capitalize on the fact that she was too old for him; it was still early to make him understand with what he was dealing with, thought Esmeralda. However, he was showing a lot of interest in continuing with their undefined but yet pleasant relationship.

Days and months went by and these two reckless loving souls would publicly display their mutual physical attraction; they would kiss and hug in a hidden corner of the bus / train terminal while multitudes were rushing in and out, the whole thing might have felt to them like those people were merely strangers and at the same time, they found themselves alone in their own exhilarating world. Esmeralda was full with vitality those days and the new lover was sort of a theriac to all her emotional and psychological afflictions; getting up before dawn was not as difficult as it used to be because she knew that same morning, she was going to see him. She was going to sit next to him and he was going to make her feel as if she was very young again; their trifling conversations many of which involved drolleries about anything they saw or imagined took the place of worries and anything that mature adults normally are preoccupied with. Esmeralda felt attractive again and she had not felt this way in a long time. After all, hanging around with a guy almost fifteen years younger than you would give you a great deal of confidence in yourself and for her it was like being administered an overdose of conceit. Those secret visits to his bachelor apartment made her feel like 'una mujer de mundo'; in liberty to do whatever she pleased, selfishly desired and unconsciously doing almost anything that he provoked her to do. Before Esmeralda knew Elijah, she always detested those adolescents to young adult males' attire; their pants hanging half way down their buttocks –showing their underpants and heavy super large jewelry, made her sick to no end. Now she was involved with one of them, but she did not ponder on this fact because she was caught in the moment — indulging her illusion with a feeling that she had found the fountain of youth. It was not as if she never criticized him; but she would do it in a humorous way and they would just laugh aloud. One day while slightly bending down his slender and tall body, tilting his head, so she could see, he told her, "Look what my friends did to me." She curiously went around him and looked; he had the word 'dick' [the vulgar name of penis] shaved on the back of his head in a pretty noticeable size. He was laughing while saying that he lost a bet with his friends and that is how he paid. This grotesque episode was just a little too much for her; Esmeralda just nodded while biting her lower lip and forcing her eyes –a signal of her non-verbal disapproval. Their colossal differences in both their disposition to life's important matters and the generation gap was manifested in this very incident; Esmeralda did not deny it, nonetheless, she was not ready to relinquish this 'locura de amor', no... not just yet.

Esmeralda was having an internal fight; she did not intend to love this guy –instead she just wanted to have fun. However, the whole thing was so foreign to her; she always had the tendency of falling in love with someone that she got so intimate with like what she was experiencing with Elijah. If one applies the concept of eros love mentioned prior and added yet another idea related to this type of love as described in the book, one might start to understand her feelings if only on the surface: '... He [Lewis] carefully distinguishes it [eros] from sex (which he calls Venus), noting how the two are often related, but not necessarily so... he claims that someone seeking sex (Venus) wants sex, and the particular person is simply the "necessary piece of apparatus" for that activity. Yet in eros a person is focused on the lover his or herself. Eros focuses a lover on the beloved, hence its exclusivity. It is indeed about the other person in particular...' and one can deduce that Esmeralda was more interested or inclined to enjoying the 'feeling' of 'being in love' as opposed to just wanting to experience the pleasure of having actual sex either via intercourse or / and oral sex. Obviously, if this was indeed the case, she was barking up the wrong tree because all she was going to gain from this relationship was a pure physical luscious activity; indeed, he was going to become for her a crazy, immature, irrational 'love'.

When she eventually was no longer able to separate her feelings from the physical pleasures, Esmeralda realized she was in a lot of trouble. It was a very dumb idea to fall for an immature, crazy young 'boy' like Elijah was. Esmeralda started thinking that one day he was going to find a young chic and fall in love with her or perhaps go back with the young mother of his daughter; that would devastate her, she was convinced of that. Even if she thought that being in love with him was just a fallacy, she was still going to get hurt or at least her pride could. So, she perhaps unconsciously initiated a process of self-weaning; she was going to reduce their encounters and stop texting for as long as she could. Time proved she was not going to be successful this way. Nevertheless, she did not stop analyzing her real feelings and putting things into perspective, she would recognize that sooner or later she needed to come face to face with reality. Besides, what she was doing was so infantile and selfish; what concept her family would have of her if any of them found out? Perhaps it would not be a big surprise for them to know she was having an extra marital affair since they all knew she was not happy in her marriage; what was going to be inconceivable for them was that she was more than a decade older than her lover. On the other hand, how would her husband react? — He could go crazy and violent, any man under this circumstance would. Nonetheless, Esmeralda was not going to be deterred from the road to self-destruction until something drastically changes her life course.

Perhaps what Esmeralda really needed to stop this insanity was to suffer another love disappointment. Now you would say: but she should not feel disappointed at all... she knew she had nothing guaranteed with this clueless fellow and she was not supposed to fall in love with him; but the fact of the matter is that she was not able to manipulate her feelings as she originally thought. That was precisely her mistake — she thought she could control the situation, but she could not. One day she got this unusual text message from Elijah stating, 'Babe, I'm sorry for asking you, but I'm really in need of some cash right now, if you could lend me one hundred bucks, that would save me, please!'. She did not like this at all — she could give him the money all right, but what about her dignity? Somehow, she intuited that he was not going to pay her back which meant only one thing: he did not have any respect for her and even worse he was under the assumption that he could very well obtain financial gains in exchange for the use of his young and super healthy body and his time. Esmeralda was quickly realizing that this scenario just turned too ugly for her to continue acting on it. She tried not to reveal her thoughts related to that sudden request of his and after a couple of hours, finally replied, 'Sorry for the delay... I was busy and did not see your message... Yes, I will give you the money... just wait for me, I will be there soon'. She went to his apartment and as soon as she appeared at the door, he grabbed her and kissed her and dragged her to the bed and without taking their clothes completely off started having sex; she was not enjoying it and it was not because he finished much quicker than usual rather it was due to her current state of mind. Then while he was putting his pants' zipper up, she coldly took out the money from her jeans' packet and pitched them on top of the dresser, saying, "Here you go... have fun!" putting a sort of sarcastic face and left. That day was officially the day when she underwent a huge transition from the 'lover' to the 'cougar'; she could not feel more humiliated meanwhile he was totally oblivious to her feelings, to the way he made her feel — so dirty, disvalued and used. Esmeralda needed to crush into the wall of her sad reality in order to wake up and get out of that ridiculous situation she put herself through. Just as military people plan their next move to defeat their enemies, Esmeralda started proactively working toward the 'detachment process' as her main defensive strategy; she went and deleted Elijah's phone number from her mobile phone and took the bus that ran either before or after the usual time they both took the bus to New York City and back, in a regular business day. The process of letting go was not easy at all as expected; she would contemplate the sun coming out through the moving trees and the more gorgeous the morning or evening was the more she would miss him sitting next to her just holding hands, sometimes taking a nap or simply conversing about silly stuff. The babble that had sustained inside this vivid and impossible to be refrained urge for sex and passion exploded and Esmeralda was once again left in a state of boredom so terrible to bear. She went back to live without desire to do so; like when you eat a meal to fill up your stomach but not having an appetite for it — in that same way she was just living. She went back to seeing the world grey instead of colorful and bright. She looked at herself in the mirror and saw this defeated old bitter woman and would ask herself, "Who is that woman in the mirror?" She could hardly recognize her nor accept her. She did not want to be that woman who was always easily irritated and would nag her husband for absurdities, but again only time and the surprises it brings with it was going to shake her up and make her see the world from the other side; perhaps that side that shows satisfaction with what one already has, content with those seemingly insignificant but irreplaceable moments in life and above all that peace that making the right or proper decision will concede. Or perhaps, she still had a great deal to live and learn.

Chapter 4

Was it all worthy?

Is a Divorce the Solution?

One fair question would be why doesn't she get a divorce? Obviously, she does not love the guy, probably never did. Esmeralda cannot make that decision for the same reason she went ahead and married Valentino. Doubts, conformism, fear were all major factors that might have contributed to her decisions or lack of them when they needed to be made. She married Valentino because she was afraid to never find a man with the same spiritual background she had; ever since she was young enough to understand she heard at church and from her own father's lips this, 'Be ye not unequally yoked together with unbelievers: for what fellowship hath righteousness with unrighteousness? And what communion hath light with darkness?' (2 Corinthians 6:14). This biblical verse was often if not always interpreted in Esmeralda's environment as the warning that God gives his people about the importance of the marriage between people with the same belief and religious practices in order to preserve their faith and avoid undue suffering. Later, advanced in her failed marriage, Esmeralda would remember this doctrine and she would get so cynical to the extent that she would secretly mock her father pronouncing these exact phrases. She was angry at her father for inculcating this 'ridiculous' concept. She must have felt this way now because she did not see this piece of God inspired scripture realized in her marriage and she had been obedient – she married 'a God's loving child, a man who feared God and walked on his ordinances' Yea, alright? Esmeralda would laugh at the whole thing now and wonder if she had married of her free will — married out of love and love alone, things would turn out to be much more different. Esmeralda recalled when her father advised her to undo the engagement if she was not sure of what she was doing; interesting enough even this very religious conservative man noticed that his beloved daughter was not being true to her most inner feelings those days when she was rushing to get married. However, at that point where she was at least emotionally, her father's unbiased and sincere advice was not good enough for her. Perhaps Esmeralda was convinced that there was not going to be another man to satisfy the powerful doctrine and she was not going to risk waiting for another guy.

One very important factor was the fact that Esmeralda was afraid she was going to end up with a dude that was going to betray her with another woman; she had experienced this in her own vivid flesh before she found Valentino and decided to cling to him as if he was the last rock standing firm in a flooded river after heavy rains. She felt secure with Valentino in the sense that she knew him for a long time and she never knew or had any reason to suspect that he would even consider being with another woman. Her insecurities were way too many and she thought that with Valentino she did not have to hide anything; they went through so much together that he became family to her, though she would not concede it. On the other hand, Esmeralda's indecisiveness was always notable; she always had this cloud of doubts lingering in her mind. She doubted that she could be happier with anybody else; she doubted whether she was ever good enough; she doubted somebody could fall in love and stay in love with her; and above of all she doubted herself — was she going to be able to make somebody else happy? This is another topic that Valentino would dare to visit with Esmeralda whenever he felt threatened, when he had a feeling that Esmeralda was getting some courage to leave him; Valentino would throw at her the infamous phrase, "You can't be happy with anybody because you don't get along with anybody, not even with your own mother... you keep fighting with her too." Of course, Esmeralda never received these words passively, on the contrary she would put a fight that would exalt her husband's assumption even more. So, even when she was not an innate conformist, she resigned herself to this life with Valentino that you could say that yes, conformism played a big role both in her decision to marry the way she did and later to not get a divorce when it was evident that was all that was left to do in her miserable marriage.

After ten plus years into her marriage, Esmeralda started analyzing some points.

• One: a good reason she chose Valentino to be her husband was because he was not a womanizer — I mentioned that before, but I need to emphasize this fact in order to compare her old sentiment with her current thoughts; now she is seriously thinking that Valentino's emotional apathy and the way she feels with him — mostly resentful and angry because 'he should have known better and not marry a woman who did not love him back'; he was after all, older than her about eleven years older and therefore should have shown a more elevated level of maturity. She thought that her current situation with her husband was far worse than if he had cheated on her with a bunch of women. And now, Esmeralda feels like she is alone — spiritually and emotionally alone, submerged in a lake of loneliness.

• Two: Valentino was going to love her more than she loved him and therefore his love for her could compensate for her meager love. However, she did not feel loved by him as she presumed, he was going to love her. Actually, the way Valentino 'loved' her was incomprehensible to her, how can she only could feel his rejection when she just wanted to talk and be listened to? How can she could perceive her husband's non-verbal criticism and no admiration and/or his lack of enthusiasm for her accomplishments when she wanted to feel valued? Esmeralda felt as if she and her husband were merely business partners working for a lousy corporation and with a difficult clientele who demanded a great deal of emotional intelligence. Of course, this skill would also need to be utilized in order to survive the bankruptcy that a divorce would represent.

• Three: As a person who loves God and follower of his commandments, Esmeralda intended to join for life that man who shared the same principles and spiritual ordinances she possessed. Very soon after their union in marriage, Valentino got as cold as a block of ice when it came down to the religious or spiritual arena; he would get up late from bed the day they were going to attend service — the day of rest, the Sabbath. Esmeralda was not able to experience that promised spiritual rest; she had to struggle with Valentino to convince him to get ready and help her with the kids in an attempt to be on time for church. There was this instance when Esmeralda was about seven months pregnant and they had such a heated argument while driving to church one Saturday morning that she asked him to stop the minivan right there at a major highway because she wanted to get out and run away from him — of course Valentino did not concede her this wish. But, by the time they made it to the temple, she must have gotten no less than seven demons in her. Esmeralda learned both by osmosis and by what the Holy Scripture taught about the role and responsibilities of the man as being the head of the household and this applied to everything including trying to be on time for the church's services. Valentino was light years away from being the spiritual father figure that Esmeralda saw in her own father when she and her siblings lived with him after their parents' divorce. Ironically, Esmeralda came from divorced parents and so did Valentino, it is like they inherited this bad gene for an unhappy marriage or simply their parents' inability to properly choose who to marry.

Now, there are of course even more reasons for not getting a divorce, the most powerful of all, the kids. Having kids was one of the things Esmeralda looked forward to once she was married; they were supposed to bring joy and happiness to a home. And then it was going to be precisely them who would help preserve the marriage — at least in papers. Esmeralda's insecurities bombarded her again, now she is thinking that no man would want her knowing she had kids, less a severe autistic son. Esmeralda found herself in a morass years later when she wakes up in the middle of the disaster her marriage was; no way out of this one. How was she going to manage as a single mother and having to deal with her son's special needs and demands? "Impossible," she thought. "That's it for me, so I will have this separate away from home little life where I could be happy for a few hours," she told herself referring to her love affairs. These last phrases sound like she premeditated her actions, but in reality, she came to the conclusion that it was a good idea to relax and distract her mind from the routine at home via the secret lover route, after the fact, after she experienced what it was like. Esmeralda felt such a relaxation during those hours of pure enjoyment that it was like she had found an oasis in the middle of the dessert. These moments were short-lived compared to the never-ending hours of spiritual solitude, scarcity of love, comprehension and harmony she was unable to obtain at her husband's side. There were times when it crossed her mind that maybe it was better for her husband to find out she was cheating on him, so he could be the one to ask for the so feared divorce and they both could move on in different directions, so they can stop hurting each other even more. It also occurred to her that Valentino had her in such a low esteem that he could not conceive the idea of Esmeralda being capable of attracting other men — much less having an affair. Yes, she would get angry at him even when the guy had no clue of the reasons she had. That was precisely the problem, he should have had at least a slight suspicion — didn't he see how beautiful she looked sometimes when she went to work? He would not say a word and when he did, it was something like this, 'Oh! You look different today' and then followed, "You are such a freaking idiot!" she would whisper in utter discontent sometimes; she sensed Valentino totally belittled all her attributes and the possibility that he simply failed to acknowledge them made no difference to her – after a while she just got used to this – One side effect of hanging around with a man who exalts even the smallest of your good features is that you learn how bad your partner is at giving you a complement. Believe it! You can get used to being admired in a blink of an eye and it feels so good!

So, to answer the question, of course a divorce should be 'a solution' though not 'the solution'. Even if Esmeralda got a divorce, she still had so many issues to deal with and resolve a few psychological and emotional dilemmas that always accompanied her since she was a little timid and insecure girl.

Esmeralda had to get rid of the huge load of bitterness that had been accumulating throughout the years; she had to learn so much, from how to confidently accept a complement to convince herself that another man in this planet could love her <u>the way she wanted to be loved</u>. Yes, because if there was one thing, she learned with Valentino was that it is not enough that your man loves you, it is crucial that a man demonstrates the love he feels for a woman in a way that she really feels loved.

Missing Her Old Self

If it is true that Esmeralda was visited by a little worm called remorse while she dwelled in her state of infidelity, she also felt at times this need to get even with Valentino. He made her so mad all the time because she felt as if he took every opportunity to make her feel out of place, undignified, and plain stupid as when he would insinuate that she 'was not able to fend for herself' so very often. For instance, she had to depend on him to transfer money to 'her' debit card account in order to take care of basic things... from buying a bag of sanitary pads to going shopping for her kids' clothes; imagine that you cannot buy that item which happens to have a huge discount and you wanted it for such a long time and not able to get it because you did not have any money left in your debit card and your husband would give you such a hard time questioning each decision you make on how to spend your money. Esmeralda was a hard-working person; she made decent earnings with her RN job, but weird circumstances prohibited her from having a normal access to her own money; she had a problem with a car she bought a while back and never paid due to the nature of how she lost it – a long and intricate story – and every time she tried to open her own bank account, it got frozen by the legal request of a mysterious group of lawyers

— in an attempt to make her pay the full price of the long-gone car. This was sort of an eternal debt because as Esmeralda inquired on her local municipal court — 'the lawyers kept renewing the case every year'. Therefore, the famous statute of limitations did not seem to apply in this case, mostly because Esmeralda did not show up at the court when she was originally summoned to appear when she was sued. Unfortunately for her, she had to ask her husband to transfer money to the card which was under Valentino's name but that she used.

One has to wonder if Valentino liked having his wife constantly under his radar; you know, when she was at the local mall, he knew and when she bought a nice piece from Victoria Secret, he knew that as well as many of her other activities. So, how did she manage to sustain this double life and not get caught? She was definitively smarter than her husband at least in the area having to do with 'common sense' and her natural actress-like tendencies helped her a great deal together with her clever disposition to play with words and phrases with which she could obnubilate the real situation occurring at a determined place and time. Esmeralda did not quite feel as if she was actually being a liar though in anybody's eyes her actions denounced at least a fabricator. She would not lie when for instance she said she was going to work. She just omitted that either before or after her work duties, she had planned other things not work related. And in this way the waters stayed becalmed in her household. Certainly not in her tormented mind; the things she had to endure to make it happen – the actual encounter with her lover – was many times a task that demanded a lot of her time and effort. For one part, she had to make herself look as beautiful as she could possibly be; have the right garment that made her look very attractive and at the same time not that obvious. Also, she had to leave everything prepared at home with the kids so she could be 'less missed' while she was away for a few hours.

So, it might be true that for Esmeralda the joy and satisfaction she felt when she was 'loved' by another man was sometimes somewhat proportional to the enjoyment she felt by taking revenge on her husband. However, at the end, it is not clear if by attempting to be vengeful Esmeralda hurt herself more than she could possibly hurt him. After all, he was oblivious to her immoral acts and like the old Spanish adage goes: 'Ojos que no ven... Corazon que no siente'. And as much as she tried to deceive herself into thinking that she could go and betray her husband worry free, no need for repentance and / or remorse, in reality at the end of the day, she was not at all comfortable with her actions. She did not like the woman she had become and again, when she took a good look in the mirror, she would see a reflection of her that was inferior in character, showed spiritual weakness and a plain bad person; she felt so terrified of what the people who knew her were going to think about her if they ever found out. Esmeralda was for most part of her young adult life [before her transformation brought about by her marriage] this exemplary figure; while serving at church she was so admired for her spirituality and dedication. For her family and all those who knew her, she was a person with a tranquil temperament, compassionate, understanding, and prone to give a helping hand to who needed it and finally 'a good God's child'. These characteristics did not fit in with her actions lately. Esmeralda felt she was being a hypocrite and a fraud to everyone around her; in order to be a good person, you must not put in danger the wellbeing of others, especially if the others are your own children, sister, brothers and / or your parents. If her irresponsible, irrational actions got revealed, everyone was going to be affected by it. Their kids because eventually when they were old or mature enough were going to resent her and, in this way, they could be marked emotionally for life; her siblings and parents would feel so disappointed in her and even ashamed if the news spread out. This was a penalty she had to endure — no one could ever jump into the water without getting wet. And now she was to her neck deep into the waters of uncertainties. She did not know who she was any more; there was a time that she could describe herself as a Christian believer, one who loved the merciful God, and simply stated: 'a good person'. The worst part was that Esmeralda got used to this new stranger she had transformed into and simultaneously she was also mostly stoic about the whole situation; like her ability to feel true feelings shot down, as though she no longer care, but deep inside she did. It is only that she did not stop to think too much about what she was doing; she did not want another confrontation with her inner, old self. She avoided going back to that woman who put others first and denied herself of the things she wanted for herself. At the same time, she also missed that former woman because that woman believed in something bigger than her troubles and her own frustrations. She believed in the promise of a far unimaginably better world after this cruel one was gone. She found joy in singing a hymn praising her loving divine father or reading a comforting verse from the book of psalms. At one point Esmeralda's strength and main reason for living was resumed into a single powerful word: "FAITH" Now her life felt so superficial, so mundane and void. No lover was going to ever fill that space that only a supreme being could. She at some point during her obstinate position to separate herself from the source of everything that had given her solace, spiritual wellbeing and peace, realized that the first thing she ought to fix was her 'personal relationship with God' a phrase so much preached while she was in church, but that now was more relevant in her life than ever. However, Esmeralda seemed to be so far away from 'the light' that it would take a real miracle to save her; to persuade her to return to her old ways.

Living a moment intensely while wasting the rest of your life
Is it possible to do it? To enjoy so much a brief moment by experiencing passion in the most intense way possible; to come close to that 'diva' kind of feeling; to abandoning the insipid and monotonous world you know and replacing it with one that makes you want to stay there forever? And then… what? Then you rebound to your previous state of mind if you are lucky; or go completely mad in a world that feels as if your misery got larger, at least 10X to the power of 10. You feel the side-effects just as a drug addict suffers during the detoxification period; the 'chemistry' that your body learned to enjoy and your senses assimilated are gone; no longer available and the withdrawal symptoms are nasty and slow to disappear. You no longer experience that feeling of looking into someone's eyes as if they were the only ones left in the world to see; kiss those lips until they distil blood and feel that incredible sensation all over your body that feels warm and cozy and makes you laugh and cry at the same time. And then you pass every minute of every hour of every day dragging the time; it feels so heavy on your back, that you almost lose your balance. You wake up with exactly the same thought as you went to bed with, "I feel so tired… when is all of this going to end?" If you have been fortunate not to have gone this far, one way to have an inkling of what this is all about is by imagining that every day of your existence is gray, the wind is blowing outside and you can see the leafless trees' branches

rocking with this almost hypnotizing rhythm; the roads are deserted and with a cold white coat, amidst of a bitter winter and there is no primavera for you to enjoy, no, not ever. And then... you live your life with a sense of abandonment so bad that you cry inside but there is not a single tear left to shed. A fear, a great fear goes and seizes you; like a frightened kid lost away from home; you are terrified to live one more minute in this solitude so deaf that it disturbs your senses. You want to get out... you are feeling trapped in a devastating desolation of anything good or pure; and you feel as if you are about to exhale for the very last time. All of a sudden, a sense of relief is born because at that point you've got nothing else to lose and then everything becomes as clear as a sunny day at noon; you look outside through the window and contemplate a beautiful American robin with its distinct orange belly, bravely and graciously holding to that fragile branch that the wind seems not to have any compassion on. And then you realize... that bird is you! And then that bird gets to see another beautiful and safe spring; the sinister winter is gone and with it your fear, your apathy, and your disdain for life itself.

Esmeralda was able to survive those periods of uncertainties and fears because when it got unbearable, that is when she would turn around and then start again fresh. She would vent her frustrations and burst of unhappiness through her writings; for her this activity helped her to discover this mysterious woman inside her. A woman who had so much to say and not a soul around to hear it; she felt that she could write her own story backwards in an attempt to find somewhere that person that she always desired to be; maybe she was still there, somewhere along the path; waiting to be rescued, found, comforted, saved! For her husband, the time she employed keying words into the word processor was a total waste of time and he would suggest things like, "Instead of writing so much… why don't you try to find an extra-curricular program for your son?" and added, "That would be useful."

Esmeralda would feel such an immense anger that would consume the last drop of patience left in her. And she would reply to him, "You freaking idiot… what do you know about what I do? What do you know about anything about me? Don't you dare tell me what to do or not to do." Yes, Valentino would bring the very, absolute worse from her. And that is how Esmeralda would sadly waste her life away; quarreling, arguing, hating her husband's guts.

If you believe in absolutism then NO, it was not all worthy to pass a good time with a semi-strange attractive guy under forbidden circumstances and then go back to your 'normal' life. Because in a world where only a black and white type of position exists, there is no room for the in between, you know, 'She is not a bad person… she has just gone through some tough times…' type of sentiment. But in the world of absolutes — again, because moral standards are elevated to the zenith, Esmeralda would not stand a chance to morally survive in it and a woman who has lost the virtue of honesty and of course fidelity will be repudiated, and cast from the unforgiving society. So, you come to your own conclusion.

Chapter 5

Esmeralda's Childhood Psychology

Missing her terribly

"Why you and Mom got divorced, Daddy," asked Esmeralda one day to her father, he was reclined trying to have a siesta and quickly got up and sat down straight; he got very attentive to Esmeralda's surprising inquiry and being careful not to quickly give an answer — after a couple of sighs, he inclined his head and supported it with an open hand, nervously rubbing his fingers against his frowned forehead, he went and said, "Daughter, your mother and I had a lot of differences... because of her beliefs and wrong practices we just could not longer co-exist with each other"

To which Esmeralda responded, "How can you say something like that?... didn't you get to know each other before deciding to get married?"

"It's not that simple, Esmeralda, there are things that you will only be able to understand when you get to be an adult." Esmeralda was not at all satisfied with her father's explanation. She insisted on knowing more, more details of the real issues that destroyed them as a family. Esmeralda loved both her parents; however, being that she had been living with her father for years now and only saw her mom when free from school, she was missing her terribly. She missed her mom to caress her hair before going to sleep so much that she used to hug a piece of clothing her mother had forgotten to take with her in one of her brief visits and she would fall asleep with the smell of it — imagining her mom was right there with her. Esmeralda and her little sister's appearance could have looked better, but they did what they could. For instance, Esmeralda tried to keep her natural curly and frizzy hair neatly arranged and as far as clothing, well, they had only two decent dresses to wear to go to church on the Sabbath and for any other special occasions. So, imagine wearing the same clothing all the time. Amazingly, they did not think about this too much and Esmeralda would make sure her little sister and she got these clothes clean, unwrinkled and intact every week. Of course, Esmeralda noticed the other girls displaying these beautiful colorful dresses, a different one every Saturday, at least it seemed to her. She could only dream of one day having her mom all for herself and she making sure that she got a beautiful dress to wear too. Not only Esmeralda wished to have a normal family with her mother around, but she had to assume some responsibilities that are normally of a female head of the household when she was only ten years old; she had to hand-wash [they had no washing machine] and iron her siblings' and her father's clothes; she was in charge of the house chores such as sweeping and washing the floor, washing dishes, making the beds and much more. Her abuelita was advanced in age and though still strong needed a lot of help in the house. You could say that Esmeralda lost part of her childhood to a premature and forced adulthood. That could have been a reason why she would go to her fantasy world and dream, dream, dream whenever she had a chance. Esmeralda's father had a good job at the time, but he would spend a great deal of money in housing – they always rented a whole family house in a nice and quiet neighborhood close to the private school Esmeralda and her siblings attended.

Paying for an education that was provided by Christian instructors and which taught the value of studying the Holy Scriptures, praying and praising the Lord and Savior was priceless. For Esmeralda's father, however, buying 'unnecessary items' like nice dresses for his daughters and modern house appliances were not in his list of priorities.

¡Es tu día madre mía!

It was May, the month when all mothers are celebrated and /or remembered, the last Sunday in May back in her country of origin; Esmeralda was so excited because she was going to see her mother on Mother's Day and was diligently preparing to welcome her and show her mother her appreciation just for being her mom. The religious private school she attended planned as usual a special program for all the mothers who were going to attend the church service held and directed mostly by the school's director, teachers and the special participation of its well-behaved pupils. One of the activities rehearsed was that of putting this beautiful corsage on each mother's chest. It was a beautiful ceremony filled with songs, poems and theatrical works all commemorating that special being, Mother. Finally, the music played by the female teacher pianist announced the special little part of the celebration when Esmeralda was going to honor her mom by adorning her even more using her own hands and fingers — this alone was an honor for Esmeralda, a privilege she did not take for granted, not for a second that her mom was there, and she was enjoying her presence at that precise instance and having the satisfaction of finally showing all the kids present there that she also had a mother, a beautiful mother. This was a rare occasion that might never repeat itself again. Esmeralda nervously, with shaky hands proceeded to put the corsage on her mom, but when she noticed Esmeralda was taking too long and awkwardly trying to secure it, she grabbed her clumsy daughter's hands, quickly removed them from her chest and finished putting the corsage on herself. The way Esmeralda felt at that moment was probably the inception of a lot of mixed feelings and resentment toward the once unconditionally adored mother of hers. This unconscious action on the part of her mother was going to stay in Esmeralda's unconscious being forever and sometimes would come up to the surface only to hunt her. It was going to be like this thread that goes through every single page of a book and unite its pages almost unnoticeable but ever present. Ines did not do a decent job on gaining her daughter's confidence; she would lie and underestimate Esmeralda's capability to understand basic stuff, such as this instance when she goes and introduces her new husband to Esmeralda like this, "Esmeralda, look, this man here is your uncle, say hello to him and give him a kiss," and Esmeralda was a nine-year-old; why would her mother treat her like a baby? Eventually she was going to find out the truth anyway. Another important factor is that Esmeralda's mother was not good at showing affection; no doubt that she loved her children very much, but she did not know or was incapable to express or even demonstrate with a kiss or caress the tender love typical of a loving mother. Esmeralda needed her mother's warmness so desperately, but this mother had a hidden agenda filled with hurtful feelings and frustrated dreams that she had not overcome. So, her state of perpetual self-pity did not allow her to notice her daughter's need of a mother's pure love.

Becoming her mother

The day that Esmeralda so much desired to come arrived; she and her siblings were going to go to the countryside and live with their mother. Her father got a USA permanent resident card because of his brother's request as a citizen of this land of opportunities. Therefore, her father conceded all rights and custody to Esmeralda's mother over their children. Esmeralda could not be more excited about this and yes, the first months living with her mother she was very happy; her mother would be as lenient as a mother could possibly be. It was almost as if she was trying to make up for those lost times when mother and children were separated. However, when the honeymoon was over, there was something that started bothering Esmeralda; it was something along the lines of the way she felt that Mother's Day putting the corsage on her. Esmeralda felt that her mother constantly talked to her in a demeaning way, the Spanish word 'tonta' was very often in the vocabulary her mother employed when addressing her and on top of this, Esmeralda would perceive at times her mother looking at her with scorn. Esmeralda did not at all appreciate her own mother thinking that she was a shy awkward stupid girl. Moreover, Esmeralda's mother had this bad habit of cursing whenever she got frustrated about something and she would not deviate from this form of outlet that easy, especially when she needed to reprimand her kids. It was like her mother learned to cope with problems this way, however, Esmeralda felt very upset and was offended by this. Esmeralda's father was a very strict person, but he would never say a 'bad' word not even when he was very upset. So, Esmeralda was not used to this new kind of talk that made her feel so disvalued and that did not show the slightest demonstration of love. Now Esmeralda is a mother herself and she is cursing as her mother used to though not calling her kids bad names, but still displaying some subtle negative personality features obviously passed on by her mother to her. The reality is that Esmeralda did not know when she started 'becoming her mother' and it looked like she had already suffered such a huge transformation that she could hardly recognize herself any more. "Oh my God!" Esmeralda cried out inside, deep inside her when she came to understand that now her thirteen-year-old daughter was probably being emotionally affected by her lack of affection demonstrated toward her. Esmeralda did not take this matter lightly; she really pondered on the why and how such a horrible thing was taking place once again, but in a different set of time and place and with characters' roles reversed. Now she was the torturer and her daughter the afflicted one. While Esmeralda had reasons to be upset with her older daughter because she would show negligence and blatant irresponsibility with her school work to a degree that she had 2+ subjects on the brink of failing, Esmeralda was being a little too harsh with her. For instance, Emma Natasha would come very often and surprise Esmeralda with a kiss on her cheek accompanied with an, "I love you mom!"

However, Esmeralda, coldly would either reply, "Me too," if she was in a good mood and other times. Well, other times Esmeralda would yell, "Why do you scare me like that?" and look at her as if she was this little monster who came from another planet and just jumped into her life.

Sometimes, she would take it back – the moment, and reflect on what just happened and be terrified of how she felt – annoyed by her daughter's cloying affection, what was that all about? Well, in the simplest terms that I could come up with I would say that Esmeralda was probably 'taking it out on her daughter' – very simplistic, right? But I would prefer to go a little be further in this 'analysis' of Esmeralda's bizarre behavior. I think Esmeralda, one: she was adjudicating her daughter's lack of commitment, procrastination and scholastic failure to her own failure; she was attributing the whole pathological situation her daughter was demonstrating to be 'all her fault'. So, she was very harsh not on her daughter per se, but on herself — in an unconsciously state. And two: her daughter's character was so similar to that of her husband who she was not being fond of and therefore, Esmeralda would redirect her anger to her daughter when she really meant to scorn Valentino.

Valentino would notice Esmeralda's weakness evident in the way she opted to let her frustration out and would often use this to prove a point, to show that he was right when he said Esmeralda could never be content or satisfied with anybody else on the face of the earth and that she could not even get along with her own mother. In vain, she would try to argue with Valentino that she just could not be happy with him that he should stop redirecting the problem to other issues when in reality they both were 'the issue... the problem'. One big problem here was the fact that Valentino never wanted to focus on his own failures or responsibilities with the real situation –the fact that they were very unhappy in their marriage. Valentino was either a citizen of Planet Oblivion or was emotionally and mentally incompetent to admit to the harsh reality of their situation. So, instead of analyzing the situation in an unbiased form and try to come up with a tangible solution, he would just permanently dwell on the 'You are such a difficult person... with so much poison inside you that you will never be happy no matter with whom you are'. This thought was beginning to make a hole in Esmeralda's mind; she probably started believing this herself. But one thing is for sure, Valentino was just deceiving himself, he was not going to get anything good out of his finger pointing — at least not in the long run. Valentino was just merely trying to prevent their beat-up fragile boat from sinking by taking the water out with a little bucket and throwing them on the immense ocean of resentment, anger, bitterness and misery they found themselves amidst of.

If there is one thing Esmeralda took out of this predicament 'of becoming her mother' is her sympathy for her; she now seems to have an inkling of what her mother must have gone through when she was little; when she would go to the door to receive her, excited and expecting a kiss and a hug and instead got quickly pushed away and was told, "Esmeralda, please not now... I have a terrible headache... I had a very bad day at work today... I need to go to rest for a while." Now Esmeralda has an internal fight with herself to make an effort to not let her daughter down like she was. But it is easier said than done; Esmeralda had been poisoned with a strange substance that had numbed all her senses and therefore her capabilities to be sensible to even the strongest stimulant — like her daughter's red flag signaling the need of her mother's attention and demonstration of love. Fortunately for Esmeralda and her offspring, the effects of this mysterious poison were not permanent and eventually she would reconsider her behavior or insensible attitude and try to amend it by telling her innocent daughter how sorry she was.

"If only my mother had the guts to finally recognize her mistakes and say she is sorry...," Esmeralda would think sometimes. Her mother was this very difficult to understand person; she was so proud and would never admit that she was wrong or that she hurt somebody. Esmeralda learned at one point when she was already a young adult that her mother had gone through very tough times when she was growing up. She experienced things that scarred her and which wounded her heart to the maximum. So, her mother seems to have carried with her throughout her life all the debris that her childhood's monstrous storms left behind. As much as she wished she could understand her mother even more, Esmeralda was incapable of accepting her; accepting the way she talked, behaved; she felt as if that was not her mother and she was swapped with another baby when she was born. Now Esmeralda was so afraid one day her own daughter felt the same way about her.

A father and daughter relationship like no other

To illustrate how Esmeralda got to interact with her father and in this way, connect spiritually with him to a relatively high degree, here is an anecdote taken from an experience with her father when she was twelve years of age: father and daughter are sitting in this unique park, located in the middle of the city and on top of an artificially flattened natural existing mountain, maybe some twelve hundred square feet –about the size of a six story building, they got all the way up there by walking the wide metal stairs. It was a typical park in the sense it had big trees, flowers, benches, light poles and many other things proper of a regular park, however being there one felt literally closer to the stars. One night of many when they were looking up watching the constellations and when even a flying star would pleasantly surprise them, Esmeralda's father, Jeremias asked, "Isn't it so wonderful what God has created?"

Esmeralda, "Daddy, do you think there are other beings in other parts of the universe?" She wondered about this not because she thought 'why so many wonders just for us, humans?' and neither this was just a product of her huge imagination; she had heard somebody maybe in a sermon in church, in a religion class in school or even her father allure to this before this night of celestial exploration with her wise father. They based their talks in part to the following biblical references among other ones mostly from the same book of Job and the last book of the bible,

Revelations, 'Now there was a day when the sons of God came to present themselves before the LORD, and Satan came also among them'. (Job 1:16). A possible interpretation of these verses could be that representative figures from different types of created beings and from different parts of the universe would regularly meet with God in heaven — the official place of God, his throne. Therefore, Jeremias's assertive reply was, "Yes, definitively, there are other living creatures of God in other planets far away from us."

Esmeralda, "But, how come we have never seen them?"

Jeremias, "That's because our heavenly father would not allow it."

Esmeralda, "Why not?"

Jeremias, "Do you remember the story of the conflict between good and evil, Esmeralda?"

Esmeralda, "Yes, of course! our religion teacher spent a lot of time covering that subject and I did very well in the exams."

Jeremias, "Well, that story explains it... but let's get a little deeper into it, let's get a refreshment." Esmeralda's eyes opened up big, she loved to hear these types of stories directly from her father's lips even though they were not new to her; her face was illuminated by the 'lesser light' that the scriptures state 'God had created to provide us with its clarity at night', Esmeralda faced her father, she crossed her skinny legs –positioning them on top of the park bench. She waited for him to talk about this mysterious subject filled with curiosity.

Jeremias, "God created this beautiful and talented angel; he was the director of the angelical choir in heaven; his voice was the most melodic and beautiful of all the creatures. They sang and played musical instruments praising the Lord all the time... One day evil originated from this magnificent, wonderful creature, he started promulgating among the heavenly angels that God was a dictator because they all have to serve him and obey him otherwise, they would be punished; in this way, he managed to persuade three parts of the angels in heaven to follow him in his campaign to rebel against God. When God saw what he had accomplished so far, he approached him and gave him the opportunity to retract from that evil path he had taken. To no avail, our merciful heavenly father tried to demonstrate his love for this being in whom an unknown horrible sentiment had been born in a mysterious way and for the very first time in the whole universe, in reality this created being wanted to take God's place; he felt envy because he noticed how God had this special meetings with the other divine members of his loving government – that is God's only begotten son and the Holy Spirit, but, Lucifer was not invited and at one point this created being begun to seek his own glory instead of the glory of God; moreover, not only he felt left out, but he pretended to be exalted above God by the angels he had the privilege of directing." Esmeralda is still submerged in this amazing story and at times she did not even blink and with her mouth agape, she would wait for her wise father to continue telling the story. Jeremias, "… After giving them [Lucifer and the other fallen angels] plenty of opportunities to abandon those false ideas and repenting, God had no choice but to throw them from heaven in order to put a halt to their damaging influences and bring peace to the now disturbed tranquil place heaven had always been."

Esmeralda, "But… where did they go then?"

Jeremias, "They went to visit numerous worlds where there exist other beings created by God; however, these creatures did not pay attention neither believed Lucifer's evil propaganda demoralizing God and painting him as an unfair father who only seeks for his submissive obedient children's praise and glory and who would not hesitate to destroy them the moment, they disobey him. So, Lucifer and his followers finally got to this planet, the last one they would attempt to convert to their new and evil beliefs and practices..."

Esmeralda, "Oh! I see... I can connect the dots; now comes in that part of the story when Eve is deceived by the serpent and then convinced Adam to eat the forbidden fruit as well... "

Jeremias, "You are correct... Lucifer through a beautiful serpent; these animals used to have wings to fly and their attractive color's hues made them look magnificent; they did not have that connotation we have now of them – we perceive them as dangerous and yes, 'evil', but it was not that way at all at the beginning... So, yes Lucifer who then became: that old serpent, Satan the enemy of God and the devil used this wonderful creature to influence the innocent woman to eat of the fruit of the only tree located in the middle of the beautiful garden that God had instructed his children to not even get close to."

Esmeralda, "I know the story, Daddy... but I have always wondered what the big deal was. Why Adam and Eve were not allowed to eat from it? Why God made such a delicious and attractive fruit to get them to sin and then they are cast out of paradise to a life filled with hardships?"

Jeremias, "Why don't we go over the details of this story one more time? So, you know that the woman, Eve, forgetting her father's advice, got distracted and wandered away from her husband and found herself in front of the magnificent tree when she heard this serpent talk; serpents did not talk as they do not do today either; it was obviously Lucifer's voice: 'So... God has told you that you should not eat the fruit of <u>any</u> tree!' stated the serpent to which she innocently replied: 'My father told us that we could eat from the fruits of all the trees in this garden except from one, the tree of knowledge of good and evil because the day we eat from it we would certainly die'. Lucifer, 'No, no, no! Your father knows that the day you eat from this fruit your minds would open up and you will know not only good but evil as well. You would be as wise as God is!'. The astonished Eve stood there seduced and beguiled by this mysterious voice, Eve took a bite of the fruit and immediately felt different – experiencing for the very first-time shame – because she had a sense of being naked, even though she and her partner had always been without the need of wearing clothes and afraid she was going to stay in this condition by herself without her beloved husband, she persuaded him to eat from it too."

Esmeralda, "I know, Daddy, I have read and heard this story way too many times; I understand that the serpent lied when it said to the woman that she would not die if she ate from the forbidden tree. Maybe not right away, but certainly one day. Still, I just don't get it… If God loved his creatures so much why he had to tempt them this way and even worse let them suffer that much after their silly mistake?" Yes, Esmeralda's father would have to accelerate and refine his thought process if he was going to clarify and make her see the real moral of this story.

Jeremias, "God gave all his creatures in the infinite and expansive universe, including the inhabitants of this planet the capability to choose what path they wanted to take or what decision they wish to make. You see? He did not create robots to love him in a programed way; he wanted his children to obey him out of love and nothing else. However, every decision and action has naturally a consequence; it has always been that way… even in the scientific world this is true, that is why science is just another subject of God to show his creatures his love for them. A 'test' needed to exist, otherwise how could God's creatures could have a chance to use their free will and demonstrate their love for his creator? After the fall of the first couple in this earth, they and the rest of God's creation would start to have a glimpse of the consequences of choosing to separate from him; since God is the one where life originates and constantly flows from him, away from him one would eventually inevitably perish... think about this... what happens when you disconnect a lamp from its outlet? Isn't its electricity cut and the light goes off because of this fact? Our bodies as complex and well put together as they are, cannot exist without a source of life, that life that was given by the creator when he introduced his breath through the nostrils of that body made out of clay and in this way, a breathing, conscious and intelligent being came to life. Therefore, in our state of created beings and dependent of an outside force, we would cease to exist without our only source of life, our creator and God. The only way to conserve life without God is by being a god oneself and that is impossible since there is only one God. In our finite minds one could not comprehend this concept of 'God' in all its dimensions, but we accept it by faith and by faith alone... "

Esmeralda, "Okay, I understand the purpose of 'the test' and that we would die without God... but what about the suffering, was it necessary? Why didn't God just destroy Satan and avoid all the terrible things that took place after his rebellion?"

Jeremias, "The suffering was necessary... and he did not destroy him [the devil] because this act would serve to perpetuate a lie for eternity; think about it... what would have happened if God killed Lucifer without giving him an opportunity to speak up his mind... without allowing the other creatures to hear his side of the story?... Wouldn't that indicate that God intended to shut up his mouth and demonstrated that he was indeed having a dictatorship as a means of governance? By allowing the entire universe to witness the devastating and sad consequences of disobeying God and / or their decision to distance themselves from their creator, the full potential of knowing evil was going to be unfolded; little by little these beings would become weak and their lights would eventually die as well. By allowing his creatures to suffer — not that God created suffering, it was merely a residue of the evil originated in Lucifer, the whole universe would realize that knowing evil was the worst thing a creature could do. After all, knowing evil was not going to make you 'as wise as God', it was going to make you suffer and one day die, that is it! How could God explain this to his children without they concluding that his teachings about the devastating consequences of sinning were just made-up fables to keep them blindly obeying and serving him? Precisely because God so much loved his creatures is that he with immense sorrow allowed them to see the ultimate consequences of evil — that is, all the horrible things we hear in the news, kids killing their parents; terrorists bombing a hospital with defenseless people in it and much more; in a way we, the ones who live in this planet and our history throughout the centuries are sort of a subject of study for other beings and they are learning together with us that sin is not the way to go. To answer another part of your question, Esmeralda... these extraterrestrial beings even though God allows them to watch what is unfolding in this planet, they have never sinned and for this reason are prohibited from interfering in our destiny and cannot mingle with us in order for them to remain holly and you know what that word means: something or someone preserved exclusively for God. But do you know something mi querida hija? Our father in his mercy and infinite wisdom made plans since the foundation of this earth, together with his son and the Holy spirit to fix this situation created by the sin of our first parents… God in his due time sent his only begotten son to take our place and be sacrificed on our behalf; being that Jesus Christ became one of us [a man] and at the same time maintained his divinity and more importantly he did not sin, not once while walking on this earth even though he suffered multiple temptations like we normally do, he was able to pay the salary of sin — that was the only way possible."

Esmeralda, "Daddy, how do you come to this the conclusion that Jesus Christ never sinned? After all, he never married, or had kids, or had a complete normal life."

Jeremias, "Daughter, remember when Jesus was tempted in the desert when he was starving, no food nor water for forty days? The devil promised him to give him everything at that moment of weakness if Christ worship him and he replied, 'It is written, the Lord your God you shall adore and only serve him'. So, you see? If you are able to endure a temptation as hard as suffering hunger is, you are indeed capable of enduring anything else, in this way it is correct to conclude that the son of God while living among us, he was tempted in all sins and yet without guilty of any. Please note that if God's son had sinned, he would have died in vain, with no hopes of resurrection much less accomplishment of salvation for humanity; father and son knew this, the immense risk they were taking, but still went ahead with the plan… you know why?" Esmeralda went into reflective mode and her father continued, "… Because of Christ's decision to take man's place and his father's acceptance of such an incredible sacrifice, one day suffering will be eternally eradicated from this planet and all God's creatures throughout the universe would have known the consequence of sin or separation from God because they watched in deep astonishment what happened to their brothers and sisters of planet earth. And God will not allow evil to be reborn ever again; peace and happiness will prevail forever and ever and we will be happy to praise the Lord for his infinite mercy and love for his creatures." Esmeralda did get it this time; she affirmed that she had comprehended the essence of God's love for his creatures and the reason why so much suffering exists in this world. This is how her father was able to influence her young, impressionable mind and this father-daughter relationship was like no other.

Chapter 6

Her Last Love Affair

Grief, a conductor of love in disguise

She is there at her sister-in-law's funeral accompanying her beloved older brother, Emmanuel, in his moment of greatest grief when Esmeralda sees this acquaintance of hers; he was standing up in a corner across the salon. He also spotted her and immediately walked to where she was sitting down next to her brother. They looked at each other with tenderness and after a brief hug and the condolences were offered then eventually during the hours that followed, they would start with some catching up. He introduced her to his teenager beautiful daughter, he sounded nervous and it was difficult for him to articulate what he intended to say, so Esmeralda finished his sentence, "Your daughter? Oh, you are so pretty… it's very nice to meet you!" Esmeralda had not seen him for about eight years, but they seemed to have picked up right there where they left off; they were both feeling like they were floating in this crowded room as if they had forgotten for a moment the reason that brought them there. Perhaps what ultimately made them appear face to face this sad day was kismet; they felt this incredible fascinating 'thing' when they met for the very first-time years back and now, they resumed that same feeling as if time had lost its power to affect them. Time merely interrupted a beautiful and of pure nature love story that was destined to be continued sometime into the future.

After a few weeks of their initial encounter, they spoke on the phone and agreed to see each other at that park where they once participated in her brother's wedding photoshoots session. One of the first things that Esmeralda asked him — went like this, "So, why you never looked for me?... never tried to contact me?" and he replied, "Well, after that gathering in your brother's home, I felt you did not wish to see me because you left without saying good bye... " to which Esmeralda added, "That's because he was there [her husband]... but, you know?... do you know what I really think?... if you had been that interested in me, you wouldn't have given up so easily like you did."

Roberto took her hands, like trying to calm her down, looked at her... he was gazing all over her face with this calmed smile while gently touching her hair and after a few moments, he really took his time to answer, he softly and pausing at every end of a sentence said, "I asked your brother about you all the time... he would tell me your relationship with your husband was complicated... that you did not seem happy with him."

Esmeralda quickly interrupted him with this, "Another reason you should have tried to find me." Poor thing, he couldn't win, but he insisted that he was afraid to cause her problems and that he was tempted many times to ask her brother for her phone number and call her. "But, you didn't and we wasted almost eight years... and if we hadn't found each other the way we did... only God knows... "

She was still talking fierily when he shut her up by kissing her intensely; then he said, "The truth is that I thought having you was impossible, something out of my reach, mi vida."

Esmeralda nodding as if affirming an absolute NO, told him, "No, it might have been a little bit difficult, but never impossible... you had won me over with a couple more smiles and looks." They both laughed. From that moment, they would kiss only stopping to catch their breath and with their eyes shut close they would forget about the world outside and one minute would become three hours in what seemed to them 'an instant'. They were crazy about each other, when they met mostly in his downtown apartment, they made love until they physically could no more and / or until they ran out of time; that place would become their get-away, their love-nest, and the only place under the sun that Esmeralda felt completely relaxed in both mind and body.

Roberto was so attentive to her and she could appreciate the sensibility with which he would do everything for her. He would prepare this soothing herbal tea; he used tropical leaves and ginger that he got in the imports section of the bodega. He would serve the hot aromatic and spicy drink nicely in what eventually became Esmeralda's tea cup and bring it to her in bed and say, "Mi vida, here is something to warm you up."

Esmeralda getting from under the blanket once said, "You make me feel like a queen, amor," just about to take a sip after gently blowing the steaming cup.

"That's because you're a queen, to me!" he enthusiastically replied. Esmeralda never felt more pampered and appreciated by a guy than now with him. He was so careful even in his selection of words; he did not want to make her feel uncomfortable in any way because he really cared about her feelings. However, Esmeralda still was carrying with her a bag filled with self-doubts and insecurities that it was taking her time to assimilate this new and refreshing emotional treatment that Roberto was able to provide.

So, she would ask way too often, "Do you love me?" and he would answer, "Tu eres mi vida!" literally, 'You are my life' in

Spanish. It bothered her a little bit that when she would say to him the phrase: 'I love you', he normally would not give the typical response, 'I love you too', instead he would tell her again 'Tu eres mi vida' like trying to reiterate something important. One day she is reading his text messages as if searching for a hint to verify he hardly tells her that he loves her. Then during her audit, she had this eureka moment; she realized that this phrase he used so much in his messages was a much better phrase than the so desired 'I love you' because 'You are my life' entails much more than a simple 'Te quiero' [I love you]. This amazing phrase means that a person's life is in someone else's hands and that the breath this person inhales depends on the other person — all related to the survival instinct to stay alive. The next time they were together, she commented about her discovery and being that he was not a talkative guy at all, he simply added, "A deeper phrase, isn't it?" They both laughed and then kissed for a long time, the way they knew how.

About eight years back in time that wonderful day when Esmeralda's brother, Emmanuel, got married, he introduced her sister to his good old-time friend, Roberto; he and Esmeralda were something like witnesses to this official marriage. It was a very simple civil wedding where only Esmeralda and Roberto were part-takers, so they have ample time to interact with each other and they did, just as if they had been setup in a blind date. But, only better, much better... they were instantly absorbed into each other; he would not stop looking at her in this permanent state of wonder. Esmeralda noticed this and that was exactly what attracted her to him the most at first because whenever she lifted up her head or turned around there was that fascinating contagious smile of his. Sometimes she would even crack a sudden smile — very close to a laugh, provoked by one of his gestures while he was trying to catch her attention. At the beautiful park in the outskirts of the city where the newlyweds went to make some good memories, Esmeralda and Roberto found the perfect scenario when surrounded by the well-maintained romantic architecture of a couple of centuries past, the mood was set for them to feel like they were living in a different time, impersonating other characters and under totally different circumstances. Roberto grabbed her hand to help Esmeralda go down the stone made stairs and she felt as if she was the bride in that instant since he would treat her with the love that only a very in love with his bride man would show.

Back to the present, Esmeralda and Roberto started living another reality, their own reality, that reality that Esmeralda felt they should have experienced long ago and they were deprived of. "Amor, I wonder sometimes why we were not given a chance to be together a long time ago, but then I think that maybe it was necessary that we met and started loving each other at the precise and due time, that is in order for us to be happy; like when the planets position themselves in a perfect alignment at a particular time in the universe," said Esmeralda with a reflective tone of voice, her lover just nodded yes while displaying a calm smile as usual. Esmeralda added, "So, maybe and just maybe it was better that we found each other at the precise time we did... I really think now is our time, it's only fair... don't you agree?" Roberto wrapped his hand firmly over her mandible and kissed her lips with all the passion a man feels for the woman he deeply loves. However, now Esmeralda was just lamenting one thing, all the bad choices she made in selecting those men the previous years; now they were reappearing in her thoughts in the form of ghosts, scary ones because any time now, she was certain her 'filthy' past was going to return to haunt her. Now she was afraid beyond words that she could lose the only man with whom she had the conviction she could be eternally happy. This is the thing; Esmeralda cared a great deal about the concept that Roberto might have of her character. It is true that it takes two to tango that they were having an affair while Esmeralda was still married to another man and that made Roberto as guilty as she was, but he was no longer married to anyone ; this fact put Esmeralda in a 'moral disadvantage' because it can be argued that the only one deceiving someone else was Esmeralda. And then you add to her long list of worries, what if he finds out? Or what if she decided one of these days to confess to him that this was not the first time, she was unfaithful to her husband; Esmeralda felt that she could not keep this huge thing from him, not him because he had become her soul mate, her confident, her best friend and love of her life. But, if she went ahead and put everything out for him to see the real Esmeralda, at least the one she was for a while that would signify the biggest embarrassment of her entire life; Roberto was such a loving person, so honest and incapable of hurting intentionally anybody. And she got the feeling that he had her in high regards as well. She had the potential to cause him a great disappointment or worse his decision to leave her. Esmeralda never felt loved this way before by anyone; at her forty plus years, finally she knew what love was, the real, genuine love, the love that encompasses all the different types of loves that exist in one together.

A penny for your thoughts

"What's on your mind? Yes, what are you thinking right now?" Esmeralda curiously asked Roberto a moment after they had made love and with their bodies still quivering and their heartbeats gradually decreasing from full potential, he just smiled and remained quiet as if letting her guess the answer. Esmeralda got a little bit impatient and told him, "So, you're not thinking anything right now, zero, nada?" He kept smiling and nodded like saying, no, not really. But Esmeralda did not buy that and she would insist on reading his mind whenever she intuited, he was awfully silent. Esmeralda had a suspicion that was slowly killing her inside; thoughts like these, "What if he is thinking what type of woman cheats on her husband? She could do the same to me one day," crossed her mind sometimes. Truth is that Roberto was not a big conversant and besides he was very cautious with what came out of his mouth. Esmeralda did tell him a couple of times, "You don't talk that much... you let me do all the talking... you know? That's smart!"

Roberto would laugh and would say, "I love to hear you talk, you say everything that's in your mind, and you are so transparent... I like that..." That is precisely what she was afraid of; when he implied honesty in his ways of talking about her, panic is what she felt.

"How can I be honest if I have omitted important details of my life that I feel he should know about?" She would eventually suspend the inquiry at least for the time being. But, in the back of her mind remained the question of whether she should open her heart completely to him even when risking losing him because he might not trust her any more.

Esmeralda seriously thought there was the possibility he would think something like, "How can I be sure she is taking me seriously, that I am not just another passing fancy?" And that was a pretty valid consideration; how was she going to explain every single relationship she happened to have — and all of them, so briefly and carelessly? She indeed would have a lot of explaining to do. Or perhaps if she just exposes for him to see the bare skeletons of her past romances and left out the rotten flesh – the 'non-necessary'– details, Roberto could accept her with her devious past and they could bury these corpses once and forever. Nonetheless, a lot was at stake; perhaps her last chance of being happy and be with the man with whom she was going to grow old with when no regrets would be waiting for them at the end of their voyage on this earth.

Wishful thinking

Esmeralda is observing Roberto washing the herbal leaves to make tea for her as it quickly became customary those bitter cold winter days, they would rob a couple of hours just for themselves. She goes and hugs him from behind as he is standing in front of the kitchen sink and whispers in his ear, "Amor, why didn't you have more kids? Were you afraid to have more? He did not answer, only smiled. "Oh, I'm sorry, I shouldn't ask you such a thing," said Esmeralda.

Then he turns to face her, holds her by her shoulders and they both slowly back off until Esmeralda sits back on the chair, he then explains, "You see? When she [ex-wife] had our daughter our relationship problems started immediately... that's what happened."

Esmeralda grabbed his face with open hands and while both were smiling and looking directly into each other's eyes, she said, "I wish we could have had a child of our own."

He agreed saying, "That would have been so great" and he proceeded to say kind of jokingly, "We're still in time, aren't we?" They both laughed and then hugged — sort of giving each other their condolences for daring to dream so much.

Sometimes Esmeralda would visit Roberto at night and leave his place very late; in case you wonder? She managed to do this using the pretext she had to work an evening shift at the hospital, so it was not strange at all when she returned home past midnight very often. Those nights that the madly in love couple forgot the world outside and it was too late for Esmeralda to safely walk alone on the dangerous streets of the old city, her very considerate lover would walk her to her car which many times was parked a couple of blocks away. When they noticed the streets were deserted and they gauged no ocular witnesses were around, they would hold their hands together while walking in no hurry, and did not worry about whether their love was going to endure forever the obstacles on the way. They would intermittently take a quick glance at each other's faces almost insinuating, 'look how wonderful we look together!', and indeed they looked like a very nice couple if you looked at them without knowing who they really were to each other. Esmeralda for the first time in her life knew how that felt, that is — holding the hand of the person one is so much in love with, outside in the open even when the only one watching is the forgiving and mute firmament. Esmeralda used to be envious of those couples and now she and her beloved get to be that couple who provokes admiration if not pure envy when they are seen together. Now Esmeralda's wishful thinking is if only they one day could be a real couple, one that does not have to occult their love and be proud to show everyone how happy a couple they were.

It is past eleven p.m. and Esmeralda is lying down on the couch alone and feeling exhausted after putting the kids to bed. She decides to text Roberto risking being surprised by her husband who was in the bedroom. Esmeralda, "Hola amor."

Roberto, "Que tal mi vida?"

Esmeralda, "I am on the couch dozing off… I'm so tired I will probably fall asleep here."

Roberto, "I feel at ease knowing you are on the couch."

Esmeralda, "Oh yeah? Do you like it when I stay on the couch?"

Roberto, "Yes, always!" As unbelievable as it might sound, this was the first time that Roberto gave Esmeralda a hint of what he was experiencing, but was afraid to tell her. Roberto is obviously jealous of the fact that her love has to share the same bed with his rival. Now Esmeralda has all of a sudden, this bitter-sweet feeling because on one hand, she just loves that Roberto is jealous and on the other hand, she is now conscious that this is a problem that might eventually get bigger as her relationship with Roberto get stronger. But, the truth of the matter is that Roberto seems to be completely oblivious to Esmeralda's uneasiness that she was anxiously waiting for him to give her a clue that he wishes she decides to separate completely from her husband. But, so far, all Esmeralda could perceive is that Roberto is cool or even comfortable with their situation. For a couple of occasions already, Esmeralda had tried to give Roberto an idea of how her marriage has been like all these years and that she does not love her husband; in one of their conversations, Esmeralda told him, "Do you have any idea how bad I feel doing this to him?" while Roberto listened attentively. "I have tried to tell him that I don't love him, but it's like he doesn't care... and he avoids this type of talk." And she continued explaining, "If I ask him for the divorce now, he will be extremely suspicious and will make my life a living hell... I know this because I attempted this route before and did not get far at all." She continued, "I will ask him to divorce me when I have a defined and definitive plan." Yes, Esmeralda was cognizant of her need to start organizing her life financially and emotionally in order to survive the aftermath of the dreaded and inevitable divorce before officially declaring the war to her husband — 'that indolent one who is incapable of acknowledging her true feelings and procuring her happiness'. Again, Esmeralda is wishing that Roberto gives her the strength, that little push to help her take that leap of faith and abandon her husband once and for all together with all her frustrated dreams and accumulated bitterness. It looks like it's a little premature yet for Esmeralda to expect Roberto to ask her what she is so much desiring, 'to leave her husband and marry him', indeed a long way to go, it looks like. Nonetheless, Esmeralda is so happy with Roberto that she will be content to have him even if they never get married. She is hopeful that it could work that way because Roberto has given her the confidence; one of those days when she was once again having these ruminative thoughts about the possibility of losing him, Esmeralda nervously and with a trembling voice asked him, "Are you still in love with me? Or are you already regretting being with me?"

To which Roberto, affirmed, "I am staying with you until you want me to, but know this… I am willing to stay with you for life, if it was up to me." That moment when she heard exactly these words, Esmeralda knew he was being sincere and serious about her. Yes, Esmeralda is being hopeful but at the same time cautious since she had been wrong so many times before when she suffered so many dissolutions and was heartbroken. This time around and hopefully for the last, she should be really taking it slowly and trying to enjoy the ride. Who knows and her final destination is a place where she will find solace and a harmonious and filled with genuine love relationship with her last lover and love of her life, at last?

Esmeralda is visiting one of her geriatric patients at his home and as soon as he opened the door, he starts weeping. Esmeralda, very concerned, asked, "What's wrong, Mr. Montero? Why are you like this?"

He replied with his voice quivering and tearful eyes, "She's gone... the love of my life left me forever!" This seventy something year old and sad beyond one's comprehension man had lost his wife a few days ago. After he summarized for Esmeralda the events leading to her death, he went and narrated the story of how his life was with his beloved wife. "She was my second wife... I didn't love my first wife the way I loved Maria. She was simply the love of my life... " The poor man continued sobbing as he spoke about her. "What am I going to do without my dear angel now?" he desperately asked Esmeralda, all the while his eyes fixed on a vase urn positioned on the fireplace mantel. She felt totally incompetent at that moment and just offered her presence and attentive ear, but she could not help it, eventually she joined him in his lament and burst into tears still holding in her hands his wife's remembrance card that the old man had handed her over moments before. Esmeralda was so touched by this old man's demonstration of love toward his diseased life partner and lover that she from that moment and forward only dreamed of one day finding a 'Mr. Montero' to be 'the love of his life and he hers'. She was seriously thinking about how wonderful it would be if she could grow old with a man she adored, respected and cared for more than her own life. The thought that at the end of her golden days, she would regret not having made the right decision when she had the chance to do so, was constantly on her mind these days. Now, Esmeralda was wishing that Roberto could be her 'Mr. Montero', that man that took care of his lover, friend and wife with compassion, love, and patience when she was fragile and afflicted by a chronic illness until she exhaled her very last breath.

Destiny

Esmeralda started another of her analytic type of conversations. "Amor, wasn't it so incredible the way we found each other again?" stated Esmeralda.

"Yes, that was something!" replied Roberto. The ironic turns of events that surrounded their encounter both when they first met years ago at Emmanuel's wedding and then about eight years later precisely at Emmanuel's wife's death. A wedding and a funeral, two contracts; if that is not the biggest sign then what is? Esmeralda and Roberto would talk about how unfortunate was what happened to Emmanuel and his wife, Sofia, she had been diagnosed with a terminal cancer which would in a matter of two years consume her vitality, render her lifeless and rob her seven-year-old girl of a loving mother and her husband, the love of his life. Emmanuel had to be strong for his little innocent girl's sake and at the same time not emotionally neglect his two older kids – from his previous relationship; he loved all his children very much – they were the apple of his eyes. Roberto and Emmanuel had been very good friends for many years, they even knew each other from back then when they were in their native land though their friendship started in the new country. Esmeralda remembers having seen Roberto from a certain distance when she was a little girl, but they never had a chance to know each other; they went to different schools — besides, the difference in their age, about seven years, could have been a factor as to why their lives did not intertwine back then. Nevertheless, Esmeralda swears that she remembers once when she went to this tailor place in her hometown to have a pair of pants altered and this young man, an apprentice, took her measurements; now she thinks that he looked like Roberto very much. She commented on this to him, but he did not remember ever seeing her before perhaps because she was about thirteen to fourteen years of age, very thin, and with a flat chest, a curly wild haired and she was this extremely timid looking girl. Esmeralda could very well have this image of this attractive about twenty-year-old unreachable guy, so she has a better reason to remember him. It is true they hardly ever frequented the same places and if they did run into each other, they never were more than mere acquaintances — if not strangers in such a minute town compared to the United States of America where they came and found each other. However, there were even more surprises that destiny had in store for them yet.

One of those instances when Esmeralda was encouraging Roberto to 'spit out whatever is in your mind', Roberto asked, "So, how many times have you been in love, Esmeralda?" She was not expecting him to ask precisely this question or anything like this. She answered with hesitation and could not hide how unprepared she was to start a discussion about her unending list of enamorados. She decided to start from the very beginning, her first boyfriend in high school back in that small countryside town where Roberto came from as well. "So, what was his name?" Esmeralda knew that the probability Roberto knew him was extremely high and when she pronounced the name, Roberto opened his eyes widely and Esmeralda noticing his surprise, asked him, "What is the matter, do you know him?"

Roberto replied, "I know him, he lived in my brother's house for a while."

"What?" said the even more surprised Esmeralda. Roberto continued by saying that Antonio had done something inappropriate; he slept with this girl, about sixteen years of age, she was adopted by Roberto's brother and his wife and Antonio betrayed their trust, moreover he found himself in some legal matters and being that he was undocumented he was deported to his country. Now Esmeralda was able to put the puzzle's pieces in their right places; she understood that the little boy in the photo that Antonio showed her was the fruit of his irresponsible act. Esmeralda felt so ashamed and for the first time did not wish to talk any more. However, Roberto did not seem to be affected by the fact this guy was Esmeralda's first love experience; he continued treating and loving her with as much devotion as before. Esmeralda told him about her casual encounter with Antonio years ago when she went on vacation to her beautiful native island but failed to mention that they had an intimate moment; that she did not have the bravery to say. Roberto might have suspected them having at least a one-night stand, but he opted for not touching that topic and putting that thought out of his immediate memory and throw it to the oblivion. He perhaps more than Esmeralda, wished not to tarnish that beautiful thing they were experiencing.

Her big dilemma

It is true that Roberto had given Esmeralda proof of his unconditional love for her; he did not judge her, at least she never felt that way. Every single word that he said to her was kind – a match to his serene temperament and even his mannerisms conveyed tenderness and sincerity. The way he would look at her made her feel as if she was the most beautiful woman in the world to him. The way he would move his fingers over her eyebrows and bring them softly down on both sides of her temples until he reached her chin all the while contemplating with serenity every contour of her face was like when an art aficionado is in front of his favorite artist's work piece. She really felt the love, she could almost touch it, love; he made it possible that love become tangible to her and she never was that afraid to lose something as she was now. After knowing that with Roberto she would never experience loneliness again because even when distance was in the way, he was ever present… he was in her mind, in every inch of her body, in the air she breathed, every moment and every day of her new-found existence.

Esmeralda had a battle with herself, should she let him know of her shameful past? Why she felt compelled to strip her soul to him by confessing something that could really hurt her is a subject of study; she indeed was debating in her mind if telling him about her previous love affairs, would mean that he was not going to look at her the same way again and if and when that happens, she would die of sadness knowing that she had everything a woman could ever want to then go and lose it. Perhaps, the mere fact that these two are having an affair themselves is a reason for Roberto to have already conceived a negative concept of her, but the love he is feeling for her provides immunity to any outside malignancy as long as the parts involved [he and she] perceive themselves as beings reserved for each other, even if just in spirit and not flesh. However, another thing would be if Roberto after knowing she had other love relationships inside her marriage interprets this as a fact that should invalidate what he has with Esmeralda now or what he thought they had anyway. Roberto might start wondering that maybe Esmeralda easily falls in love with a man given the number of lovers she had before him and therefore presume that he is just one in a bunch and who could easily be replaced. How then can she convince him that he is the love of her life? That she never experienced love this way before; a love that does not cause pain, that is pure as a baby's smile and tender as the gentle fresh breeze in spring, a love that wakes up that woman she longed to be for so long.

A God sent punishment?

"Why should I deserve all this happiness? If I have broken every moral rule that there is? Besides... how could I have conceived the idea that his world and mine could mingle together without creating chaos?" Esmeralda was asking herself. "Who am I kidding? I am in the middle of a dream and any minute now I will wake up," she whispered while feeling this horrendous knot in her throat. Esmeralda was never driven to think that God enjoys punishing the human race, on the contrary she believed that God only allows evil to run its course sometimes to demonstrate to the universe the far-reaching consequences of turning away from him, 'the source of life'... and once disconnected from this source there is only eternal death, eventually. God leaves Homo sapiens to decide which path to take even when it would lead them to perdition or death... God wants his creatures to obey him out of love not terror. These are spiritual concepts or doctrines if you will that Esmeralda had inculcated since she was little and now, she regresses to them. So, her reasoning is not that God is punishing her now, but that she sooner or later will reap what she sowed; it is just a matter of cause-and-effect type of thing. Now, once again she is faced with another choice, a chance to change the way she has conducted her life so far. She could get a divorce and automatically stop the cheating and then see if she still has a chance to be happy with Roberto; perhaps he could find it in his heart forgiveness for his 'vida' as he would call Esmeralda so very often.

A big sigh of relief

They are both looking at each other the way people who are deeply in love with each other do; I heard 'the eyes are the windows of the soul' and these two seemed to be searching into the soul of each other very often. It was during one of these sweet moments that Esmeralda while firmly rubbing her fingers against Roberto's lips and he is mimicking to bite them as if trying to eat the most delicious apple that she softly interrupts the silent ritual with this, "Is there anything that could change the way you feel for me now?"

Roberto rephrased what she said in an attempt to understand what she was trying to say and then finished by saying, "No, nothing could ever change the way I feel about you, mi vida!" And looking somehow concerned he continues to say, "Why do you ask that?"

Esmeralda's semblance had changed from happiness to worrisome and hesitating to go straight to the point continued with 'the strange talk', [it seemed to Roberto]. "I have not been completely honest with you, there is something you need to know about my past…"

Roberto interrupted her, "About your past?… I don't care about the past," but Esmeralda insisted that if he knew about what she was afraid to confess, he was not going to look at her the same way ever again — that the concept he had of her was going to drastically change. Roberto repositioned himself in bed like trying to get comfortable and a little intrigued reiterated that he did not believe anything could change anything at this point.

Esmeralda stopped looking at him, she did not turn to look at him not for a second while with watery eyes, looking at the ceiling and trembling voice said, "You are not the first man with whom I am unfaithful to my husband." There was a brief silence and she still did not want to look directly into his eyes afraid to see his reaction.

Roberto sounding calm asked, "How long ago? Do I know him?" and she replied, "A few years ago and no you wouldn't know him or any of them [her other lovers] for that matter… I was unfaithful with more than a guy in different occasions throughout my marriage; this last one you would not know him since he is not in your or even my circle of friends… he was a complete stranger when I met him on the streets." And as if trying to belittle that last shameful love affair, she added, "It was a mistake, a crazy thing I did… he was so young for me and I didn't love him anyway… I didn't care about any of them, they were just a pastime for me."

Roberto looked at her and smiled and then said, "Well, I wish it didn't happen but like I said before, your past won't change how I feel about you."

Esmeralda still doubtful asked, "Not even your concept about my character, my persona?" Roberto looked at her being careful not to sound judgmental while Esmeralda continued with her litany. "Do you know that you are like my brother [Emmanuel]? He has always put me on a pedestal; he thinks that I am incapable of behaving like a bad girl." However, Roberto would insist on that she is a wonderful woman and nothing was going to change that for him. They kissed and made love for about the third time that evening. Indeed, Esmeralda had a sigh of relief hearing him affirm his love for her even after hearing her confession. What happened here did not necessarily mean that for Esmeralda the picture was totally clear, she still had to forgive herself in order to leave her past in the past.

Is it too good to be true?

Esmeralda still has the savory taste of those moments in which Roberto demonstrated one more time how much he loved her; his love, of a special kind — one that is unconditional, that forgives everything, that endures anything and which main objective is to make his loved one happy. Esmeralda could not believe such a love was even allowed, that such a fortune was intended for her and she would debate in her mind, "What could possibly be amiss with this scenario?" One day during one of her son's usual tantrums, and hearing his disturbing loud and persistent screaming, she could not help it and thought that even if in her future was him, the love of her life, they were not going to be completely happy together. Not under the same roof, anyway. *"How could a man other than her Mateo's father withstand the heavy and agonizing load of dealing with such a situation? He would go mad in no time and run away, for sure,"* thought Esmeralda. That is when a dreadful feeling grabbed her almost by surprise and she needed right away a confirmation that Roberto's love could withstand such a test. The next day, as soon as the coast was clear in her house, she sent Roberto one of her filled with I-love-you text messages; that morning she typed: 'Do you know something? I love you more than ever!' His reply was: 'Good morning!' His following text, 'It's cold today' and yet another text, 'Are you home?' At this point Esmeralda was on the brink of an emotional breakdown; she could contain herself no more and replied to his mundane short comments like this: 'Why do you have this tendency to deviate from the conversation? Is it that you are not really sure of what you are feeling for me? Or are you simply afraid to say it? Oh! I know, I tell you 'I love you' way too often. Don't worry, I won't say it any more, I promise you!' Roberto texted her back, 'Can I call you?' Esmeralda answered, 'No, lest leave it like this… Everything is perfect the way it is, it cannot get any better otherwise it would get spoiled', these last words meant in a sarcastic way. Roberto insisted, 'Mi vida, can you talk?' Esmeralda, 'No, the more I talk the more I sink myself'. Roberto, 'I am surprised, mi vida, I need to speak with you'. Esmeralda, 'I am an idiot, just forget it'. Roberto, 'Mi vida!!! Please! What's going through your mind?' Esmeralda, 'Go over my previous messages and you will find out what's going through my mind'. Roberto, 'I am your property, completely, can you consider that if only a little bit?' Esmeralda, 'It is not going to work, your world and mine cannot unite, sooner or later I will end up hurt. I can't change my life. I am only living a fantasy. Did you want to know what I was thinking? Now you know!'. Roberto, 'Can I call you?' Esmeralda, 'What for?' Roberto, 'I need to hear your voice'. Finally, Esmeralda agreed and he called her right away. "Mi vida, I was about to go to Bella Villa [Esmeralda's town] and drive by every road until I found you." Roberto did not know where exactly she lived, but he got so 'tormented' as he tried to explain to Esmeralda that he needed to find her. Roberto was in the dark about Esmeralda's sudden change of mood; he did not understand as he put it, "We had such an unforgettable time just yesterday and today you sound so different; how can you ask me to forget? Can you forget just like that what we have constructed together so far?" Esmeralda was ashamed that one more time she had over reacted, but she was still in a very depressed mood to apologize and when she tried to talk, she would start crying. Roberto tried to reassure her of his real feelings for her, he apologized and added, "I was going to tell you 'I love you too' later in the text message, but I got really busy in the store [his business] and lost track of my thoughts." Here the real issue was not that Roberto did not respond as she wished he would; she just used that to parry her mental attacks, to deviate her mind from what she felt was the real threat, that is the thought that given her convoluted family dynamics she would never be happy in a new relationship. Roberto seemed to deem time as his best ally and asked Esmeralda to give him some time and he will show her that his love for her is sincere and real. However, Esmeralda being of an anxious nature wants results, proof, and actions right on the spot; she did not dare to tell him what she really needed him to do, not six months down the road but now – she was dying for him to ask her to separate from her husband and become his woman either by marriage or just by common union. It seems that Esmeralda was viewing this refreshing new love just as a temporary fix, for her the whole thing she was experiencing was just too good to be true.

The way she loves him

"Do you want to know why I tell you so many 'I love yous'?" Esmeralda was asking Roberto while her head is resting on his chest; she could hear his heartbeats — it sounded like a beautiful symphony which conveys that simple but crucial feeling of being alive; and his arms around her made her feel protected from all the outside struggles, fears and uncertainties. He waits for her answer and then she lifts her head slightly, looks into his eyes and tells him, "That is because there are one hundred billion I love yous crammed in my heart that need to be released and they are all reserved just for you." He is still attentively listening and with a big smile lifted his head slightly and kissed her, and that kiss lasted for a good while. Esmeralda had this urgency to express what she was feeling for him as if her affection was trapped in a steam compression pot, so the minute the lid was lifted just a tiny bit, a lot of suppressed emotions and very strong sentiments would inevitably escape. So, she also felt the need to hear him say that three-word phrase and that is why she would ask him very often, "Do you love me?"

On more than one occasion he would reply, "Mi bella, don't you feel it?" his face with an accentuated expression as if by stating: 'Do I need to put into words what is so obvious?' Esmeralda had to believe it and leave it at that, afraid to become a nuisance. Truth is that for Esmeralda hearing from him, the most satisfying statement of love that ever was pronounced was vital for her in order to nourish her soul. At the beginning of their relationship, yes, she needed to hear it as a confirmation of his love for her and even as a reassurance that he still loved her later on, especially when she was feeling under the weather. However, she already had reached a point when hearing him say it simply gave her so much pleasure as eating a cup of her favorite ice cream, only better. For instance, there was this time when she texted him, 'Sometimes I need to hear you say it [that he loves her]... '; in another text, 'So, my life could make sense... ' yet in another text, 'Please tell me that I'm not just a pastime for you'. Roberto, 'Mi bella, I know I neglect you too often [to call her daily]... but it's true that I'm yours'. Esmeralda, 'Love, I'm not complaining... it's just that I wish to understand you a little better... like what you just said... what does that phrase mean to you [I'm yours]?' Roberto, 'It means that I'm loving only you!'. Esmeralda, 'That's the most beautiful thing you have told me in a while... See how easy it is to make me happy?' That was all she needed to go to sleep that night with a peaceful heart and hopeful that sometime into the future she could fall asleep with her lover and wake up with him the next morning under the same roof.

One fine spring morning while Esmeralda was jogging in a local park and listening to one of her favorite singers out of the incredible Pandora, a classic beautiful song, 'Tu de que vas?' written by one of the big names of the Latin music world, Franco de Vita, and which she had not heard in a good while suddenly interrupted her singing along routine. The lyrics of this song helped her clear some gray clouds from her mind; an accumulating precipitation forecast created by those unreasonable doubts of whether the love her Roberto professed to feel for her was real or if it was going to last. The whole thing sounds like a contradiction since at times she is so sure of his love for her and then out of nowhere despair seizes her. A couple of verses of this Spanish song go like this:

https://youtu.be/VSSIsb6FfmU [Franco de Vita – Tu de Que Vas (Live)

'…I need your kisses so I can breathe, there is not a motive or reason to doubt it not even for a second, because you have been the best thing that ever touched this heart of mine and that between heaven and you, I would rather stay with you… If I have given you all that I had until getting in debt even with myself and still you ask if I love you?… what's going on with you? If there's not a minute of my time when you don't cross my mind… if this is not love then you tell me what would be?'

Esmeralda stopped to breathe and bending down to stretch she then raised her arms and upper body with a new energy because she remembered that one time when she asked Roberto if he loved her, he answered with something similar to the essence of this song, he said, "I know I love you because I am thinking of you every instant of every day…" Again, this is the way Esmeralda was capable of loving him, sometimes walking over floppy white clouds when she felt loved and other times she would stray away to a dark and cold place to wonder or rather anguish over the thought that nobody will ever love her for real not even Roberto.

Fortunately for Esmeralda this time around it looks like she was not fantasizing loving someone, and better yet she was not alone loving the one – 'to whom she had pawned her love and who had also taken possession of her soul' – as she once declared in a love verse, she wrote dedicated to him. Now Roberto was reciprocating this love only that he would do it in a way that she would discover slowly but steadily with every interaction they had. Esmeralda was going to learn another love language, the one that he spoke and eventually she was going to comprehend how much he loved her. "Who do you belong to?" Roberto asked her in a cunning tone of voice, one good day. She was surprised to hear that expression, and she had to employ a few seconds to process it in her mind meanwhile he was anxiously waiting for her to react, say something.

When she understood where he was coming from, she with a huge smile replied, "You, I'm all yours!" Esmeralda later noticed he would ask her the very same question often and that is when it dawned on her that maybe this was his way of getting reassurance of her love just as she needed it herself when she asked him if he loved her.

Esmeralda without realizing it started feeling this need that she had to make sure she was being faithful to her lover not only in spirit since that was a given, but in her flesh as well; she was not only avoiding her husband, but she would reject him right on the spot giving him a lame excuse and other times just a 'because'. Esmeralda would feel she was betraying Roberto if she allowed Valentino to touch her even when Roberto knew the name of the game; one day they could be happy together for the rest of their lives though in the meantime he was cognizant she was still married to his oblivious opponent. Every day that passed revealed the impending task of Esmeralda having to define her situation and the way it needed to be executed was by talking to her husband frankly, but this was such a dreadful thing for her that she would not dare to do it, not just yet.

Esmeralda's text goes like this: 'I'm thinking of you right now, amor', and Roberto answers, 'I'm thinking of you as well, mi vida... with the difference... ' She is waiting anxiously for the rest of the sentence then he continues in another text, '... that it's all day long'. These words, the way they were organized had an impact on her emotional state that she remained quiet for a few minutes like in a temporary state of shock. Esmeralda had him in her mind every hour of her day too, but she opted to not acknowledge this at this moment with the intention of maintaining the momentum; she wanted him to take credit for a well-done job romantically courting her. That was the way she was loving him, counting the days, hours and minutes when she was going to see him again and re-living every moment, they shared by seeing flashing images of those passionate kisses they gave to each other among other things.

After Roberto experienced how it would feel like if he ever went to lose Esmeralda – when she got so emotional that day and told him things like, 'I won't tell you that I love you any more', his text messages were sprinkled with much more 'I love yous' and romantic phrases and he would now respond to her 'I love you' with an 'I love you too'; they were truly learning their own dialect of love. Roberto realized that in order to make Esmeralda happy he needed to learn fast and know how to follow her tacit directions on how she liked to be loved. Of course, Esmeralda was learning his preferences in loving matters as well, and she was a dedicated and disciplined student; she would observe all his gestures and reactions in hope of discovering his likes and dislikes. Although this new kind of love she is experiencing, at times has a foreign feel, Esmeralda is quickly adjusting to it. For the first time in her entire life, she feels loved back and it is so easy to get used to it but at the same time impossible for her to take it for granted. If one were to describe Esmeralda's love for her Roberto, one can start by saying that: it is peaceful as a beautiful Sunday morning sitting around the park's fountain filled with birds singing and flapping their wet wings; desiderative as when a woman in her pre-menstrual period is craving a piece of sweet dark chocolate; certain as knowing the sun will come out tomorrow again. Esmeralda feels valued as a woman because Roberto procures her satisfaction in every aspect of their relationship; he wants her to enjoy their intimacy to the full potential and he is not taking a short cut in order to accomplish this. Roberto shows a profound interest in knowing the mystery that her thoughts guard because he desires to understand what makes her hurt and what she fears; he wants to be her protector, her confident and her faithful servant in delivering a pure and genuine love to his bella Esmeralda. Esmeralda is now much closer to being capable of loving with confidence because her love is being appreciated; she loves without reservations because she is not afraid to love him even under the circumstances. Esmeralda loved him really knowing what love was, and she knew love through him and by loving him.

It is undeniable that Esmeralda had to kiss many frogs before finding her prince; she had so many infatuations yet never a true love. Roberto was not another mash; he was the one and only real love for her. Roberto came to be the object of her most sublime inspiration; thinking of him she felt as if contemplating a beautiful blue sky filled with birds making their skillful acrobatics; absorbing the warmth radiating from an autumn panorama with trees of a great variety and its beautiful hues; observing the snow falling and spreading its huge white floppy blanket all over its path and many other wonders. Esmeralda's love for her Roberto was expressive, it was communicative, it conveyed insights from her most intimate thoughts and her voice would penetrate his heart when she opened up to him like she never did with anyone else before. It might sound that at times the two of them were talking in an affected kind of way — that is, they would say to each other the silliest things like 'Will you love me forever, amor?' and the answer would be 'Forever and ever, mi vida'. However, for them these words were true and they meant what they said. They would also talk to each other by the way they looked into each other's eyes; they would get lost in themselves in this way abandoning the outside world and submerging themselves into their own created universe. The way Esmeralda loves him cannot be described in its plenitude with words since words have a propensity to express ephemeral meanings and her love for him seems to be of an eternal nature.

Sometimes I reinvent you over my pillow

One more time Esmeralda is enjoying her lover's company and while they are submerged in their own kind of tranquility since their love creates this invisible barrier that impedes anything or anyone to enter their territory while they are loving each other, lost into each other tender looks and caresses, she goes and tells him, "Amor… do you know something? I do this thing when I'm alone and desiring to be with you…"

Roberto sounding somewhat intrigued, "Oh yea… what would that be?"

Esmeralda: "Sometimes after I have showered and I'm in my bedroom, he [her husband] is at work and the kids are in school, I lay down in bed and touch myself while thinking of you; you see? I have to visualize you, re-invent you in my mind, over my pillow, yes! Pretend that you are with me… and it feels so good!"

Roberto, "Amor… you are incredible!" He kissed her with so much passion that her lips turned purplish after a while.

She explained, "Amor, I need to do that in order to survive just another minute without you, without your kisses, your hugs, do you understand?"

Roberto, "Mi vida, there's really nothing to understand!... I do the same... but, it sounds like you are able to do it much more gracefully than how I could ever possibly do it." They both laughed and continued loving each other in this way creating yet another memory to revisit when they were apart from each other physically, certainly not in their minds and spirits. So, that is how Esmeralda described those moments when she would twist her body laying down and trembling out of pure pleasure; she would get the ultimate climax just by remembering love scenes with the man of her dreams, Roberto. Ironically, she did not used to do this activity when she was young and naïve. Maybe, again her religious strict upbringing while living with her father helped to shaped her character early in life; this could reflect her innocence in certain normal aspects of the love life or just sex when she was an adolescent or even a young adult. Now, she has learned how to indulge herself by exploring her own body and using episodes of her already lived romance and from her new secret life.

Will love conquer adversity?

Esmeralda is one more time trying to caress Roberto's reasoning and attempting to touch his most inner thoughts; she goes and tells him, "I know... you told me to give it time and things will fall into place and that things will get better, but this waiting is killing me." Roberto keeps listening and Esmeralda continues saying, "What if I tell you that I am going to ask him for the divorce?" Roberto seems to be pensive and slow to react like trying hard to come up with the proper thing to say to her in such a pivotal moment. However, Esmeralda is interpreting his prudence as a sign that he is not excited about the news as she presumed, he would be, consequently he has no intention to have a 'normal' relationship with her in the foreseeable future.

Roberto finally replies like this, "If I tell you that you probably need to think about this more in depth... just because it is a long and tedious process, I know, been there and done that, you would think that I am not acting like a man in love would normally behave... "

Esmeralda interrupted him and said, "No, now you are over thinking this, so your answer will not be spontaneous, you will say what you think I would like hearing, not what you really think," then Roberto could perceive from her sad countenance that she was not taking his well thought answer well. Unexpectedly, she turned her back at him while in bed, covered her eyes, and a few seconds later started weeping, Roberto seemed impotent, he did not know what to do or say to console her, he saw her shivering, in a fetal position in bed, so he went and got the white T-Shirt and gray sweat pants she loved to wear to feel cozy when visiting him for a few hours, helped her put them on and threw her favorite warm wool blanket over his fragile and vulnerable Esmeralda. It took her a good while to calm down and then finally she tells him that she over reacted again.

The next morning, she decided to text him and said: 'Do you know why I cried last night? During those moments, you were trying to give me an answer, it occurred to me that you did not care having to share me with another man and that you could very well continue with this occult relationship forever'. His reply was, 'With time I will show you how mistaken you are... what happens is that what you need to do is something very delicate and personal'. He called her to make sure she was fine and again managed to allay her doubts about him. Roberto elaborated a lot more on the phone; he talked about his experience divorcing not one woman, but two. Esmeralda knew about his most recent divorce, but now she was surprised to hear that he had been married twice and was wondering why. Roberto gave her some insights into his previously failed marriages by telling her a couple of anecdotes and the nature of the most prominent conflicts he endured with his ex-wives. Roberto's confessions generated more questions in Esmeralda's volatile mind and he said he was going to answer every single one of them to the best of his abilities. Indeed, Roberto was going to need lots of luck in order to abate the strong winds of her tempestuous and sometimes unpredictable character. It seems like Esmeralda's ups and downs are not about to go away anytime soon. It remains to be seen whether her sudden and frequent mood swings will wither their romance or their love will conquer adversity.

Jealousy

When does being jealous about your lover, partner or significant other become unhealthy? I will go ahead and assume that we all sometimes like to be the subject who provokes the feeling that inevitably connotes something negative, but that at the same time has that capability to serve as a condiment to enhance or make more interesting a loving relationship — that is jealousy. If words were associated or linked to colors, I would think that this word, jealousy, is 'black' just like love is 'red' since this state of mind could really awaken that dark side that one has and depending on the degree or intensity of such a feeling, jealousy could make a person reverse the love they profess to have for a person to a pugnacious and even punitive type of sentiment. That being said, one can understand why then Esmeralda was a little bit concerned about her lover's tendency to be jealous a person as he admitted to be. So, that is why she became even more inquisitive and went to – kind of – interrogate Roberto with the intention to find out if the 'accused' had logical grounds to base his jealousies. At one point when Esmeralda and Roberto started feeling more comfortable about speaking openly and without reservations, they also talked about Roberto's previous relationships and that is when jealousy appeared in the map. It all started when the madly in love couple innocently were teasing each other with trivialities such as what made them jealous; Esmeralda said that the idea of him having some contact with his ex-wife would cause her that feeling and he confessed that imagining her interacting closely with the physicians at her work place provoked in him jealousy. Esmeralda laughed at this and she actually felt flattered. Nevertheless, she foresaw – based on this feature of his character, a potential problem for them later on. This is the thing, if you like black pepper, you would put it in your soup, but if you put too much you will not be able to eat it. So, yes if Roberto's jealousy got to be moderate to severe that could very well spoil a normal or healthy relationship. So far all of these jealousy talks are hypothetical conversations and / or past experiences; their future reaction to a perceived or real thread is an unknown at present time. "So, you said you were jealous of your ex-wife... what made you jealous?" asked Esmeralda.

Roberto replied, "She would let her ex-husband into our house when I was not there... I had expressed to her my dislike but she didn't care."

Esmeralda, "Were they by themselves?"

Roberto, "No, I don't think so... her daughter was there too."

Esmeralda showing empathy then told him, "Oh, why did she do that? If she knew you did not like it?" Esmeralda wanted to find a justification for Roberto's jealousies and so far, she had been successful. This sticky topic had yet to be explored to the fullest and Esmeralda having this insatiable need to be ahead of the game, she did not hesitate to dig into it; she then asked him, "So, you know I have kids and they will need to see their father probably on a daily basis, when Valentino is no longer living with us… Would it bother you if he comes to visit and you are not there?"

He responded, "That would be different to my previous situation with my ex-wife… her daughter was a grown-up woman and she didn't seem to like me. I do understand that your kids still need their father close to them – they are still so young." Esmeralda was glad to hear him say that; she loved Roberto, but was not willing to maintain a conflict-free relationship with him at expense of their children's emotional wellbeing. So, then again one could say that Jealousy is a two-edged sword; you can either benefit from that happy feeling knowing that you are important to someone or endure a nasty tempest out of nowhere, under a perfect beautiful blue sky.

A jittery feeling in her heart

It was one of those inexplicable lugubrious days for Esmeralda and once again she was anxiously waiting for Roberto to call or text her. When her patience was no more, she decided to text him, 'How is your day going, are you too busy? I am dying to see you today!'. Roberto would never turn down a proposal of this nature when it came from his bella Esmeralda even when it was clear he could not afford to do this all the time. She sensed this wherefore she would always be somewhat apologetic when asking him if they could get together because she was conscious of his demanding job. On the other hand, she was wondering why Roberto seldom would take the initiative and ask her to see each other once in a while for a change. So, they got together that same night, Roberto downloaded from YouTube the songs of Esmeralda's favorite all time Spanish female artist, Paloma San Basilio, and they slowly danced, hugging each other very tight as if they were afraid to let go of something very precious to them. And she sang to him with her sweet melodic voice part of her favorite song, 'Beso a Beso Dulcemente'. When the evening grew old and Esmeralda saw the propitious moment, she shot the question that was lingering in her mind forever. "When are you going to be the one who asks for a date with me?"

Roberto was looking a little bit confused but managed to give an answer, he explained it like this, "I let you decide when to see me to make it easier for you... don't you think it's better that way?"

Esmeralda backfired by saying, "What are you afraid of? If you tell me 'I need to see you today', it is not like I am going to abruptly interrupt what I am doing and rush over here... What I mean is that it would be nice if sometimes you show me, you really want to see me... that would mean a lot to me." While he was there still not knowing exactly what to say, Esmeralda continued trying to make her point and stated, "I'm the one chasing you around like a desperate woman... at least that's how I feel." Roberto was disconcerted hearing her say that and as usual tried to convince her that he really cared about her and would only wish she could be happy. But you see? Esmeralda was having a jittery feeling in her heart, as if she had this ominous sensation that her luck in love was running out one more time therefore, she was compelled to take action pronto. So, she proceeded to do what she usually did when she needed to test one of her sentimental type of hypotheses by creating a fictitious situation where she could manipulate the human subjects and variables. So, she said to him the following utterance without any warnings, "I have been thinking the whole day how I was going to tell you this…" At this point Roberto seemed intrigued and Esmeralda continued saying, "I was planning to say adios to you today — that is… forever."

Roberto was surprised to hear that and responded, "What? Can you do something like that for real?"

She explained, "Yes, if I feel trapped against a wall, with no choice." Nonetheless, Esmeralda fearing that he could really feel bad attempted to repair the damage by assuring him that after being with him that evening, she was convinced she could never leave him because she would not be able to live without him. It did not end here because Esmeralda still had another 'subliminal message' for her lover; after Roberto got emotionally stable – not that he lost his composure, on the contrary he remained pretty calm, but he did look just a little bit perplexed, Esmeralda told him, "When I stopped calling you and we did not see each other for about three months, you did not call, but only once and I get it… you decided it was best to not try again. The thing is… if I hadn't called when I did, we wouldn't have come back together." Roberto said to his defense that he was afraid to call and somebody else answered her phone since she was not expecting his call and got her in trouble and that he at one point got so desperate to see her and know something about her that he went to Facebook in hopes of finding her. He did and that helped a little and two days later Esmeralda called him, he thought that was a fantastic coincidence and he was so happy that she called.

He also told her something that made a lot of sense, "I wondered all the time what made you go away without even saying good bye." Roberto was probably very afraid to find out if the reason she had to leave him was because she realized she felt nothing for him, and you know? If you think about this, it is better for one to stay in limbo than to hear from that person you fell for the torturing confession 'I'm not in love with you any more'.

After hearing his explanation, Esmeralda asked him, "If I were to disappear from the map, would you look for me, would you fight for me this time?"

His answer, "My feelings for you are much stronger than when we first started seeing each other and now I can't stop thinking about you all the time, so yes I would show up at your house if it came to that."

Esmeralda very surprised told him that he should never do such a thing, he asked why not and Esmeralda replied, "Because I would die from a heart attack!" Roberto was a mellow guy; he did not get all bent out of shape for hardly anything and this was not an exception.

He then jokingly told Esmeralda, "I need to know your home address, you know… In case you disappear." They both laughed out loud and the results of her test? Well, they were inconclusive and perhaps lacking credibility due to Esmeralda's biased involvement with it.

Beso a Beso… Dulcemente
by Paloma San Basilio
http://lyricstranslate.com/es/beso-beso-dulcemente-kiss-kiss-sweetly.html

Te acercas tan despacio que casi me impaciento
Me quemas con tus manos, me abrazas con tu aliento
Amor de horas ocultas, bendito amor secreto
Mi cuerpo te desea, yo también.

Es tarde y en mi casa me espera la tristeza

El fútbol, mi marido y un vaso de café
"¿Qué tal en la oficina?", "Prepáreme la cena"
"¿Me quieres?", "claro, claro," ¡Rutina indiferencia!"

Coro

Beso a beso, dulcemente, abrázame que quiero
Sentirme diferente, el mundo no perdona y yo
Paloma infiel prefiero estar contigo y no morir con él. [bis]

Es triste, se hace tarde, se está durmiendo el cielo
El tiempo se impacienta y tira de mi pelo
Las ocho y el en casa, ayúdame a marchar
Me espera mi destino, me espera soledad...

Kiss by Kiss Sweetly
Paloma San Basilio

You come close so slowly that I almost lose my patience
You burn me with your hands, you hold me with your breath
Lover of occult hours, blessed secret love
My body desires you, so do I

It's late and in my house, sadness waits for me
The football, my husband and a cup of coffee
"How did you do in the office?" "Make dinner for me."
"Do you love me?" "Of course, of course."
Indifferent routine!

Chorus

Kiss by kiss sweetly hold me
Because I want to feel different,
The world doesn't forgive

And I, unfaithful dove, I'd rather be with you
And not die with him.

It's sad, it's getting late, and the sky is falling asleep
Time gets impatient and pulls my hair
Eight o'clock and he is at home, help me to leave
My destiny waits for me, solitude waits for me…

The nitty-gritty of their love affair

Roberto's father passed away in his country of origin and he had to immediately prepare to travel to partake of the funeral services and accompany his mother and siblings during such a hard time. Esmeralda was cognizant of that crucial decision that Roberto had to make — that is abandoning his business and his only source of income so abruptly without any planning. But the thing that was actually agonizing for her was the idea of not seeing him for God knows how long. She did feel a little bit uneasy given that she had a feeling Roberto might distract himself so much as to not find the occasion to call her while he was away. She refrained from warning him not to do such a thing — she tried not to sound obsessive and unreasonable and just wished him a safe trip. About a week before the news of his father's passing, Roberto had commented to her that as per his conversations with his mother on the phone his father was not doing well. They had just finished making love when Roberto goes and sits up in bed and while caressing Esmeralda's back and looking kind of embarrassed, in an apologetic kind of way said, "I finished way too soon this time… didn't I?"

Esmeralda rolled over to face him still resting her head on his lap and then she passes her fingers over his fleshy attractive lips, smiles at him and tells him, "No, amor… the simple act of being with you gives me all the satisfaction and pleasure I have ever desired."

Nonetheless, Roberto appeared worrisome and he stated, "I am worried about my father."

Esmeralda, "What about him? Is something the matter?"

Roberto, "You know, he takes so much medication, all different types, especially for pain…"

Esmeralda, "Why? Is he in a lot of pain?"

Roberto, "I don't know… he had prostate cancer once, but he was able to overcome that… the thing is that my dad is so afraid of dying, he will take anything to prolong his life and he is very old."

Esmeralda is attentively listening and with a big smile takes a look around his dresser and nightstands which had bottles of medicines all over and then she says, "I don't know, but I got to say that the apple does not fall too far away from the tree," in a sort of sarcastic way.

Roberto with a curious tone of voice replies, "What do you mean?"

Esmeralda, "Come on! Mira all that stuff all around… looks like you have a pharmacy of your own." Roberto just cracked a laugh, kissed her and wrapping his arms around her cold body evidenced by the way her nipples got perked right up, pressed her tight against his naked chest. They stood hugging each other with the strength a nail gets attached to a magnet until Roberto was forced to answer a business phone call. Esmeralda's mood changed to a resignation type and she quickly jumped out of bed, got dressed and while putting on her coat threw a kiss to Roberto meanwhile, he was still engaged talking to a client on the phone; he waved good bye with his free hand and smiled and looked at her as if telling her 'I'm sorry love' and she left.

A couple of days passed by since this last encounter and Esmeralda did not receive a text message or call from her lover; she was growing impatient and texted him, 'Hola! Where are you? Did you decide to become a stranger again?' Roberto, 'He passed away [his father]'. Esmeralda, 'Ah! I am so sorry to hear that... I wish I could be by your side at this moment and give you a hug'. Roberto, 'I will take a plane tomorrow in the early morning'. Esmeralda, 'I understand amor... you should be with your mother during moments like this... take care! Te quiero!'. Roberto, 'Gracias... te quiero'. After three days of Roberto being gone, he called her, "Mi vida, how are you?"

Esmeralda, "Amor, I am fine, what about you, how are you holding on?"

Roberto, "You know... it's sad, especially looking at my mom, she never separated from my dad for too long before and he was the only man she ever knew. But I am fine... it is refreshing to feel your own land's breeze and see old dear friends."

Esmeralda, "Have you seen a lot people already?" Esmeralda was somehow worried that he might run into her teenager-years' boyfriend and with whom she also happened to have a one night-stand on her vacation trip to the island years back — she had talked about him to Roberto before, but she did not want to go into details of what really took place while she was married and she saw Antonio again after many years. However, Roberto did not give any signs this was the case and she was relieved for the time being; she was afraid that if Roberto ran into this guy again [they knew each other both from back home and also in the USA], he was going to be tempted to ask him about her past relationship with Esmeralda and Antonio would say things she would rather not want Roberto to hear. Then after this call which she should not have taken for granted, Roberto called her one more time two days later and spoke for maybe a minute or so and then no more. He spent seven more days away and that Thursday Esmeralda was anxiously awaiting by the phone for an indication that he was back. Roberto had told her the last time they spoke that he was coming back a week from that day; so, she counted every day until the day he was supposed to return. Friday came to be and no call, so she was getting worried, she thought, "What if something bad happened?" She reassured herself that bad news travels quickly and she should hear if something terrible like a plane crash took place. Then she started thinking too much and this crossed her mind: "He spent almost two weeks there, with so much time he could have met a beautiful young woman and who knows probably fell in love… Oh my God!… This is pure torture… why don't you bother to call me?" There was nothing that annoyed Esmeralda that much as not getting a text message or call or any signal of life from Roberto. She could no longer stand it and quickly without thinking texted him, 'Hola! Are you back?' Roberto, 'Mi vida, can I call you?' Roberto called her and Esmeralda took that opportunity to get it all off of her chest; after she asked him how he was doing and how his mother was feeling. Roberto was acting a little bit clueless and Esmeralda updated him with how she was feeling given that he stopped calling her while he was so far away. He downplayed the whole situation and kind of conveniently forgot that he indeed had not called her for over seven days already not even to let her know he was back. Esmeralda insisted, "Why didn't you tell me you had arrived already?… I was getting worried."

Roberto, "I am sorry… you know? I brought my mother with me to spend a couple of weeks here and I have been so busy…

as a matter of fact I was going to call you last night... "

Esmeralda "Yea! And as usual things got complicated in your business... I can imagine because you were away from it for so long and now you have a lot of catching up to do." Esmeralda had this tendency to speak for him, to make excuses on his behalf, kind of helping him out since he was not a talkative guy at all. So, she probably felt compelled to forgive him way too fast. On the other hand, Roberto was this kind soul that even though he did not do a good job defending himself, he was nevertheless so transparent in the sense that he did not know or like to lie and one could very well perceive this. Roberto would neglect to call her, but he was not a womanizer, he was merely a man that loves one woman, Esmeralda, with all his heart and soul. Esmeralda did well on trusting him because she could not find a reason not to; she knew key people who could talk about him if he was getting involved with any woman and she could not find a clue that he was with anybody else but her; she had many Facebook friends from their native island – right there from their hometown, so she could see remotely if something peculiar was going on while he was over there.

Even the way Roberto reacted when she confronted him a couple of occasions such as this time after his trip was something out of the ordinary; they were in the kitchen of his apartment, he was preparing a pot of tea and she was hovering around him looking kind of pensive as if she was afraid to start something that could eventually interrupt their harmonious time together so far that day; he quickly grabbed her by her waist, lifted her up and sat her on the counter top; he started lifting her blouse and goes, "Where is it? Where is it? [her belly button] while he was biting her all over her abdomen; she was laughing and kicking her legs and then when they stopped their silly play and looking tenderly into each other's eyes, she asked, "Why are you so cruel with me sometimes?"

Roberto, "Mi vida!... What are you talking about? Why do you say that?"

Esmeralda, "You did not call me for seven days... don't you think that is what a torturer does?" lowering and softening the tone of her voice while pronouncing those sad sounding words.

Roberto, "I did not call you for that long? I am so sorry!... Mi vida..." He took her face in his hands and kissed her.

Then she still had something else to say, "I thought you had met someone there... a young and gorgeous chick... "

He quickly interrupted her with this, "Impossible! mi vida... you are a woman very hard to find a replacement for." She just bit her lips while shrugging her shoulders and looking a little bit confused; that thing that she does when she does not know what to say or think. Esmeralda secretly reconciled with her lover since he never seemed to have noticed she was very upset with him. They shared their warmth that evening and loved each other like they had not done so in a good while and they had so much to offer to each other, so much more than just complaints and regrets. Their bodies were able to take revenge of all the distance and time apart that they were subjected to so unfairly. Their souls found each other again as they always did and nobody or nothing could change how madly in love, they were with each other. ¡Un amor tan fuerte que nada iba a destruir jamás! Not even the nitty-gritty of an illicit relationship such as theirs.

He should be your rival!

On their second encounter after Roberto's trip back home to bury his father, Esmeralda is caressing his chest while laying down in bed and out of the blue asked him, "Did you see anybody you'd rather not see… when you were there?"

Roberto took a couple of seconds to digest the question and then said, "Um? Oh! I saw him [Antonio – Esmeralda's first love]… I got to tell you… he still got it! He is looking good." Kind of joking and smiling. Esmeralda's face filled with curiousness and she waited anxiously for more input. Roberto continued saying, now with a different semblance, a reflective one, "I noticed Antonio tenderly holding my mom's arm while trying to console her during that difficult moment that it was necessary to abandon the burial ground and leave… you know? That was one of the hardest moments." Esmeralda could not believe her ears, the man that she was so in love with had just described such a disarming beautiful act on the part of this guy who he should view as a rival – it occurred to her. Apparently, Antonio was still deemed a friend of the family [Roberto's brother and sister-in-law] in spite of the circumstances involving the young woman getting impregnated by him years back; after all, a couple who were not able to conceive a child of their own [the adopted parents of the young lady] helped very much raise the loving boy and that made them very happy. At the same time, Esmeralda could not help to think about Antonio in this new light, this image that he could be so compassionate and caring. After she left that night and got home, she continued remembering Antonio; flashbacks from about thirty years back went through her mind and she thought, "Why did you have to mention him now?… He was dead for me for such a long time. And besides, don't you care a bit about the fact that he was my ex-boyfriend, my first love? For God's sake!… plus, you're ignoring the fact that I was with him a few years back when I shouldn't have done that." Esmeralda felt very uncomfortable whenever she did not understand the logic behind certain things such as Roberto not caring that much about her ex; it felt to her that it should bother him – just the idea, you know… What if she still had feelings for him? When Esmeralda asked him if he had seen somebody that 'he shouldn't see' back there, she was referring to Roberto's first wife who happened to be living still in the same town he visited and Esmeralda knew from a solid source that Roberto loved her very much and suffered tremendously when she terminated their long relationship. Also, Roberto had helped raise his first wife's kid from a previous relationship even though he was so young, that fact was hard evidence of the strong feelings he must have felt for her — Esmeralda secretly deduced. She decided not to clarify her inquiry and just went along with this unforeseen story that Roberto so distinctly verbalized. Once again, Esmeralda was tormented, thinking, "What if they talked about me and now Roberto has this negative concept about my persona… and he is just not telling me about it?" There was this thing that occurred when Esmeralda was this immature and clueless adolescent and going out with her first love, Antonio. They had a very tortuous and conflictive relationship; Antonio was this womanizer type of guy. He would be with other girls in high school at the same time he was with Esmeralda. Being that they lived in such a small town, rumors would fly very quickly and everything one did would be known — no matter how hard you try to hide it and even more so when he was so reckless with his insinuations to pretty girls around him. Esmeralda's self-esteem was totally annihilated by his behavior. Unfortunately, Esmeralda at one point decided to take revenge at Antonio by "Pagandole con las misma moneda" – responding in kind; she would start openly flirting with other boys that showed interest in her and even agreed to go on a date with another boy from their cohort just to provoke Antonio's jealousy. She thought it was only fair that he felt in his flesh what he made her feel whenever she found out he was once again spotted with another girl. Only, that one day Antonio had the audacity to write a long and demoralizing letter to Esmeralda. One important thing worth noticing in this letter was this, 'Esmeralda you are the type of girl that one day will be a filthy adulterous wife to her husband... ' These exaggerated remarks and unscrupulous words stayed in her memory forever as if encrypted in stone. As you might imagine, she now feels annoyed to no end that Antonio's words did become a realized prophesy, after all. And now she gets this feeling that Antonio could had mentioned to Roberto something along these lines. After a while, Esmeralda decided to give this whole weird thing a final rest; they did not touch that subject of her ex- again and/or Roberto's ex and continued with their forbidden, passionate romance.

An unhealthy monologue

They finally were able to see each other after a couple of weeks because Roberto was way behind in his business and they simply could not coincide on having free time to meet. Esmeralda got there around six p.m. and as usual texted to let him know she was parking her car and to make sure he was home already and not in the store which was located a couple of blocks from his apartment. He called her when he saw her text and told her to please go there, that he was waiting for her. He also told her, "I need to tell you something when you get here."

She replied with a kind of perspicacity in her voice, "Oh yea? What would that be?" So, she got out of the car and looked around to see if anybody she knew was in her proximity and then with steadfast steps walked about a block down the road packed with cars to meet with her lover. She entered the front door which was ajar and walked down the narrow hallway that led to his bedroom; Roberto was wearing formal dark pants and naked from his waist up; he was holding two shirts hanging from hangers, a white and a light blue dressy shirt; he looked at her when she let herself in his bedroom and he immediately dropped the shirts over the bed and quickly went to give her a kiss and a hug. Esmeralda could not help but feel attracted to this man who had just finished taking a shower and had put on a pleasant aftershave — to finish her off. She was caressing his chest with her long fingers interlacing his masculine nipples and appreciating the beautiful contrast between her fair-skinned and his darker complexion — proper of his ethnicity. She was thinking "how cool that he is getting all dressed up just for me." It occurred to her that perhaps he planned a surprise special dinner for them and he was just running late; she could very well forgive this minor thing. Oh! But she had forgotten that he was supposed to 'tell her something' and he eventually did. "Mi vida, please forgive me… I really need to go to this friend's wake… I just found out about his death a little while ago." Esmeralda swallowed dry, closed her eyes tight for an instant while taking a very deep breath — as if trying to fill her lungs with air before jumping into a deep lake and then glimpsed at the incredibly low ceiling and the four neglected bare cream walls which she failed to notice before. She did this for a few seconds almost as if trying to contain herself and not show pure displeasure right there and then. She was able to fake it — that is, that feeling of realization that she was not the center of his universe.

She swiftly grabbed the white shirt which still was holding the price tag; she quickly removed it and goes, "I want you to wear this one… I bet it will look very nice on you!" She was all smiles and looking assertive when she made her unsolicited suggestion, all the while, Roberto was kind of oblivious to her sudden elusive demeanor which if examined closely, it would certainly show at least a fit of pique. He started to put on the white elegant shirt and Esmeralda surrendering to this forced situation, helped him to button it while fixing her eyes on his erect torso, like when a mother tenderly does with her adorable little boy. He could not help it, he took her face and started kissing her mouth passionately. Esmeralda told him kind of wondering, "Aren't you leaving?... you are going to be late... you said the wake is just until eight p.m.... " He ignored her and quickly took her to the bed, undressed her and made love to her. Esmeralda did not realize that the way she was helping him to get dressed provoked him to do what he was not planning to do at that moment. She then was looking a little bit worried and asked, "Did you finish inside me?"

Roberto looked surprised and told her, "Mi vida... You should have let me know." [that she was not using protection and as she explained after the act, she was supposed to be ovulating around that time].

Esmeralda, "You took me by surprise... I was going to tell you... but everything happened so fast!" She did not intend to shock him even though her instinct was to take revenge, so she then sort of retracted and said, "Nothing to worry about... I can take the morning-after pill tomorrow." Well, it was unlikely she could get pregnant at her age, but she just intended to be spiteful — if only for a second. He smiled and quickly put on his clothes, he said he was coming back real soon, no more than forty minutes all together. Esmeralda asked him to hurry noticing that he kept hovering around as if forgetting what he should be doing next. He finally left after giving her a kiss and looking tenderly at her as if asking for forgiveness.

He added, "If I don't do this, I will see one of his relatives when they go to the store one of these days... they are clients of mine and then I will feel really embarrassed that I didn't go to pay my respects... do you know what I mean? Mi bella." Sounding very apologetic. He was looking very handsome with that black suit that fit him so well — noted Esmeralda.

So, she told him, "You are looking good... be careful!" They both smiled and he left.

Esmeralda went to the kitchen and served herself a cup of the fresh herbal tea that Roberto had left slowly boiling on the stove. She then went to the bedroom and started watching TV, however, she was way too anxious and started to think about what just took place; she was so happy that finally they were able to be together and she had fantasized that moment when they were going to share time, quality time together, enjoying themselves like there was no tomorrow. She took a deep sigh and turned around in bed, her eyes got fixed on the night table at her left side when she saw the small weathered wooden trunk with poems inside that she had written for him; she had carefully prepared this gift for Roberto's birthday a couple of months before. She went and opened the metal hinge slowly as if afraid she was invading his privacy, then lifted the cover and noticed the love letters and a dark blue aromatic candle positioned neatly as if they had not ever been touched — it looked that way to her. She thought, "He didn't read them yet... he does not care about my stupid sentimentalism... he must be thinking that I'm such a cursi idiot!" She put the box back exactly the way she found it and remained sitting on the edge of the bed, dangling her cold feet and folding her arms, touching her back with the tips of her fingers, and slightly bending forward – the way you do when feeling a chill. She continued with her unhealthy monologue:

"Who the hell do you think you are?... You can't imagine all the things I have to endure to just make it here... I was so naïve to think that you were going to make it up to me... all this time away from you to only come here and stay alone in your home, without your warmness, and wondering why in the world a dead person has to take precedence over me?" She wanted to cry perhaps she could find some relief in doing so, but was unable to do it. If she felt so hurt by Roberto's decision to go out and leave her alone why she did not make it known to him somehow? The truth is that she did not expect things to turn out the way they did and she was not quick to react, to show her true feelings and her first instinct was not to make him feel even more unconformable to how he was feeling already. However, the unwelcomed solitude that the quiet and cold apartment incited in her created a totally different scenario where she could not help it but feel sad and completely out of place. Esmeralda's monologue was perhaps an attempt to vent out some repressed feelings which did not — amazingly! originate that evening, but certainly escaped from her subconscious being at a moment when she felt so vulnerable. "How many times do I have to explain to you that what I intend with being with you isn't to have pure and exclusive sex? It is much more than that, stupid! I can surely have sex with my husband... if I wanted to; his erection can really last for a good while!... But it's not sex what I'm craving all the time... silly... I need your closeness... I need to feel that you belong to me and you need me as much as I need you."

Her mobile phone rang and it was him, "Mi vida, I'm on my way there now... did you wait for me for too long?" A silly question, but he did not know exactly what to say.

Esmeralda released a deep breath and attempting to quickly move out of her moodiness then told him, "No amor... don't worry... just come here." A few minutes later he arrived, quickly changed his clothes and put on the pajamas Esmeralda had told him before he looked so sexy with. They cuddled in bed, and kissed for so long that their lips showed the undeniable marks of unrestrained passion; eventually they fell asleep so peacefully in each other's arms looking like a pair of loving doves. In spite of all the unforeseen and stressful events of her visit that day, Esmeralda went home that night refreshed and totally recharged with love and tenderness, exactly what she was looking forward to when she arrived that evening to his apartment thirsty for his kisses and orphan of his warm hugs.

No amour propre?

Could it be that the intensity with which Esmeralda felt in love has something to do with her low self-esteem? What does one have to do with the other? You might ask. Esmeralda's need to constantly get a confirmation that she is being loved is almost like an obsession to her; it makes one wonder if she received sufficient attention from her parents when she was little or if she felt their love. But just wait a minute! It might be relevant to know that she used to ask her father if he loved her. You do not usually see a twelve-year-old asking that of his/her parents, however, Esmeralda's behavior and expectations in the love arena differ greatly from the average people. But still, isn't she melodramatic way too often? What could possibly cause that? Truth is that for Esmeralda hearing her lover saying that he loves her, misses her or any of those affectionate phrases was like a security blanket which she would grab and hug during those moments when she was feeling kind of blue. It got to a point that for Esmeralda that divisory line between her need to satisfy her ego and her real feelings for her lover became so blurry for her to distinguish one type of feeling from the other. Indeed, there is a high probability that what exacerbated her often-exaggerated emotional state were her own insecurities routed from early childhood. Esmeralda was this timid girl who was isolated from her school peers and that hardly ever participated in any extracurricular activity. Esmeralda lived mostly in a world she had created, and where she went to dream, fantasize and hide from the adverse external environment. To make matters worse she never went through that normal stage in life when one as a young adult has a steady relationship with the person one falls in love with, instead she experienced a series of extremely short-lived situations where she was infatuated with someone and that someone would eventually break her heart. This created a vicious cycle where her 'amour propre' suffered greatly due to these failed love relationships and at the same time she would rush to 'fall in love' again with the wrong guy almost as if that was the way she could fill that void in her heart. And when she finally had a permanent relationship, she did not love him; she simply kind of accommodated her feelings to accept the man who for the first time was able to stay with her for the long run and she did not feel that he could ever betray her. Esmeralda liked to feel at ease with her own internal self, she used to for a good while avoid putting herself in a situation where she was crazy about a guy and as I mentioned before, she found in her fiancé the man who was going to love her for what she was, without wanting to change her, at least that was what she had in mind those days; eventually this also became just another mirage since Valentino did find a ton of flaws in her and worst, he let her know this one way or the other. Perhaps after all, Esmeralda had a little advantage concerning her insecurities issues with Valentino being that her long-time boyfriend and who later on became her husband was himself this extremely timid guy, Esmeralda did not ever feel threatened by him, as a matter of fact, Valentino gave her the illusion that she was such a confident person because you know what? — like the adage goes, 'In the land of the blind, the one-eye man is king'.

What about her love for Roberto? No doubt that she felt something very special for him and perhaps he is the only man she has loved with such a strength and conviction for the very first time. However, even during the climax of their love affair, she had moments of self-doubt not only she questioned his love for her at times and without any logical explanation, but she would analyze her own feelings fearful that she might be submerged in another fantasy of hers and her love for him was not even real. That time when she was pretending to break up with Roberto, she was examining her ability to leave him and she would know once she had him in front of her one more time.

A secret shameful tendency all women have

'The man that I love sometimes is like a little boy, he has a wide smile and a tender look, he has the voice of a thousand men together and I love him crazy like he is, but my crazy lover, wise, intelligent. The man that I love is not afraid of anything, and when he loves everything around trembles, he is a tireless warrior in search of adventures, he has strong warm pure hands... the man that I love, he knows that I love him... he takes me in his arms and I forget about everything; he is my motivation, my own sun, he gave me happiness that nobody was able to give me before... '

https://www.youtube.com/watch?v=1ddK89KqVe8

[Myriam Hernandez – El Hombre Que Yo Amo]

These are lyrics of another of Esmeralda's favorite romantic ballads, interpreted and made known by Chilean singer-songwriter Myriam Hernández. What woman has not ever dreamed of that man, that man who is wise, sensitive, makes her laugh, doesn't wish to change her, and loves her more than anyone or anything? Even though she might be married, that does not prevent her from longing to have that ideal man in her life. Hence, one could say that there are way too more women out there than one can imagine — who are unfaithful to their partners, not necessarily physically, but in their minds, souls, or spirits, whatever you want to call it. Of course, most women will not admit it not even to themselves because they do love their husbands, love partners, or significant others and having these feelings or thoughts is just plain shameful. These virtuous women and perhaps self-sacrificing mothers would go about their lives repressing those forbidden feelings. I do not see anything wrong with this as long as they do not end up full of regrets toward the finalization of their natural womanly vitality. I do think nevertheless that women who are not happy or satisfied in their love relationships should speak up their minds, let them know how they wish to be treated, talked to, loved in all the sense of the word. And if still their partners with all these improvements are not sufficient to make them feel happy then these women should not stop trying to reach what is only a right, they have, what does that mean? It means an array of different things to everyone; the answer to this problem is specific to every single situation. Religious people have impregnated in their psyche that marriage is forever, for as long as they shall live even when it is not a happy marriage and if abolishing this divine rule would terrify you, and makes one even more unhappy then there is nothing to be done, but accept resignation as your best buddy. In the case of those people who at a time in the past were in love with each other, I believe there is a significant probability of them to be able to fall back in love and some might even have their love transcend a higher level with the tests of times. Therefore, in these instances it is worthwhile the fight to keep one's marriage and leave the word divorce out of the equation. For a person to whom religion does not play a significant part in their behavior or decision making and who have no indications of ever loving each other again if they ever did, then the logical thing to do is start fresh again with a different but qualified partner. Yes, I know, it is definitely easier said than done, but hey! It is either doing something to repair the damage or doing nothing. In the peculiar case of Esmeralda where she did not precisely fall out of love with her husband, she simply married without love, more over the irony that involved her reason – to marry a man of the same faith and in that way, satisfy a doctrine – can one criticize her for wanting something different to the bitterness that her life turned out to be? There was this instance when Esmeralda heard a woman angrily say, "I hate cheaters!" She said it in a beauty salon filled with other agreeable women. This woman was more than likely hurt and she pronounced these words in the context of a conversation a couple of other women were having.

However Esmeralda took this remark very personally and imagined for a minute a bunch of women who enjoyed a high social position talking badly about her, so she confronted them with these words, "All of you puritan women out there take a very good look in the mirror and if what you see is a happy, fulfilled woman alongside a loving husband with whom you feel happy? count yourself amongst the blessed ones and do not dare to judge that woman who is not as lucky as you are and just wants to be happy even if that means breaking a few moral rules."

Esmeralda was thinking this way while faking a smile that could signify her empathy with the hateful woman or simply an expected form of social etiquette. Esmeralda could very well understand this woman because she also has been betrayed in the past, but now she was the aggressor and she obviously did not assume this realization of what she had become well.

Esmeralda did observe at some point, husbands and wives who exemplified that ideal couple; they possessed all the necessary tools to live a happy and fulfilling long marriage, well? maybe being in love with each other helped. One afternoon in a Sabbath day, the pastor's wife addressed her sisters in faith who had gathered for a rehearsal of the Christmas cantata and confessed, "… I am in the habit of elevating a prayer to my heavenly father giving thanks for the blessing of allowing me to enjoy those intimate moments with my husband, and I don't take it for granted." Esmeralda was already married to Valentino for almost two years when she heard the wise woman express the way she felt about her husband, especially during and after their sexual intimacy; she could not help to ponder upon her own circumstance where she did not feel any pleasure whatsoever during her closeness with her husband. Far from congratulating this lucky wife, Esmeralda was envious of this woman's fortune and angry at herself for settling for a precarious love relationship. Esmeralda saw other middle-age couples at church who demonstrated they loved each other even after going through hardships and experiencing the challenge of bringing up kids in a strange land. Perhaps, she only focused on the spiritual or religious aspect of these harmonious marriages and did not care to inquire about the insights related to their feelings or the love they had for each other before she got married. Esmeralda might have assumed that these couples' merely religious profession and

/ or strong spiritual conviction were the automatic answer to a happy marriage. Indeed, she had it all wrong in her mind and failed to make it a reality in her decision process that love was the moving force and always will be in every single relationship in order to succeed. A very important piece of the puzzle was missing; Esmeralda had lost the heart card in a risky and dangerous game where her happiness and spiritual wellbeing were at stake and ended up losing like an addicted gambler tends to do, very badly and without hopes.

Esmeralda also saw the other side of the coin, sadly, there were those lonely married women in church but that were never seen with their husbands because they were nonbelievers and many of them not only disliked church altogether, but also would make these poor women suffer greatly at home; some of these husbands were heavy alcohol drinkers and that meant this activity would take precedence to anything else even to the extent of their submissive wives becoming second or last in their lives. Esmeralda used to have compassion for these unfortunate spiritual sisters and she was terrified to one day join their group. Esmeralda understood that if she did not choose a Christian man to be her partner for life, the cruel destiny these women had could be hers as well. So, if you were to choose in what side to be, what would you decide to do? You would not want to be that woman whose husband is absent during those San Valentine's Day celebrations at church; it is a very ugly scene and Esmeralda could not digest how they could bare this, year after year; how did they manage to avoid feeling envious of their happily married counterparts? Yes, Esmeralda was tricked into believing that marrying someone in her faith would spare her the pain and suffering these martyr women had to go through, but she did not foresee that she could equally be one them. Not necessarily for everyone to notice her loneliness since Valentino was going to be sitting by her side in one of those long church benches though it was going to become very real for her. She would secretly endure her solitude while putting a wide and warm smile with her husband by her side in front of that audience who expected her to be the happiest woman around; they had the false impression that Esmeralda had everything in her favor since she was a beautiful young woman who married one of them and was this dynamic member and even leader of more than one department in the church. What else could she ask for? A heck of a lot more! I would say and only time would make this evident; all of a sudden, it appeared, Esmeralda was never to be seen again at church and eventually she became just another lost soul out there. In her present world, Esmeralda is simply behaving like any other woman would; what she is experiencing might just be that secret shameful tendency all women have at some point in their lives. In her case it seems more notorious given that she never felt for her husband what a woman should feel when they are at the dawning of their relationship. Unfortunately, Esmeralda skipped that natural step and jumped into a tedious life of old-couples type of situation. But, maybe now it is her time to be happy and she would not let this opportunity slip away. Maybe?

Calm in the eye of the storm

There is not a day that goes by without a feeling of discordance in Esmeralda's home. The quarrelling is ongoing and the reasons mostly unjustifiable. It is of course worse when they get heated up outdoors, in front of strangers; everybody has experienced it, it is so embarrassing for the ones watching, mostly — For these pair of squabbles? Well, they are used to it. A good example, they go into this new bagel store to get a take-out breakfast on a

217

Sunday morning, the place is crowded, Esmeralda took a glance at the signs high up on the wall behind the counter and noticed there are two lines, one to order plain bagels and the other for hot grill sandwiches. Valentino had mentioned that he only wanted a bagel, no sandwich, so Esmeralda tells him, "You should stand up on the line over there and I will stay here, I want an egg and ham grilled sandwich." Valentino ignored her simple suggestion just to provoke her despisement, she thought, and as expected she looked at him in a way that if looks could kill, he would have dropped dead right there and she said aloud, "Fine, as you wish!" More than one person standing there turned their faces. But, one day the inexplicable happens; Esmeralda asked Valentino, "Could you please transfer money to my account, my annual special keratin hair treatment is due?"

To what he has the nerve to object by saying, "No way, I have way too many payments to make this month." He pronounced these words with an angry tone, so it is surprising that Esmeralda quietly walked away without creating an altercation which usually followed an interaction of this kind between these two. Something very unusual was on the forecast, a phenomenon that was going to take Valentino by surprise and was going to make him wonder what on earth was going on with her quarrelsome wife? "I have gotten in trouble with her for lesser things, and now she is all of a sudden, mute!"

Esmeralda's attitude these days was probably due to a combination of factors: one, she was getting exhausted of so much fighting and thought it was not even worthy. Why she did not come to this logical conclusion sooner — that blows my mind or perhaps she did, but was not successful in curbing her temper. Two, she really wanted to be a different woman — the one that her Roberto has described with her in mind sometimes and why not embrace that gentle and pleasant personality he attributes to her? Maybe it could become a real thing the more she practices self-control in the anger management department. And three, maybe it was becoming clear in her mind that if she was going to go through something as complicated as a divorce process, she needed to learn how to have 'discussions' in a wise manner with her soon to be ex-husband, hopefully. No question that in order for her to get out of this horrifying situation with a sound mind, she needed to exercise tolerance and patience and these attributes do not just appear out of nowhere, it is necessary to practice them in ordinary life only then it eventually gets to be part of one's nature or character. Obviously, Esmeralda's new resolution was going to be a slow and painful task, but with a great motivation to embark on such an undertaking, it could be possible; the thought of sharing her days with the man she was in love with and with whom she wished to spend the rest of her life, would help her endure every minute and survive every day. Esmeralda could now smile again while watching the flowers bloom early in spring a simple act that she used to skip way too often; while still having her hopes high, Esmeralda is able to understand that it is true: 'the essential things in one's life are fundamentally simple', yet of invaluable significance to uplift the soul, so she now would try to take a day at a time and appreciate those little sweet details every new day brings with it even though they might be mingled with not so pleasant things and therefore difficult to discover. This couple were no doubt in the middle of a furious hurricane though apparently enjoying a temporary calmness, the worst was yet to come.

Exactly what was going to happen at that moment when Esmeralda finally has the guts to pull out the plug could represent that unpredicted variable in a person's life that nobody wants to ever undergo. In this story though everyone must have seen it coming; it was an obvious result of an ill made decision. American romantic films usually portray the story of either a male or female protagonist where they have a chance to realize just in time before they tie the knot that his or her fiancé is not the love of their lives or simply not the right person for them to marry and the happy ending gracefully shows that moment when they finally meet the one. This story you are reading is different because the main character here unfortunately totally missed her opportunity to avoid a life commitment with the wrong guy for her. In this story, you go and see how the life of a person changes drastically for the worse by going ahead against every possible insinuation of an impending bad turning point; through glancing every chapter of this book one is able to mentally palpate the answers to the 'what ifs' most people have before making the biggest and important decision in one's life. Esmeralda needed to swallow the bitter sip now, be strong as she ever could be and persevere until the end. She needed to confront her fears, go ahead and just do it, quickly so it can be less painful – at least in perception, but nevertheless painful for all parts involved. Esmeralda experienced agonizing moments just thinking how she was going to tell him and the way he was going to take it. How their kids were going to adjust to the new situation Mom decided to put them in — though not on purpose; Esmeralda did think about the typical pedagogical psychology which explains how innately selfish young kids tend to be, so she was not expecting any empathy from her own kids. There is simply no right way to prepare to see in your children's eyes the look of resentment and pain that their own mother who brought them to this world would cause them. Yes, there were definitely some severe gusting winds approaching Esmeralda's whereabouts and she needed to hold on tightly to someone or something much stronger than she was, perhaps her love for Roberto or simply a profound desire to change the course of her life.

Un día a la vez

It is Sunday late in the afternoon, the kids went out with their father to eat ice scream and Esmeralda has a little alone-time. She turns to a melancholic sort of mood, takes a glance at her mobile phone, and whispers, "Why bother? Of course, he wouldn't text me on the weekend unless I do it first." She then in one of her impulses, texts him the following, "Do you know how many times I check my phone to see if I got a text from you? Way too many times." In another text, 'Then I think that maybe I expect too much from our relationship or whatever we have'. Another text, '… and I arrive at an inevitable conclusion that what we got together cannot have a future'. In another text, 'and that's why I try to live a day at a time. But, it's still very difficult for me this whole situation', and in the last text, she simply states, 'Have a good day, amor' and this last part she meant it as a sarcasm. As expected, when she sends Roberto these messages which seem to come out of nowhere, he gives his typical answer, 'Can I call you?' He always would ask for her permission to call her; his prudence gets in the way every time and Esmeralda wishes he could be a little bit bold even if risking their secret romance be disclosed. Roberto insisted, 'When you are able to talk on the phone, please let me know'. Ten hours later Esmeralda still did not answer him, so he had no choice but to text her again, 'Are you asleep yet?' At last Esmeralda deigned to answer his text by saying a lonely 'No'. He sends another text, 'You know you're in my mind every moment, don't you?… Are you angry at me today?' Yes, Roberto could be a little bit naïve sometimes or perhaps as usual just trying to smooth out a rough time. However, Esmeralda still not out of her depressive mood, answered him by asserting, 'It doesn't look like' [that she is in his mind all the time]. At this point it is not clear to Esmeralda if Roberto's patience finally ran out or if he was just kidding when he texted, 'What did you eat today?' This expression perhaps conveying a kind of sarcastic feeling because he did not seem to know what was causing Esmeralda this apparent change in mood, and this annoyed her even more and she replied, 'Don't worry... just like you said once before, one can't have everything in life'. Esmeralda told him once that she wished they could see each other every day and that was his answer, a cold and insipid answer — it seemed to her. Roberto being a pacifist type of guy did not continue with this absurd argument and told her, 'I love you, have a good night'. About an hour after Roberto's futile attempt to remove Esmeralda from the dark gray cloud she was under, Esmeralda texted him, 'I can't sleep', to which he replied, 'What's tormenting you, mi vida?', she said, 'The same thing as usual... the way I am living my life... I think that soon I will have to make a decision... and I don't want to lose you, but at the end I don't know if my destiny is to live without love... just sticking to a tradition... and the possibility that I will stay with him because it's my duty and nothing else... that's why I'm terrified of my future and you don't seem to understand that', then she asked Roberto if she could call him and he said 'yes, of course'. They were on the phone after midnight, she on the sofa and Roberto doing much of the talking since she shouldn't talk that much otherwise, she could be heard by her husband who was as customary of him, browsing the internet catching up on the latest prominent daily news. In case you wonder the reason, her husband seemed not to care that much about his wife preferring the uncomfortable sofa to his company, most nights, it was because he was cognizant that his loud and annoying snoring would disturb her sleep as she has complained numerous times.

The holidays were the worst for Esmeralda because her lover would be busier than ever in his business. Whenever Roberto got a lot of orders from his faithful clients, he would try to take care of every single one in a timely basis in order for them to get those orders ready just on time for the holidays even if that meant putting all his time to accomplish it at the expense of sacrificing time with his loved ones including his 'vida', Esmeralda. She had not seen him for a couple of weeks, there was simply no time to meet and she was getting lonelier each hour that passed by without him. That Thanksgiving evening while Esmeralda was having quality time with her children, husband, siblings, her mother and friends, she still felt something was missing. Amidst the noise of laughter, loud and cheerful conversations referring mostly to remembrances from their childhood's unforgettable events, Esmeralda's mind would wander, lost, thinking how wonderful it would be to have him by her side during moments like this. Just sitting next to each other on the couch while drinking a glass of wine or doing just about anything, it did not matter as long as they were together in the same room, listening to the same silly conversations, smelling the usual smells of 'La Noche Buena' with its distinct odor coming from the kitchen that Christmas Eve that also soon came and passed displaying the same scenario where Esmeralda felt so lonely at the same time that she was surrounded by so many loved ones. There she was thinking that perhaps it was always going to be this way; that they would never be able to be a couple for real. Above of all, Esmeralda would start to doubt once again if Roberto indeed loved her. A few days before she had talked to him on the phone and she told him, "I am getting tired of sounding like a teacher giving you a lecture... " Roberto kept silent just like an obedient student would behave. She continued, "tell me one thing... do you really believe me when I tell you that I love you? Or you can't do that because of the things I have confessed to you? Is that what's going on here?"

Roberto, "No mi vida, I believe you... I already told you before... it's true I was not happy to hear you say certain things you said, but I just want us to live the present and hope good things for our future... "

Esmeralda, "You really think that way?"

Roberto, "Positive, mi vida," and then he added, "Of course, I would not like you to do anything of that sort [what she confessed to him about her past lovers] while you are with me."

Esmeralda quickly responded, "No, amor... how could I do that to you?... I would not do something like that not just because we are together... the thing is that I don't want to hurt you because I love you very much... just for that simple reason, mi amor."

Roberto released a deep sigh and said, "Mi vida, that's really something... it makes me feel so good to hear you say it like that." Esmeralda was still not satisfied because she intuited that once they were off the phone, she would have to wait patiently for the next time he deigned to call her again. So, this time she was not about to just let him go so easily without first giving him a sort of ultimatum.

Esmeralda, "I don't believe a man that is in love with a woman can spend so much time away from her... our relationship seems to be like those people have remotely, you know, when they live apart in different regions of their country or abroad... but you know what? Even those relationships are better than what we have right now… because I bet, they talk on the phone all the time or send each other love letters very often."

Roberto, "Mi vida, I recognize that I neglect calling you but it has nothing to do with not caring or loving you… I do think of you all the time."

Esmeralda, "Not true… why don't you call me one of those moments that you are supposed to be thinking of me… if you don't call me there is no way I could know for sure that you really think of me sometimes." And she added, "From now on if you don't call me or text me, I will assume you are not thinking of me regardless of what you told me that you admit to be neglectful and the sort." At that point Roberto let escape a nervous laugh and Esmeralda did not let him talk any more, she just said goodbye.

But really, what was going on through her mind this time? Esmeralda has been exactly on this life big interception before; it seems like she ends up right here every time she senses a need to choose a direction different to the one, she is on, however the heavy traffic of indecisions, self-doubts and conformity to the established norm, win over every time. At times her surroundings look so familiar like when she ends up sometimes in a remote part of the highway lost — she has been lost in this same area before, so yes, she does remember it. The thing is that she seems not able to find her way back home for a good while; maybe she does not wish to return to the same old same, to the vain, to her profane habitual life. All of a sudden, it feels to her, she is in the middle of nowhere semi-paralyzed in need of deciding which cardinal direction to take; wondering which way would lead her to a life of peacefulness and happiness. True is that she is now having flashbacks of times past when she had a gut feeling she ought to diverge drastically and forcefully from the direction she was heading and instead fear of changing the status quo of her life and a profound apathy because she opted not to get out of her comfort zone, positioned her in a stagnant place which she has not been able to abandon so far. Will she ever be strong enough to make the decision and take real action to finally change the course of her life? Esmeralda seems to be in desperate need of having Roberto's unconditional support and more importantly his open and clear position that he will stay with her, loving her when and if she goes through that horrifying thing, they call divorce. The thing is that she is not convinced that Roberto is being enthusiastic about her intention or mere desire to getting a divorce at this time. And in all fairness, who could blame Roberto for not wanting to rush through anything given that he has suffered not one but two painful divorces? Yes, it's very unfortunate that when Esmeralda finally has in her life a suitable partner whom she sees herself happily with for the rest of her existence, this guy has emotional scars himself that render him practically incapable of committing to her the way she wanted him to be. He might eventually overcome his fears and as time passes by, and their love gets stronger, his attitude changes in Esmeralda's favor and she is then able to leave that forlorn state that she tends to be, so often head on. Meanwhile, she will have to acquiesce to her lover's passive disposition when it comes to her divorce issues. She will need to learn to live a day at a time in order to avoid madness and entertain peace in her mind and soul. The next day after their conflicting texting, these lovers got together, made love passionately until they would get exhausted as usual, but hardly any mention of their talks from the day before; indeed, Roberto did not allude to Esmeralda's behavior, perhaps he did not want to resuscitate that subject for peace's sake and because he was not ready to deal with that at the moment. However, Esmeralda did try to bring the uncomfortable subject up again and she asked him, "Did you get mad at me for the way I behaved yesterday?"

To which he answered, "No, I understand now that when you get in that mood, you eventually get out of it."

"What if one day I don't?" said Esmeralda in a defying kind of tone, he just smiled and kissed her tenderly as if telling her there were more important and exciting things to focus on than to waste precious time dwelling on hopeless pettiness. That evening they were together turned out to be a good one for them and it ended like this, a romantic dinner Roberto had ordered to bring home from a local restaurant for them and she complementing him on the gorgeous tan he unintendedly got when doing some shores outside on the sun, "Oh! I see… you got your gorgeous color back." They once again enjoyed themselves like there is no tomorrow and Esmeralda as usual having a hard time trying to leave that place where for a couple of hours, she felt immensely happy. It was one more memorable night to remember and treasure in their hearts to revisit later in their senile years whether or not they would be together in their final destination in this life.

In a Moment of Weakness

They finished making love that night, but Esmeralda felt as if he just did it to satisfy a basic human need and not really loving her; what pushed her to this conclusion was her perceived idea that he was rushing through it. If there was a thing, she detested was this feeling 'of being used' because she has been this instrument that has served more than one guy to do just that: make him reach a sexual orgasm. It was probably her perception of a reality seen through her biased mind and trauma-filled-life in the love arena, and not the real thing. However, she could not explain it to him without sounding vulgar and demented, so she opted for letting it go, in this way repressing her feelings to the max. This was not a good procedure at all, for she was going to find an unsuitable outlet sooner or later. Yes, then the solution to her problem was going to be worse than the problem itself. May I explain? Sure! Pay attention to what happens next. Soon after this last hurry-love-making sort of night if you will, at least in Esmeralda's mind, she was feeling down, blue and miserable to no end. She waited for his call or text, checking her phone constantly, three days passed by and nothing. So, she then goes and sends him this text, 'Once, you told me that time was going to demonstrate how mistaken I was [she believing that he did not love her] and true is that time has only served to convince me how insignificant I am in your eyes... I do not wish to continue like this. I know I probably deserve this for being such as moron letting you take advantage of my idiocies... I don't want to see you ever again! Don't bother to call me, now I'm determined to end this once and for all... this time I won't change my mind, I promise you!'. Then a few days later, Roberto still was not answering her fiery monologue which infuriated her even more. And just as a miraculous apparition she sees this friend request on her Facebook, it was him – that crazy young guy with whom she had an affair some years back. She hesitated to click the confirm tab and then, she would come back and stare at it. So, she decided to tip toe the attractive waters in front of her and proceeded to click on his profile picture which said, *'One day you will see me pass by and would say: There goes the only man who truly loved me'*. This phrase sounded so mature and romantic to her; she could not believe it could had originated from the same mouth that the closest thing to romance he could ever enunciate was something

like, 'Babe, make me cum, please... make me cum!!!'.
Esmeralda felt in the trap and in this way created a cascade of
eventualities that she would later regret; she went and said,
'Hello, Elijah', he answered, 'Hello love'. It was down the hill
from here. Elijah would say things like, 'remember when I used
to touch you and made you see the stars out of pure pleasure?...
I can do that again, love... don't you want it?' She would reply,
'Shut up!... you did not change at all... don't talk to me like that'.
Elijah, 'why not? Just knowing I'm talking to you look! How you
put me', and immediately she saw this picture of him having a
penile erection. Esmeralda was red in the face after seeing this
and got out of the chat in a flash and feeling ashamed she went
into pensive mode. "I should have not contacted him... I just
betrayed the love of my life... what am I going to do now?" Now,
she was being tormented thinking how she could had fallen so
low like this? Thinking that she had told Roberto how much she
loved him and nobody else that she was his completely. And now
she went and just sold her soul in the blink of an eye to someone
so inferior to her Roberto the one she loves. But why? Why
would she do something so monstrously? Like I said before the
'solution to her problem was going to be worse'; this is the thing,
she thought that she was going to be strong enough to say good
bye to Roberto and never look back, so when she dared to contact
Elijah, she unconsciously did it out of spite for Roberto ignoring
her all this time.

"Enough already! This insanity has to stop," thought
Esmeralda and that night when Elijah texted her again, she told
him, 'Elijah, darling, I will be honest with you... yesterday, I
made the mistake of flirting with you... that was wrong because
now finally I have found the love of my life... there is this man
that I love so much! Elijah, 'Oh... that's awesome! I'm happy for

you... so in that case I apologize... I won't bother you again'. Esmeralda, *'No, it's not your fault... I am really glad that I could find you and know you're doing so well... look! You are such a handsome guy and full of energy... I want you to be happy, all right? Take care!'.* Elijah, *'Thanks, you too'.* And that was the end of this short-back-to-craziness moment in Esmeralda's world. Then she goes and sends Roberto a text, yes after she had told him that she promised 'not to see him again'. *'I think you will lose me forever if you do not react soon enough, but maybe you do not care a bit about that... it hurts to realize that you never loved me enough... how could you not call me for so long? Every single time I put you to the test, you fail...'* then after waiting a few minutes and no answer, she says, *'Okay, I will leave you in peace'.* This is when he finally, answers, *'How are you, mi bella, tell me how are you feeling?'* Esmeralda, *'Why... why are you so cruel with me?'* Roberto, *'I get sad when you are angry at me and fighting without an apparent reason'.* Esmeralda, *'I fight with you because I feel you don't love me and worse, you don't even try to convince me... it's like you don't care!'.* Roberto, *'I am yours! You don't have to worry about a thing... when you get mad at me, it kills me'.* Esmeralda, *'Then... why don't you react? Don't you know your silence angers me even more?'* Roberto, *'Just know this, I will be here for you... and when and if you get angry at me again, I will wait for your anger to go away'.* Esmeralda, *'I hope one day it does not get to be too late for us... a flower that is not cared for would wither eventually, likewise love'.* Roberto, *'That is true... I agree with you, mi vida'.* Well, after this sort of reconciliation attempt, they as usual made a date to see each other the next evening. However, she had to add just one more thing, *'Love, please remind me to confess something to you when we get together, only that I might have not the strength to do it'*. Roberto being this super calm and patient guy just said, *'Okay, mi bella'*. Esmeralda, *'Do you still love me?... If so, please tell me when I see you'*. Roberto, *'Yes, love, I will'*. And yet, she still added something else, *'I love you, no matter what happens, I will always love you. Remember this those days when I won't be able to avoid hurting you'*. Roberto, *'I will keep that in mind, mi amor, always.'*

They got together and enjoyed each other in the most intense way possible; their faces showing the unmistakable signs of pleasure so immense to put into words; the sound they produced, were quiet sounds of inner soul jubilation – consisting of a million compressed feelings being released slowly – and their embrace so strong that nobody or any external force could break. When finally, their bodies, minds and souls succumbed to the climax of an act so incredibly executed, they exhaled and looked into each other's eyes as if saying 'Thank you for transporting me to the firmament, my love'. After these amazing intimate moments, they went and sat down at the kitchen table to have dinner and that is when Roberto with a calm smile, as usual, asked her, "So, you wanted to tell me something?"

Esmeralda sighed almost like with this sensation as when one experiences a fainting spell, she answers, "Oh! I thought you had forgotten." She got up and stood in front of him, took his face in her hands and told him, "Amor, do you believe me when I tell you that I love you?" Roberto just looks at her tenderly and nods his head affirming a non-verbal yes. Esmeralda was not ready to tell him what she had told him that she needed to confess to him before in her text. So, she changed the subject and then grabbed his hands took him back to the bedroom and they laid in bed, cuddling, and kissing only stopping to catch their breaths. Then she suddenly stops, takes her smart phone and tells him, "I need to show you something… I did something stupid… I accepted as a friend on Facebook this guy I once told you about… the crazy young dude I had an affair with, remember when I told you that?" Roberto was very quiet, you could not tell how he was feeling since his face remained kind of neutral; definitely not happy, but not angry, at least not how Esmeralda expected him to be. Esmeralda goes and starts reading the exchange of text messages she dared to have with this guy and as she is showing him, Roberto is trying to find his reading glasses that had fallen on the bed, mingled with the linens, so she says, "Don't bother, I'll read them to you." Esmeralda explained that she had deleted a couple of things that were kind of obscene. After the showing of the hard evidence that she opted not to conceal to her lover, even at the expense of risking all she had constructed with him so far, as usual, she goes and tries to read the reaction in his face, but was unsuccessful because he is just being himself and not saying a word or showing any emotions whatsoever. So, she asked him, "Please, amor, tell me what you are thinking, I need you to react to this… your silence is killing me, tell me something even if you think I won't like it."

Roberto finally said something, "Do you think what you did was a bad action?"

Esmeralda, "Of course! What I did was a grave mistake… I am not denying that at all."

Roberto, "How would I know that you will not do this again?"

Esmeralda, "Amor, te quiero con toda mi alma… didn't you see that part when I told him [Elijah] that I had found the love of my life that I love you… and you see how he responded, he is not going to try to call me again because I made it clear I loved you!"

Roberto, still calm, but kind of sad or leaning toward

resignation, says something else, "Why?"

Esmeralda, "Why I did it? Um, I was very vulnerable that day, feeling that you did not love me because you did not seem to be bothered at all when I told you in a text message days before that I did not want to see you ever again... I heard nothing, not a word from you... how did you expect me to feel?... So, I saw his profile and friend request and accepted him in a moment of weakness."

Roberto in a reflecting mode says, "So, it is not good when you feel vulnerable... not good at all."

Esmeralda nervously smiling says, "No, it is not good when I am vulnerable, I tend to do crazy things, but don't worry love, I won't do this again, I love you, please forgive me!" Roberto did not answer with words to her plea for forgiveness, but he did show that no matter how bad her behavior was, he still loved her; they continued hugging and kissing in bed, utilizing that little body member to experience pleasure rather than to generate spoken language; they remained in silence as if afraid one more single word could spoil those magical hours they were enjoying; it seemed that Roberto even as hurt as he could be, he was willing to not let this sour confession undo all the love they had given to each other this day. This is how Esmeralda felt his love, a love that was able to put love before self-pride and she understood now more than ever how lucky she was to have him, to have his love. Then time dictated for her to depart home to her daily insipid life.

A privilege to love you
It's nine a.m. and everybody is asleep in Esmeralda's home because it's a cold, quiet morning and they are in the middle of a winter blizzard, no school, Daddy and Mom are off work like

many people are, due to a declaration of a weather emergency alert in some areas of the Northeast of the USA. It is also mid-March, spring is supposed to start soon, but seems reluctant to show its beautiful face. Esmeralda is contemplating the snow falling down and listening to the crispy sound of ice hitting the window and this scenario transports her to thoughts and feelings she presumed were non-existent by now. Now that the winter of her life's struggles, lack of love and long desolate hours were finally dissipating, all of a sudden something starts fluttering around in her mind and heart. How is this possible? She should be content with her life right now — at least in that area that pertains to love, even if that love has to remain a furtive one for the time being, instead she is doubtful again that what she has with Roberto is just a bird of passage and that she has been deceiving herself all this time. The night before was probably the big precursor that led her to arrive to this sad conclusion; "… no, it is not his fault [Roberto's], it's just that he cannot help it" — to be a workaholic, to put his duties first, before her and she adds, "… just like I cannot help it to be this hardened romantic girl." Esmeralda continued talking to herself again; she was trying to listen to reason and ignore anything else this cold snow-day, late, very late in winter. So, could it be that when Esmeralda is close to finally see a beautiful spring in her life, she is also inclined to have to make an about face? "I wish you could always be able to dedicate time only and exclusively for us, to be together, to see into each other's eyes without regard of time, to caress each inch of our bodies and not think about what's outside those walls [his apartment] which are merely an accomplice to our love." This was Esmeralda's silent cry of lament because with each day that passed, Roberto dedicated less time for her — it seemed to Esmeralda. What was eating Esmeralda was the fact that Roberto

234

did not quit to attend to his business even when they had agreed to see each other later than usual that night precisely to allow him to finish up his work-related duties before Esmeralda got there. However, it looked like he was not able to accomplish it this time. Needless to say, Esmeralda felt very disappointed in him and most importantly in her for failing to foresee this repeated action becoming a reality again. So, this quiet morning she went and dragged from her deepest sentiments and thoughts the following: "I thank you for giving me the privilege to love you, amor... even if just for a brief moment, a moment which has interrupted my long, long state of complete boredom and destitution of love... You opened for me a door to the impossible, to wonders and things I could only dream of... oh! Yes, you made me forget for a good while that love was not meant for me, but now your attitude is forcing me to believe that I should resign myself to loving and caring for my kids, my home and nothing else... I should find happiness in doing this... why not?" You could say that Esmeralda was sort of rehearsing the farewell to the love of her life. She was tearful and her throat got in a knot while trying to force out these words. She put her hands open to cover her face and sobbed, then watched through the window time regressing to darker and colder days evidenced by that huge blizzard that came out of nowhere late, very late that winter. A couple of days after a big snow hits the ground everything that at the beginning looked beautiful and amazing about this white matter starts to transform into trouble, trouble and more trouble; no place to park your car in the city roads; delays in schools and consequently delays in your work and the list of negative stuff goes on and on. However, these are trivialities compared with the real aftermath of a nature's phenomenon; the TV News Commentator expressed something related to this: "... The cherry blossom trees in

Washington, DC were affected by the unforeseen and extreme seasonal weather change; these trees which provide beautiful canopies full of light pink flowers and that decorate the national mall, experienced earlier than usual blossoms caused by a warmer for the season climate amidst winter. Therefore, when the temperature dropped drastically low late in winter and the winds hit them to the point of breaking many of their branches, these trees which are a real delight to watch might not have all their flowers alive when they are supposed to just a couple of weeks ahead, at the beginning of Spring… " Listening to these remarks, Esmeralda started wondering if something similar happened to her; could it be that she got warm and cozy in this unbelievable love affair too prematurely and then was surprised and hit by the frigid winds of self-insecurities and a realization that even when he loved her, she still did not feel loved. Truth is that she was getting tired of finding excuses for him as for why she had to wait for him in bed antsy for his caresses while he answered a client's phone call even when out of business hours; made her wait for an 'I love you too' and attributed his inscrutable demeanor — that tendency of not openly expressing verbally his feelings for her, to a merely timid personality trait. It occurred to her that perhaps she should learn a lesson from nature; sometimes when you experience a very nice weather when you are not supposed to, you are bound to face the harsh reality when the real climate proper of such a times resurfaces and it is indeed so hard to re-adjust to this sudden change given that you had probably put away all your winter gear, all the needed protection. Therefore, failing to recognize this unbelievable mild weather in winter as atypical and getting used to its pleasantness could be dangerous. That is why Esmeralda decided this cold and lonely morning to take out that heavy coat that she had put away; this action could well represent an unnecessary resignation to something good because yes, winter was about to come to an end pretty soon, even when it felt to her as if it was never going to go away. Or perhaps she is just feeling once again under the weather, so when she manages to recuperate her mental health by getting out of this state of perturbation, she will continue to have the privilege of loving him with all her heart and with all her soul.

The last time we were together...

The last time we were together, my hair got soaked with our sweat because that cheap motel room lacked a suitable air conditioning and had no ventilation. We made love that hot and humid evening in a way that you could say, we left our souls there. Our bodies trembling, stuck together due to not only the uncomfortable moisture in the air, but our inability to stay apart from each other for long and our respirations in a constant state of acceleration, and during those moments, those precise moments, I wished those moments could last forever. As usual he pronounced hardly any word unless I asked him one of my silly questions, 'Do you love me?' To which he would reply, 'I do, I love you very much, mi vida', in a soft low voice. At one point his smart-phone rang, he took a pensive look while staring at it. I knew how particular he was about answering a business call, so I took him out of his misery by suggesting he should take it. I took advantage and ran to the bathroom to urinate, this sad place looked dated, with presumably white walls which time had turned into yellowish, nonetheless, I still felt my emotions very alive just like my heat-induced rosy cheeks that evening, thinking that we were under the same roof. I knew that while that was the case, I would be happy, imperfectly happy, but happy like I was never before in my entire life. When I came back to him a minute later, he seemed to be struggling to 'fix' the AC; he was pressing different buttons on the wall apparatus which had certainly seen better days, but it was a futile attempt. No point in asking the person in charge to remedy the situation; we had barely enough time to just love each other. So, we went ahead and enjoyed a refreshing shower together, appreciating our bodies – how they were so impatient to come closer and give in to their deepest desires! After this, we returned to the undone bed. My head was resting on his shoulder, my fingers playing with his coarse dark hair, which he hated when it appeared on his chest, but he had no time to shave as he apologetically confessed. I found him as handsome as ever, anyway. He was almost sitting down, with a pillow against the off-white wall, folded in half engulfing his long neck and attractive to no end shaved head, oh, maybe he is bald? I don't know and certainly, I couldn't care less! I looked into the darkness his eyes evoked me, trying to search deep into his soul, a habit of mine when we are together. But, the more I searched the more I realized that he was looking at me radiating this tenderness as if he were looking at something very cute, like a little soft bunny. I asked him once again, only seconds away from caressing his well-defined virile jawline and again enjoying myself, kissing his sun-bathed face, and my lips feeling the roughness of his sexy short beard, "Amor, what's on your mind? Tell me... what are you thinking?" I whispered these words very close to his ears and in a supplicating manner.

He bites his lower lip – I think it is so sensual the way he does it – and then turns his head to look directly at me and with a smile asks me, "Who loves you more?" I understood the ambiguous question, I had gotten used to his way of communicating with me; he would employ as few words as possible and would stay quiet longer than my patience could tolerate.

So, I immediately told him, "I wish the answer to your question were that you loved me more than what he [husband] could ever possibly love me." He is still there patiently listening, but not smiling any more. At this point I deduced by that bizarre question of his that he was trying to read my mind – which I found strange since reading minds is indeed my job! – I think he wanted to know for sure if I was not tempted to accept my husband back being that during those days, as I had mentioned to him recently, my husband was treating me more delicately and showing me a great deal of affection. I did not mean anything by telling him this, it was just a casual conversation. Obviously, he was now pondering this which main idea got stuck in his head without my knowledge. I switched position in an uncomfortable manner to raise my upper body to sit up in bed, his semblance changed to a sort of sad demeanor, perhaps he sensed that his question triggered something in my psyche that he was not prepared to deal with. I had not finished my answer to his short and to the point weird question, so I proceeded to unleash my disturbed thoughts about the annoying and yet necessary topic. To be frank, who knows? If what my mind was able to generate was no more than a distorted reality; by the time I saw the clock on the wall, I was already going mad because I knew it was time to abandon that place, that moment, that reality and I had no idea when I was going to be able to be with him again.

Just a hope remains, it has to do with his last words that evening, "Amor, one day it all will be the way you wish it to be." He enunciated these words with a positive tone of voice and looking at me as if saying, 'Please believe, please just believe it'. He probably knew how I was feeling evidenced by how sad I looked toward the end of our brief encounter. So, based on the sympathy he showed me this last time we were together, I have reasons to believe now that he suffers when we are apart, that I am not alone in this cruel reality. And finally, one day we will love each other freely, with no clouds of doubts in our heads, without mortifying thoughts and anguishing long interruptions.

Esmeralda made a narration of this particular meeting with her lover in her smart-phone notes as soon as she had a chance; they had to see each other this time around in a motel room because Roberto's mother was staying in his apartment while visiting from abroad for a few weeks. Perhaps Esmeralda was somewhat and unconsciously annoyed that her lover had picked precisely this place; however, she did not complain. She did dwell on — if just a little tiny bit, the possibility of Roberto not giving enough importance to their supposedly planned romantic date by rushing to reserve whatever he managed to find at his first attempt. She felt compelled to jot down these memories, perhaps in this manner she would know she was not dreaming, imagining it when time once again passes so cruelly without her love. Their situation was a bitter-sweet type because those moments were NOT forever, at least not in real time. Therefore, with these brief notes, she could sort of put these last remembrances in a time capsule which she could check once in a while and in this way cope with her loneliness. A solitude caused by the unfair physical separation from her lover. Also, she intended to come back to the subject that ironically Roberto initiated, but that Esmeralda felt she needed to explore even more. This account of events of these particular hours in this day in Esmeralda's life could be well perceived as that future reference when she would need to self-analyze her and his actions later on. It is as if she needed a reminder that she should confront him or somehow make him feel he was not off the hook yet when it comes down to her insecurities regarding their love relationship. Yes, she just had to keep on sabotaging that incredible love story with her Roberto; she was not going to accept something this good in her life that easily because she would have to learn to finally do that. She still needed to be convinced that she was deserving of his love. And what can be done when a person is his / her own worst enemy? Or simply is unable to stop fighting windmills? Yes! she was full of self-doubts and Roberto was clueless as to the reason she had to feel that way. In vain this man would try to convince her of his love, but I guess he was not that good defending himself and she was very good at arguing about how right she was about his coldness, his negligence to dedicate time to her. Well, only time was going to determine who was right. Who was just panicking? Or who was being realistic? Who was being sincere, yet not effective convincing the other? That sometimes sadistic or other times benevolent factor, time, yes… only time was going to tell.

Chapter 7

A Desolate Space without Her

The News

One evening of many that Esmeralda was going to see Roberto at his downtown apartment she never arrived. Roberto texted her a few times asking her if everything was okay, but no answer. He was worried about her because if she did not cancel their date and she did not show up, something had to have happened. This tormented man did not have anybody to turn to who he could confide his secret to and ask about her. Esmeralda's brother and who was Roberto's good friend, Emmanuel, lived in another state, so he could not help him and Roberto was hesitating to call him and worry him unnecessarily, besides Emmanuel was not aware of Roberto's affair with his sister, so he did not consider it wise to give any clue to his friend as of what has been going on between him and his sister without Esmeralda's consent. The next day came to be without Roberto hearing anything from her, it occurred to him to ask Esmeralda's stepfather, in an indirect kind of way about her; Henry happened to work for Roberto in his shop, but he did not know of Roberto's relationship with Esmeralda and he had no reason to even suspect such a thing; he, like everyone else could not even conceive the idea of his sweet Esmeralda having a different and secret life of the shameful sort. Henry with tearful eyes told him that Esmeralda was hospitalized after suffering a terrible car accident the night before. Roberto could not help feeling totally shocked and plummeted to a nearby seat; Henry asked him if he was alright noticing how pale he turned all of a sudden. He did his best to recover and assured Henry he was okay; he quickly informed his nocturne employee to take over because he had something important to attend to and flew to the hospital where Esmeralda was. Once there he asked the main lobby's receptionist the room Esmeralda Vignota was in and he was told Esmeralda was currently in the intensive care unit, so no passes were being given to visitors other than her immediate family. She asked, "Are you family?" Roberto nodded saying no and with a very sad demeanor slowly turned his back and walked away. Roberto felt so incompetent and frustrated because he could not do anything to assist her and he was desperate to see her, touch her, feel her, but nothing, he was going to have to wait and see, just hoping she was going to overcome this somehow. He went home that night but not before going to that park where he had the opportunity to start knowing her some years back when Emmanuel asked him to go there for one of his wedding photography sessions. He parked his car near the entrance and reclining back and closing his eyes, images of her gracious smile came to his mind, he remembered when he asked her to go out to have dinner together when they happened to be alone for a few minutes, and she just laughed as if by what he said was a joke; she was indulging in a flirtatious moment and did not wish to spoil the irreverent provocation this man in front of her was capable of generating in her, so she went and omitted to him her marital status at that time. All the while, the clueless and totally infatuated Roberto just stood there watching her, and refraining from kissing her right there and then. After a couple of hours of remembrances and having cried on and off, Roberto went to his now sad and desolate apartment because every space there enclosed a memory of his bella Esmeralda and he had no way of knowing if she was going to ever be there with him again, loving each other immensely and without any reservations. Exhausted, he got into bed and extended an arm to reach out from his night table a piece of lingerie Esmeralda had forgotten there sometime back. He took it and hugged it tight against his chest, he burst into tears again while holding on to the only thing that smelled like her and which was a symbol of their happy times together.

The conversation

After a very long week, Esmeralda was transferred out of the ICU and moved to a regular room. Even though she was stable, she was still in an unconscious state. Roberto recognized this opportunity and went to visit her in his role as a friend of Esmeralda's brother, this was the explanation of his presence there in case he was caught in the act. When he got to the hospital it was the evening and everybody was there, the immediate family – including her husband, many relatives and friends – because it was the time when most people had gotten out of work. Roberto saw from the large window and from a decent distance how crowded it was in there and decided to come later that night hoping he could have a moment alone with his love.

Roberto was afraid he was not going to be strong enough when he saw her for the first time and in that way, show his true feelings for Esmeralda in front of people. So, he left the hospital for a few hours and then returned; he waited hidden until he heard everyone say good night. Once he deemed it was safe, he went in the room and he saw her laying there, looking so peaceful and so quiet. After a few seconds of just standing there paralyzed, nonplussed, watching in disbelief that scenario where tubes, machines, and all the other equipment proper of such a setting, he felt overwhelmed. When he got over the impact, he could look at her, just her and then he hurried to her side to hug her, he wanted to embrace her whole body and he wept incessantly, kissed her, and then he sat down by her side and told her, "Te quiero mucho mi vida... I want you to ask me if I love you like you used to ask all the time and I promise you I will tell you how much I love you as many times as you want me to say it... but please talk to me again." Roberto was hurting so badly; the annoying silence because Esmeralda would hardly ever stay quiet was unbearable and the fact that he was alone suffering with nobody to offer their shoulder to cry on made this sad situation even sadder. That night Roberto did all the talking; he remembered how Esmeralda would try to guess what he was thinking all the time and now he was willing to answer every single question he did not answer before. At times, he would just gently touch her face and tenderly look at her as if by waiting for her to wake up any minute.

Time was up so quickly – it seemed to him – and the nurse softly and with due compassion because that is what he inspired, tapped his back, he raised his head showing his reddish eyes and a somber semblance that was not to be missed, and then she said, "Sir, the visit time has finished for today."

Roberto immediately asked her, "What is the earliest time that I could be back to visit her tomorrow?" She said eight a.m. Roberto continued asking the sensitive lady, "Is it all right if I bring flowers?"

Nurse, "Yes, that would be okay."

Roberto, "What about something to stimulate her brain a little bit? I heard people in her condition can benefit from soft music... "

The nurse was touched by the devotion he was displaying for this woman and wondered who he was to her, why he was the last one to come and all alone? So, she asked him, "How are you related to her?... you seem to care a lot." Roberto looked surprised and could not answer right away, the nurse noticing his weird behavior told him, "Oh! I'm so sorry... it's really none of my business..."

Roberto, "Don't worry I will leave now, have a good night... thank you very much!" and left.

The following day Roberto presented himself to the hospital at eight a.m. and just how he predicted, there was not a single visitor; either he was the first to arrive or nobody was going to show up until later in the day. Roberto took a chance and entered the room carrying a bunch of dark pink margaritas, Esmeralda's favorite flowers. He put them on a table next to her bed and took some water from the bathroom sink and poured it in the crystal base. After taking all his winter gear off because he did not want to bring the cold from outside close to Esmeralda, he then kissed her forehead softly being cognizant that she was more fragile than ever. Roberto was just being himself when he was attending to his bella and dormant Esmeralda; he did his best to serve her as if she was a guest of honor when she visited him and now, he would still try to make her feel special even when he did not have to impress anyone. At some point, he put on Esmeralda's favorite songs that he found on YouTube on his smart phone. The night nurses were in the process of handing over patients to the next shift, Esmeralda's nurse reported, "Room 307, Esmeralda Vignota, Spanish, forty-six-year-old female, car accident, head contusion and brain trauma, some fractured ribs, right broken arm, left leg fractured in two pieces, respiratory distress, unconscious seven days. She has many families and friends, but the guy you now see in her room came first thing this a.m. and was the last one to leave last night; there is something strange about him, yet it is so romantic the way he treats her, I have no idea how they are related."

Relieving nurse, "Why didn't you ask him?'

Night nurse, "I tried... big mistake... I wouldn't ask if I were you."

Relieving nurse, "He must be her husband or boyfriend."

Night nurse, "Nope, I met her husband yesterday and that's not him... and why wouldn't he tell me he was a relative or friend? What's up with that?"

Relieving nurse, "You are right, it is so strange."

Roberto continued with a monologue in the presence of his now inert Esmeralda. "Mi vida you got to wake up soon... I will prepare the best tea you ever tasted and you will feel invigorated and warm inside, you'll see... we will be together for eternity just like you once told me... remember when you asked me if I was going to love you when you were old and using a walker?... yes, we are going to grow old together and I will die being in love with you." Roberto was holding her hands and, in an instant, when he was tenderly kissing the lifeless limbs, someone came into the room without Roberto noticing because his face was totally engulfing Esmeralda's hands. She cleared her throat in an attempt to make herself known and he was startled, quickly got up and recognizing Esmeralda's only sister, awkwardly tried to dry his eyes and said, "Hola, Anne Marie." He gave her a hug, and told her, "I'm so sorry... this is a tragedy."

He could not go on without getting choked up and decided to go to the cafeteria, he offered her a cup of coffee, Anne Marie said, "Yes, please I appreciate it... I was rushing to get over here... I was running late preparing my kids for school and then the traffic!... I just didn't have a chance to drink my coffee."

Roberto, "How do you like it?"

Anne Marie, "With sugar, black... yes not like she likes it, with sugar and definitely half and half, don't you dare give her black coffee..." They both smile simultaneously getting their eyes filled with tears of sadness. A few minutes later he came back with the beverages and Anne Marie firmly asked him, "Please, sit down, let's talk." Roberto and Anne Marie knew each other for years, she was a client to his business. He was feeling uncomfortable and afraid that she was going to inquire about what she saw when she quietly entered the room. His intuition was right on the mark, Anne Marie goes and tells him, "I think I know my sister very well and I know for sure she does not love her husband," nodding her head like saying, 'no, no!' Roberto was engrossed in her talk, she continued, "... and I know she is that type of woman who gets all excited when she smells romance... she is the euphemism of infatuation!" Roberto could not believe she was talking this way while his Esmeralda was there indefensible and mute. However, the clever little sister was not done making her point – the conversation was not over – and when she sensed he was trying to escape from her by the way he got up and was heading to reach his coat, she grabbed his arm, looked straight into his tired eyes, smiled at him and said, "Please, Roberto, sit down... I really need to know what's going on between you and my sister."

Roberto sighed a couple of times almost as if hyperventilating then sat down and said, "I love your sister with all my heart and she loves me." Anne Marie had this serious look on her face, those who did not know her well would think she was very angry, but in reality, that is the face she would put when she was speaking about something that she was passionate about and her sister's occult life was not a laughing matter to her. If you thought Esmeralda was a tough cookie, think again, Anne Marie was very different in character to Esmeralda, but they had in common their persistence in getting to the bottom of something and their perseverance in the process of making it happen.

So, she went on and asked, "For how long have you been seeing each other?"

Roberto, "Close to four years now... ever since we found each other again at your sister-in-law's funeral."

Anne Marie, "What are you saying... at Sofia's funeral?" She was momentarily surprised but not for long; this is the type of thing that Esmeralda would experience; this is the sort of situation that Esmeralda would strive on. She smiled and while holding her sister's hand told her, "Why were you so afraid to confide this to me? I thought there were no secrets between us." The truth is that Esmeralda sincerely thought that by leaving her out of her messy and complicated life situation she was doing her a favor; it occurred to Esmeralda that if her sister knew she was having an affair, she would be putting at risk her sister's own reputation; she reasoned that if she was ever discovered her little sister could end up being accused of covering her up and in this way, mar her untouchable integrity. You see, Anne Marie loved her husband very much, she did marry him when she was very in love with him and in spite of the fact her life has not been a nice path of flowers while joined to a guy who had a couple of previous relationships with women who conceived and brought to this world his children, but that he refused to marry, he obviously had a serious issue with commitment, so marrying Anne Marie was almost a miracle. Because of her husband's Peter Pan sort of personality and his lack of maturity in the love arena and on top of everything else his heavy drinking followed by his infantile and absurd annoying behavior while under the influence this was putting a toll on Anne Marie's emotional being. So yes, she would suffer humiliation and emotional hardships especially at the beginning of their hurried marriage, and amazingly they already have celebrated their fifteen-wedding anniversary. She endured with bravery and patience – that is, she assumed the position of the typical wife who eternally and unconditionally will love her husband until the end – Therefore, Esmeralda really believed that if she loved her sister, she should not do anything to jeopardize her solid marriage. Esmeralda really admired her sister and wished she could be able to emulate her strong and wise personality, her constancy in her feelings, her dedication to her 'undeserving' husband and her loving care of her children. Life can be so unpredictable sometimes, now Anne Marie was going to assume that role Esmeralda tried to prevent her to fulfill; she believed in Roberto's sincere and genuine love for Esmeralda and moreover she had a good vibe about him. Therefore, now she has become all of a sudden, his accomplice and Roberto has a friend to share with memories of his love, with whom to vent out his frustrations and cry together when it would turn out unbearable for him.

A face-to-face encounter

Early one Monday morning Roberto is sitting by Esmeralda's side in the hospital's room and as always tenderly gazing at every inch of her face and gently caressing her hands. Meanwhile outside the large glass this man abruptly stopped, stood by the window and looking surprised, inside he saw this strange scene; he was trying to figure out who the guy holding his wife's hands and looking at her like not even he would do it – not in ages, anyway – was. This Monday was a holiday, one of those not observed widely, but Valentino being a government employee got to enjoy many of them and the clueless Roberto did not even imagine it. When Valentino had the bravery to go in and find out something that was so undeniable therefore impossible to ignore all together, he goes and while quickly removing his jacket as if this piece of clothing was bothering him a lot, said, "Hello, I'm Valentino Vignota, Esmeralda's husband." Valentino extended his arm trying to reach Roberto's hand and the very surprised Roberto also extended his, they shook them. Valentino was probably giving this whole situation the benefit of the doubt; his wife had a huge number of relatives and he had not met half of them, so he thought that this guy might very well be one of her cousins that she talked fondly about on a few occasions. Valentino asked him, "Who are you?"

Roberto turned to see Esmeralda sort of asking her for help on how he should answer, but no reaction from her, he opens his mouth wide and he puts the palm of his hand all over his face and after pressing his fingers anchoring his mandible, said, "I don't mean any disrespect, I wished it wasn't like this… " Valentino is seriously and attentively waiting for Roberto to articulate the impromptu requested answer, Roberto, "That unresponsive and indefensible woman laying down there… I love that woman!" Valentino immediately puts his hand on his head, pressing his lower lips tight with his teeth and making a fist with his other hand, makes a sudden swirl as if by wanting to hit something, but he refrained himself. Roberto is just standing there as when a boxer is in the ring on guard, prepared to receive a hit.

Valentino all a sudden approached him grabbed his shirt and once very closed and face to face furiously told him, "Look! I want you to get the hell out of here and if I see you here again, I will ask for security to throw you out!" Roberto gathered his coat and hat and attempted to give her a goodbye kiss, but he was impacted by a quick force from his back and thrown to the floor.

Roberto slowly got up and when he finally was able to recover his balance amazingly calmly said, "I don't respond the same way out of respect for her, the circumstances and the place we are... Alright! I'll leave now, but know this... I won't give her up... what we had cannot be undone... I don't know whether you deserve her or not, all I know is she was immensely happy when she was with me." He left and Valentino stood there for a while very pensive and looking at her from a distance; he was upset and angry at her as expected, but what else could he do now? Esmeralda was unable to respond to him for her transgression and he continued to love her – in his own kind of way – in spite of all he just found out. In the end Esmeralda could not know how lucky she was to have two men loving her; a very ironic situation because she always had the tendency to believe she was incapable of being loved for real and forever by anyone.

A sudden awakening

That same day that Valentino discovered the truth and Roberto was forced to leave Esmeralda, something incredible happened, she woke up from her long dream of exactly two weeks and one day. Was it a mere coincidence or all the commotion between the two men in her life transcended to her unconsciousness and compelled her to come back to a world where she has left some unfinished business? Valentino is taking a sip of his third cup of coffee and reading the latest issue of his favorite computer technology magazine when he saw through the corner of his eye a movement, it was Esmeralda turning her head as if having a bad dream, so he went to her side and looking perplexed held her hand and yelled, "Esmeralda, Esmeralda, can you hear me?" She then opened her eyes while Valentino was like in a trance for a couple of seconds because he just stood there staring at her and she is looking at the ceiling and then side to side as if trying to figure out where she was and then she sees him. Valentino could not believe she was looking straight at him. When he got out of his astonishment, he got closer to her and said, "Esmeralda... you woke up, at last! I am so happy to have you back." He kissed and hugged her all the while she has not said anything; Valentino noticed she was acting oddly as if he were a stranger. So, he said, "Esmeralda, are you okay? I'm going to call the nurse," and he ran outside to the nurse station and filled with emotion exclaimed, "She is awoken... my wife is not unconscious any more... please come quickly!" The nurse quickly went into the room and found her sitting in bed.

Nurse, "Mrs. Vignota, how do you feel?"

Esmeralda, "Where am I? Is this a hospital? What happened?"

Nurse: "Mrs. Vignota, you suffered a car accident and were unconscious for a while."

Esmeralda was anxiously looking at everyone and stopped at Valentino and realizing he was not part of the clinical personnel, said, "Who are you?" Valentino took a deep breath and turning around as to hide his reaction burst into tears.

The nurse told her, "Mrs. Vignota, I will call the doctor right now, he needs to make an assessment and he will give you some answers... please wait just a bit... don't worry, you're in good hands here." The nurse hurried and paged the doctor on duty and he quickly came to the unit after knowing what had just happened. The whole medical team with the neurologist as the main medical professional arrived at the unit and analyzed her clinical profile and after carefully studying the MRI results came to the conclusion that Esmeralda was suffering a condition of hopefully temporary amnesia caused by major edema in her skull. Esmeralda's family sat down in the unit conference room to hear the prognosis and treatment to be followed for Esmeralda. The hardest part for her loved ones obviously was going to be how to approach her being that they were now complete strangers to her. Since Esmeralda was now in a perfect physical stable condition and conscious, she was discharged and transferred to a short-term rehabilitation facility near her home for her to benefit from physical and occupational therapy with the goal of acquiring her previous level of functioning.

If only from a distance

Anne Marie texted Roberto, 'Did you hear the good news yet?'.

Roberto, 'No, what is going on?'

Ann Marie, '"Esmeralda woke up'.

Roberto, 'Please call me we need to talk'. She called him and he says, "How is she doing?"

Ann Marie, "She is physically okay, but unfortunately she does not remember anything or any of us."

Roberto, "Oh! No, how is that possible?"

Anne Marie, "Yes, the doctors think it could be a temporary state of amnesia due to all the swelling she got to her head."

Roberto, "I'm dying to see her."

Ann Marie, "Frankly, I don't think it's a good idea since she does not remember anybody and she might not remember you either."

Roberto, "I understand, but I have to see her somehow even if just from a distance." Ann Marie informed him that the plan was for Esmeralda to finish recuperating in a place where she could strengthen her muscles and get stronger; she advised Roberto to not visit her there, fearing he might run into Valentino and create another scene and Esmeralda needed peace of mind and an ambient suitable for the betterment of her health. Roberto accepted Ann Marie's proposal with resignation and with great sorrow, but his desire to see his bella Esmeralda — if only from a distance, remained unchanged. Truth is that Roberto was not going to renounce to her great love and he was going to find a way to be close to her; he started planning in his head a strategy, it had to be perfect, so he would run it in his mind over and over again and modify it as he deemed it necessary.

The weeks turned into months and just like that it had passed two painful months since Esmeralda lost her memory. Roberto would be very busy working in his business and now he would dedicate even more hours in his work place and doing errands with the intention to distract his mind and by the time he got to his lonely apartment he just succumbed to his bed most of the time even without taking a shower. You could say that Roberto suspended his life as he had known it until the unfortunate accident and assumed a life where he would eat and satisfy other human basic necessities, but as far as taking care of his soul, his spirit that, he neglected. His appearance demonstrated the way he was feeling inside, a feeling of mental disarrangement because he did not comprehend how destiny could be so cruel to take her away from him so sudden, without warning. Roberto was fortunate enough to have Ann Marie on his side; she became his confident and when he saw her, he focused on the resemblance that both Esmeralda and her sister had and not on their differences. For Roberto being able to appreciate Ann Marie's mannerisms or body language and even the way she would look at him in a way that for a moment he saw his bella Esmeralda in her, was a source of solace, a way to relax his traumatized senses and dream she was there with him. Ann Marie also would clarify certain things that would bother him here and there. For instance, after their conversation about why he should not visit Esmeralda in the rehab, he was preoccupied with the potential consequences of Esmeralda's state of oblivion and the possibility of her husband taking advantage of this. Ann Marie told him in response to his worries the following story, "I will tell you my version of the story when Esmeralda got hooked up with Valentino... you see? She had experienced a terrible love disappointment those days... she would cry all the time and we could no longer stand to see her like that... one day Valentino came to our house, obviously to visit her because he was not a person known to the family other than Esmeralda and my father knew him from church and I and the rest of my family did not used to attend church. Esmeralda had gone to a youth camp in the mountains and Valentino was there as well; he approached her and started talking and sharing time together in the beautiful and isolated place; they sat by the big fire in the evening and sang songs, heard stories, while putting marshmallows on the fire. The problem with this scenario consisted on the fact that the perfect idiot, that imbecile that broke her heart was there too, he was right there in the human circle around the fire together with his new girlfriend, the one who he was seeing simultaneously with poor Esmeralda. So, these circumstances fomented a situation that forced Esmeralda to lean on Valentino and accept his company out of sheer spite because she was never in love with him and that became evident very soon, but me and my cousin could have a little bit of blame for Esmeralda ending up with a guy she did not love and could not love no matter how hard she tried."

Roberto, "What do you mean by you are to be blamed?"

Ann Marie, "Well, that night that he [Valentino] came uninvited to the house, my cousin and I were watching TV in the living room, heard the bell ring and there he was; I let him in and even though he didn't ask for her, we knew she was the only reason he had to be there. My father was in the kitchen table reading one of his spiritual books and Valentino went directly for it that is, he went and warmly greeted him and attentively listened to one of my father's usual and unsolicited sermons for a good while. It occurred to us [Ann Marie and her cousin, Emily] that maybe Esmeralda should get some distraction and what better way than go out and have fun with a guy, after all he was to be trusted, he was a regular member from her church. So, we went and practically dragged her out of her bedroom where she was still crying and told her that Valentino came to visit her to what she immediately and firmly objected with the argument, 'I don't want to see him, he is not even my type', we should have listened to her; she said right there the most truthful statement she has ever said in her life and we oversaw it, we did not pay attention, perhaps due to our desperation to do something to change her depressed state and take her out of that helplessness she was experiencing those days. Yes, we did manage to get her out of her hidden cave and interact with Valentino a little bit that night and that is how they started seeing each other."

Roberto, "Wow, that was interesting."

Ann Marie, "Do you see now why I feel kind of guilty?"

Roberto, "To be perfectly honest with you, I don't think it was your fault that she decided to go out with him, it was her prerogative and you did not force her to do so."

Ann Marie, "I know but if we had not created the environment for her to start knowing him and had listened to her plea to leave her alone, God knows what a different outcome her love life had turned out to have?"

Roberto, "Don't anguish yourself dwelling in the past,

especially when you don't know if anything you did or didn't would have made any difference, destiny has a strange way of arranging everything in one's life that one just can't foresee nor prevent, look at me... who would had thought that after two divorces I would madly fall in love just to lose her one day like this."

Ann Marie, "Don't say that... you have not lost her, she will get her memory back and her love for you as well, just be patient and wait a little bit longer, please. Esmeralda will need you once she is back to her reality... the purpose of telling you this story is so you could appreciate a little bit the fact that no matter what Valentino tries to do now, he won't be able to entice her to his arms; there was simply no attraction there and never will be." Indeed, Esmeralda was definitely going to be needing her love with her once again when she finally had returned from her trip to the forgotten land and had to face the same or worse world she left; she will need to resume her decision process, plans and actions to get independent from Valentino and try to be happy with the man that she loves; a major undertaking for sure, but that she should not prolong any more.

'The perfect couple'

Esmeralda was admitted to the Rehabilitation facility as planned and quickly made great progress on her path to going back to 'normal' at least as far as the basic activities we take for granted as walking and holding a fork. Valentino would go to visit her every evening, and this evening as he was waiting in front of the first-floor elevator to go to see Esmeralda on the sixth floor, the nurse on the unit was running to catch a ride and got in with him, Valentino said, "Hi! Coming to work? It's the change of shift, ah?"

Nurse, "Indeed it is… now the fun begins!" They smiled and the nurse said, "You know? I really enjoy watching you and your wife together, you get along so well, you are the perfect couple; it's unbelievable how some couples just fight all the time, they don't seem to agree on nothing at all."

Valentino, "Un uh!" How hilarious this clueless young woman sounded, the thing is that now Valentino and Esmeralda would treat each other totally different to the way they did prior to the accident, when Esmeralda was this woman who the years shaped into someone she did not like, she was certainly not proud of herself and secretly resented her husband for it. Another negative taking place before this couple's drastic life change consisted of Valentino's daily frustrations caused mainly by his failure to satisfy his wife – evident by the way she was with him and that made him so tired to the point of not even trying to gain his wife back that is if he ever got her. But now while Esmeralda's memory was being reset — sort of speaking, this allowed her to re-learn without her knowing how to deal with her husband, but now with no bias because all his 'failures' were deleted from her immediate memory, at least for now. So, in this surreal world, they now were courteous to each other and never argued, just like when couples who are getting to know each other would behave. You know, withholding their true take on certain issues to avoid controversy and displaying a nicer personality than their real ones, a fallacy. Valentino was enjoying this new Esmeralda; she was non-argumentative, stopped being 'so needy' — as he would think she was many times, albeit her partially physical disable temporary condition and now he had an opportunity to make her fall in love with him. That is what he thought, anyway. Truth is that they have not been intimate, not even a kiss so far. It looked like Esmeralda was just trying to be nice with this guy who she knew hardly anything about. It is funny because Valentino used to accuse Esmeralda of being so urbane with anybody from outside, especially when they were strangers, but him, she treated 'con la punta del pie' meaning 'to treat someone like dirt'. Esmeralda is now back home and Valentino is trying to impress her just like he did when they first started going out; she was so young and it was easier to catch her attention back then; now he will have a challenge or maybe Esmeralda still has that sensitive girl inside her. Valentino used to prepare special dishes for her as his main recourse when trying to conquer her heart; he might not have gotten her to love him for real, but he did get her to feel very special when she was so vulnerable and heartbroken. Will he be able to re-create that atmosphere and wake up in Esmeralda something beautiful, make her see him with different eyes to the way she has been doing for the last fifteen years?

Valentino is busy in the kitchen and it is smelling good; he has cooked for Esmeralda one of her favorite Italian dishes, linguine with vodka sauce and shrimp al ajillo; he set the table nicely and opened a bottle of white wine. They sat at the table, just the two of them because Valentino had arranged with his sister to stay with the kids for a couple of hours. Exactly the way he imagined, he asked Esmeralda, "Do you like it?"

Esmeralda, "Yes, are you kidding me? It's delicious... I absolutely love it!"

Valentino, "I'm so glad to hear that... that was the idea, that you liked it."

Esmeralda, "Thank you very much... this means a lot to me."

Valentino, "No! it's nothing... you deserve so much more than this." Esmeralda smiled at him and he saw this as a sign that she was opening her heart to him, so he took her hand and caressed it, but she retreated it slowly as if afraid to hurt his feelings.

They ate her favorite dessert – tiramisu – of course she did not remember that was the case, and as expected she enjoyed it very much; she then asked, "What is this I'm eating, it tastes like coffee, so interesting!"

Valentino, "I cheated, I knew you would like it because it is your favorite."

They both laughed and Esmeralda then said, "I am having a lot of fun, but I am really exhausted and would like to go to bed." Valentino faked to be perfectly okay with Esmeralda's early retirement from their special evening together and felt kind of disappointed in himself — the plan to dazzle her worked until a certain point, but the effects did not seem to last. The still hopeful husband did not desist from his obsession to create this different and improved image of himself in his wife's eyes; however, he was forgetting about something important, eventually Esmeralda was going to go back to being herself once she recovered her memory. She was going to remember the way he would look at her sometimes, when his face transformed into this savage looking animal; he would grind his teeth showing them all and his eyes would be fixed with an expression of hate so pronounced that made her cringe. He would become this fearsome creature whenever Esmeralda attempted to have a peaceful discussion about something she had in mind. Like this, 'Valentino, I was thinking that we are better off if I apply for bankruptcy to solve that problem with that old debt... '. Valentino, 'Don't... don't bother me now, I have enough in my head, can't you leave me alone for once?' That is how Valentino would try to shut her up just like that. Esmeralda then would get her blood boiling and would raise her voice, saying profanities in this way becoming that woman she hated so much; that woman who belongs in a psychiatric unit and she felt her nerves were so disturbed that this rendered her incapable of regressing to a calm state until hours later. Eventually, Esmeralda was going to see Valentino as her enemy and the one who has been sabotaging her happiness since forever, it feels like.

A beautiful spring Sunday morning, the Vignota family is having breakfast on the back deck of their semi-suburb house; Esmeralda is enjoying the soothing sun rays and contemplating the pink and purplish hydrangeas in her garden and she says, "Boy! I wish I could be an artist to draw what I am seeing right now."

Valentino, "I can draw... I could paint it for you."

Esmeralda, "For real? You are not kidding?"

Valentino, "Sure, I can do it... I will do it if that makes you happy." Exactly the same offering Valentino extended to Esmeralda way back when she was impressed by the fact, he was an artist of the small brush; she got to see a couple of his very old drawings and asked him to draw something for her. Fifteen plus years later she was still waiting, except for two simple pictures of flowers and fruits that he did in a hurry after Esmeralda's unending supplications; apparently, she wanted to save money on art and she needed some when they first moved to an apartment shortly after their marriage, and he also managed to work for a while on a couple smaller panorama pictures which remained unfinished. The bottom line is he did not bother or took time to give his wife this simple pleasure. What annoyed Esmeralda the most was Valentino's lack of motivation to create something beautiful with his talent and artistic skills; she could not understand why he wasted those beautiful sunny weekend mornings or those magnificent sunsets watching a silly movie or just taking a long and unnecessary nap. If she could recall the disdain that his apathy provoked in her every time, she wished Valentino dedicated time to do art at the time Valentino cordially insisted he could paint those beautiful flowers for her, she would sarcastically laugh at him. The thing is, he was obviously taking advantage of Esmeralda's accidentally imposed innocence, at least for the time being.

Attraction all over again.

Anne Marie invited Esmeralda for a latte in a nearby café, they sat on the outside tables because it was a nice afternoon and the ambient was just suitable for these sisters to do some catching up along with some silly conversations and remarks. As Esmeralda was ready to take the next sip of her delicious drink, she noticed this gentleman across her table looking straight at them; after a few more gazes, she knew it was not just a coincidence that she had been spotted by this interesting looking stranger. So, she curiously asked Anne Marie, "Don't look yet, when I give you the signal, turn around to see the guy behind you."

Anne Marie, "Esmeralda, who? What guy?"

Esmeralda, "The guy staring at us!"

Anne Marie, "Are you sure?"

Esmeralda, "I'm sure... I'm not fancying this... I want to know if you know him... perhaps we even know each other and I just don't remember him as I don't remember anybody!" Anne Marie did not want her to get too anxious and agreed to the plan, so when Esmeralda lifted up her cup, Anne Marie slowly and discreetly turned around and took a glance at the mysterious personality observing these two beautiful women. She then quickly turned her head to face Esmeralda and partially covering her mouth – a sign of surprise – confirmed her sister's lucky guess; Anne Marie told her that she indeed knew this man, so Esmeralda says, "Please, don't be bad... tell me all you know about him." Esmeralda was filled with curiousness waiting for her sister to start spilling the beans.

So, Anne Marie said, "You guys were introduced to each other by Emmanuel."

Esmeralda, "How come?"

Anne Marie, "They are good friends... Emmanuel is his daughter's godfather."

Esmeralda, "Wait a second... he has a daughter?"

Anne Marie, "Yes, from his previous marriage."

Esmeralda, "Oh, so he is divorced?"

Anne Marie, "Yes, my darling, twice."

Esmeralda, "Twice?"

Ann Marie, "What's the matter? What do you care?"

Esmeralda, "No, nothing... so tell me why if we know each other and obviously he recognized me he has not come over and greeted us?"

Anne Marie, "Oh! That's not a problem!" Anne Marie suddenly got up and went to Roberto's table while Esmeralda smiling kind of surprised followed Anne Marie with her eyes and with anxious anticipation. Ann Marie returned to Esmeralda holding Roberto's hand and he showing this huge smile, Ann Marie goes like this, "Esmeralda, I want you to meet Roberto."

He extended his hand to Esmeralda and still smiling said, "Hi! It's very nice to meet you! One more time."

Esmeralda is shaking inside for reasons behind her comprehension and replied, "I'm glad to meet you... I'm sorry I can't remember anything since that stupid car accident," said Esmeralda while striking her head with the palm of her hand as if reproaching herself.

Roberto, "No worries, Anne Marie told me all about it… the important thing is that you are here with us and in good health."

Esmeralda, "Would… Would you like to sit down with us for a little bit… that is if you don't have to go or do anything…" Esmeralda was kind of nervous and it showed in the way she was stammering and playing with her hair.

The three of them got comfortable, Esmeralda looked at Anne Marie with this expression as if saying: 'what now?', so Anne Marie interpreting her sister's gesture went to her rescue and said, "Roberto, please tell Esmeralda how you both met."

Roberto without any hesitation went and stated, "It was a beautiful sunny summer day and your brother had taken us to the park so we, the witnesses of his wedding could have pictures taken with him and his new wife, right after we left the Municipal Court."

Esmeralda, "So you mean to say that we are 'los padrinos' in Emmanuel's wedding?"

Roberto, "Yes, indeed we are… we are attached by a holy link." They cracked a smile and Roberto continues, "So, when Emmanuel goes and says, meet my sister, Esmeralda, I was totally shocked because I never saw so much beauty all in a single woman."

Esmeralda started laughing nervously; she tried to belittle that last part of his remark and said, "Oh! Aren't you exaggerating just a little bit?"

Roberto, "No! not at all… on the contrary, like you told me once, I'm a man of few words… unlike you, I am not good with words and I wish I could be able to express half of the things you are capable of provoking in me."

Esmeralda opted for ignoring this last bold phrase this man

said to her and asked, "So... I said that you were a man of a few words? Why would I tell you such a thing?" Esmeralda's face was saying something like: 'Why am I feeling this way with you? What is this warm feeling traveling throughout my whole body? Why my stomach is all in knots? Who is this guy in reality?' It seems that Esmeralda was experiencing this attraction for her Roberto all over again as if she was programmed to always feel the same thing for him no matter what happens; so even when her brain was rebooted somehow it managed to detect previous deep feelings and sensations that at some point were directed to him and generated in her by him. The truth is that Anne Marie and Roberto had confabulated together to meet at the same place and time so Esmeralda could meet Roberto and 'see what happens?' Their efforts to ignite a spark in Esmeralda once she met him was a total success; all Roberto needed to do now was simply continue to be himself and everything was going to eventually fall in its proper and due place, or so they presumed.

A nostalgic place

Esmeralda went jogging as she used to early in the morning after the kids were gone to school and day-care respectively; but this time she chose a different place for her exercise routine. Esmeralda had flashbacks of many years back – before she was even married – of this huge and beautiful park located in the outskirts of the old city she spent most of her youth and decided to go there to relax. She was also hopeful that perhaps since she is remembering that place it could help her remember more things and who knows, she could finally gain her precious memory back. After running for a mile or so, she stopped to rest and as she was contemplating the green fauna and the richness of the different variety of stones found everywhere, she spotted an antique looking building, so she decided to get closer to appreciate it even better. Esmeralda got distracted, enticed by the serenity and organic sounds that only undisturbed nature, even if partially, could provide and while looking at the wonder scene – consisting of sun rays filtering through the very tall tree's branches, birds trying to secure their nests, and all the natural elements and the man made as well, harmoniously hanging from the magnificent blue clear sky and white soft clouds – she blindly tried to walk up the stone stairs leading to the main entrance of this mysterious castle when she almost stumbled into someone. Still looking down trying to regain her balance, she saw the feet of a man who grabbed her by her waist as if attempting to prevent her from falling backwards, she then looked at him and he smiled and said, "Hola mi vida... I'm so glad I was here to hold you... truth is I would hold you in my arms forever if you only wished." This last part he only said it in his mind. Esmeralda could perceive Roberto's tone of voice and demeanor as way too familiar and tried to ignore his affected kind of talk; perhaps because she was afraid to embarrass herself by realizing later, she was mistaken about what she felt and heard.

"Roberto! What are you doing here? I didn't see you; I was... "

Roberto, "... You were immersed in all the beauty surrounding us, you being one of them!" Esmeralda looked at him and frowning her face, sort of asking herself why Roberto was addressing her that way; it was so obvious he was utilizing a romancing tone and choice of words.

Esmeralda could not repress her inquisitive side any longer and when she was sure that she was not misinterpreting his signals then told him, "Why do I get this sense that you are trying to woo me?... You know I'm a married woman, don't you?"

Roberto, "Yes, I am very well aware of that." Roberto did not say more and his eyes wandered around for a minute; Esmeralda took his quiet response as a sign that her talk affected him in ways that she could not understand right then but nonetheless the change in his mood from sheer enthusiasm to sadness were noticeable. Esmeralda decided to curb her curiosity and just use this moment to get to know this guy in another way, hoping to find the reason behind her prohibited attraction for him.

Esmeralda is looking up admiring the more than a century-old Medieval Revival architecture of the castle which was seated on a rocky mountain and one could see from there the whole city of Paterson plus all the other bordering towns and cities. A gentle breeze is playing with her hair and Roberto is once again doing something he enjoyed doing a lot, he was letting her do most of the talking while he was looking at her as if she were the most beautiful thing there was and as though nothing else mattered. Esmeralda is moving around in the same place and using her hands a lot – words were deficient to express what she needed to say – exaggerating her facial expressions in a particular own kind of way and taking a glance all-around said, "I don't get it… I feel kind of nostalgic in this place… and it isn't just the normal melancholic feeling such a historical place would conjure, it is more than that… it feels like I was here before and experienced things, but I just don't remember what…" She then turned around and looked at him just the way she used to, making herself irresistible in his eyes; she looked so innocent and yet coquettish. She seemed to be waiting for his insight – what he thought of the place.

Roberto noticing her tacit inquiry then said, "Yes! I think I know what you mean… because I kind of feel the same way…" and while they are still standing there, face to face, he gently combed her hair from her face with his fingers, and when they were both smiling to each other as though enchanted by the tangible still standing remembrances of an era past, he kissed her. It was one of those seemingly eternal kisses they would give to each other.

Right after this kiss there were no questions, no verbal remarks, they just continued holding hands and looking at each other's eyes for a good while; Esmeralda hesitated to question what took place fearing breaking these magical moments that might not come back again, however, sooner or later she had to confront her fears and assume her responsibilities, so she went ahead and asked him about a 'suspicion' she had, "Roberto, we were having an affair before the accident... weren't we?"

Roberto, "Mi vida! Are you getting your memory back?" He jumped and laughed thinking that he finally got her back, but his jubilation was short-lived; Esmeralda was just considering the possibility of a prior relationship with him after having analyzed his behavior with her and his 'coincidental' appearances to the places she frequented.

Esmeralda, "No, I wish... it's just that the way I feel when you look at me and talk to me reveal something hard to deny, an attraction that is trapping me and I don't even feel the need to escape."

Roberto, "That's my Esmeralda... I missed her so much!"

Esmeralda quickly diverted away from the conversation, realizing that she was walking on shaky land, so she asked him, "By the way, how did you know that I would be here today?"

Roberto, "Anne Marie..."

Esmeralda, "Anne Marie? Is she your accomplice? My sister! no way."

Roberto, "Why not, your sister is a great person and she

loves you very much! Your plan to come here just came up in our conversation this morning; she said you were asking her how to get here."

Esmeralda, "No wonder she just dropped me and gave me the pretext that she needed to do something that could not wait."

Roberto being such a resilient guy was able to come back to earth even after noticing Esmeralda's coldness compared to her usual warmth, so he said, "It's okay, I will wait whatever time is necessary for you to recover your memory... but at least now I know you still feel for me something even though you are not able to recall any of our times together."

Esmeralda, "Were there many of those times?"

Roberto, "Yes, at least a couple of times per month, Well... I know that's not much, but that was what we could afford at the time. We saw each other in my modest apartment and there we were very happy... You used to tell me: 'Please, amor, help me get going... I don't want to go... but if you throw me away, I will have no choice but to leave'."

Esmeralda, "That sounds so silly."

Roberto, "I wish we could go back in time... I really miss you in my lonely place."

Esmeralda held a surprise sigh and taking a glance at her smart phone said, "Where time goes? I need to get going." Roberto accompanied her to the main road where she was going to wait for Anne Marie to pick her up. Roberto offered her to give her a ride home, but she did not accept and asked him, "Please leave me here... we should not risk people seeing us together... especially just the two of us."

Roberto, "It did not bother you that much before..."

Esmeralda, "What do you mean... that I did not care if people saw us?"

Roberto, "No, I'm sorry I guess I was remembering one time when you told me: 'Amor, I really enjoy walking on the streets holding hands together... it makes me feel as if we were a normal couple... it really feels so good!'.

Esmeralda, "We used to walk on the streets holding hands?"

Roberto, "Well... it was late at night and those streets were mostly filled with factories and business buildings which by that time were already closed... I live in a downtown apartment."

Esmeralda, "This is a little overwhelming for me and..."

Roberto interrupted her and said, "I understand... It's a lot to have to assimilate all at once... I will leave you alone, please just call me if you need my help... or if you want anything, anything at all!" Esmeralda smiled at him – sort of out of pure courtesy – turned around and walked away while he stood there watching her disappear on the curving mountain road.

Trying to find out who she really was

Esmeralda stepped into a hidden walking closet at her house one day, and discovered a couple of cartoon boxes filled with old albums, papers with writings on them and other memorabilia. She started to read some loose old papers, they were romantic poems and songs written by a female and directed to a man. She was truly impressed by what she read; some of the papers had the author's name on the bottom of the last page, her name. She could not believe she wrote those things, things like: 'So many people passing me by, but you don't appear... I'm feeling very lonely here, thinking that nothing could ever be the same, because you estranged from our beautiful sunsets and now, I need to succumb to the idea that our kisses and me... you plumb forgot... ' Who is this mysterious woman? When and why did she write these things? Who and what circumstances triggered her to convey such deep feelings and the way she did? She had all these questions. She continued trying to find herself in that little room, sitting on the floor, a tall mirror on the back of the shut door and which she could not avoid and browsing curiously the hundreds of photo pages, most of them containing her kids' birthday parties and other significant events. Then she found on the bottom of one of the boxes a smaller white and well-kept box, she opened it and saw on the cover of this white album a picture of this young and happy looking woman in a wedding dress; she was the bride. As she continued studying these photos, she started all of a sudden having these flashbacks of her entering the church on the arm of her father and looking at all these eyes fixed on her. She got so scared, she did not understand why she did and then she remembered something; she was sitting on the white sand of a beautiful shore crying and then she is transported to a hospital where she is straining trying to push something out of her, one of her babies. Yes, Esmeralda was finally remembering everything, now she was going to know who that woman in the mirror was or perhaps this was just half-way true since she did not have the answer to that question before she lost her memory. Perhaps, she was soon going to regret getting back and having to face Valentino now that he knew her big secret, only that she was not aware he already knew that. Esmeralda was still trying to connect all the loose ends; the way she felt with Roberto and the way she felt with Valentino. Too different type of feelings, how was she going to withstand the currents of tormenting thoughts and anguish that her constant ambivalence and fears would produce?

That evening when Esmeralda and her family gathered to have dinner, she was pretty much aloof; she was not asking the typical questions she would ever since she came back home with a deleted hard-drive as a brain, you know, things like: 'So, what do you guys usually do at this time?', or 'What's your favorite type of ice cream?' There were no sparks in her eyes any more because everything around her stopped being novel and all of a sudden turned into the same old same, the mundane and the boring. She saw her husband with the very same eyes she saw him before the accident that is, with that desire to run away from him and undo the knots that kept her attached to him. But how could she do that without dragging her kids together with the mud slough her life could hardly contain any more? She would try to put anew the pieces of the complicated puzzle that her life is, in their right places. She needed to decide what to do with Roberto, should she relinquish to that love flame that was going to divide her family or hold on to him as her last chance to be happy? Esmeralda went back to be the same Esmeralda, the doubtful, the fearful and above of all the unhappy one. Or perhaps she just needed to see Roberto and feel secured and loved in his arms again.

Soon after Esmeralda got her memory back, she would change her mind from one moment to the next. At one point, she was seriously thinking that her accident could have been that sign that she always wanted in order to decide what to do with her life. So, now she is sort of having a contrite heart, she is leaning toward resignation and pure abnegation to her family, no room for self-pity, self-denial would serve her better. Was she going through a stage? A change of heart caused by a near-death experience? And then return to the old woman inside her, the one who resists settling for a simplistic life deprived of passion and true love? As Esmeralda is slowly and steadily remembering her past, she is trying to keep it to herself for as long as she can; she cannot deal with her family one more time shifting gears emotionally as they find out that she is going back to normal as far as her memory is concerned. She is learning in the process of remembering how to readapt to her new old-life, it is not easy for her because she has been a curious tourist in her own home for a while; that was way better than all of a sudden being well aware of every single issue or problem she had been fortunate enough to put off for a while without even realizing it. But now her respite is about to end and she would react to daily events and circumstances such as this when she confronted her oldest daughter at an instant when she unconsciously got in an autopilot mode, "So, Emma Natasha, did you finish the social study assignment that is due tomorrow? Please don't procrastinate as you usually do... you know you cannot afford to have points taken off for submitting it late because you did not do well in the last two marking periods... your average will simply not add up!"

Emma and Valentino were left speechless for a moment and then Emma exclaims, "Mammy, your memory is back, you are talking to me exactly the same way you used to before the accident!"

Valentino, "Is it possible, do you really remember everything now?" Esmeralda is hesitating to answer them and looking somewhat pensive asked to be excused as she gets up from the table and retreats to her bedroom. Valentino and her confused daughter looked at each other shrugging their shoulders and wondering what was going on with her.

Esmeralda is sad to rediscover that older self and realized that great part of her is just this kind of melodramatic woman who switches from a sweet lady to a 'bitch' in a matter of seconds. How can anyone stand her? How can she live with so much bitterness in her system without collapsing? She is reflecting on the scene that had just taken place at the dinner table; why she goes and reacts that way immediately after getting

274

her memory back? Should not she have something nice and positive to say to her family? Something along the line of: 'I am so glad to have you with me and grateful that I am now able to remember all of you and our past times together', but, no she did not say that. Again, she is extremely busy tormenting and overthinking her life and where she wishes to be, a place remote from what she knows; it is the most selfish thing to think even though it is just a passing thought. Now she is trying hard to come to terms with her disorganized, scattered and unstable feelings. Esmeralda is having an internal conflict that of whether to remove Roberto out of her map and finding a substitute activity to take over and help her survive her every day's depressive moments. Maybe she was using Roberto as a way out, an outlet to divert her frustrations, maybe after all, she was confused thinking she loved him and in actuality he was just a means to isolate her mind from the monotonous and tedious days of her life.

Who is that woman in the mirror? She is a very brave woman, but she does not know it; it takes courage to get up from bed every day in spite of feeling totally out of sync with one's reality; having sorrow as your ever-present companion and when happiness finally knocks on your door if just to stay momentarily, you feel guilty and totally unworthy of it. It could be that the religious concepts or doctrines if you will greatly and inevitably shaped Esmeralda's thoughts to such an extent that even when she departed from that pious life and decided to ignore the norms and rules she learned since she could ever remember, they were still scratching her conscious. Esmeralda used to hear often through sermons or even casual conversations a passage of the Holy Scriptures that says: 'No man can serve two masters: for either he will hate the one, and love the other; or else he will hold the one, and despise the other. You cannot serve God and mammon'. [Matthew 6:24, KJV]. Esmeralda learned to love God at an early and tender age and the way she knew how to love him was by being faithful to his word – not just obeying his commands in a legal kind of way, that would connote something different – yes the bible is filled with urgencies to follow God's commands, but Esmeralda understood that when one loves God you would walk in this world according to his ordinances, happily – meaning one would behave out of love and not fear and act God-like – and you would know how God is through his son, Jesus Christ, who being God himself was also a man at the same time and therefore could show us his father's character and demonstrated that another human being could also imitate him. Now Esmeralda is not happy because 'she stopped loving God', she arrived to this conclusion based on her definition of 'loving God', she still wanted to love him but was unable to do so. The reality is that she is not enjoying this world without her God. So, she is in a sort of state of limbo and it has been established already that one is either with God or against him. She feels a deep void in her soul, heart and mind that no one could ever fill. Perhaps that woman in the mirror got lost a long time ago when she abandoned her faith, the only life she knew and the only way she could ever find peace in her heart. How could it be that after submerging so deep into the dark ocean of incredulity and spiritual glacier, she still feels a little, tiny something in the most remote corner of her mind that is calling her, persuading her to come back to 'the admirable light, the source of all life'? At least this is still true for her even though she would not admit it. This is the way she feels, but she does not acknowledge it. Perhaps, it is true another spiritual thought she was also exposed to very often: 'When a person rejects the voice of the Holy Ghost for too long [exactly the lapse of time not known] this person will eventually be left alone by it [the Holy Ghost] abandoned to their own fate'. If one were to believe this concept then one could conclude that Esmeralda might just have rejected that voice in her conscious for so long that she is now incapable of softening her heart because there is no one whispering 'good' thoughts in her ears. All she is able to think and therefore do is carnal and scarcely spiritual; she has no influence from above and is attached to the secular and the profane, so she has been left alone with her own bitterness and frustrations. I dare to say all these things mentioned and the following as well merely in light of Esmeralda's deep, deep, inculcated spiritual teachings. The real woman in the mirror might be dormant, in such a spiritual stupor that she needs an external and superior force to awaken her, to bring her back to live among the living, those who still see the glass half-full, appreciate the beautiful roses while ignoring their thorns, and who, yes, still love their creator above all things and in spite of all the adversities this world might provide them with.

Her odious look

Esmeralda decided to re-unite with Roberto and talk, so she contacted him through Anne Marie since she had lost her phone with all the contacts in the accident and did not remember his numbers, not his cell, home, or his business. They got together in a café, she refused to visit him at his apartment perhaps with fear she would end up doing something she was going to regret later on. After letting him know that she had recovered her memory and allowing him some time to celebrate, she goes like this, "Roberto, I asked you to meet here because I think we need to define our situation…"

Roberto, "Mi vida, you sound the way you used to talk about

'the situation with your husband'... Am I sensing you don't love me any more?"

Esmeralda, "I don't want to do this to him any more... I don't even want to imagine how he would take this... and my family... how could I forgive myself if they hate me for breaking up our home?"

Roberto, "Esmeralda, you are wrong... "

Esmeralda, "No, I was wrong to stay with you in such an unhealthy relationship!"

Roberto, "So, now you're calling it 'unhealthy'?" Esmeralda swallowed hard and he continued his argument, "Your husband knows about us... he is just pretending not to know, God knows why."

Esmeralda, "What are you saying? Valentino knows I'm having an affair with you?"

Roberto, "Yes, he caught me holding your hands in that hospital room and I had no choice but to admit to him my love for you."

Esmeralda, "Are you crazy... couldn't you just come up with anything else? How could you do that to me?"

Roberto, "Mi vida, what is important is that he already knows and he is fine, don't you understand? Now we could have a real chance to be happy together... now you can ask him for the divorce."

Esmeralda, "Let me see if I'm hearing you correctly? You're telling me now to ask him for a divorce? You, who wouldn't mind sharing me with him."

Roberto, "I thought I had clarified that issue to you before... of course I was jealous to know you would go and sleep in the same bed with him... but I did not want to force you to do anything, to rush through something so delicate and personal... I told you that before."

Esmeralda, "Yes, and I pretended to buy it… the truth is that I was very disturbed to know that you did not love me sufficiently as to jump with happiness when I told you I was thinking about divorcing him… How do you think that made me feel?"

Roberto, "Why didn't you confront me this way back then? Why now?"

Esmeralda, "Look! I don't know what will happen with my life now… I need to go." Esmeralda grabbed her bag and got up quickly, Roberto did the same and attempted to stop her by holding her elbow, but she looked at him in a serious way and he gathered from her odious look he had to let her go.

Roberto was in pure anguish, the way she looked at him, he could not get that look out of his mind. "What happened that changed her so drastically?" he was wondering and could not believe that now that she was able to remember how happy they were – or was she? – She would react so cold and angry at him; was he now the one to be blamed for her troubles? Poor man, it is not a good thing to fall out of grace with Esmeralda because she is capable of despising with the same intensity as she loves. Or it could be that now Esmeralda is so angry at herself that she is being forced – as a result of a self-inflicted punishment of some weird sort – to detach from the man who is capable of loving her. Roberto started to lose hope that Esmeralda would come back to him one day. He would hesitate to even attempt to see her again, not if it meant having to bear the disdain that she seems to have for him now and he does not have the slightest idea why. Roberto got to his sad place filled with resignation, ever since he lost her for the first time, he never thought of giving her up. But now he has finally decided to let her fly away. Who knows, if she still loves him, she will come back because a bird that is used to being caged and tenderly cared for, would not be able to survive on its own for long. Esmeralda knew happiness with him; she experienced unending pleasures with him and that could not be unlearned that easily.

Sleeping with the enemy?

Esmeralda is acting strangely; she is awfully quiet and has not contradicted her husband, not once. Valentino came home from work earlier than usual and cooked one of his interesting dishes for dinner; everything seems to be fine in this household which has passed through very tough times lately; imagine the kids missing her at bedtime and her father gone for hours when he was visiting her at the hospital instead of coming home directly from work. Esmeralda thought about this and she was admiring Valentino's calm disposition during hard times. At the table, she would take a glance at him once in a while like trying to get a hint of how Valentino is feeling now that he 'knows'. She feels embarrassed and awkward in her husband's presence even though she knows he does not know she knows he knows. What a predicament she is in this time! A lot of things are making nests in her head; for one thing, it crossed her mind: "What if he is just waiting for the right moment to avenge me?" but other times she would say to herself: "I wouldn't have thought in one million years that Valentino would forgive me for doing something like betraying him so badly like I did... does that mean he loves me more than what I ever was able to even imagine? Oh God! What's going on?" She was more confused than ever, her husband's unexpected or should I say? 'bizarre' behavior was not helping her. How could Esmeralda know for sure if her husband's noble attitude was genuine or if she was sleeping with the enemy?

While I was gone

It is a gorgeous Sunday morning and about to become a glorious day for Esmeralda due to this single but yet peculiar occurrence; "Esmeralda, I have a surprise for you!" Valentino said enthusiastically.

Esmeralda, "Oh Yes! What is it?" Valentino suddenly showed her a large rectangular shaped thing wrapped in brown paper that he was trying to hide behind his back. She is looking at it with a smile and then ran and grabbed it. She quickly opened it; It was a drawing of an old bridge located in close proximity to their neighborhood and this river would transport her to childhood pastimes she enjoyed in another river shore in the countryside of her native land. The river in Valentino's picture had maple trees' branches that provided a cozy green canopy in spring and a few duck families had their homes there. In this picture of a small antiquated bridge but that still functioned well Valentino incredibly depicted that sentiment that she wanted him to bring in the drawing; it came out picturesque displaying the old greenish color of the bridge with most of the paint coming off and underneath showing proudly the rusty metal that time and nature allowed to happen like they always do with everything else. The bridge in this painting showed a scene of a rainy day and one could appreciate the whitish and reddish cars' lights in motion like running away — a natural special effect produced by the rain; one cannot tell weather is early morning or around sunset — one could say this picture is timeless due mostly to the fog and lack of sunshine. The old wood-light-pole which was lucky enough to shed a dim light and located right at the entrance of this old thing complemented that feeling of tranquil country scenery that Esmeralda longed for and now could go back to through a painting hanging on her living room's lonely wall.

"When did you do this painting, Valentino?" asked curiously Esmeralda.

"While you were... "

Esmeralda noticing, he was looking for a word to finish his sentence, finished it for him "... gone, while I was gone."

Valentino, "Well, I couldn't say you were gone because I always felt your presence in every corner of our home." Esmeralda kept looking at him with this particular smile as though she did not know exactly what to think about this new Valentino, nevertheless she now likes him. What is happening, the way Valentino is behaving is what Esmeralda only wished it could happen and now as it was a miracle, she is able to experiment that part of her husband that she tried in vain for so long to awaken in him. And more importantly, Valentino is being incredibly spectacular with her even though he discovered her long-time infidelity. So, now Esmeralda feels compelled to remedy the situation, to give an explanation of her acts at least. But she is cognizant that it will take more than an apology on her part; actually, what can she say to justify her irresponsible and filthy actions? Nothing at all because this is a case where the afflicted one either accepts the situation, forgives and tries to forget or would do exactly the reverse of this. It seems Valentino was able and willing to grant his forgiveness to the only woman in his life since forever, it seems anyway, and way before she would seek it. This in and of itself should mean a huge deal to Esmeralda. If his unselfish behavior does not win her over, what will? This couple now has a new and fresh avenue to mend their past failures and invent a way to live in harmony by giving each other all the hidden goodness they sure must have and leave out their cheap pride. Esmeralda's proximity to that dark side that no human being seems to know anything about should be a starting point. It should mean the end to all vain and cruel remarks, purposeless actions and plain waste of so much precious time. It should…

Numb

One of those in-home movies' nights, after the kids went to bed, Valentino and Esmeralda were laying down in bed watching the huge screen on the white wall from a projector. They allowed themselves to be submerged into the romantic atmosphere the story conveyed and at one point Esmeralda asked him out of the blue, "Valentino, when was exactly that you stopped loving me?" Valentino laughed kind of surprised and she assured him, "No, it's not a tricky question… really I am curious to know when that happened?" she went and insisted in a very calm and subdued tone of voice.

Valentino, "I never stopped loving you… it's just that you distanced yourself from me, you put a barrier between us, it felt as if you were hating me."

Esmeralda, "That's probably because you would treat me as if I were a crazy woman, you would ignore me or simply make me feel so undeserving of anything… don't ask how you would do that… it has been so impregnated in our daily lives that it eventually became one with nature."

Valentino started reminiscing of very old times when they first started going out; Esmeralda was this clueless skinny young woman in her early twenties and he goes and says, "I will never get out of my mind that breath-taking girl… you were wearing these tight skinny burgundy jeans that accentuated those beautiful curves and laughing while your curly hair was uncontrollably beautiful that fall afternoon."

Esmeralda, "Really? You remember those jeans, I know! I

used to wear them often… my ass is ten times larger now."

Valentino, "You are still beautiful to me." Esmeralda sighed and looked up to the ceiling sort of wondering where time went and how they got to this point in their lives. She is not feeling desperately unhappy, but she is not feeling a sense of complete satisfaction with life either, not even close. She is kind of numb and wishing something could make her feel again, feel anything, feel a desire to go back to that girl who had so many dreams and imagined herself loved like one of those female protagonists in a Spanish soap opera she used to indulge with. Having Valentino next to her and he trying to bring old memories back served only to make her realize that nothing could be like before; and by before, I meant those few seconds of the infatuation Esmeralda experienced back when she started getting to know Valentino. Esmeralda is cognizant that they had gone way too far and things could not be undone, forgotten. They had sex that night and Esmeralda felt it was so mechanical the way they did it. Actually, she never knew another way with him; she hardly ever enjoyed it, but it seemed that he never realized this. However, this time around Esmeralda had a point of comparison, her body and soul remembered how she felt when being loved by her Roberto. She would have flashing images of when she made love to him and they were light years away different to what she was experiencing right then; she just felt this heavy load on top of her chest that was asphyxiating her and this feeling left her incapable of moving, she just wanted it to be over. They were used to treating each other so badly that the next day when they went back to their normal routine, they quickly and unconsciously assumed their respective roles of being alternating a victim and / or a torturer. So, they were going to be enemies until death or maybe until they finally agreed to terminate their irreparable marriage.

There is an old Spanish song by the tittle: 'Para Vivir', interpreted by Sonia Silvestre, she was a very talented singer in The Dominican Republic, now diseased. This song was a hit when Esmeralda was a teenager back in her native country that for some reason she would sing or just hum it once in a while over the years. It goes like this:

https://www.youtube.com/watch?v=7kVkz6Tz2zI
[Sonia Silvestre, Para Vivir]

Muchas veces te dije que antes the hacerlo
Había que pensarlo muy bien,
Que a esta unión de nosotros
Le hacía falta carne y deseo también.
Que no bastaba que me entendieras
Y que murieras por mí,
Que no bastaba que en mi fracaso
Yo me refugiara en ti.

Y ahora ya ves lo que pasó
Al fin nació, al pasar de los años,
El tremendo cansancio que provoco ya en ti,
Y aunque es penoso lo tienes que decir.

Por mi parte esperaba
Que un día el tiempo se hiciera cargo del fin,
Si así no hubiera sido
Yo habría seguido jugando a hacerte feliz.

Y aunque el llanto es amargo piensa en los años

Que tienes para vivir,
Que mi dolor no es menos y lo peor
Es que ya no puedo sentir.

Y ahora tratar de conquistar
Con vano afán este tiempo perdido
Que nos deja vencidos sin poder conocer
Eso que llaman amor,
Para vivir
Para vivir....

The lyrics of this song worked in her mind as if she knew all along, since she was very young and single that one day, she more than likely would end up living the essence of this precise song. I will try to translate it, but some meaning might get lost in translation.

In Order to Live

Many times, I told you that before doing it
We had to think about it really well,
That this union of us
Was missing flesh and desire as well.
That it was not enough your understanding
And that you were willing to die for me,
That it was not enough that in my frustrations
I could take refuge in you.

And now you already can see what happened
At last, it came to be, after the years have passed,
I cause you to feel a tremendous fatigue
And even though it is shameful,

you have to say it.

On my part I hoped
That one day time would take care of the end,
If that had not been so,
I would have continued pretending
Making you happy.

And even though it is a bitter weep,
Think about the years that you still have to live,
That my pain is no less and the worst is
That I am not longer able to feel,
And now trying to conquer
With a vain urgency
This lost time
That leave us defeated without knowing
That which they call love,
In order to live
In order to live...

The value we attach to things

Seven months went by and now the Vignota's home is upside down; the house they bought a few years ago was a fixer-upper kind of house and Esmeralda has wanted to start the process of 'beautifying' it for a long time. Esmeralda is talking with the contractor when Valentino found her in flagrante. "I'm thinking of putting nice wood panels, you know, those with square or rectangular boxes... very high ones all around the dining room walls."

Valentino, "What are you talking about, Esmeralda? I thought we were doing the hardwood floors, and now you want the celling re-done, plus new walls and who knows what else?"

Esmeralda answered with this embarrassing smile, "I am just telling him an idea I have [signaling with her hand the worker up on the ladder]... you know, asking for his advice."

Valentino, "What about the budget... do you have an idea how much that is?"

Esmeralda now sounding really annoyed, "As usual... so typical of you, you don't want to plan anything or discuss anything with me... if only you would listen, you would realize that I am not asking for a lot; the panels I am thinking about are not that expensive and not only they would make this room sophisticated but the walls would be more durable." They are having this argument in front of the guy while failing to take heed of an unmistakable sign of social embarrassment – the redness on the outsider's face – Esmeralda removed herself from the room and left the two guys alone to discuss 'male issues', mostly money. After the contractor left, the dispute over their home sort of renovation between Valentino and Esmeralda continued; Esmeralda, "Why do you always try to embarrass me in front of strangers like that?"

Valentino, "Why do you embarrass me? Why don't you ask how much things cost to be built your way? Their labor is not free... you know."

Esmeralda, "We will always live as miserable people... "

Valentino, "You will always be miserable no matter what because you're never satisfied with anything... you always want more, more!... We are not rich! You know?" Esmeralda left the room so upset she was about to burst into tears but did not want to appear fragile in front of him.

You guessed it! Things after a while returned to the usual series of emotional turmoil for Esmeralda. Contrary to what her husband thinks of her – a woman with this unquenchable desire for material stuff, a money vacuum machine, and an unrealistic above-the-clouds dreamer – in the end, Esmeralda just wanted to create an atmosphere around them that was warm, fresh and inspiring; a place where she could get up every day and be able to enjoy a cup of coffee sitting down on a strong — not on a lose leg chair, getting lost in the beauty of a piece of art instead of staring at a hole in the wall, yes that sort of things. Esmeralda was not clueless about the importance of sticking to a budget, but she did not believe that having even ten thousand dollars sitting in a vogue while they did not have a decent stove to cook with was smart. That saying that one should save for a rainy day made absolutely no sense to her since every day was practically a rainy day for her. One thing that could have saved them from quarreling and the verbal cruelty they would inflict on each other was that of 'listening'. Why Valentino could not for once shut his mouth and hear her plan? Quietly let his wife put all her visionary beautifying work out in the open? That single action would have helped her feel at ease by releasing so much tension and anxiety even when perhaps only half of what she envisioned for their home to be was going to actually be accomplished. Esmeralda sadly realized that Valentino never ceased to be that dream annihilator, that insensitive guy who would inflict her with pain to the bones because his smart-ass remarks made her feel so cheap as a person, an idiot, totally alone with her frustrations and devastating spiritual misery. Esmeralda did not value things for their intrinsic worth but she thought that when she chose an object to be utilized at home, it had the potential of acquiring a place and a purpose; things are valuable when we make them valuable because they eventually become an important part of one's household. After all, don't we all attach feelings, memories and meaning to things around us? Especially those things we need in order to live in a comfortable, clean, civilized manner and not less important, at least in Esmeralda's view those things that are aesthetically indispensable. If the old adage: 'The eyes are the windows to one's soul' is true then Esmeralda does well in wanting beauty displayed in her home maybe this would influence greatly her mood in a positive and happy way. Sure, Valentino wanted beautiful things as well, but that was not a priority for him; well, it was for Esmeralda.

What made Esmeralda think that anything at all could change between them? How was it possible that Valentino was going to forgive her and go on with their lives as if nothing happened? A living hell that is what she should have expected; now Valentino is suspicious all the time and treats her like another piece of furniture in the house; he ignores her except to get her to satisfy his natural basic human needs as a man. Esmeralda feels she ought to pay her dues; that she should endure the consequences of her acts for as long as she possibly can. If she continues on this path for much longer, she will end up in a psychiatric unit very soon. So, she started her self-talks again: "What am I going to do? Emma and even little Bianca who happens to be a soaking sponge of knowledge, are old or mature enough to notice how her dad and mom treat each other. Is that an example that I want to give them? Maybe it would be better if we decide to separate amicably… at least that way their mom will be happier and they could enjoy having a fun and energetic type of mother." Again, wishful thinking. Not to take Valentino's side, but who can assure Esmeralda she would be happy after divorcing him? Valentino surely did not make her happy and his absence would not necessarily make her happy either because her happiness should not depend solely on a man, period. It is about time Esmeralda learns a way to find happiness on her own without a male intervention, she needs to make peace with her own self in order to be happy and that is the end of it.

Love should be let free

He started shaking, became pale and with a trembling voice told her, "Please… let's not do this… the kids, think about them."

Esmeralda, "Precisely because of them is that I have stayed with you for so long… don't you understand that I no longer wish to live like this… fighting, hating each other?"

Valentino, "I don't hate you and I never will."

Esmeralda, "Your actions and even the way you would look at me sometimes say the opposite to what you are affirming."

Valentino, "I admit I get way too frustrated and angry… but you know it is mostly because all the tension we have got, especially dealing with Mateo."

Esmeralda, "Yes, I understand, but you just don't realize that people who love and respect each other would unite and be even more compassionate and understanding toward each other under circumstances such as the ones we have been through." Esmeralda seems to be in an amazing serene mood and at the same time sounding firm as if this time around nothing would make her regress to a previous state of conformism; now she is putting the money where her mouth is, so she is stopping her speeches about how unhappy she feels in their relationship and finally materializing the so much feared divorce. Valentino is trying to hold on until the last minute, trying hard to appeal to all of her sentimentalism and her love for her kids. However, he is not being successful; Esmeralda would not back off even an inch.

Everything has been settled in a court and at last she is free; Esmeralda is now a new woman. Valentino moved out of their home and the kids stayed with her. She assured him that he could visit any time because she did not want their kids to grow up without a dad. They also forgave each other for all the suffering and mutual maltreatments all these years. No, Valentino did not die, that was a fear that Esmeralda had because he reacted so badly whenever she broke up with him in the past. So, now she is happy for him as well, she hopes and wishes that he could also find that woman that would restore his confidence in love and make him feel things that could really elevate him as a human being, a man that feels he is loved and respected and he is able to feel and demonstrate that for someone as well. They both had the right to be happy even if happiness meant to be apart from each other. 'Love should be let free, if you love each other indeed, love will grow happiness even among the weed'. This was part of a poem that Esmeralda wrote one day when feeling trapped and wishing to abandon her unhappiness.

Chapter 8

A New Beginning

The way one's soul should be

It is so wonderful to witness nature renewing itself; from the dead comes life like the blooming of the flowers every spring. That flowers are not only beautiful but fragile as well is common knowledge, but I think they are powerful nonetheless. The power of the flowers consists very much in their beauty; both the beauty that is captured by the sense of sight and the one that is assimilated into one's soul by the sense of smell or perfume made from them. Think about it, besides their decorative qualities, flowers do not serve other major roles; they are not meant to be eaten and hardly any well-known remedies are made from them if any at all that I am aware of. Oh! Yes, they serve to propagate their pollen which then will become seeds and germinate into plants that bear fruits we enjoy so much, however, many flowers do not have this function and they are the most beautiful flowers we know — like the divine breathtaking red roses whose only purpose is to entice us with their charm. Beauty in nature is prominent and this is not due to chance; it must be this way so humans can experiment through their senses of sight, smell, hearing, and touch that feeling of appreciation of something that mysteriously makes one utter: how beautiful that is! Esmeralda was contemplating the plants that grew tall due to their relatively strong long stems, at the side of her house; it was as though they had something of value to protect or even show off. These plants had flowers consisting of simple small white pedals. "They look so humble and pure, the way one's soul should be," thought Esmeralda. If these flowers were cognizant or reasoning creatures, they should feel proud of their foundation – so strong and deep rooted. Most human beings even those who are presumably humble still feel proud of having as their foundation a supreme, omnipotent, omnipresent and invincible creator. These flowers that Esmeralda was appreciating are synonyms of simplicity, however, their austerity is not the sole reason for their humility rather it is the fact that they are ephemeral; they must know that they would wither immediately after the first extreme summer sun's rays hit them. So, being humble means knowing our own limitations as mortal beings and at the same time be able to keep one's head high – thinking about our beautiful and mysterious origin – until that day when darkness decides to wither us. Esmeralda had this flash thought, "Indeed the most beautiful feature of Homo sapiens is a pure heart." If you comprehend this abstract definition of something you cannot prove exist by scientific means then there is beauty in that too. A beauty perceived and transmitted from one to another in every act of mercy, sincere smile and comforting words. Indeed, there is beauty everywhere, tangible and intangible beauty, a powerful beauty, a far-reaching beauty — that of the soul of a renewed person. It is possible now for Esmeralda to undergo a new beginning; her soul could be reborn; after the cruel bitter winter of her life, she could have a new spirit and a pure heart – like those simple little flowers had a chance early in spring – when she sees through a different lens and feels with a fresh and broader ken everything around her, now that she should have not an ugly spot to hide and nobody to despise.

After the so awaited divorce, Esmeralda had to go through a process of re-defining herself; she needed to discover how this new woman was going to continue to move forward on her own. Esmeralda had to undergo a double bankruptcy in order to make sense of her life, and in this way make a hundred and eighty degree turn around; it was necessary for her to become bankrupt to get rid of an expensive debt she could not afford to pay and her divorce also in a way constituted that means of a person's liberation of a debt, a moral debt. It is almost impossible to satisfy this debt because it is not a monetary one, but a condition that demands one to forgo something that cannot be bought with money; now this family was no longer having Dad and Mom together and the kids would wonder why their world suddenly looks different and they feel something is missing that cannot be replaced. Esmeralda saw this scenario as a kid as well; their parents got divorced when she was about six years old and she lost something during that process and she never got that something back. So, then again Esmeralda suffered a bankruptcy involving feelings, emotions, and memories. Now, this whole new process was a necessary evil if Esmeralda was going to drastically change her life in order to feel happy and fulfilled at last.

Another thing to consider was who she was going to love and how? Should she love a man at all? Can a woman live life to the fullest without a male exemplary of love? These questions would have their answers as she went along this new path though not too far away, she started to feel that need to have that someone she could tenderly look into his eyes and touch his lips and tell him I love you. She has not met anybody who is able to awake in her anything worth noticing; she is not seeing sparks or feeling any butterfly sensations in her belly just yet. Only that whenever she remembers him, yes Roberto, she inevitably would sigh and wonder how he is doing. She would think, "What if I see him again? Will everything be just like it was when we used to love each other in our hide-out place?" She would torture herself by wondering if he ever thought of her. Roberto seemed to have completely disappeared after she told him she had made up her mind and was going to give her marriage with Valentino one last chance; she needed to do this not just for herself but most importantly for her kids' sake. Roberto respected her decision though he did not think it was right and promised to not interfere in her life. He said good bye with profound sorrow and she as tough as a turtle's shell let him go without mercy. She needed to show herself strong and firm when speaking with him that last time so the process could be quick though not necessarily less painful.

Two souls destined to love each other

One fine day Esmeralda got this urge to just go there, to Roberto's business locale and surprise him. It occurred to her that since she is free to love anyone now, she would want to experience what it feels like to go and kiss him in front of whoever happens to be there at the time. She was going to risk being humiliated if by any chance Roberto already had moved on and had a new woman in his life; however, she was so thrilled with this new impetuous idea of hers and without giving it much thought went for it. She arrived there, it was around noon and she could see through the large glass his silhouette standing erect with his upper body in motion behind a counter top; she stopped for a few seconds solely to observe him, she was smiling as if expecting something good – that kind of anticipatory excitement kids have when waiting to be handed over their favorite ice cream cone – her face was glowing; her cinnamon hair was bouncing while the sun's rays made it sparkle; she was wearing a cotton spring dress with a floral design and her waist accentuated, she looked as beautiful as she could possibly be. Roberto looked outside maybe he saw something out the corner of his eye and instinctively lifted his head. He abruptly stopped what he was doing, jumped over the now only obstacle in his way – the counter top – and got out of the store in a fly, he ran and stood right in front of her like waiting for her to confirm to him that yes! She was there to see him. Esmeralda smiled at him and he immediately hugged her, raised her in the air by holding her by her waist and then they kissed each other without any fears or worries or any care whatsoever right there on that blessed-to-be sidewalk. The people who were inside curiously gathered at the window and witnessed the reunion of two souls who were destined to love each other and that now have a chance to do just that.

Esmeralda still shaking inside confessed to him that she was so afraid he would reject her. He replied, "Never mi vida… I told you before that I was your property and I meant that, forever!"

Then, Esmeralda did not hesitate to utter, "Perdóneme mi amor… nunca más nos vamos a separar… Te lo prometo." Roberto happily took her by her hand and proudly walked her inside and introduced her as his girlfriend to everyone there. This day was one of the happiest days Esmeralda has yet lived with Roberto. Esmeralda had commented to him a couple of years earlier while she was visiting him at his apartment, "Amor, I wonder sometimes how about if we had been in the past boyfriend and girlfriend… if we had known each other while we were both single… imagine going to see a movie in the theater or go out to dinner… doesn't that sound wonderful?" Roberto would just look at her in a tender way and just the way he knew how to do so while she went on reciting her wish-list. He was always attentive to her words; she seemed to be always enunciating a suppressed desire to change her life around and be happy. Roberto would contemplate her face displaying a range of emotions and hear her voice with varying intonations of expression, this was the way she normally reacted to the ordinary nuances in her life and served as a constant reminder to Roberto that she was there with him and nobody else. He did not feel vexed by any of her bursts of anxiety on the contrary he always showed his sincere understanding. It was very important for Esmeralda to count on Roberto during those moments when she needed to unscramble her convoluted mind and fill it with positive thoughts. Now finally there is no more fickleness, what ifs or wishful thinking. This new reality is all that Esmeralda one day hoped and now is here to stay. She finally found a man who loved her in good times and bad ones and who was willing to grow old with her. She had introduced him first to that idea and soon he adopted it as his own because it just made sense to him that when two souls love each other that much, they deserve to pass every minute left of their existence together. Not a second to be wasted and all their love sealed for eternity in their flesh, mind and spirit until that final hour of bodily separation though in spirit united forever.

It was NOT just another day
Esmeralda went to the park – the one with a castle at its center – to jog; she has this renewed vitality and a desire to go out there and become almost one with nature though this time she is not in need of distraction rather she only intended to indulge in a temporary solitude. During this process, she would sort of wash off the impurities that daily life brings normally attached with it.

Her thoughts would reach unexplored dimensions where she could acquire a new perspective or way of seeing things around her and in her as well. After all, we humans are volatile thinking creatures, this is a good feature; imagine not being able to change your mind, ever? Now, too much volatility is not good either. However, the perfect amount of change after a moment of reflection contributes to the maintenance of a healthy homoeostasis of one's spirit or mood if you will, don't you think? Esmeralda has already made up her mind; she knows what she wants to do and with whom she wants to spend the rest of her life with; now she is just assimilating her new life and detaching from her former state of negative emotional ambiguousness a little bit each day. So, she – in a sort of automatic mode – goes to the castle where she could stretch her body while leaning against the stone walls and enjoy the magnificent view of the valley below – filled with city life; she could see a marked contrast between what took place down there where people struggle to live in harmony with one another and the tranquility and solace innate in that beautiful place she adopted as her spiritual sanctuary type of thing. Not to be implied that Esmeralda had converted to any religion that worships nature per se; but it is true that she enjoys nature very much, even when she has not dwelled on this thought because she is not even aware of this tendency of hers, if you will. She is merely participating in a natural self-renewing of the mind –influenced by the power of the beauty around her and in an unconscious way.

Esmeralda continued with her jogging routine while still lost in the alluring beauty and spiritual comfort that the place provided. At one point, she is turning from one side to the other, and then bending down her body from her waist and lifting her arms and upper body — stretching up, and that is when she saw him coming from inside of one of the walls of that faithful castle; yes, because she could count on this place to accomplish that sense of utter relaxation every single time she went there. Roberto was standing up there at the entrance and waiting for Esmeralda to decide to come up the stone stairs to where he was. Esmeralda first got this smile – looking somewhat surprised – and cheerfully waved at him and then noticing he would not move from where he was, her smile turned into a reflective one; she was wondering what he was doing up there, so she then widens her steps firmly and went to meet with her love regardless of his reason to be there. The moment she made it to that spot where Roberto hoped she would, all a sudden she could hear the buzzing sound of something being dropped from above, it was a huge sign which once completely unrolled showed an antique cursive writing with the question: 'Esmeralda, mi vida... would you marry this poor soul who only lives for you?' The dropping of the sign was done simultaneously with Roberto's gracious kneeling of one knee and holding a little red velvet jewelry box and looking at her eyes as though imploring for the so much desired yes. Esmeralda's eyes immediately filled with tears, tears of the immense joy she was experiencing. She lowered herself to his level and grabbed his face and kissed him; Roberto then asked, "Is that a yes?"

Esmeralda, "That is me offering all that I'm to you and accepting with all my heart... ¡Te amo!"

Roberto, "Gracias mi vida... ¡Yo también te amo!" This was not just another day; it was the day when everything negative and that made her feel inadequate with her own life passed and everything else was new and fresh. Indeed, a new beginning for the both of them. Now their main purpose as opposed to a meager task, was to make each other happy and that was going to be so easy since it was just perfectly normal for them to impart only good things in their relationship as if they did not know how to do it otherwise. Even though they had flaws as anybody else, they were perfect for each other or maybe life molded them to be this way; yes, a combination of the right timing of their encounter when they both had lived through many things that would refine their characters and made them stronger and wiser. It might sound as a cliché, but yes, they seemed to have the right keys for each other's hearts. And this I am afraid is a rare occurrence, a weird and yet beautiful phenomenon in nature, I would say.

The most important destination

Shortly after Esmeralda was surprised by Roberto with that incredible proposal of marriage, she stopped to think for a minute about the nonsense that her first marriage was. She now is able to look back and say, "What the hell was I thinking? Valentino did not ask formally to marry me... I was the one insisting on hurrying to tie the knot!" The whole situation surrounding the enormous mistake of her entire life flashed through her mind – from the absurd reasons for marrying him to the ridiculous wedding that she spent so much time and energy on. But why? For the sole purpose of not delaying the right time for her to become a married woman, have kids and yes, keep up with her cohorts — all the other young women from her family and friends that were also on their way to the altar. Everybody seemed to be getting or planning to get married those days and she did not want to be the exception. Who else should she wait for to be her husband? If not the guy that she promised to herself — after that very last time she was humiliated and betrayed by a guy she fell for; "the next man who dares to cross my path will have to love me more than what I would love him," she used to think...

"this guy should not be a super star" in this way she would avoid the risk of catching a womanizer and besides, being in love with him was not a requisite for this vulnerable poor girl. She could not have acted more immature and she thought, "I was so foolish thinking, at least unconsciously, that I was engaging in something that could easily be undone and forgotten if it did not work out... marriage is not like getting a lease of a car that once you get bored of it, you return it." Another thing Esmeralda could have not ever guessed is that when a man or woman stays in a relationship where only one-part loves, there will be devastating and unforeseen consequences. For one thing, when Esmeralda found herself hating her life with Valentino and loathing his every gesture and action, she realized that sharing your life with a person you do not love, at one point, would be worse than suffering a love disappointment. When one has a heart deprived of love for whom is supposedly to be your life partner, something else has to inevitably fill that void; and eventually, hate, resentfulness, and other negative feelings would take the place of love. So, yes... if you think you are saving yourself from suffering by avoiding an engagement with the person you really love out of fear to get hurt, think again. Those who decide to give themselves to someone in marriage or just by common union for any reason other than genuine love would end up hating themselves and their partners as well; they would lament their stupid choice to the point of wanting to inflict 'a well-deserved' punishment on themselves and they don't forgive those idiots who could not perceive the real situation and / or did not have the courage to reject a bad deal; those who apparently are the victims but that they should have known better and noticed that they were not being loved back; come on! Whoever is not capable of realizing that their love has not been reciprocated is because either they are deceiving themselves or temporarily blinded by love; notice I said 'temporarily' because this bandage on one's eyes eventually falls, love's power to entice to the point of blinding someone is in fact short lived in many cases and in a few cases, lasts longer than what it should. However, once one recognizes that one is not being loved in the same way one loves, something has to click in one's head and you need to take action. Leave the freaking situation for good! But, no, these conformist people stay and are unhappy and, in a way, impede the other person to go and be free to at least try to find happiness somewhere else. I know this sounded harsh, but it is the plain truth. Besides, should not be deemed questionable the love a person affirms to feel for someone when this person is not willing to let him / her fly away? That is… when it's evident this person is not being loved back.

Esmeralda struggled with her dubiety about the positive role of the institution of marriage for a while; I suppose this is a common reaction of people whose marriages were complete failures and need therefore someone or something to adjudicate blame. Fortunately, this time around she wanted to exalt love; one way of doing this is by admitting that comprehension ought to be a key component between those who say they love each other and this quality is just a result of loving each other – not the other way around. Also, she finally saw crystal clear, the importance of the consecration of one whole self to the other person who one intends to share one's life with in the sacredness of marriage. Esmeralda reflected on those moments during her first marriage, in front of the altar when she was physically there while the pastor was preaching, however, her mind was absent. Therefore, this time around, she was going to not pay attention to the vain, the frivolous and the prosaic customs when it came down to the celebration of their love — their wedding. She is a mature woman at this point in her life and knows exactly what she wants out of a marriage; she will focus on demonstrating sincere love to that man who also has proved his love for her. Now Esmeralda is trying to find out how to embark on this hopefully wonderful trip with her lover that she is determined in her mind will be her last and which final destination is a fulfilling life due to the happiness of giving herself to that person she loves and that she does not mind to be attached to for life; that person that she desires to be a prisoner of; that person that she could laugh her heart out with and never hurt each other not with a hateful look or nasty word. The man that she loves is convinced that she loves him and she knows he is crazy about her. This couple is like no other at least they feel that way because they can perceive the very special treatment, they are able to provide to each other. Esmeralda feels her love for him will endure anything and his love for her has already gone through fire and came out victorious. There is nothing else to be said other than God bless their union!

They made it to one of the most important destinations one could arrive to in this life; there against the majestic water curtain in the outback of the land that saw them be born, were Esmeralda and her beloved Roberto. They were celebrating their nuptials in the midst of nature; a soothing background sound coming from the calming waterfalls, the Antillean siskin birds chirping a gracious melody, the flora consisting of red hibiscus, ferns, orchids and numerous more plants adorned and perfumed that tranquil place. These two souls decided to come precisely here to promise to each other... well, let's put it in their own words. Roberto, "Mi bella... I feel so fortunate to have you by my side as the love of my life and I know in my heart that you will be my eternal companion. I promise to love you as I have never loved anyone before, with a pure love and so strong that nobody and nothing could ever diminish. I promise to be faithful as the moon to the earth and be with you in good times as well as bad times. I will be forever in love with you."

Still looking straight into her lover's eyes, Esmeralda pronounced her vow, "Mi amor… before you came into my life, I knew nothing about what love truly was… with you I learned to love and be loved. I promise you to love you until the day I die with the same intensity and strength I feel for you today. I will be yours and completely yours in spirit, mind and body. I will be with you during health and adversity as well. You will be my eternal and only lover." They were both standing face to face, holding each other hands, and before the Marriage Officiant could ask the groom to kiss the bride, they were already at it, so she had no choice but to pronounce them husband and wife. There was no crowd in this wedding, the only witnesses were Anne Marie and Emmanuel; this couple intended to display and promise true and enduring love to each other surrounded by the beauty and innocence distilling from the air of a pure and virgin territory. They did not wish to be just another couple swearing to engage in something they were not truly meaning to do. They wanted their promise to each other to be made in freedom so they could remain in this state loving each other forever; without the commonalities of formal unions and the presence of people who knew nothing about the feeling they had for each other. Only the precise people needed were there and there needed not be anyone else.

In that magnificent place, they began a journey in which they intended to enjoy their crossing through this life together with a same sentiment and appreciating every single moment they shared. Every day would be a new opportunity to see their love mature and grow even more. This was possible just like the way the muscles of a physic culturist get larger due to the heavy lifting; love being exercised by continued caring, comprehension, patience between them had the potential of getting stronger each day. Esmeralda and Roberto had their different points of view of certain things; for instance, while Roberto was a Republican, Esmeralda had always sympathized a great deal with the Democratic ideology. Even during Trump's era, their love and fondness for each other kept going stronger. They would not fight about their differences rather they would exchange ideas and even laugh at themselves realizing that there were things they would likely never agree on, nonetheless they would not dwell on this insignificant aspect of their healthy relationship.

Esmeralda woke up one morning and noticed in her backyard growing a lot of undesired plants and bad grass. Her immediate response was to start pulling them all up with her bare hands, she did not bother to go and try to find her gardening gloves, and there was no time to waste. She was thinking how these plants came out of nowhere with the only intention to take over; they would engulf all the other beautiful plants until it caused them to die of suffocation or lack of nutrients because these horrible types of flora would suck all the good substance from the soil without regards to the other less strong and delicate plants and flowers. She perpended this experience in her garden and deduced an analogy from it: 'Bitterness, frustrations, hate, disdain, pride, all of these are the weed in any relationship; love is the fertilizer that makes a couple grow in tolerance and maturity to deal with issues where it is inevitable not to differ in opinion or belief. And also love could serve as the insecticide that kills any mal-intentioned behavior and even those vestiges of resentfulness due to real or perceived hurtful acts against each other because no one is exempt from causing pain to someone even when that someone is a loved one'. She thought again about how wrong she was to have neglected considering love as her main objective to base her marriage on the first time. Now they have a good and strong foundation; her love for Roberto was capable of keeping off all the weeds and damaging plants in the garden that was going to be the home she and Roberto are now forming, nourishing and protecting. They will not let anything or anyone kill or harm their love. They intend to honor and respect that crucial cell that is supposed to bring life to a healthy society, that sacred entity called marriage.

The happy newlyweds are walking bare foot on the white sands of a gorgeous tropical beach; pretty soon their souls become nude and so do their flesh when they let their clothing drop without a care in the world. They stop for a moment and stand face to face while holding their bodies close together and losing themselves into each other's eyes as if wanting to hold on to these moments forever. This loving couple had nothing to envy the splendid panorama, not even the soft salty breeze which whispers a sense of tranquility and calmness nor the palm trees' fronds with their dancing dark shadows against a vivid orange background trying to say good bye to the sun before it goes to sleep. Then, they would feel attracted to the solitude and gentleness that the ocean conveys and they do not resist, they just go in deep, deep into the waters of feelings, sensations, and emotions so strong that they do not attempt to dismiss nor withstand. The wetness of the warm clear waters bathing their excited bodies — these calm waters still reflecting the lingering sun rays, and this incredible feeling, these eternal lovers will never be able to forget; they will forever remain submerged in the pureness and delicateness of an ocean that loves peace and celebrates solace.

Roberto and his bella Esmeralda woke up to a new life together after a night when ardent desires were extinguished to only re-ignite the moment oxygen — which is their mutual attraction, comes to the surface again. It is the most beautiful morning on earth and since forever — they are convinced of that, and this couple continues to enjoy each other's warm company; they are inseparable, not wanting to forgo a second when they can honor love. They persist in their mission to create unforgettable memories to treasure in their hearts until their now still healthy and young bodies become weak. The love that they are imparting to each other now will serve as a great foundation in which to erect a loving companionship until death comes between them. Meanwhile they are understanding their own natural tendencies and remarkably adjusting themselves accordingly. They are recognizing their need for each other and trying with resolution to attend to their most inner calling: to love and nurture one another.

The faithful earth went around the magnificent sun many, many more times and two of its inhabitants were still together making every hour count; Roberto and Esmeralda are taking a hot shower, enjoying themselves; he is behind her holding her by her waist and tenderly kissing her neck when a frank and spontaneous, "I love you" is whispered into her ears, Esmeralda has this satisfying smile while feeling she was being loved the way she always wished to be loved; her reflection on the blurry glass shows a woman who has no reason to envy those happy-looking couples any more, no more wishes to be granted and no regrets; a woman whose days are filled with a desire to be with him and when apart from him she looks forward to seeing him come home and receive him as her king. So, then again... Who is that woman in the mirror? That woman in the mirror is an immensely happy woman.

El Fin